HAMMER
OF
FATE

BOOKS BY G.N. GUDGION

HAMMER
OF
FATE

G.N. GUDGION

SECOND SKY

Published by Second Sky in 2023

An imprint of Storyfire Ltd.
Carmelite House
50 Victoria Embankment
London EC4Y 0DZ
United Kingdom

www.secondskybooks.com

ISBN: 978-1-83790-180-7
eBook ISBN: 978-1-83790-179-1

For James
Adelais's first fan.

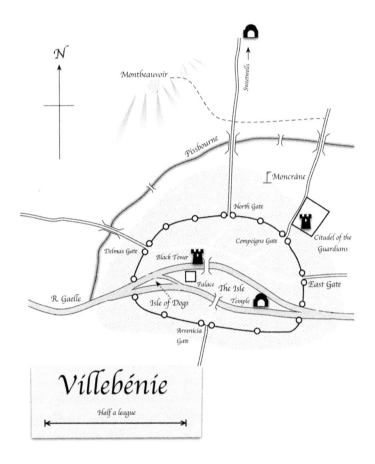

N

Montbeauvoir

Sweetwells

Pissbourne

Moncrâne

North Gate

Compeigne Gate

Citadel of the
Guardians

Delmas Gate

Black Tower

Palace

The Isle

East Gate

R. Gaelle

Isle of Dogs

Temple

Arrenicia
Gate

Villebénie

Half a league

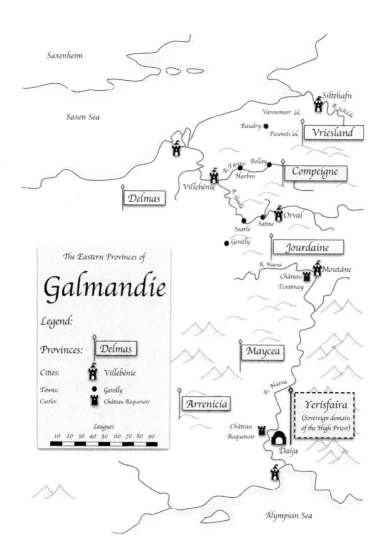

PROLOGUE

They would come for her soon. The ravens were telling her. As Yrsa left her cottage they flapped around her head, screeching their agitation. Clever birds, the ravens.

So be it. If the morrow was to be her dying-day, then what mattered was how she faced it. And now Yrsa wished the birds would be quiet. She wanted peace; a time to reflect and prepare. A chance to breathe the still, salt air of a final evening. Sit on the crest of the island's one, low hill and watch the creeks empty in the slow breathing of the marshes. Yrsa tried, and failed, to remember how many years she had been custodian of this place. Long enough for her hair to fade from pale gold to grey, and for her daughter's daughter to grow to young womanhood.

Where is the girl? There was so much Yrsa would like to say to her. So much that now would never be said.

They would not come before nightfall. The tide was full, and beginning to ebb, so the priests and their soldiers would come with the morning flood. No outsider risked the treacherous mud around Freyjasoy; they waited until a boat could land them on dry ground. On this long evening of the flower moon, she could allow herself the luxury of walking the island's paths one last time. She'd say farewell to the place she loved.

The ravens quietened when Yrsa reached the blackened ring of standing stones above a beach on the western, seaward shore. She closed her eyes, thinking of dead friends whose bodies had been burned here, with the village gathered around. They'd drunk mead and ale until the eulogies turned to stories, and the tears turned to laughter, then scattered the ashes onto the next ebb tide for their loved ones' final journeys. Now the priests insisted that bodies must be buried in the ground to rot, and people feared death as never before.

Only *seidhkonur* were burned now; her sisterhood adept in rune magic. Burned alive as 'witches'. The 'cleansing of Vriesland', the priests were calling it. Three days before, it had been *Frú* Sigrid, just three leagues away. Half a day's walk. Now only Yrsa was left, on this island between the land and the sea, at the edge of the world.

She pulled herself back from that line of thinking. Bitterness would not help her. Anger, yes. Defiance, certainly. Above all, she needed to find the courage to step into the unknown. Not to run from death, but to embrace it and go beyond it.

The broadening foreshore told her it was time to start.

Yrsa touched the rune-carved lintel of her door as she entered her cottage. Another farewell, of sorts. Her home was large enough for her pigs to be penned inside during harsh winters, where they could share the heat from the central firepit and in turn yield theirs. But the far end of her cottage was immaculate; a polished wooden deck was kept free of all clutter and utensils save those needed for her *seidhr* work: a chair, sturdy enough for a lord; a chest with herbs and tinctures for healing; her bag of runes and her cat-skin cloak. And her staff. Chest-high, it was thick as a man's forearm at its top, tapering to an iron-bound thumb's width at its base. Its whole length was carved with an intricate pattern of runes, overlaid one upon the other until their meanings melded into incoherence for any who had not spent a lifetime steeped in rune lore.

When that staff was struck into the boards, the boom would resonate for half a league in still air, and the world would know that great *seidhr* was being wrought. The high, keening voice of her rune song would also carry, easily as far as the village. No villager would dare disturb her work, but if there were soldiers nearby, they would kill her before her spell was wrought.

And there was a priest of the hungry god in the village. He would stop her if he could.

She ate no food, for the body must be weak if it is to yield its spirit, but she sipped a thin infusion of mushroom and mandrake root, with a little precious opium. These measures were important; enough to help her mind travel into the spirit world, but not so much that she would lose focus.

Yrsa sat on her chair, holding her staff, with her knees man-wide, waiting until she judged that her island would be surrounded by impassable mud. Perhaps her whole life had been preparation for this moment. Was she capable? She was attempting the stuff of legend. The magic would bring her either death or rebirth – as *fylgja*, a spirit guide. No *seidhkona* had ever returned to show the way.

And even if she succeeded, became *fylgja*, the girl had received almost no training. Knew so little. Understood nothing. She'd not even learned the ways of listening to the warp and weft of fate. The runes said only that she *may* be the one, but they said it strongly enough for Yrsa to lift her head, put her shoulders back, and slam her staff into the boards at her feet as she began her song.

'*Reidh er sitjandi sæla...*'

She held the outline of *raido* in her mind, the rune of journeys.

Except that she was journeying into the spirit world.

'*Ok snúdhig ferdh...*'

The rune dissolved into an image of a horse cantering in time with the drumbeat of her staff. **One** - *two* - *three*, **one** - *two* - *three*...

'*Ok jórs erfidhi...*'

As the herbs and the chanting took hold, her awareness faded beneath the rhythm of her spell. Only the chant itself changed, from the journey of the spirit to the purpose of the journey. Time lost its meaning.

'*Odhala er gjöf höfdhingjans...*'

Odhala, the rune of ancestral right.

The rune of hearth and heritage. The old ways.

'*Öruggur aflinn og löglegt frels...*'

She was flying like a bird, able to see for leagues. Down below, she felt the awe of the villagers, hearing the forbidden booming of rune song from the island.

'*Réttur allra kynslódha...*'

She knew the fear of the priest, cowering alone in his temple. Rune song battled with prayer.

'*Odhala er gjöf höfdhingjans...*'

She saw boats crowded with soldiers, rushing downstream on the ebb, and her song changed again, to the victory rune *tiwaz*:

'*Týr er einhendr áss...*'

And in the midst of the soldiers was a black-and-white-robed priest, his face sharp with a hatred more implacable than steel.

'*Ok ulfs leifar...*'

Against all reason, her vision blazed as full dark settled on the world outside. Now cloak-wrapped soldiers sat in barns, waiting for the dawn and the tide. Villagers huddled behind barred doors, their resentment palpable, all symbols of the old gods hidden. Children whimpered. None would sleep this night.

'*Ok hofa hilmir...*'

And two priests knelt together. Yrsa faltered, not from their prayers but from her own exhaustion. She was too weak to continue, and too strong to die. The spirit wanted to fly free, but the animal within her refused to let go. The smells of the world of men began to intrude as the effects of her infusion faded; the rot of low tide was drowning under the salt of the flood. Time had passed. A half-tide already.

In the first ghost-light of dawn, Yrsa knew she had failed. Her voice had faded to a whisper and the mighty pounding of her staff had become a weak lift-and-drop. It was still too dark to see within the cottage, but her fingers could trace the runes carved into her staff. *Ansuz. Ehwaz.*

The staff was too precious for the priests of the hungry god to defile. It had been her mother's, and her grandmother's before her, through all the generations since the gods were young. It should be buried beneath living water.

Yrsa's rune song faltered and stopped. With the last of her strength she staggered outside, light-headed and sick with defeat. A light mist lay over the waters, softening the outlines of trees and reed banks into spiderweb shades of grey. The tide was already over halfway to flooding; she did not have long.

She followed a scarcely visible path into the marshes to a place where logs allowed her to step down into the water. Mud sucked at her bare feet but she kept wading, out to where she could dive deep, below the lowest of tides. The cold tightened her chest but she dived again to weigh the staff down with a sack she'd brought for the purpose and filled with silt.

The yearning loss as she climbed out, empty-handed, was the hardest farewell of all, but the cold had sharpened her mind. She staggered back to her cottage as fast as her faltering strength would allow, with the wet skirts of her kirtle slapping against her shins. She knew now that she must not simply yield herself to the gods; to be *fylgja*, spirit guide, she must bond herself to the girl.

A man and a woman waited outside her cottage, both muddied to the knees. Njal the fisherman knew the places where a light, flat-bottomed boat could land long before the soldiers' heavier craft. Estrid was a trusted friend. Both their faces were tight with concern.

'They are here, *Frú* Yrsa.' Estrid's warning was unnecessary, and their caring presence an intrusion. Yrsa needed to work *seidhr*. Urgently. But Njal held Yrsa's shoulders, staring into her eyes. 'Come with us.' He was a slight man, slightly shorter than her, with grey eyes and hair that had once been as fair as hers. His skin had weathered and aged until it looked like folded leather.

Yrsa shook her head with real regret. 'There is something I must do. Here.'

He tightened his grip. 'I know how to live in the marshes. Or I could take you north across the river, where the old gods are still honoured.'

'Njal, I must stay.' This was hard. She and Njal were

friends, in the way of solitary people who honour each other's aloneness. Occasional lovers too, though usually apart.

'I could stay with you.'

Then he would die too. They both would, if they stayed. 'I must do this alone. It is *seidhr*.' Rune magic.

Njal held her gaze. 'How did it come to this, Yrsa?'

'They defeated our army and banned our gods. You know this.' Yrsa was torn between a last, precious contact and the pressure of the creeping tide.

'And where were the old gods when we needed them?' Njal sounded bitter.

'One shall come.' Yrsa's reponse was almost ritualistic.

'That prophesy? They say *Frú* Sigrid screamed it as she died. So has every *seidhkona* that they've murdered. *One shall come, born of wolf-kind and of mud, who shall roll back the borders of the hungry god.* Do you still believe it?'

'It is because I believe it that I must stay. If I did not, I would leave with you.'

That made him look at her more sharply, his eyes brightening.

'It is you?' Estrid asked. Yrsa had come from the Wolf People of the north, so many years before.

'Not me. But perhaps my blood. Perhaps Adelais.'

'The girl?' Njal grimaced. 'But the conquerors took her south, to serve in one of their god-houses. She will have forgotten our ways.' The hope faded from his eyes and became a frown. 'What are you planning, Yrsa?'

'I have one great task ahead of me, one I must do alone. And I must do it here.' On the sacred isle, where the veil between the worlds was thin.

He stared at her long and hard, his face slowly softening in sad acceptance that this was truly farewell. Around his eyes, the lines in his dry, weathered skin began to glisten.

'Go, my friends,' she urged them. 'They will kill any they

find with me.' And Njal's never-spoken love would weaken her. Yet despite the urgency, she clutched at Estrid's arm to give one last message. 'I carved a *taufr* for Adelais before she left. A talisman to bring her home. If it fulfils its destiny and she comes, tell her to burn it in my hearth. Tell her that if it is in my power, I will watch over her. Tell her...' All the things Yrsa wanted to say. So little time. 'Tell her that if the gods find her worthy, I will show her the way. Now go, if you love me.'

Njal was hunched as he left, pushing angrily at his boat's pole. Estrid sat wide-eyed in the bow, staring back. Yrsa did not wait to see them lost in the mist.

Her staff had given her the answer. Perhaps in her moment of despair, the untold generations of her ancestors had guided her fingers in the darkness, and let them rest on the runes that *might* be the portal. *Ansuz* the god-rune, to invoke the power and wisdom of Odhinn.

ᚠ

And *ehwaz*, the rune of unbreakable bonds, like that between horse and rider.

She allowed herself another steaming infusion. This time Yrsa added a little hemlock and henbane. Medicinal measures, not fatal. Life must be yielded as a gift, with rune song, not taken in an act of self-murder.

And she had no staff. Hardly enough strength to stamp. But

she could tap the tempo with her fingertips on wet thighs. She inflated her chest once more, and found the power to sing.

'*Hestar eru gledhi adhalsmanna...*'

At the limit of her hearing there was the sound of oars rumbling against a boat's hull. It had to be now.

'*Andabundinn...*'

Spirit-bonded...

Ehwaz, the rune of soul travel. And spirit guides. The rune of the *fylgja*.

'*Ok hradhvirkur hófar...*'

She felt herself soaring upwards again. Hovering like a hawk over the soldiers wading ashore. Feeling their fear. *So many swords against an old woman!*

And the priest in black and white, holding the hand emblem of his god before him like a shield as he pushed open her door.

She looked down on herself, head slumped forwards, grey hair hanging lank and wet all the way to the soaking boards, her hands still twitching on her thighs.

The priest was shouting something. An invocation or a warding against evil, but she could scarcely hear; she was filled with a terrible agony. As the priest reached to touch her empty body, the pain ended, as sharply and finally as a cut thread.

PART ONE

THE STRAWBERRY MOON

CHAPTER 1

1.1 ADELAIS

Adelais knew the winds by their smell, even when she could not feel their touch on her cheek. From the east they arrived at the sisterhouse along a slow-flowing stream that carried so much sewage that it was called the Pissbourne. It curved around the capital's walls, a stinking barrier between the hilltop hamlet of Montbeauvoir and the crawling mass of Villebénie, half a league to the south on the plain. Veer a little south of east, and there might be hints of a richer corruption from the great gibbet dangling its thin fruit outside the city walls at Moncrâne. The west wind was cleaner, though laced with wood smoke from the sisterhouse and the cluster of houses around it, but to Adelais the rare northerly breeze was the fairest, no matter how strong or cold or wet, for it carried memories of home, fading but bittersweet, the way incense clings to wool.

On a morning in the last quarter of the strawberry moon, the wind blew from the foulest quarter of all, for the south wind reached Montbeauvoir across the great, crenellated midden of Villebénie. It choked on a thousand fires and festered in the city's tanneries and slaughterhouses; it eddied in fetid, piss-trickling alleyways and flowed over the encircling bone-grey walls into the slums piled against them. The wind pushed soldiers, merchants and wagons along the Great North Road at the foot of the hill, and had no time to lose its smell even over half a league of summer-lush fields. It broke like an invisible wave against Montbeauvoir's slopes, and when it reached Adelais, tending the sisterhouse's vines, it still carried the taint of packed humanity, living and dead, from scented lord to manure-footed stable boy. Today she didn't mind the stink, for if the gods willed, it was a breath that would blow her homewards, away from enforced servitude in this *fordæmdur* sisterhouse, and back to Vriesland where she belonged.

She'd tried before. Fool that she was, she simply stole a sisterhouse cloak, and as much food as she could carry, and walked out. Within a league, two priests had spotted the novice's habit under the cloak and seized her. Novices did not leave sisterhouses unaccompanied, not unless they were on an errand. The beating that followed had put her in the infirmary, face down, for six days. Adeifi Fabianne enjoyed administering punishments, particularly on a novice's bared backside; she had a range of pliable willow switches for the purpose.

Adelais had learned one thing from that whipping, though. It had been thrashed into her, one cutting stroke at a time. *Did. She have. Any idea. How a lone woman. Would be expected. To pay her way. On the road?* Adelais wondered if Adeifi Fabianne relished that thought, too, but it had rung true enough for her to plan her escape differently this time. This time she'd be dressed as a man. They'd seek a novice, and not see a peasant.

That old cow Fabianne was 'supervising' the novices in the vineyard now from a bench in the sun. Her back rested against the orchard wall and the white hood of the Daughters of Salazar was angled to shade her face. Her mouth hung open, and at the top of each breath came the faint catch of a snore. There would never be a better time. Adelais worked her way steadily away from Fabianne, down the hill towards the head-high stone wall that enclosed the sisterhouse's land. She hoed assiduously as she went, dry-mouthed with nerves even though she hadn't done anything wrong. Yet. From time to time, just in case anyone was watching, she'd pick up a weed and drop it into the gardeners' sack slung around her shoulder. Beneath that light litter of greenery lay her cloak, her *own* cloak that she had been wearing when she arrived nearly two years before and had stolen back that morning from the eldest daughter's private rooms. There was also some food, mainly cheese hoarded from her meals. Enough for two days, if she was careful. It would take her eight or ten days to walk home, but she'd thought of that, too. This time it was going to work.

Adelais had a cache hidden down the hillside, below the vineyard's lower wall: a peasant's linen cap; a loose, belted coat of the style they called a cote-hardie; hose for her legs; flint and char to make fire; and a knife. The corpse in the infirmary hadn't needed them any more. She was tall for a woman, and slender enough to pass as a youth. She'd even had a fellow novice trim her hair that morning. The novices did that for each other; it was almost their only permissible grooming. One or two of them even liked the boyish look, though Adelais still felt the loss of the tresses that she used to plait into a honey-gold crown of maiden's braids. Fate hadn't given her much of a figure, but it had given her hair, and it still hurt that it was hacked so short that she only saw wisps that had escaped the shears. Long hair was vanity, the eldest daughter had shouted at the assembled convocation the day Adelais arrived. She'd made Adelais stand in their midst, weeping, humiliated, with her head rough-shorn into tufts that were bloodied where she'd struggled. Vanity! And the punishment for vanity, she'd thundered, was leprosy. It was written. Those who thought they were fair would end their lives as outcasts, watching their own faces rot away.

Soon Adelais would not have to put up with this *skit*. In Vriesland men and women stood tall before their gods; gods who laughed and drank and *fjakked* like people. The old gods walked this world, unseen but mighty like the great bears in the forest. They did not hide beyond the stars or demand worship in temples. And in Vriesland she'd grow her hair long enough to have maiden's braids once again. Maybe she'd find a man for whom she'd comb them out, as she had once for Jan.

That was another hard lesson; Ischyrian priests don't take wives, and women who fall for priests are called harlots and sent to sisterhouses a hundred leagues away.

At least no child came of it.

Adelais tugged at her habit where the coarse, undyed wool scratched at her skin, slick with new sweat, stale with old. She'd learned to live without fashionable dresses, but she'd never lost her yearning for the touch of clean linen against her body, encircling her waist and slipping over her backside like a lover's caress.

Soon, girl.

Adelais was nearly at the lower wall. An old, twisted fig tree grew in one corner, thick with leaf and heavy with unripe fruit. The sturdy branches within provided a natural, hidden ladder. She paused, working her hoe, her eyes up the hill. Two hundred paces away Adeifi Fabianne showed no sign of waking, even though some of the younger novices were now playing 'catch-me' games between the vines, running to and fro in the way the geese darted and squealed when Adeifi Elodie threw scraps. No one was watching. Adelais backed into the tree and climbed until she could lie flat along the wall, knowing she should go, right now, but putting off the moment. Lichen crumbled under her fingers. Her heart was pounding. The sisterhouse was at least some form of security. Food. A few friends. Two hundred paces below her, across a steepening hillside too rocky to farm, was the Great North Road, and it was flowing with people; farmers rumbled towards the city in produce-laden wagons. Other carts rattled north, empty. Further away a stream of people emerged from beneath the towers and battlements of the capital's North Gate, like maggots crawling through the teeth of a skull. Within the tree she was between the worlds, invisible to all.

What would the eldest daughter do to her if she were caught again? At that thought Adelais swallowed to force saliva into her mouth, and reached around to touch the pouch hanging from her belt, feeling for the hard square in the lining that was her grandmother Yrsa's hidden talisman, her parting gift. Yrsa had carved a flat piece of yew-wood, rune upon rune, to make a bind-rune, stained with her blood, whose destiny was to bring Adelais home. Back in Vriesland, before the Galman conquest, folk touched Mjölnir pendants in times of stress, invoking the protection of the gods with the hammer of Thor. Now the old gods were proscribed and their symbols had to be hidden.

The precious scrip on her belt hid one other treasure; within its lining was the pouch to Adelais's sling, and the leatherwork around its top unravelled to yield the sling's thongs. Typical Yrsa: honour the gods, then give them a little help. Adelais had been good with a sling, the best in her village. And with the knife, flint and char in her cache she could live off the land. She could do this. And she had to do it now, for when the bell sounded for noon office they would all be expected in the temple and her absence would be known. She had to be long gone by then.

Deep breath. One last look, all round, and Adelais slipped off the wall, beyond the sisterhouse's boundaries. There were footholds on the far side. She knew her way down; she'd done this before. Her cache was twenty paces away, where loose stones masked a hidden void. Now she must be swift, and transform herself from escaping novice into a lanky peasant before anyone saw her. She crouched in the low scrub at the wall's base, looked around, and let out an involuntary yelp of fright.

A huge she-wolf sat just below the hiding place. Adelais's

mind raced at this impossibility; she had not seen a wolf since she was taken from Vriesland, and even there only in the depths of winter when hunger drove them out of the forests into the domain of mankind. Never here, in the warm south, in summer, with a nation's capital half a league distant. Adelais stooped slowly, making no sudden movements, until she could grasp the hoe she'd dropped from the top of the wall. She'd been intending to knock off the metal end and keep the shaft as a staff, but it made a weapon of sorts, and she felt a little safer with it in her hands.

They eyed each other. The wolf made no move to charge; it sat on its haunches with its mouth a little open, panting, tongue lolling. After several heartbeats it lifted a hind leg and scratched at its neck, sending a dandelion-puff of dust floating on the wind. Adelais began to relax. But she had to get to her cache and the wolf was in the way. *Need must conquer fear*. She took one step towards it, the hoe levelled like a spear.

The wolf stopped scratching, dropped its head and growled, a low, menacing rumble. It did not move away. Adelais stopped. *Impasse*. She was now visible from the road: a novice, outside her bounds. She had no time to assemble her sling, and no room to swing it anyway from this animal track between scrub and wall. In one controlled, fluid movement she picked up a stone, hefted it, and hurled. The wolf dodged, but stayed in position, snarling, more like a guard dog than a wild animal. Adelais took one more step towards it, and the wolf seemed both to grow and drop its head at the same time. *By the gods, it is big*. Now the fangs were bared and the warning was clear, as if the cache held the wolf's cubs, not old clothes and a knife.

Adelais retreated a pace and waited, squatting to hide from view as much as she could, but still exposed. She threw another stone, earning herself another snarl. The wolf was not going to move. *Skit*. She risked a glance at the road below, where some kind of procession had emerged from the North Gate, led by two mounted clerics in the white robes and black cloaks of the anakritim. Adelais swore again in gutter Vriesian and retreated into cover below the fig tree. To be seen by a cleric would be bad; to be seen by the anakritim could be fatal; the order charged with maintaining the purity of the faith of Ischyros would probably burn her as a witch if they found the *taufr* in her scrip. Adelais glanced up at the sun, climbing towards noon and the bell. She did not have long.

And the wolf was still there. Its head was twisted over its shoulder as if it, too, was watching the anakritim. It turned back to look at her, staring as if there were something she should understand.

The anakritim were close enough now for Adelais to see that the priest in the lead rode a destrier befitting a great noble, and the one riding half a horse's length behind sat on a grey too fine for any vow of poverty. Two mounted soldiers cleared the road in front of them, though their task was easy; traffic scrambled out of their path into the verges and ditches, the way a pond's shoals of little fish will part and reform around a hunting pike. She could make out the blue of the royal badge on each of the soldiers' surcoats, even at this distance. Two more soldiers followed, bunched on their horses behind a wagon with a solitary prisoner sprawled across its boards. He might have been chained, but it was too far for Adelais to be sure. She wondered if there was to be an execution, for prisoners who had been put to the torture often had to be carried to their deaths, but no crowds followed to see the spectacle, and there were quicker routes to the killing ground at Moncrâne.

The wagon rolled in a rut, close enough now for her to see the prisoner contort as if in pain. He was definitely chained. The priest on the grey reined in until he was alongside the wagon, looking into it as if concerned before spurring back to join the leader. A slight unease began to grow in Adelais's mind; the anakritim had no baggage, so they were making a visit to somewhere nearby, not starting a journey. The unease grew into a terrible possibility: what if this was the anakritis-general himself? What other cleric would be escorted by king's men? She only knew the head of the most feared order of the Ischyrian faith by reputation; she'd never seen him. Nobody ever *wanted* to see the anakritis-general, Ghislain Barthram.

People called him the Angel of Death.

Adelais looked up at the fig tree, calculating her chances of climbing the wall without being seen. Maybe she'd have to delay her escape to another day.

Cries of alarm carried to Adelais even across three hundred paces of hillside and she looked back towards the procession. A man had sprung onto the moving wagon and was crouched over the prisoner. Soldiers were spurring to intercept him, drawing swords or levelling lances. Sunlight flashed on steel as the assailant drew a short sword, reversed it into a two-handed grip, and struck downwards at the man chained at his feet.

1.2 MALORY

When the prisoner groaned, Pateras Malory d'Eivet reined back alongside the wagon, leaving his master to ride ahead. He could not quite rid himself of regret at causing pain, and this one's body was in truth too broken to be moved. It was sad, but necessary. There was always so much suffering before truth, and usually even more before Ischyros could be glorified in a sinner's repentance. 'You are saving his immortal soul,' Pateras Ghislain Barthram always said. 'Without repentance there is no unburdening, and no pardon. Without pardon he would fall from the bridge of judgement into the fiery pit of Kakos. His pain now is as nothing to the infernal pains he would otherwise endure for all eternity.'

Malory d'Eivet knew the anakritis-general was right, but still Malory felt twinges of guilt. Their prisoner had cradled his hands claw-like across his chest, hunched over to the limit of his chains, and was making the high, nasal, keening sound that was his usual response to agony. Strange how deep must be the instinct to reach out for support as the wagon lurched, even with broken hands.

'We will soon be there.' Malory caught a trace of the man's

smell, and tried not to let his disgust show in his voice. The brown robe that had once identified Carel de la Tour as a lay brother was threadbare, stained to the colour and texture of a dung-heap, and it stank like one. A ragged flap hung loose where the lion badge of the Order of Guardians had been torn from his chest, exposing an irregular patch of dirty skin. The shirt beneath had long since rotted away.

Carel de la Tour looked up, cowering like a dog, but Malory smiled in the way he would indulge a child who feared a beating. Reassured, his prisoner spread his legs wider on the wagon bed to brace himself against further lurches, lifting his feet along the cloak rolled up under his ankles. The cloak had been Malory's idea. He was still not sure whether it was to show compassion or minimise his own guilt.

'Thank you, Pateras.' The words disintegrated into a coughing fit that sprayed droplets of blood upwards, though none came near Malory's robe. Carel de la Tour wiped his cheek against his shoulder and managed a small, nervous smile; it folded the dirt on a parchment-white face and lifted his beard into bristles over the cheeks. A bond was growing between them. Malory had seen it before, that link between a prisoner and his interrogator. It came when any hope of their former life was gone, and all that was left was utter dependency. For as Assistant to the Anakritis-General, Malory could be cruel or merciful, feed or starve, reward cooperation or fail to intercede. A prisoner's wilful failure to cooperate, after all, made them complicit in their own agony. But that look of fearful, grovelling hope always told him the prisoner was ripe to spill whatever secrets were left. They just had to keep him alive for long enough.

The dog comparison was good; some might even call this bond a form of love.

'The Daughters of Salazar have an infirmary.' Malory spoke as if his main concern were for his prisoner's care.

Carel de la Tour lifted his head so he could look down the length of his body, past the chains, towards the remains of his feet. Was that a silent comment? Was there still a spark of defiance in there? The chains, Malory knew, were entirely symbolic. This one would never walk again.

'Thank you, Pateras.'

But the subservient tone reassured him. *Pateras.* Malory's consecration as priest was recent enough for him to smile inwardly when a man who must be over forty called him 'Father' in the High Tongue.

'And you have a son, yes? Guy, is it not?'

De la Tour nodded his head cautiously.

'Yes, my son is Guy.' The tone said 'as you know'. The face was fearful, clearly wondering what role this son might play.

'He is full grown, now.' It was, after all, five years since de la Tour was incarcerated in the Black Tower, along with every Guardian knight in Villebénie. 'You would be proud of him.'

De la Tour's eyes widened. 'You have seen him?'

'The faith can be merciful to those who abjure sin. We will bring him to you at the infirmary.'

Oh, that light of hope in the man's eyes. The wonder, quickly masked. He could work with that.

'Pateras Malory.' Ahead of them Ghislain Barthram turned, lifting an arm so that his black cloak fell away from his white habit. He beckoned imperiously.

'Pateras Ghislain.' It was Malory's turn to show respect. He spurred his horse into a trot to catch up.

'You are too soft, Pateras Malory. He is a heretic.'

'*Láthos mou*, Pateras. My mistake.' Malory inclined his head as he made the ritual apology. The roles they played as anakritim were now deeply ingrained, even shaping their speech when no one was listening: the implacable anakritis-general who smelt heresy, and the gentler assistant who would plead on a prisoner's behalf. Sometimes Pateras Ghislain listened to Malory's intercessions. Sometimes it would be easier for Malory to stop a water mill with his bare hands. At first, Malory had doubted their work. Could it really be Ischyros's will to hold a man's feet in a fire? But he doubted no more. The abominations they had uncovered must make even the prophet Salazar weep. Mistakes would be understandable, in a way, in territories newly brought to the faith, for they might be only *mistakes*; it took generations to purge all traces of the old gods, and there were whole realms to the north that resisted the blessings of Ischyros. There were times when the anakritim chose to educate as well as punish, but not with the Order of Guardians. Lapses were utterly unpardonable in the faith's own knights.

There was much work to do.

A shout from behind made Malory turn. At first it was simply a soldier's '*Oi! You!*' but within two heartbeats it was '*Stop where you are!*' A man was climbing onto the wagon, using a moving wheel to launch himself upwards. He was plainly but respectably dressed in a good-quality cote-hardie and a woollen cloak that had fallen open as he sprung, revealing a short, two-handed hunting sword hanging from his belt. He was old enough to have grey strands in a well-trimmed beard, and he stared down at Carel de la Tour as if suddenly unsure. There was something in that wide-eyed, pasty look that reminded Malory of men he'd seen on the scaffold in the moments before their execution; this was a man reconciled with his own death. Malory turned on his grey, knowing he would be too late to intervene; already the soldiers behind were spurring forwards, one levelling a lance.

The drama was unfolding with skin-prickling slowness, all within a few heartbeats. The assailant had time to say, 'Brother Carel?' followed by, 'Forgive me, Brother', for Carel de la Tour had smiled, knowing him. Carel even opened his arms, welcoming death, for the man kneeling above him had drawn his short sword, reversed it into a two-handed grip, and plunged it downwards in a killing blow.

The soldier's lance caught him in the chest from behind before the blade could strike home, throwing him forwards and sideways so that the sword's point slammed into the wooden boards by Carel's shoulder. The man hunched over his own weapon, supporting himself on it, his body twisting as the soldier's momentum carried him past. A spray of blood blossomed briefly from behind him as the lance was wrenched out, and the man coughed once, massively, bloodily.

Malory lifted his hand as the second soldier drew level with the cart, swinging his sword.

'No!' Malory needed to talk to this assassin, while he lived, but knew instinctively that the man was dead, even before the sword bit into his neck, crumpling him into the corner of the cart like a poleaxed bullock.

For the time it takes to draw several breaths there was near-silence on the road. Apart from the soldiers, wheeling their horses back to the cart, everyone had frozen, staring inwards. Then blood began to flow through the boards of the cart into the road, and a merchant's wife screamed.

Malory stared into the cart, his mouth working, unable to think. The assassin had fallen across Carel's arm, curved around the sword still embedded in the wood, his almost-severed head at an impossible angle and the beard now red, clogged, dripping. A miniature silver Hand of Salazar lay near his mouth on a broken chain; the man had been a devout Ischyrian. Half-closed eyes stared at Carel, who was spattered with blood but seemed to be unharmed; he was breathing deeply, rapidly, like a man saved from drowning. Carel was the first to move. He lifted his free arm and touched the dead man's face with the back of a clawed, broken hand.

'They knew each other.' Ghislain Barthram had arrived at his elbow. He seemed more angry than shocked. 'How did that happen?' he shouted at the sergeant, who'd dismounted and was hitching his horse to the wagon's side.

The sergeant didn't answer at first, but swung onto the cart and tugged the two-handed, short-bladed sword from the wood. He examined it with a soldier's eye before glaring at his two men who'd been in the rear, demanding an answer.

'He just walked past, like he was in a hurry,' said one.

'Couldn't see the blade,' pleaded the other. They were all looking about them as they spoke, weapons ready, watching for another attack.

'It's easily hidden beneath a cloak, Pateras.' The sergeant did not sound apologetic. 'It's a hunting sword, see? Draws quickly. Useful at close quarters when a charging boar might come inside the swing of a fighting blade. Double grip to strike true through the hide.' He held the sword with both hands, pointing it at the body. 'And this one was prepared to die to kill the prisoner. He had no chance of escape.' He bent to unbuckle the dead man's belt, pulled it free, and sheathed the sword. Carel looked almost wistful as he took it away. 'My guess is that he'd have fought until we killed him rather than be taken alive.'

There was truth in that. In captivity the man would have died slowly, in unspeakable pain, and only when the tormentors had squeezed every last drip of information from his body.

'Do we go on, Pateres?' The sergeant glanced between the two priests.

'Yes.' Barthram's response was immediate and emphatic. 'We will take our guest to the infirmary at Montbeauvoir, as planned.'

'And do we send for more men?'

Barthram turned slowly in the saddle, staring at the crowd. Some people flinched from his gaze. None seemed to worry him. 'No. But you will ride in the wagon with your sword drawn. Come, Pateras.' He beckoned Malory alongside him once again.

'Why do you not send for more soldiers, Pateras?' Malory asked quietly. He was still in shock. Fearful for Carel, not for himself. No one would attack a priest.

'I think this man was acting alone, on impulse. And if we surround the heretic with guards, our plans will not work.' He made a dismissive gesture that required silence, and they rode in a calculating quiet almost to the crossroads below the sister-house. The anakritis-general was thinking. He did not sit easily in a saddle but hunched forwards, so full of tension that when he began to speak it seemed that cords in his neck were pulling his jaw down.

'Tell me, Pateras.' Barthram sounded like one of Malory's tutors at the seminary, talking him through a difficult question of religion. 'Why would a man sacrifice his life to kill our prisoner?'

Malory had been pondering that. 'At first I thought he might have been a devout man who hated the Guardians for their heresies.'

'Enough to die for that hatred? Unlikely.'

'And the assailant cried, "Forgive me, Brother" before he struck. What's more, he delayed his stroke to be sure he had Carel de la Tour.'

Barthram's head swivelled at that. 'So he was a Guardian. There were a few who escaped the net. Now why would a Guardian kill one of their own?' Barthram had a way of asking questions that implied he already knew the answer.

'To stop him telling us something.' Malory knew they were on the brink of a great truth, and the dying man behind them held the key.

'We have held him for five years. He might already have told us.'

'Not if the knowledge was so significant that our possession of it would be known to the world.'

'Exactly.' Barthram straightened in the saddle as they

turned at the crossroads, taking a climbing, lesser road. A novice was running uphill through the lines of vines stretching towards an orchard; the sisterhouse of Montbeauvoir must lie beyond its leaves.

'Was he working alone, do you think?' Barthram was testing him.

'It was a desperate act,' Malory replied. 'The Black Tower must have been watched.'

'Which suggests a small group. Enough to keep one man always near the gate. Who knew that we were going to move the prisoner?'

'You. Me.' Malory had learned to answer crisply. 'The garrison captain, yesterday. The men, this morning.'

'Anyone else?'

'The boy. The heretic's son. But his hope of seeing his father again was beyond words. I cannot believe he would be part of this.'

'But his friends might. After all, he is the son of a Guardian, and he would have shared the news. Will he come, do you think?'

'Oh, yes.' Of that Malory was sure. And all their plans depended on that boy's hope.

1.3 GUY

'Since when did an anakritis show kindness, eh, boy?'

Guy winced at the words even though he knew they were not meant to hurt. In front of him the master armourer shifted a hot iron plate on the cutting surface with his pincers, aligning his scored mark with the blade of the great shears.

'There must be decent men in the priesthood, master?'

'In the priesthood, maybe. But the anakritim?' Arnaud l'Armurier nodded and Guy heaved his weight on the long lever arm, feeling the softened metal yield steadily until the blades closed with a snap. The handspan-long cut was as smooth as a honed knife through leather.

'He says Papa was forgotten in the dungeons.' Guy lifted the arm of the shears over his shoulder, releasing the plate, leaving Arnaud to move the iron for the next cut.

'So why has he found him now?'

'Because I asked, and maybe he is a good man.'

'You just walked up to an anakritis outside the Black Tower and asked about a Guardian? You're lucky you're so young. Otherwise, he'd have hauled you inside and put your feet in the fire. Besides, we heard your father was dead. Cut.'

Again, Guy swung his weight on the shears. They both had to shout in the workshop's din. At a bench against the wall, three apprentices assembled chain-mail, hammering rivets to close each alternate row, for Arnaud l'Armurier specialised in the prized double-linked mail, heavy but proof against even a windlass crossbow. A fourth apprentice stood by the master, watching and learning. Beyond the doors, the clatter of the workshops of Villebénie's armourers' quarter competed with the lowing of cattle from the butchers' quarter across the Great North Road.

'He was not among the four-and-fifty, master.' Four years before, Guy had run among a line of Guardian prisoners, searching their faces as they were marched from the Black Tower to Moncrâne. He'd dodged the swipes of the guards, so unaware of what was to happen that he was actually excited, hoping to see his father among them.

'Perhaps he hadn't confessed. Or wasn't alive to confess. Again!'

Guy had been about the age of the watching apprentice when the fifty-four were led out; proud of the first downy hair on his face, innocent. Until that terrible day there'd been hope. Hope that the high priest would see justice done for his own knights. Hope that his father would be released, and they'd go back to the life they'd had within the citadel of the Guardians.

He'd known some of those knights all his life: great, bearded warriors whose scabbards tapped at their legs; the Lions of Ischyros who'd ruffled his hair and called him 'Carelet', the little son of Carel. What could have brought such men to that shuffling, chain-clanking walk? 'What news,' he'd called, 'of Carel de la Tour?' They'd all shaken their heads, their trapped eyes darting anywhere but at him. 'Go,' one had hissed. 'Run. Hide. Save yourself.'

Arnaud l'Armurier, his father's friend, had found him afterwards, weeping, stained with soot, and blackened still further inside where the taint of burning flesh had stuck to his throat and lungs. 'Why?' Guy had cried, staring at the smoking, contorted debris where fifty-four Guardian knights had been roped together on a platform of wood and straw, and burnt alive. Arnaud had slid his arm along Guy's shaking shoulders. 'Because they trusted the high priest,' he'd said. 'Now come away, boy.'

Something else had burned, that day: whatever faith Arnaud had left. And if Guy had had any adolescent piety, it was snuffed out.

Arnaud looked up from the metal they were working, the light of the furnace reflected in his eyes, and waved his pincers at Guy's face to emphasise his point. 'Trust gold, lad. Trust good steel, and trust the friend who'll wield it beside you, but don't trust priests. They burned our friends, and maybe your father.'

'Priests didn't order the burnings,' Guy protested.

'No, boy, that was King Aloys. It was the king who accused the Guardians of heresy and had them all arrested, but it was those anakritim bastards who tortured them into confessing.' Arnaud turned back to his work, aligning the metal anew. 'Our most holy high priest sent his own chamberlain from far-off Daija to find out the facts, and when the Guardians told the chamberlain that they'd only confessed to stop the torture, the king had them burned as relapsed heretics. Quite legally. End of all arguments. Cut!'

The last edge of iron fell away from the plate as Guy snapped the shears.

'And now you're talking to an *anakritis*.' L'Armurier's voice was sour with scepticism.

'He works with Ghislain Barthram. I have seen them together.'

'The Angel of Death himself. All the more reason to stay clear.'

'But he insists that my father lives. He is moving him to an infirmary. He will take me to him tomorrow.'

Arnaud snorted. He turned the newly cut plate in his pincers, sighting along its edge, and nodded his approval. Next would come the shaping – hammering the hot metal into a curve. When finished, pierced with eye-sights and breath holes, and riveted shut, it would become the great helm for a knight, case-hardened until it was strong enough to turn a lance point.

'Did you tell this priest where you live and work?' There was an edge to Arnaud's question, hard as his steel.

'No!' Guy wasn't that stupid. A few Guardians had escaped the net through the random chances of journeys or warnings. Arnaud's brother Parsifal was one of them; Guy would not dream of bringing anakritim to the door. Some of those lucky ones had fled the realm. A handful of others had been released, dragging mutilated limbs and the dark shame of tortured confessions. They all lived in the shadows, trusting only each other.

'Good. Keep it that way. Where will you meet him?' Arnaud returned the unfinished iron to the fire.

'Outside the fire temple on the Isle.' Guy worked the man-high lever that rocked the double bellows, forcing air into the furnace. 'After the public confessions.'

Arnaud snorted. 'What a display that will be. Three great officers of the Guardians, all lining up to confess their heresies and to be pelted with filth by the crowd. It's tragic that the grand master is brought to such a pass. He is too great a man to be so humiliated.' Arnaud stared into the furnace as if he sought wisdom within those glowing coals. He had a habit of scratching at an old wound on his wrist when he was concerned. 'This will be like the mummers' plays at the spring festival. Each knows his words and the part he must play. Confess or die, and there will be witnesses. Episkopes from Daija.'

'So it will all be false?'

'Think of your father, boy.' Arnaud's voice rose in a rare

flash of anger. 'Think of Parsifal and answer your own question.'

Guy pumped the bellows harder, cross with himself for asking a stupid question. Guardians like his father were heroes, not heretics. And Parsifal had been idolised by every apprentice in Villebénie; the craftsman's son who'd been made a Guardian knight for his prowess in battle. Before the persecution Parsifal had been an upright, pious man who prayed much and smiled little, close-shaven, with linen clean as his soul. These days he wore a grey-threaded, slightly matted beard and looked haunted. The kind of man in a threadbare cloak that you'd step around in the street.

Arnaud turned the iron with the tongs and sighed before he continued. 'The Guardians could be arrogant, but you could wish for none better beside you if it came to a fight. Lions, they were called, and they earned that name in every battle since the time of Salazar. But heretics? Idolators? No, by Tanguy!' He was silent for two strokes of the bellows, his eyes on the iron in the coals. 'The king's men arrested every Guardian they could find on the same day, without warning, all on the same detailed charges. They'd even prepared their confessions in advance, and the anakritim were waiting with their fires for those who resisted. No wonder they found some evidence.'

Arnaud pulled the reheated plate from the furnace with the pincers, and spat on it to test its heat before resting it on the bickiron, an angle of blackened iron like an upended foot. He offered the pincers to Guy.

'You do it.'

Guy aligned the plate and began the steady, laborious process of beating it into a curve with a heavy, flat-head hammer. It was an uncomplicated task that left time for thought. It was even possible to converse, in between blows.

'So why—did—the king—seize them?' Guy had asked this

question a lot when his father was taken. Perhaps now he was a man he'd be given an answer that satisfied him.

'The Order grew too rich. Simple as that. Noble families gave their second sons, and nearly every joining knight came with an endowment of land to support him in the sacred cause. After two hundred years, the brotherhood was rich enough to lend money to kings, and King Aloys needed money more than any, especially after the war to conquer Vriesland. Always growing his borders. Wars cost money. When you were a boy, he threw all the Yddayim out of his realm and took their money, just to avoid paying his debts. He owed the Guardians even more, both in money and honour. Remember it was a Guardian charge that broke the Vriesian line at Vannemeer. So they say he had them all arrested and called them heretics just so he could cancel his debt and take their gold.'

Guy finished one line of beating; the edge of the plate now curved by perhaps half a finger's width. He knocked out a minor irregularity and started another line.

'But—the anakritim—work for—the high priest—not—the king.'

'Ghislain Barthram is also the king's pardoner, and takes little notice of the high priest, who hides two hundred leagues away in Daija. King Aloys is here, and strong. He's a surer and faster route to the purple robe of an episkopos.' Arnaud touched Guy's arm to pause the beating. 'Enough! It's cooling. Work it cold, and the metal will harden. Then you won't be able to pierce it for breaths and rivets.'

This was the lore of the master. The right heat for working, gauged by spit. The much higher heat for hardening, judged by the colour of the flame and the hint of blue in the metal. And above all, the recipe for the quench, the liquid into which the hot steel was plunged. Arnaud's quench was a secret known only to him, but it involved vinegar and the piss of a beardless boy.

Arnaud sighed as they watched the furnace, coming to a decision. 'When you go tomorrow, I will come with you. I will make sure there are others in the crowd to watch you. Some you will know, like Parsifal. Make no sign of recognition.'

Guy swallowed, humbled at the thought that former Guardians would risk arrest to protect him. Or would they take that risk anyway to watch the charade of public confessions?

1.4 ADELAIS

Adelais stared open-mouthed at the scene of violence on the road below, too shocked to move. She'd never seen a man killed like that. It had almost been silent, after those initial shouts. A lance, jabbing like a youthful game; a sword flashing; a body that fell like a dropped cloak. A wider awareness crept back slowly, of her own panting, the wolf fading into the undergrowth. She could not go downhill into that chaos and must go back, now, while everyone on the road was staring at the cart.

Once over the wall she ran up the hill with her gardening sack thumping awkwardly against her thigh, and wondered why the little world of Montbeauvoir carried on so *normally*; the orchard was still lush with green apples, and novices still played between the vines, oblivious, running like her but with less urgency. She hissed a warning as she passed. Adeifi Fabianne still snored against the wall.

She touched the old adeifi on the wrist. The snort of waking became a frown as Adelais pointed down the hill. The little procession had already turned off the main road at the crossroads and was climbing towards them.

'They were attacked, Adeifi, just below us. I think a man was killed. They are coming here.'

Adeifi Fabianne reached for her stave and began to heave herself upright.

'Go. Tell the eldest daughter. Quickly, girl.'

'The mitera has gone to Sweetwells, Adeifi.'

The novices thought that the eldest daughter must have a great weight of sin, to walk twice weekly to the clerical complex of Sweetwells, a league to the north. Her unburdening would take half the day and she'd return flushed, 'from the hill', she'd say. One or two of the girls, the ones who'd known a boy's love, understood that look of fulfilment. They wondered, giggling, who pardoned the pardoner.

'Fetch her. Now. And *run*, girl.'

Adelais realised the gods were playing with her that day. As soon as she abandoned her attempt to escape she was *sent* out of the sisterhouse, on her own, by the woman who would have beaten her half dead if she'd been caught a few moments before.

She ran past the infirmary on her way out. It was outside the sisterhouse's area of seclusion in the small square next to the temple, where all people might come. She needed to warn Elodie that anakritim were arriving. Just as importantly, she needed somewhere to leave the bag with her incriminating cloak inside.

She wouldn't have survived the sisterhouse without Adeifi Elodie. When Adelais first came, delivered like a prisoner, she'd been crushed. Humiliated. Paraded before them all as the harlot who'd seduced a cleric. It hadn't been like that, she tried to say. Jan was young, he was beautiful, he was *Vriesian*. They'd grown up together, before he went away to study for the priesthood. He was just a junior cleric, anyway; he wasn't even consecrated, and when they were together the world had sparkled like sunlight on dew. She hadn't expected sympathy from the eldest daughter; she, after all, had the task of keeping Adelais here, a hundred leagues from temptation. But Adeifi Elodie had listened, even to her impossible dreams of a life with Jan back in northern Vriesland, beyond Galmandie's borders. She'd have fled to the shores of the Ice Sea with him if necessary. It was Elodie who'd held her in the darkest times, when that creeping realisation grew that Jan wasn't coming for her, couldn't come for her, and it was Elodie who'd rekindled her will to fight. *Be strong or go under, girl. Fight or sink. This is your life now.*

Adelais paused in the infirmary's doorway, letting her eyes adjust to the darkness. A double line of low wooden cots stretched away from her on the bare earth floor, four against each wall, although just one had been laid with straw and linen for a patient. Elodie knelt beside it, helping old Perrin to retch into a bowl. Perrin was wasting away with a bloody, stinking flux, and they kept him in the far corner lest the bad airs of his sickness contaminate others. Adelais slipped her bag with the incriminating cloak under the empty bed nearest the door, hoping that Elodie did not see. She couldn't run with it. She had to leave it somewhere, and in the infirmary with her friend was the least worst place. She called out her warning and ran, leaving Elodie's shouted questions unanswered.

There was a path along the ridge to Sweetwells. She had no need to run past the anakritim, and no wolf blocked her way. No one would have believed her if it had; after all, there were never wolves this close to the city, were there?

The pounding of her feet helped her think.

She could keep running, beyond Sweetwells, but she was still in a novice's habit. No cloak. No money. No knife. No food. One hundred leagues. Ten days at least. Bad idea.

Fjakkinn wolf.

That wolf was disturbing. Her grandmother Yrsa came from the Wolf People on the shores of the Ice Sea where the winter nights were four moons long. Yrsa would see the wolf as an omen, or a warning. She'd sailed south on her own father's boat forty summers before to trade furs and swords for Vriesian cloth. Back then a rune-marked, spell-wrought blade was prized above all weapons. She'd fallen for a Vriesian and stayed. Yrsa would treat the wolf with respect and make some obeisance, not throw stones at it.

But it was weird. In a strange way that wolf had not seemed wild.

It was almost as if it knew her.

1.5 MALORY

'It seems we are causing some alarm, Pateras Malory.' Ghislain Barthram pointed with his chin.

Ahead of them, a novice was running north, away from the sisterhouse, along a track on the ridge of the hill. She'd gathered the skirts of her habit into her arms to free her legs, and the anakritim's escorting soldiers whistled and cheered at the sight of female flesh – 'Fly over here, little bird!' – as if the attempt to kill their prisoner had never happened. Malory's heart was still pounding.

The girl ignored them. Her kerchief had fallen back from her head, revealing bright yellow hair, hacked short. Her legs were lean, almost white from the lack of sun, and lithe, like a boy's. Malory d'Eivet looked away before his interest was noticed. Ghislain Barthram took their vows of celibacy most seriously.

'She should be whipped, exposing herself like that.' Malory pretended outrage.

'And you'd like to administer the punishment?' Barthram turned, lifting an eyebrow, his smile hard.

'You jest, Pateras.' Malory blushed, despite himself.

'That is for you to say.' Pateras Ghislain kept his eyes on
Malory. Beyond his shoulder, the girl disappeared along the
ridge towards Sweetwells, leaping obstacles with urgent grace.
Malory reined in behind his master, his eyes cast down.

The sisterhouse of Montbeauvoir proved to be a poor affair,
trapped halfway between Villebénie and Sweetwells, and off
the main northward thoroughfare. They arrived in a square
bounded by low, wooden buildings that Malory guessed would
be the public areas: a travellers' dormitory, perhaps, and an
infirmary. They were all timber-framed, wattle-and-daub struc-
tures, roofed with humble thatch rather than tiles. The adeifes'
quarters and the working areas would be beyond a gated archway. A building that he might have mistaken for a headman's
hut formed the last side of the square, though the carved hand
pointing skywards from its roof and the single bell over the door
told him it was a temple. Even that was built of wood, with a
cone of thatch rather than a dome over its sanctuary.

Both temple and infirmary would serve only the local peasants who could not afford the donations expected at the great
fire temple of Villebénie. There, for gold, the sick could touch
the relics of the Blessèd Tanguy, the first disciple, who brought
the teachings of Salazar out of Alympos. They could even gaze
upon his skull, encased within a reliquary on the high altar, or
hold his holy texts in their hands. The relics made healing so
much more worthy, so much more likely to be effective. And if
they failed, the episkopos of Villebénie himself would intercede
for the sufferer to be accepted into the ranks of the blessed;
value was always given. No one of rank or wealth would visit
Montbeauvoir, just a league away.

It was perfect for their purposes.

A young adeifi stood in the doorway to one of the buildings,
staring at the anakritis-general, one hand lifted to her mouth in
consternation. She wore the flask badge of a licensed healer on
her breast, and Malory understood her reluctance to approach;

much medical knowledge had its roots in heathen, herbal lore. Though healers were taught the prayers to make their work acceptable to Ischyros, they all feared examination by the anakritim; they worked on the fringes of doctrine, and they all had something to hide, some experiment of healing that took them close to witchcraft. That adeifi's hesitancy would become outright fear when she learned who was before them. Ghislain Barthram never warned establishments that he would come. It was much more productive, he said, to catch people unawares.

Their escort spread out around them, rocking in their saddles to see under the thatch and through open shutters, until another, older adeifi came labouring through the archway, leaning on a stick. At least she had the courage to approach, though she froze as she came close enough to see into the cart. She tore her eyes from the body, now pushed into a corner, and looked up at them.

'Welcome, Pateres. I am Adeifi Fabianne.' Her eyes flicked sideways; Carel de la Tour had moved. Perhaps she'd thought there were two dead men.

'And I am Pateras Ghislain.'

'The Anakritis-General of all Galmandie,' Malory added, herald-like. He wondered if he should unburden his frisson of pleasure that came from such encounters. He so enjoyed the deference that came with reflected power.

The old adeifi's face paled almost to the shade of her hood. Just two spots of colour remained on her whiskery cheeks, perhaps from her recent hurry, comical blobs the size of ripe cherries.

'And how may we help you, Pateras?'

'I would speak with the eldest daughter.'

'She is unburdening her sins, Pateras, in Sweetwells. I have already sent for her.'

'Then we will wait.' Ghislain Barthram managed to say 'we' as if it were singular, the way the king said it. But then, he was also the king's pardoner. He waved dismissively at the cart. 'We were attacked on the road. The assassin is beyond your help, but I have brought a prisoner who would benefit from your care.'

'Of course, of course. May we offer you refreshment, Pateres? Wine? Bread?'

Pateras Ghislain swung out of the saddle and called towards a soldier who was edging his mount closer to the younger adeifi in the doorway.

'You. Carry the prisoner to the infirmary. Stay with him. And if any one of you so much as touches one of the adeifes, I'll have you all gelded.'

Pateres Ghislain and Malory were shown to a bench in an orchard that Malory guessed would be the eldest daughter's place of contemplation; the panorama of Villebénie spread across the southern horizon, with the dome of the fire temple piercing the smoke of the city.

Some would argue that the fire temple had fuelled Ville-bénie's growth more than any of King Aloys's conquests. Pilgrims came from afar, even from countries beyond the seas, to worship at the shrine of the Blessèd Tanguy, and his relics in Villebénie's temple lent authority to Aloys, their illustrious king, whose vast realm now stretched from the Alympian Sea in the far south to the Saxen Sea in the north.

The shadows shortened. Adeifi Fabianne brought wine. A bell tolled from the crumbling temple behind them, and in the vineyard below half a dozen novices shouldered their tools and trudged up the hill for the noon office. Pateras Ghislain rose to join them, signalling for Malory to stay.

'Watch for the eldest daughter. Tell me when she returns.'

Malory was content to sit in the sunshine. The scent of the flowers was almost strong enough to mask the city's stink, and in truth he found it tiresome to observe all six offices in a day. His uncle, the episkopos of Villebénie, had told Malory that some years with the anakritim would be good for his career, but

Pateras Ghislain did take life so very seriously. Besides, the adeifes' wine was good. And after that morning he needed it.

He still could not quite believe that a Guardian would try to kill one of his own. Malory toyed with alternative, political motives; the rivalry between the king's chancellor, Othon de Remy, and Pateras Ghislain was legendary. Secular power against spiritual power, both whispering in King Aloys's ear. De Remy could conceivably kill a prisoner if that would prevent Barthram gaining advantage. What was less likely was that de Remy had someone willing to sacrifice his life to do it, not when he could have simply bribed a guard to smother the prisoner in his cell.

No, all his reason said this was a Guardian attack, and a desperate one. That meant they were close to a great prize. Malory sat forwards on his bench, eager for activity. Between the trees of the orchard he could see the citadel of the Guardians rising outside the city: a great keep, a temple with a cluster of buildings around it, and a whole estate of fields and vegetable gardens enclosed within a curtain wall. Villebénie's slums lapped against those walls, making the enclosure look like an emerald mounted in filth. If he had been a Guardian and wanted to hide anything, he'd have put it in their keep, with their treasury. The citadel was more than a fortress, it was a self-contained town on the outskirts of the city, and a testament to the disgraced Order's former wealth and power. Now it was empty, with only a nominal guard to keep the rabble from looting it for stones and timber, or finding precious secrets where five years of official searching had failed. And it seemed the citadel really did hold some last secrets.

For now.

Away to the north the yellow-haired novice appeared over the brow of the hill, still running, and Malory moved to the gate to watch her arrive in the square. She bent to rest her hands onto her knees outside the sanctuary, breathing heavily, until the elderly Adeifi Fabianne hurried out to her. As the novice straightened Malory saw she was tall for a girl, with strong cheekbones flushed from her run, and double-bow lips held slightly apart for air. That rosy-faced panting stirred un-clerical thoughts in Malory and he looked up at the sun, measuring its passage. It must be two leagues to Sweetwells and back; the girl had made good time. He allowed himself another look as the girl whispered in the older adeifi's ear. She had an unremarkable figure, but what there was lifted her habit very prettily.

Adeifi Fabianne stepped back, nodding her approval. 'Go, help Adeifi Elodie in the infirmary. We have a new guest.'

The girl caught sight of Malory at the gate and glanced levelly at him before she left; a curious, unafraid, almost hostile stare that told Malory she needed taming. Her eyes were striking – a pale, ice blue rimmed with a darker shade where they touched the whites – and they seemed to look into him. A slight dimple on the point of her chin gave character to a heart-shaped, high-cheeked face. Dangerously attractive.

In front of him Adeifi Fabianne lowered her head deferentially. 'The eldest daughter is coming.'

Malory muttered his thanks, though his eyes were on the young novice as she stooped to enter the infirmary; her robe clung to her body, perhaps with sweat. It was a burden to him, this desire. By the God, if He wanted His priests to be celibate, why did He put such temptations in their sight?

'Will your prisoner be staying with us, Pateras?'

He had forgotten that the old adeifi was at his side. 'That is for the eldest daughter to say.' He forced his mind down a more pious road. In all his musings he had forgotten his priestly duties. 'Where is the body?' The man had been devout enough to wear a silver hand on a chain around his neck. Even a murderous Ischyrian deserved the Office of the Dead.

'In the infirmary, Pateras.'

'Then I shall pray over him, and offer the print of pardon.

The prophet tells us that even sinners merit the last office.' So now he *needed* to follow that novice into the infirmary; he had work to do there. He paused for as long as he might take to say the Prayer of Atonement. 'And then I will unburden our prisoner of his sins.'

The unburdening would be just the first step, a necessary preparation for all that must follow. It was time to set plans in motion.

1.6 ADELAIS

Adelais rested her hand against the infirmary doorway, letting the breeze cool her sweat. A body lay on the bed in the far corner, its face covered by sacks. The old man Perrin had lifted himself on one elbow and was staring at it, wide-eyed. Elodie knelt in a pool of light beneath a window, tending to the new arrival, and she glared at Adelais with untypical anger. Adelais groaned inwardly, looked towards the cot where she'd hidden her bag with the incriminating cloak, and swallowed at the sight of a soldier sitting in the shadows. He'd pushed his chain-mail coif behind his head, and was watching her with a half-smile that undressed her as she stood. A helmet shaped like a bowl lay on the cot beside him, and a length of chain that had probably bound his prisoner was piled at his feet. He licked his lips and spread his legs a little further apart, making the skirt of his mail hauberk clink as it fell into his groin. Adelais smiled sweetly, made the sign of benediction, and swore at him in filthy Vriesian that this *fjakkinn svín* would never understand.

Adelais knelt beside Elodie and risked a glance towards her bag. It was still there, behind the soldier's heels. The man mistook her look and opened his legs a little further. Adelais turned away and picked up a cloth, wishing she and Elodie could speak. Normally they worked well together, understanding each other with little need for speech. Adelais had never told Elodie that she'd been raised by a grandmother who followed the old gods. The 'hungry god', Ischyros was called in their village, because he would tolerate no other faith, not even Odhinn or Thor.

As Adelais leaned forwards with her cloth, the man looked up at her with deep, dark eyes that had sunk in the depths of his pain. When the face was cleaned to the colour of old chalk, she and Elodie took off the filthy brown robe and wiped a body that looked like a temple's wall paintings of the early disciples of Salazar: emaciated, wounded, loin-clothed, suffering. The man did not speak, but lay passive until a bubbling began deep in his chest that erupted into a retching cough that left a trickle of bloody sputum running from his newly cleaned lips. Adelais wiped his face again.

'Thank you.' He spoke with the cultured tones of a man of standing – a merchant, perhaps, or even a knight. The voice did not match the ripped, verminous robe or the dirty loin cloth that barely covered his modesty. His feet were useless, malformed, shrivelled back to the bone, and the colour of pus. One of them only had three toes remaining. It looked like a dead bird's claw carved in candle wax.

'May I have a little water?'

His silence had made Adelais think him simple. She fetched a fresh bowl, helping him as he gripped it between his wrists, with his fingers splayed in odd directions above its rim like the legs of a dead spider.

'What is your name, messire?' Elodie asked.

He looked at her as if he hadn't understood. His eyes flickered; perhaps the question was menacing.

'Who are you?' Adelais was more direct.

'His name is Carel de la Tour.' The young anakritis that

Adelais had seen in the archway darkened the entrance. The soldier stood in respect, clutching his helmet, and the priest dismissed him with a jerk of his head. 'He was a Guardian lay brother and is a heretic.'

Carel de la Tour shuffled backwards on the straw, watching wide-eyed and fearful as the priest crossed to the dead body in the corner. The anakritis picked up a drying-cloth to protect his robes from the dirt and knelt to lift the sacking from the face. Adelais turned away, swallowing the urge to vomit. The words of the Ischyrian Office of the Dead filled the room, in the High Tongue of Salazar, though the priest faltered at the part where the dead are named to their God.

'His name was Mauger,' the prisoner whispered. 'Brother Mauger of the Knights Guardian.'

'... *min petáxete ton adelfó Mauger apó ti géfyra tis krísis...*' Cast not Brother Mauger from the bridge of judgement...

There was silence behind her as the sacred ash of pardon was pressed into the man's forehead, and a rustle as the sacking was replaced. Adelais breathed more easily, until the priest came to kneel beside them at Carel de la Tour's cot.

'Carel, the time has come for us to part company.'

Was the man to be executed? But surely not, for the priest's face was suffused with kindness. A handsome face, some would say. The black hood of the anakritim should have made Adelais fearful, yet this one's eyes were gentle and his dark beard was freshly trimmed and oiled. The hood pushed back on his shoulders, revealing the blood-red cap of a consecrated pardoner, tied tightly to his head so that he seemed to wear a crown of curls. The other novices would nudge each other and giggle if they saw him. Adelais wasn't so taken; she wondered if he was too conscious of his own beauty.

'I have interceded for you with Pateras Ghislain, Carel.' The anakritis spoke almost lovingly. 'He has agreed that you may remain here, if the eldest daughter agrees. The adeifes will tend to your wounds.'

Carel de la Tour stared back, frowning, clearly bewildered. The cleric reached forwards and touched him on the shoulder to emphasise his words.

'Carel, I shall hear your sins, unburden you, and then you will be *free.*'

The words sounded stilted, and there was still no reaction. The man must have lost his wits. Elodie and Adelais backed away, giving them privacy for the unburdening, though as far as Adelais could tell, Carel de la Tour said little before the anakritis nodded to them to return.

'I have a last gift for you, Carel.' The priest spoke with the forced jollity of an adult encouraging a child. 'You have confessed to the grievous sin of heresy.'

Now fear leapt into Carel's eyes. The punishment for heresy was death.

'Carel, do you abjure heresy?'

Carel nodded, panic tightening his face.

'Say it.'

'I abjure heresy.'

The anakritis opened his silver box of sacred ash, reached forwards, and made the print of pardon on Carel's forehead with his thumb.

'*Apó ti chári tou Ischyros, sas xefortónomai tis amartíes sas.*'

Adelais knew the ritual words in the High Tongue. She heard them every time a pardoner visited. By the grace of Ischyros, I pardon you of your sins.

'*Zíste mia kalí zoí apó aftí ti stigmí. Sto ónomá Tou, amín.*' Live a good life from this moment on. In His name, amen.

Pateras Malory rocked back on his heels. 'Carel de la Tour, you are free of your sins. I welcome you back into the faith.'

Carel lifted his right arm, attempting to make the ritual sign of the faithful – a touch to the forehead, the heart, and the stomach, *mind, soul, and body for the God.* Carel's mangled hand turned the act into a parody.

'I may go home?' De la Tour spoke softly, as one not daring to believe.

'The citadel now belongs to the king. Your son must care for you now, when you are well enough to leave the infirmary.'

Now de la Tour became more animated. 'Guy will come?'

'I will bring him tomorrow.'

As the realisation sank in, Carel de la Tour's face began to melt, leaking tears like ice in sunshine. He lifted both hands to his face and crossed his forearms in front of his eyes. The wrists were raw with shackle sores and his body shook. The priest touched Carel's shoulder with great gentleness and looked at him with eyes that were so full that Adelais thought he, too, was going to cry.

Elodie tugged at Adelais's habit, pulling her to her feet and away.

'Forgive me, Pateras, but I must send the novice on an errand.' Elodie sounded as if she was forcing calm into her voice. Behind the priest's back she dragged Adelais's sack from under the empty bed. She glared at Adelais and pushed it into her chest, forcing her through the door into the square. The closing chants of the noon office sounded from the temple. Two guards stood beyond the entrance, their hands resting on sheathed swords. They looked over their shoulders at the movement in the square before turning their attention back to the road.

'I don't know what you were planning, but this must go back,' Elodie hissed. Adelais had never seen her so angry. 'While everyone is in the temple. For the God's sake, the anakritis-general is in there. The Angel of Death himself. Do it now.'

Adelais swallowed. The pause earned her another shove. 'Now!'

The eldest daughter's house formed the fourth side of the

small square, facing the temple, the infirmary, and a small travellers' dormitory. Elodie watched as Adelais climbed the two
steps to the door into the single, ground-level room that was
Mitera Chantalle's office, living area, and dining chamber; an
oak table that might seat eight was also her desk. Wooden steps
led up to a sleeping chamber in the roof space. A window had
been cut into the walls on both the northern, temple side and
the southern, garden side; it was a light space when the sun
shone. Iron-bound chests lined the walls, some big enough to
have cushions on their lids and to double as seats. One held
documents, which Adelais couldn't read, and another clothes
that were awaiting the needy poor. A third stored clothes that
were thought to be too fine for peasants, like the kirtle that
Adelais had been wearing when she arrived.

And her cloak. Adelais had risked much to find it, the last
time that Mitera Chantalle had gone to be unburdened at
Sweetwells. She'd carried a jug of flowers as an excuse, though
no one normally entered this room uninvited. But that cloak
was warm, and lined with squirrel fur. She'd need it walking
north. It might be the strawberry moon with the longest days of
the year, but the nights could be chill in the open.

Folding the cloak and putting it back was the work of a
moment. Adelais glanced through the window before she left;
Elodie had stayed in the square, watching. Adelais gasped and
backed away into the shadows as the anakritis came out of the
infirmary and began talking to her. He seemed to be making
conversation and in no hurry to move. Elodie was trying to lead
him back into the infirmary. He gestured at the sun, smiling.
She lifted her hand towards the garden. He shook his head, and
called for the guards, loudly enough for her to hear, and pointed
towards the infirmary. Two to be on duty at all times. There
may be another attempt. *Fjakk.* Now what could she do? The
window into the garden was mullioned; she could not escape
that way.

And now the mitera herself rode into the square on a borrowed horse, swaying uncomfortably in the saddle in the way of someone more used to walking than riding. Adeifes and novices were leaving the temple to help her. The older anakritis watched from the temple steps.

Sætur Sif. Sweet Sif, what now? They would come into this room, she knew. It was the only place. Adelais looked around her, her heart pounding. Hide above, on the mitera's own bed? No. The consequences would be unthinkable. But she might fit into the largest chest. Adelais lifted the lid and climbed in. It was just possible, with her knees drawn up like a newborn baby and her head rammed against one end. The lid would not quite close until she twisted, flattening herself into the clothes beneath, pushing her face into her own squirrel fur.

As the latch of the door to the eldest daughter's house rattled open, Adelais resisted the urge to sneeze.

1.7 MALORY

'*Sas efcharistoúme gia...*' Ghislain Barthram's brows furrowed in concentration. Malory d'Eivet had noticed that the anakritis-general gave thanks before food with the same intensity that he read the holy texts, frowning in his effort to squeeze meaning from the words. On the opposite side of the table, Mitera Chantalle had also closed her eyes in prayer.

'*Tóso charagméno epáno mas...*'

Mitera Chantalle's steepled fingertips were touching her lips. Quite sensuous, expressive lips, Malory thought, unusually so for an eldest daughter. She was nervous, but that was to be expected. Malory had known eldest daughters collapse in tears when the anakritis-general paid an unexpected visit to their sisterhouse. They always had something to hide, some petty iniquity, some laxity in their rule. And this one had been flustered when she returned, hurrying, gabbling her excuses like a child caught stealing food.

'*Kai gia aftó to fagitó...*'

She was younger than Malory expected, with a face whose faint lines showed maturity rather than age, and curves that filled the habit and scapula of her order rather well.

'*Prosefchómaste gia ouránio fagitó...*'

Winter forage, perhaps, but not unappealing. He wondered if her hair had begun to grey; adeifes' hair was always such a disappointment, cut short and flattened under their hoods.

'*... na mas ypostiríxei...*'

Ghislain Barthram believed in long prayers of thanks, perhaps because they demonstrated his command of the High Tongue. In front of them lay a simple meal of bread and vegetable broth.

'*... ston agóna mas...*'

... which was cooling rapidly. Did Pateras Ghislain never feel hunger?

'*... enántia stin aíresi...*'

The interminable prayer was drawing to an end. Malory eyed the jug of wine at the eldest daughter's elbow.

'*Me ti chári tou Profíti...*'

They chorused the *amín* in unison. Ghislain alone kept his eyes closed afterwards, feeding on heavenly food long enough for Mitera Chantalle to bring her hands back together. She had already dismissed the young novice waiting to serve them.

'I hear you were attacked on the road. You are unharmed?' The eldest daughter poured wine, with her own hand.

'Our prisoner was attacked but escaped injury. Our assailant was killed.'

'Thanks be to the God. And now you have brought us this prisoner to tend.' The eldest daughter hardly touched her spoon, keeping her eyes on the anakritis-general. He too waited, perhaps to demonstrate his disdain for matters of the flesh, and returned her stare.

'A heretic.' Pateras Ghislain made the word sound like a lowly form of cattle.

'Who has abjured his heresy,' Malory corrected gently, playing his part, 'and who is now reconciled with the faith.'

'And what was the nature of his heresy?' Mitera Chantalle

relaxed a little, perhaps suspecting that her sisterhouse was not the object of the anakritim's visit.

'He was a Guardian.' Ghislain Barthram spoke as if that were condemnation enough.

'We hear terrible stories of their practices. Can they all be true?'

'Such heresies as you would not believe.' Malory sighed. 'At their reception into the Order they were compelled to deny Ischyros and to spit upon the holy texts.'

'Salazar protect us!' Mitera Chantalle made the warding sign against evil, though her gaze was level and unconvinced.

Ghislain Barthram pulled his cloak closer around him and shivered as if in horror at his own revelation. 'And brother lay with brother in the foulest of perversions.' Barthram never seemed to shed that black cloak, even when a fire had been lit in a room. Hunched over the table, beak-faced, he looked like a roosting crow.

'Yet the Guardians were the high priest's own knights,' Mitera Chantalle challenged, 'owing allegiance only to the head of the faith. They were the vanguard of the army in every holy war since the Blessèd Tanguy brought the words of Salazar to the west.'

Malory lifted his head from his food. 'The issue is not the Guardians' willingness to fight, it is their heresy and idolatry.'

'Five years ago, before the arrests,' Mitera Chantalle persisted, 'the Guardians were seen as exemplars, the Lions of Ischyros, beyond all taint. Knights who welcomed death in the service of the God. How could it be that there were no whispers of such misdeeds?'

Barthram straightened on his bench, smiling slightly. If the eldest daughter knew the anakritis-general better, she'd realise how dangerous that smile could be.

'They were a closed order, Mitera. Initiates were sworn to absolute secrecy.'

'Yet, and forgive me, Pateras, half the noble families in the Ischyrian world gave their younger sons to the Guardians. Surely some word would have...' Mitera Chantalle's voice faded. She'd seen the warning in Barthram's eyes.

'It did, Mitera.' Malory tilted his bowl to scrape the last of the broth into his spoon. 'It reached Aloys, King of Galmandie, who asked the anakritim to investigate.'

The eldest daughter turned towards Malory, apparently more comfortable with challenging him than Barthram. 'Though I heard that His Holiness the high priest was most displeased with the king's intervention. The Guardians were, after all, a religious order. They owed no allegiance to any secular power, not even the faith's most powerful king.'

Malory was beginning to find this woman tiresome. It would be hard for the anakritim to remove her from her post without proof of heresy, but, even so, she must feel very secure.

'It is worth remembering, Mitera, that the anakritis-general also reports directly to the high priest.' Malory eyed the scarcely touched bowls in front of Pateras Ghislain and the Mitera Chantalle. If Pateras Ghislain ate a little more, he might not feel the cold so much.

Chantalle inclined her head towards Barthram. 'And it is an honour to welcome you, Pateras. I am sure you will soon tell me why so exalted a priest has brought us a patient wearing the robe of a humble lay brother.'

'This man was no ordinary lay brother.' Ghislain Barthram held her gaze. 'Carel de la Tour entered the Order after his wife died. As one who had been married, he could never be admitted to full brotherhood, but he became the Guardians' treasurer of Galmandie. He employed a small army of bookkeepers, and knew where all Guardian wealth was held. He understood money better than even the Yddayim.'

'It is curious how frequently conversations about the

Guardians turn not to heresy or idolatry, but to money, and the king's need of it.'

Malory sat forwards. 'You go too far, woman.' He wondered if her aggression was a way of asserting that she had nothing to hide.

'But is that why he was put to the torture?' Mitera Chantalle barely concealed her distaste.

'How else are we to learn the truth?' Barthram had a way of lifting that thin, pointy face as if sniffing for a response when someone might betray themselves. Malory enjoyed imagining his superior in unflattering guises, and decided the crow was now a hungry rat. A slight smile pulled back Barthram's lips, a look Malory knew well; the anakritis was playing with the woman. He was challenged so rarely that he may even have been enjoying himself.

'We serve Ischyros in different ways, Pateras. Here we show the God's love by easing suffering, not adding to it. So why have you brought him here? To heal him of his wounds? Surely the infirmary at the fire temple of Villebénie is better staffed, and blessed with the sacred relics.'

Barthram took his first sip of wine, as if considering his words.

'As you say, the Guardians were the swords of the faith. Before they became corrupted by Kakos they carved a path westwards for the holy texts of Salazar, and they defended Alympos against the Saradim hordes in the east. However, they acquired certain arcane items through conquest that they needed to keep secret, for the Ischyrian faith would not tolerate their existence. Many have said there is an idol, a golden hand, that their commanders adored at secret ceremonies and called their god.'

'The Hand of Salazar sits above every temple.' The eldest daughter shrugged.

'It is a symbol of the prophet, and points to the God. For the

Guardians, this golden idol *was* their god. They were heretics and idolators.'

'Can an order of Ischyros behave thus?' Mitera Chantalle made the warding sign again, this time with a little more conviction.

'We know this idol exists,' Pateras Ghislain continued. 'Too many have unburdened of it for it not to be true. The cords that each Guardian girded around their waist were touched to it to bind them to their vows.'

'You have held every Guardian in Galmandie for over five years, and put many to the torture, yet you have not found this *hand.*'

'The idol was shown only to a select inner circle, a third degree you might call it, above the knights and the lay brothers.' Barthram was losing patience. Malory knew the signs. 'These few are willing to die to protect it, and they would see such a death as martyrdom. They revere it as they should Ischyros, and fear it more than any torture.'

'Might it not be a sacred relic? We venerate the bones of Tanguy in the great temple. His skull is encased in a golden head.' This time, the eldest daughter's challenge was reasonable; Malory had asked himself the same question.

'Then why not share such a relic with the rest of the faith?' Malory gave her the same answer as he'd been given himself. 'A true relic would have immense value. Villebénie's wealth flows from Tanguy's bones.'

'The Guardians vowed personal poverty. They owned nothing. Perhaps they did not desire such wealth.'

'Yet their order was rich enough to be the moneylender to kings.' Barthram's voice became quieter, yet very clear, when he wished to end a discussion. 'The only possible reason for them to hide their hand was idolatry; they would be damned for revealing it.'

Mitera Chantalle breathed deeply, absorbing Barthram's

words. 'If the man you brought is only a lay brother, he cannot have been part of this third degree.'

'Yet he knows as much as a knight, perhaps more. He has said only that he was not worthy to look upon it, but that it was a treasure beyond price. What were his words, Pateras Malory?'

'Such a treasure,' Malory watched Mitera Chantalle for her reaction, 'that all the wealth of Galmandie was as a single crown in comparison.'

Mitera Chantalle blinked.

'That is gold beyond imagining. What makes you think this lay brother knows where it is?'

'As I said,' Malory replied, 'the Guardians' treasurer knew where everything of value was to be found.'

'And we believe,' Barthram added, 'that the attempt upon his life was made by a former Guardian so he could not divulge his knowledge.'

'He must already have told you much.'

'Indeed. But if he revealed a treasure of such value, the world would know about it. This Guardian knew the prisoner had more to tell.'

'So why bring him here? With king's men?'

Pateras Ghislain broke a piece of bread and dipped it into his congealing broth. 'Remember, Mitera Chantalle, that King Aloys was persuaded to move against the Guardians by terrible tales of heresies and idolatry. We have ample confessions, but there will always be some misguided souls who say that such confessions were only made to end the torture. Proof of their idolatry, and to be able to show the idol itself, would be highly desirable. In this the king and the anakritim are working together.'

'So, again, why bring him here? I will allow no torture in this place.'

Pateras Ghislain lifted his hands as if horrified at the thought. 'He is dying, we fear.' He sighed as if the prisoner was a loved uncle. 'The damp humours affect some of our guests at the Black Tower. Once they begin to cough blood, there is little hope.'

'And this man would die with the knowledge you seek locked inside him.'

'Just so.'

'And you have brought him to an infirmary in the cleaner air of Montbeauvoir, that he may die in comfort.'

By Salazar, this woman must really be taught to show more respect, Malory thought.

Pateras Ghislain pulled his lips into a snake-like smile.

'Not quite.'

1.8 ADELAIS

In some ways, her old cloak was comforting; it reminded Adelais of happier times. She could imagine she smelt her home: the tang of salt from the tidal Schilde, the crisp, nutty odour of flax seed before the spring sowing. The touch of fur against her cheek was an echo of childhood, of soft voices above an infant's cot rather than the menacing grate of the eldest daughter or, worse, anakritim. If she could have seen them properly, she might have watched their faces as they spoke, but within the chest there was only a thin split in a panel to peer through, so she listened to their voices as carefully as a blind woman.

'The damp humours affect some of our guests at the Black Tower. Once they begin to cough blood, there is little hope.' That was the older one, and he spoke with a quiet, chilling evil.

In other ways, she could have wished for anything but the cloak to lie upon. Each gentle breath, so carefully quiet, stirred the fur beneath her nose and made her want to sneeze.

'And this man would die with the knowledge you seek locked inside him.' Mitera Chantalle. Steely. Disbelieving. Strong. Adelais's respect for the eldest daughter was growing.

'Just so.'

Besides, the cloak reminded her that her own father had brought her here, bound and thrown in the back of his cart with rolls of cloth for the priests of Villebénie. He'd been the first in their village to convert, back when the duchy was free and all faiths were allowed. That conversion had brought him a thriving business weaving and selling fine linen for vestments. He could not afford to upset the priesthood. Useless daughters who *fjakked* a cleric must suffer the consequences.

That betrayal still hurt.

'And you have brought him to an infirmary in the cleaner air of Montbeauvoir, that he may die in comfort.'

Adelais's scrip was digging into her groin, but she could not straighten her legs. That hard edge might even be her grandmother's *taufr*. In her mind Adelais reached out to Yrsa, remembering how she'd sung rune song the night before Adelais was brought south.

It had begun with a slow drumbeat that resonated through the village as if the earth itself made sound, and none dared intervene, not with a staff-woman practising her art, for Yrsa was a *seidhkona*, one who could read the warp and weft of fate in the casting of runes. Yrsa would have been seated on the *seidhr*-platform in her house, with her knees man-wide and square, and her shoulders back, strong in a way that had little to do with muscle. Her ash staff would have been between her legs, twisted, rune-carved, itself a representation of the *isa* rune, and so thick at its top that she could not fully close her hand around its grip. She'd have been lifting it and letting it drop onto the wooden floor, beating time to her song and punching her will into the woven fabric of fate. And all the village, from disbelieving weaver to quivering priest, had fallen silent in the way that the world falls silent at the rumble of coming thunder.

All to make the *taufr* in Adelais's groin. Yrsa believed she could change fate with runes, and she'd carved the fate that would bring her beloved granddaughter back to her.

'Not quite.' The older one again. So cold.

Adelais wished she knew a rune that would get her out. Now. Before she twitched or got cramp or sneezed. She shifted her face, just a little, enough to bring her eye closer to the crack and take her nose off the fur. The faintest draught carried the tang of strawberries. *Strawberries!* The anakritim were honoured indeed; the first fruits of the sisterhouse's carefully tended beds were reserved for the eldest daughter and a select few adeifes. Never a novice. Unless, of course, they were on gardening duties and unobserved. Adelais's mouth watered. If she moved her head from side to side, very slowly, she could build up a partial picture of the room.

Mitera Chantalle sat with her back to the chest, at the head of the table. The younger priest was silhouetted against the window so she could not read his expression, but the older one was smiling across the table at Mitera Chantalle in a way that had more menace than warmth.

'Not quite,' he said again. This must be Ghislain Barthram, the one they called the Angel of Death. He held himself very still, hunched within a black cloak with the hood pushed back; dark eyes flickered within a thin face, like some creature peering from a cave. Adelais could see the rims of bowls over the edge of the table, one still heaped with fruit, and realised she was hungry. 'Pateras Malory has devised a solution where no one need suffer. He hates violence, you see. He intercedes for the prisoners, and pleads with me to stop the tormentors. He begs the prisoners to talk to relieve their suffering, and his distress is real. You might almost think the instruments were being used on him.'

The one he'd called Malory shifted in his seat. 'You shame me, Pateras.'

'On the contrary, I praise you for your gentleness. Ischyros works through you to achieve His aims.' Barthram turned back to the eldest daughter. 'The time we learn most is after I allow a prisoner to think that his ordeal is over, and that Pateras Malory has persuaded me to relent. The prisoner thinks he has won, and that he's held on to that precious pearl of information. We let his hope rise.'

'Only to take it away.' Mitera Chantalle's shoulders were high with tension.

'There! You understand. When a prisoner realises that all hope is false and that the anakritim are implacable, *then* he will talk.'

'So you will let us nurture him, then take him back to the Black Tower.' Adelais listened to Mitera Chantalle with respect. She'd loaded her words with distaste. And this was the anakritis-general of Galmandie.

'I fear, Mitera, that he would die.' This was the young one, Malory. Adelais would remember that name.

'Then I do not understand.'

'Pateras Malory's plan is elegant. I have taught him well.'

Adelais shifted her head to bring Barthram back into view.

'Carel de la Tour has a son, Guy. Just a boy when the Guardians were arrested, but now a grown man who is searching for his father. We will reunite them, here.'

Mitera Chantalle slowly straightened in her chair. Her hands went to the tabletop, fingers splayed. 'By the Blessèd Tanguy, you will torture the boy to make the father talk!'

'The mere threat will be sufficient.' Pateras Malory sounded confident. 'No man who has known torture could tolerate it being inflicted on his own son, not if he has the means to stop it.'

'And if the Guardian really does not know where this hand is to be found?'

'Then we will be sure of that fact.'

'But the boy is *innocent*.'

Barthram looked back at Mitera Chantalle with a face that

held no emotion. 'There are times, Mitera, when hard decisions must be taken for the good of the faith. Did not the Blessèd Salazar himself say that the path to Ischyros is through sacrifice, even of that we love most? Remember it is written: "Thus the Earth, the pearl of Ischyros, was made. It was precious to Him more than all in His creation, yet He would offer it in sacrifice as a snare for the Destroyer."'

Adelais knew that passage from the Vision of Salazar. Every novice must be able to recite it. *When the Destroyer reached out his hand to take the Earth, Ischyros cast a shining net of stars around him that bound Kakos to the Earth for ever, that he might no more cause havoc in the Heavens.*

'And consider what is at stake,' Pateras Malory added. 'Proof of the Guardians' idolatry.'

'And riches that would found a city, perhaps even a realm.' Mitera Chantalle almost spat the words at them. She stood and moved out of Adelais's vision, towards the window. The priests hardly moved, though Barthram brushed a crumb from his sleeve. His eyes came to rest on the crack in Adelais's hiding place, and his face showed neither patience, nor anger, nor guilt. Nothing. Those deep-set eyes could convince Adelais that he already knew everything there was to know about her, every sin, great and small. He lifted his face slightly as if sniffing, and she had a sudden fear that he could smell her, or could see movement in that tiny split in the chest's wood. Adelais pulled her face back, stifling a gasp. Her mouth was suddenly dry. Very dry. The dryness of running two leagues in a novice's habit, without water. Or maybe it was fright.

Mitera Chantalle murmured a passage from Salazar so quietly that if Adelais had not known the text she would not have understood. '... that the battle for Eternity might be fought on the Earth and not in the vastness of the Heavens. Thus it shall be until all that is evil is destroyed, and the hearts of men are once again pure. And on that day shall the bounds of Earth be loosed, and all people, whether they be living flesh or spirit, shall cross the bridge of judgement to sing the songs of eternity with Ischyros beyond the stars.'

Mitera Chantalle's voice strengthened. It sounded as if she had turned to face the priests. 'Pateras Ghislain, sometimes the boundaries between good and evil are hazy and we must look into our hearts to pray for the answer. I fear to offend you, but I must ask you to remove your prisoner. Plans such as this should be hidden within the walls of the Black Tower, and I want no part of them.'

Adelais risked another look through the crack. Malory had just bitten into a strawberry, and its scent oozed through the split panel. Mitera Chantalle came into view and stood behind her chair, her backside blocking her view of Malory, though she could still see Barthram. The anakritis-general now had a humourless smile on his face; clearly he had expected that sort of answer. 'Mitera Chantalle, your sensitivity is commendable. So few of the sisterhouses that I visit would dare to question us. Most are simply keen to conceal their own iniquity. Why, we have found adeifes with lovers, and even nursing their babies.' The anakritis's voice hardened. 'And, saddest of all, an eldest daughter receiving a very carnal form of instruction from her pardoner.'

Mitera Chantalle sat heavily on the chest. Puffs of dust sprayed into Adelais's face and she held her breath, straining. She moved one hand, too swiftly, to push her nose and block a sneeze. The anakritis was still talking.

'We, the anakritim, have long battled to free the faith of heresies, and to bring discipline back to all realms. In pursuing the great heresies, such as the Guardians', we often uncover individual failings that are just as grievous. That eldest daughter's order reacted very harshly. I believe she was sent to tend lepers in some distant corner of Galmandie, far from Sweetwells.'

'Pateras, I, I...' Mitera Chantalle seemed lost for words, and Barthram spoke over her.

Adelais stifled a sneeze with her fingers. *Gods help me!* Mitera Chantalle stood, widening Adelais's view. Adelais held her breath, again, expecting the lid to lift.

'Naturally, we will respect your decision, Mitera Chantalle, and remove our prisoner. But would you like to reconsider? After all, Pateras Malory and I do the will of the high priest...' He waved at the table, inviting her to return and sit.

Chantalle stepped to the table as if in a dream. As she turned, pulling at her chair, her face moved out of the shadow of her hood. She looked suddenly old.

'Why do you not simply arrest the boy? Why does this have to happen here?' Chantalle sat, heavily, as if her legs were newly weak.

'We know little about the boy, only that he approached Pateras Malory in the street. By his garb, he is an apprentice, but we do not know his master or where he lives. If we sent soldiers for him, we'd lose him in the alleyways of Villebénie. He must go willingly where we can be sure of seizing him. And few go willingly into the Black Tower.'

'Then how will you find him?'

'Tomorrow, the last three officers of the Guardians, including Grand Master Bastien Guerin, will make a public admission of their idolatry in front of the great fire temple of Villebénie.' There was a hint of pride in Barthram's voice; perhaps his first sign of emotion. 'Pateras Malory and I will naturally be there. Pateras Malory asked the boy to come to him afterwards. He will then bring him here. My escort will remain here, in the travellers' dormitory, to secure the boy and ensure the prisoner is not killed or removed in the meantime.'

The silence in the room was broken only by the sound of Malory moving the bowl of fruit, wood on wood. Mitera Chantalle pushed herself upright against the table, and turned towards the door.

'I think I need a little air.'

Mitera Chantalle paused by the chest on her way to the door. Adelais was about to exhale in pure, wonderful relief when the chest filled with the noise of its bolt being shot home, locking her inside.

Adelais had no way of measuring the passage of time. She was hungry. She was thirsty. And worst of all, a cramp began in her leg that had her squirming inside the chest, all thought of concealment gone, but she was unable to straighten and had to endure the agony. The pain was bad enough for her to make a high keening and thump at the lid, begging for release, but either no one heard or no one came. It faded, eventually, leaving her gasping into the fur of her cloak. The space by her mouth was now wet with her drool.

The bell tolled for afternoon office and the chest filled with the muffled sounds of novices and adeifes in the courtyard on their way to the temple. Instinctively, Adelais made no sound.

The silence stretched. *Sweet Sif, help me.*

Finally, footsteps into the room. The clump of thick, sister-house boots on a wooden floor, and there was urgency in their pace. The bolt shot back and Elodie looked down at her, unsmiling.

'Get up.'

Elodie had to help her. Had almost to lift her out and massage Adelais's legs into movement. Her frown softened as she worked and realised Adelais's state.

'Can you stand?'

Like a crone, only by leaning on Elodie's shoulder.

'She knows, doesn't she?' The eldest daughter. About Adelais in her room.

'She'll talk to you later. Brace yourself.' Elodie's look said *'this time, I can't protect you'*. 'She sent me to let you out while the courtyard was clear. The anakritim are in her garden. And if anyone asks, we're changing linen.' Elodie pushed a pile of it at her. 'And don't even think of running.'

'I don't think I could.' Adelais had to circle the table twice before she could even walk without stumbling. Elodie linked arms under dirty linen to keep her upright as they crossed the courtyard, smiled sweetly at the guards outside the infirmary, and let Adelais slump onto the bed by the door. She sat alongside her and, unexpectedly, reached for Adelais's hand.

'So what were you doing?' Elodie did not sound angry any more, just hurt.

'I was going to run away.' There was no point in lying. Not to Elodie. 'Then the anakritim came.'

Another squeeze, acknowledging the honesty. 'I'd have missed you.'

'And I you. Above all, you. Sorry. But I couldn't say goodbye...'

'Of course. Tell Mitera Chantalle that you changed your mind. That may help.'

'What will she do?'

Elodie shrugged, sadly. They sat together watching Carel de la Tour's chest rise and fall in sleep. It was a laboured, struggling movement. Perrin also was asleep in his corner.

'He's dying, isn't he?' Adelais nodded at Carel, breaking the silence.

'Even with care, he would not last a moon. He's coughing blood.' Elodie sighed. 'I gave him hemlock, henbane and opium. It is probably his best sleep in years.'

'He will need strength tomorrow.' Adelais took a deep breath and told Elodie what she'd heard. By the time she'd finished Elodie had buried her face in the bundled linen.

'In the great fire temples, they have choirs to sing the

offices.' Elodie lifted her face. Her eyes were wet. 'Men and boys, their voices weaving together in harmony that rings beneath the dome as if angels were singing. It is so beautiful it is impossible not to believe. How can that produce this.' She gestured at Carel.

Adelais had no answer. She was simply waiting for the summons to Mitera Chantalle and untold punishment.

'He told me the tormentors held his feet in the fire to make him talk.' Elodie had hunched over, rocking slightly. 'They smeared them with pig fat first to make them burn better.'

Adelais put her arm around Elodie and drew her into a hug, a frightened novice comforting an adeifi.

'And now they expect me to heal him with prayers and salves, so he can watch them do it to an innocent boy.'

Elodie sniffled into Adelais's side and pushed herself upright on the bed. She patted Adelais's thigh in thanks.

'We do not serve the same God.' Elodie's fingers fretted with her rope belt for several breaths with her head lowered before she spoke again. 'There's a question I wanted to ask you. How do people heal the sick in the pagan lands, where they don't know the power of prayer?'

Adelais took a deep breath. This was dangerous.

'With herbs and salves, just the same.'

'And?'

'Runes.'

'Tell me.'

Adelais stood and looked out of the door. One guard was sitting on a stump, sunning himself with his sword across his knees. Another stood in the road. Neither was within hearing. She returned to the bed, thinking of the lessons she'd learned at her grandmother's knee. She spoke so quietly that Elodie leaned close to hear.

'My grandmother Yrsa is *seidhkona*, a wise woman. She says that a rune is a shape—what she calls a "stave"—and a song, and above all a mystery.' Adelais bent down and drew in the dust.

'This is *bjarkan*, the rune of the birch tree, but the stave is only a drawing that tells of mysteries beyond. We could never climb that tree's branches nor cut its wood.'

Adelais rubbed the rune out with her foot and looked over her shoulder. This was madness. There were anakritim nearby.

'Keep going. I want to understand.'

And Adelais was trusting Elodie a great deal. Rune lore was not permissible in Galmandie. 'A rune is also a song, and the song of each rune is different, as the sound of wind through the trees is not the music of the stream.'

In a strange way it was exciting to share this knowledge. She and Elodie were like girls complicit in some great naughtiness.

'The *seidhkonur* teach us that all life is connected, and that the web of fate is one great song: the harmony and disharmony of this world. It is rune song, richer than any fire temple choir.'

Adelais had expected Elodie to be shocked, but her friend smiled and said, 'That's beautiful.'

'Women with the gift of prophecy, the *spakonur*, cast the runes for someone and read the fate that is being woven for that person at that time. The runes are like a window onto the web of fate.' Adelais paused, watching for her friend's reaction. This was dangerous talk. 'Yrsa says that those who are adept at rune lore, the *seidhkonur*, can alter fate with rune song. They can literally change the web of fate.'

'Ah.' Elodie's shoulders sank a little. 'That's witchcraft.'

'It's *seidhr*. It has been our way since the gods were young. It is the way a *seidhkona* heals, with herbs and the rune songs of healing.'

'Show me a healing rune.' Elodie had recovered quickly. She was genuinely curious.

Adelais drew in the dirt again.

ᚢ

'*Úruz*, the rune of the aurochs, the mighty cattle. A *seidhkona* can sing its strength into her healing.'

'Will you sing it for him?' Elodie nodded at Carel. Adelais was shocked. She had never seen Elodie in this rebellious mood.

'He is beyond rune song and I am not *seidhkona*. Besides, you will get us both burned as witches.'

Although she had once whispered the song of *úruz* over a dying child in the infirmary.

'*Úr er skýja grátr, ok skára thverrir, ok hirdhis hatr...*'

The child had lived, against expectations, but Adelais had no idea whether that was her rune song or Elodie's ministrations.

A clatter of hooves interrupted them, making them both look over their shoulders. The anakritim were leaving. Adelais felt a sense of dread; there was nothing now between her and the eldest daughter's wrath. She breathed deeply and stood in the doorway, meeting her fate, knowing what must come now.

Mitera Chantalle was crossing the courtyard. She stopped, pointed at Adelais, and crooked her finger.

'You. Come.' Contained fury tightened her voice.

Adelais followed Mitera Chantalle up the steps, back into her office. She swallowed, feeling a little light-headed. The eldest daughter's shoulders were braced as if she already held a whip. Adelais flinched as the mitera rounded on her.

'Of all the souls in this sisterhouse, only you would have the impudence to do such a thing.' Chantalle was shorter than

Adelais and had to tilt her head back to glare up into her face. 'Why?'

Adelais lowered her head. There seemed no point in lying. 'I took my cloak because I was planning to escape, Mitera. I changed my mind. Then I could not get out.'

'Did you hear it all?' Chantalle's voice was cold as iron in winter.

'Yes, Mitera.' No point in denying it.

'And you have told Adeifi Elodie?'

'Yes, Mitera.'

'Then we are all bound by a terrible knowledge. We are in each other's hands.' Chantalle paced the room and looked out into her garden as if looking for inspiration. The sunlight through the window was lower now, softer, polishing the wood of the shutters with gold. She turned, glaring as if she might turn Adelais to stone. 'And do you have an opinion about what should be done?'

Adelais's head snapped up. The eldest daughter was asking *her* for an opinion? Adelais breathed deeply and swallowed, letting her answer rise from a point of calm within her. 'Did not the Blessèd Salazar himself write, "whatever ye do for the sick and the helpless, ye do for Ischyros?"' Adelais felt a fraud; one who still called on the old gods and had just quoted Salazar to an eldest daughter. It was Elodie's favourite verse. She was noble-born and could read, and one day she had taught it to Adelais. Dear, devout Elodie, who would kneel beside a dying man and bathe the face of her God.

Mitera Chantalle's stare slowly softened until she nodded, satisfied. 'I should have you beaten, girl. But if I beat you as you deserve the others will ask why. So instead I have a task for you. But if one word of this gets out, I'll have you flogged so hard you'll wish you could die. I have an errand for you. It might prove dangerous. And yours will not be the only life that depends on your success.'

CHAPTER 2

2.1 ADELAIS

Adelais sang the responses for the dawn office with such enthusiasm that her fellow novices glanced at her curiously. *They* were still puffy-eyed with sleep; *she* was to be allowed out, and she'd been awake before the first bird song, hugging herself with excitement. *She* would be allowed ordinary clothes for the day, to blend with the crowd, for no novice would ever be let out unsupervised. Unless, of course, it was to fetch the mitera from Sweetwells. *She* could make choices. She might even choose to turn north, towards Vriesland.

In front of them Mitera Chantalle knelt to feed the sacred fire with sweet-smelling wood, exercising the eldest daughter's right to lead the office in the absence of a consecrated priest. As she rose to dismiss them, she unhooked the veil that had covered her mouth and nose to protect the holy flame from desecration by mortal breath. The face she revealed sent the convocation on its way swiftly, in silence. All save Adelais.

They stared at each other, not speaking. Only when they were alone did Mitera Chantalle reach into a hidden corner of the sanctuary and pull out a pile of folded clothing. Adelais's heart sang as she recognised her own chemise and kirtle. She

even laughed at the touch of fine linen, so soft against her skin
as she buttoned the chemise to the wrist, until she caught
Mitera Chantalle's disapproving glare. She hid her face in her
bundled kirtle, inhaling its scent to smother her smiles. There
was no smell of home, only the too-familiar scent of the cedar-
wood chest.

The kirtle was of good quality, as befitted a merchant's
daughter, and had been dyed a rich green to show off her golden
hair; people would see she had some status even if it hung
unfashionably loose from her shoulders. There was even her old
belt that would sit low on her hips, still with its small knife in its
sheath – the kind any woman carried to cut food. Adelais
threaded Yrsa's scrip onto the belt, squeezing it gently to feel the
resistance of the bind-rune *taufr*.

No cloak. 'The day is warm,' Chantalle said with an edge of
distrust. She was not going to let Adelais have anything that
would help her go further than the capital.

Mitera Chantalle touched Adelais's roughly cut hair and
tutted. Not enough was left to form maiden's braids, so she must
go with her head fully covered, as a wife. A simple linen cap
was found for her hair, and a kerchief with a veil that could be
pinned across her face to complete the disguise.

'Acceptable.' The eldest daughter eyed her critically. 'But
unfashionable.' The ladies of Villebénie now had their gowns
cut to fit, and laced across their stomachs to display their curves.
'What trade did your father follow?'

'He is a weaver, Mitera.'

'Then if you are asked, you must be a Vriesian weaver's
wife, come to sell cloth. Vriesians always were behind the
times.'

The eldest daughter had explained her logic the evening
before. She saw torture as a sin, even if she set herself at odds
with the mighty anakritim. If she was to prevent this sin against
an innocent boy, in her own sisterhouse, Carel de la Tour's son

must not come. So now Adelais had to find a boy called Guy that she'd never met, and persuade him to believe her rather than a consecrated priest. She could but try.

'Watch the young anakritis,' Mitera Chantalle repeated her instructions, 'and when the boy makes contact, follow and warn him.'

'But what if Pateras Malory takes the boy with him?' Adelais did not have high hopes of success.

The only solution Mitera Chantalle could offer was to give her a single coin, enough to bribe a child to take a message to Guy and bring him to her if she could not approach.

'Don't fail me, girl.' The eldest daughter gripped Adelais's shoulders, glaring up into her face. 'And don't get caught.'

She handed Adelais her staff, not noticing how tenderly Adelais received it; this too had been a gift from Yrsa. Only Adelais knew that the pattern of lines carved into its shaft were also runes, overlaid until they formed a continuous, apparently innocent, decorative band. But Chantalle was already at the temple door, checking that no novices or adeifes were in sight. She sent Adelais on her way, warning her again about the consequences of being caught; the eldest daughter would deny she'd sent her, saying Adelais had overheard the anakritim and taken it into her own head to warn the boy. Her punishment would be in the hands of the anakritim. Serve her right for eavesdropping.

As soon as Adelais was out of sight of the sisterhouse she paused, glanced around to make sure she was alone, and turned her scrip inside out until she could remove the yew-wood *taufr* talisman. She handled it carefully, for the delicate black crust in the carved depths of those runes would be Yrsa's blood. Rune carved upon rune to multiply their power, making a lattice where no single rune was dominant. She could make out *thurs*, the rune of Thor, a rune for strong defence:

A single stroke turned *thurs* into *raido*, a rune of journeys both of the body and mind:

Cuts that mirrored *raido* added *odhala*, the hearth-rune, a rune of heritage and ancient right:

There were others. Yrsa had not had the chance to explain, except to whisper that the *taufr's* destiny was to bring her home. 'You too have a destiny,' Yrsa had told her. 'And you have power; the threads of fate pass strongly through you. Come back that I might teach you. And because I love you. But first you must endure much.'

Had she endured enough, yet? Two years in a sisterhouse? The prophecies that had seemed so real, so possible when Yrsa had spoken them, had faded like a fireside story told in childhood. And after endless chanting in an Ischyrian temple, even her memories of rune song were fading.

Adelais returned the *taufr* to its hiding place and walked on. At the crossroads below she must make her decision – north towards Vriesland or south towards Villebénie. She let her staff tap out a rhythm as she walked, like the slow canter of a horse, and dragged the memory of the rune song of *raido* from deep within her mind. She even dared to whisper it.

Reidh er sitjandi sæla,

For riding is the joy of horse folk,
Ok snúdhig ferdh,
And the speedy journey,
(*Would she have a speedy journey?*)
Ok jórs erfidhi
And the toil of the steed.
(*But she didn't have a steed.*)

And Yrsa had told her never, ever to sing rune song, not until she had spent many more years learning the lore. 'You have power, child,' she'd said. 'You are like an infant with a sharp knife, more a danger to yourself than anyone else.'

Adelais stopped singing. To sing a rune without knowing the full mysteries of its lore was too dangerous.

So what if she walked north? Jan would be a consecrated priest by now; he'd feel bound to the Ischyrians by gratitude for taking an innkeeper's son and teaching him to read. He wouldn't want her, and she was no longer sure she wanted him. He'd been part of growing up.

Her father wouldn't take her back, not when he needed the clerics so badly. But Yrsa had held on to the old gods. Yrsa wanted her home. Perhaps they would go beyond the Schilde together, where the laws of Galmandie did not apply. They could take a ship back to Yrsa's homelands in the far north. Adelais remembered ships blowing upriver from the sea, lean dragon-headed vessels full of Northmen with their furs to trade, or fat-bellied cogs stuffed with Saxen wool. But she hadn't enough money even for a single meal, and her scrip held only bread and cheese for one day. And there was Adeifi Fabianne's brutal warning about how a lone woman without money would be expected to pay for help. She'd rather die than that.

But she had her sling, still folded within her scrip. She'd been good, before the sisterhouse, able to bring down one sitting pigeon in two from a tree at twenty paces; better with a sling-

shot than most of the boys were with a crossbow. They'd hated
that. Her cache on the hillside held more clothes, and flint and
char. She stared at the crossroads and the stream of people
flowing both ways. A knight rode proudly north, with three
more horses in his train: his squire, his baggage, and a great war
horse – a destrier – prancing along with a leather roll of chain-
mail and a great helm tied to its saddle. A merchant drove a cart
full of sacks of grain south, ambling slowly behind a small herd
of bullocks being driven to the slaughterhouses in the butchers'
quarter. A humble cleric walked north with a bag slung over his
shoulder, swinging a stave. Villebénie sucked in food and spat
out priests and soldiers.

And loose among the travellers' feet was a dog. Not a wolf,
but the wolf-like Theignaulter breed that were good for hunting
or guarding. It stopped and lifted its nose at her, sniffing, until
its master whistled and it ran after the cart. South. As omens go
it was as good as any. Adelais could almost hear Yrsa say it.
'South, *mynn litla Sif.*' My little Sif. Yrsa had always called her
that after Sif, the golden-haired wife of Thor, the thunder god.

South, then. Adelais turned her back on Vriesland and
joined the stream of humanity flowing into the capital, crossing
the bridge over the open sewer of the Pissbourne. She felt her
spirits lift, despite the stench. It felt right. Besides, she might
save a boy's life. She would let this fate be woven. She even
laughed again at being outside, unwatched, unknown, herself. A
passing priest frowned at her, clearly disapproving of this feminine jollity. She put her shoulders back saucily and giggled at
his deepening scowl. Today she was allowed to be Vriesian; she
did not have to kneel, hunched under a burden of guilt that only
a priest could lift.

Adelais knew the way to go. She'd visited the infirmary at
the fire temple of Villebénie with Elodie to buy supplies.
Behind the city's gates the Great North Road led directly to the
bridge over the Gaelle onto the Isle, the ancient heart of Ville-

bénie, and the fire temple was on the Isle. Elodie had tugged her along while she'd stared open-mouthed at the greatest city she'd ever known; the Vriesian capital of Siltehafn was a village in comparison. Today she had time to dawdle, *must* dawdle, for the southward flow moved at the pace of the merchant's bullocks. She looked into the shops as if she might buy; none need know how empty was her scrip. Pies, ale, boots, cobblers, clothing, all offered on shutters that folded along their bottom edge to make a counter. A blacksmith plied his ringing, fiery trade in a small square.

Adelais's wonder did not last. The streets stank of shit. Bullock shit. Human shit, tossed into the back streets by those who couldn't afford the ordure carts. Piss. Adelais walked in it, slipped in it, breathed it, and somewhere ahead was an abattoir and a tannery, perhaps the only trades with a strong enough stink to cut through. A stall by the road was doing a good trade in herb and flower nosegays, wrapped in linen. The buildings themselves trapped the smell; a road that was three carts wide narrowed to half that above her head where upper stories, two levels above the road, projected out to make an arch above.

The crowd was slowing. The bullocks had been driven down an alley into the butchers' quarter, but now the flow was choked by a narrowing of the road. High above even the over-hanging houses she could see the towers of a castle. Once its walls might have been the clean grey of newly worked stone; now they were grimed with soot for over half their height, as if the fortress itself waded through filth. This, Elodie had said, was the Black Tower, and it earned its name not from its colour but from the deeds that happened within, for this was both the king's prison and the home of the anakritim and their tormen-tors. Its massive walls encroached into the road, and as Adelais came closer the crowd fell quiet in awe, or fear, or simply the crush. They shuffled forwards with the nearby lowing of cattle from the slaughterhouses almost muffled by the mechanical din of hammers from the armourers' quarter on the other side of the road.

And from within the walls of the Black Tower came the deep boom of a drum to unsettle the murmuring quiet. It beat slowly, ponderously, demanding attention. Every head turned to stare as the dread gates swung slowly inwards.

2.2 GUY

Guy had heard that in his great-grandfather's day the whole city of Villebénie could be contained on one island in the River Gaelle, and that the Black Tower had guarded the landward approaches to the bridge onto the old quarter of the Isle. Now, Villebénie's walls lay a quarter league or more from it, and the Black Tower had become a prison. It squeezed the Great North Road into a narrow passage opposite the butchers' quarter. Guy and Arnaud watched each other's backs as they waited; there was no love lost between the butchers and the armourers, who faced each other across the neutral frontier of the road. Apprentice fights were common, and a packed crowd was an ideal place for someone to even an old score. On the whole, the armourers were better fighters, but the butchers were better fed.

They were not the only loiterers. Arnaud's brother Parsifal was hunched in a corner. He flinched away, almost guiltily, at the sight of his brother and Guy.

Yet he glanced at others. Guy followed the looks, becoming aware of one or two similarly haggard men waiting in doorways, all watching the Black Tower as a drumbeat, slow as doom, announced the opening of the great doors of the prison. Soldiers with the royal badge on their surcoats, a yellow sunburst on a blue field, beat a path through the crowd. More mailed men followed with spears held flat across their bodies to keep the way open. Behind them, the drummer stepped out, flanked by mounted spearmen, so that the procession forming behind was hidden at first.

When he was a boy, Guy's father had let him meet Bastien Guerin, the Grand Master, and in that meeting Guy had known that his father was truly an important man, for he walked and talked with this legendary knight. What was more, Guy saw that his father's counsel was valued. Together Carel de la Tour and Bastien Guerin met the ministers of King Aloys, with his father sitting at Guerin's right hand. Guy remembered a tall, sunburnt knight whose long beard was already greying. That day Guy had been disappointed that Guerin wore no armour, only a sword at his hip, but his pure white surcoat bore the proud lion salient of the Guardians – a red lion, rearing on his hind legs, with both forepaws raised and clawed in front of him. Best of all, the face that had been furrowed with the affairs of state softened as he rested his hand on Guy's shoulder. Like his knights, he'd called Guy 'Carelet', and Guy thought his chest would burst with pride.

None of the three men led out from the Black Tower could be him. To be sure, they wore threadbare, once-white surcoats whose lion emblems announced they had been Guardian knights, but these men were old, even pathetic. Their wrists were bound and they flinched from the light, hiding their eyes in the crook of their arms, but even if their faces could not be seen clearly, such men could not be the heroes of the Order. They wore no mail, and no hose, so that their dirty surcoats flapped against bare shins. One was barefoot, and all three staggered as if walking was a skill they had half-forgotten. They looked like beggars newly roused from sleep in a ditch. Then one of them lowered his arms and straightened, forcing himself upright even though he still screwed his eyes at the sun. He pushed his shoulders back and spoke, astonishingly, in the voice of one who had commanded armies.

'Come, Lord Brothers, let us make an end of it!'

And Guy recognised Bastien Guerin. The giant of his childhood had shrunk to his own height. A thin white beard trailed from a face as pale as dawn clouds, but now, as Guerin stepped out from the gates, the first in a trio of ghosts, he had the bearing of a king in rags.

More spearmen walked beside the prisoners, ready to encourage them forwards or to keep the crowds back with the butts of their spears. A woman in the crowd screamed '*Rahoul!*' and one of the Guardian knights lifted his head, seeking the sound. A noblewoman tried to reach through the men-at-arms to touch him, but was knocked back and almost trampled by the crowd until her steward cleared a space above her with his stave. A boy of about twelve helped her to her feet. '*Courage, Isabeau!*' the Guardian called as they were swept apart.

'Rahoul Cheyne.' Arnaud had to shout into Guy's ear over the noise of the crowd. 'He was Grand Commander of Jourdaine.'

But Guy's attention had turned to the anakritis on the fine grey horse bringing up the rear of the procession. He'd thrown back his hood, leaving just a priest's blood-red cap tied under his chin, and he wore a smile on his face that was almost triumphant.

'Pateras Malory!' Guy tried to push through the crowd, calling, his eyes on the anakritis so that he did not see the spear butt until it thumped into his belly, dropping him gasping to his knees. The man-at-arms marching at the priest's stirrup cursed Guy for getting in the way, while, beyond him, Pateras Malory waved the sign of benediction at the crowd, oblivious.

'Smug-looking bastard, ain't he?' Arnaud lifted Guy to his

feet, but held him back from following. 'Let's not get too close right now.'

Guy stared at him, still finding his breath.

'Look around you, lad. Parsifal ain't the only Guardian here, even if none wears the lion badge.' Arnaud lifted his chin towards a man-at-arms in a threadbare cloak that had weathered to the muddy brown of winter-bare fields. He wore no identifying device on his surcoat, and had lifted the cowl of his cloak over his head, shadowing his face. Although old enough for his beard to be wholly grey, he carried himself like a veteran in his prime; one gauntleted hand steadied the sword on his hip with easy familiarity.

Arnaud frowned, concentrating. 'That's Humbert Blanc, who was Grand Commander of Arrenicia. I thought all the high officers had been taken. And I've seen that one before, I'm sure.' He pointed at a broad-shouldered, heavy-set greybeard for whom the crowd instinctively parted. 'Something tells me that today won't run quite as the anakritim intend.'

2.3 ADELAIS

Adelais kept her face lowered as Malory d'Eivet rode past, hunched over her stave like a crone. Finding the priest had been easy; she just had to wait with the crowd outside the Black Tower and follow when the procession emerged. She was able to keep his grey horse in sight as she was pulled along within a press of bodies by the slow beat of a drum somewhere ahead. Between her and Pateras Malory was a group of apprentices, also following the procession; perhaps one of them was Guy? Or knew him? As they flowed out over the Great Bridge towards the Isle, Adelais plucked up her courage, picked a pleasant-faced young man who might be the right age, and touched him on the arm.

'Do you know Guy, son of Carel?'

The apprentice looked at Adelais and called to a nearby youth in a way that made her grip her stave more tightly.

'Guy! It's your lucky day!'

The youth pushed through the crowd towards her, his stained apron and abattoir smell telling her he was a butcher. Two companions turned with him.

'You are Guy, son of Carel?'

'Yeah, I'm Guy.' He reached past her face and unhooked her veil before she could flick his arm away. 'What d'ya think, lads?'

Four apprentices now stood around her, hands on hips, taunting. The crowd divided and flowed past them, squeezed between the apprentices and the silversmiths' booths lining the bridge. Already the priest would be drawing away from her.

Adelais breathed deeply, remembering another river, near her home. She'd upset some village youths by being better at 'boy's' games like running and hunting with a sling, and boys don't like to be beaten by a girl. They had wanted to reassert their manhood in the worst way possible. There she had been surrounded on a dyke, not a bridge, but the circle of young men had the same cat-with-mouse manner.

'Bit scrawny.'

Then, she had been truly alone. Here, she might as well have been; she was ignored in the multitude. The threat was the same. Between the booths lining the bridge she could see barges pulled up on the River Gaelle's north strand, unloading their goods. Watermills turned between the stone piers of an old, wrecked bridge, powering unknown workshops – armourers, by their din, she thought. On the bridge itself silversmiths' hammers tapped rapid patterns against tiny anvils in their booths. The stink of sewage rose from the river. She was irrelevant to the life and the decay flowing past.

A hand groped her backside and she spun, jabbing her stave towards the apprentice's face but not striking home; a warning, for now. She breathed again, forcing calm into her body and her mind. She had learned her lesson that day on the dyke: stay calm, act tough. She'd even prayed to the goddess Sif. Today she might do it again.

'Tight little arse, though,' the apprentice behind her smirked.

Adelais snarled at him and turned back to the one who'd called himself Guy.

'I have a message for Guy, son of Carel. What business did your father follow?'

'He wields his chopper, like me.' He moved menacingly close and pushed his pelvis towards her. 'Big choppers run in our family, see?' The surrounding apprentices sniggered.

No way could this lout be Carel de la Tour's son. Adelais closed her eyes and breathed. *Sætur Sif vera medth mér. Sweet Sif be with me.* It had worked on the dyke. She tapped her staff lightly on the ground, picturing the *tiwaz* rune in her mind.

Tiwaz, the rune of victory.

Týr er einhendr áss...

Swift as a heron striking for a fish, she swung her stave point upwards between his legs, hard, and jabbed backwards with the other end until it hit something behind her. 'Guy' sank to his knees, white-faced, mouth gaping, clutching his crotch, no longer a threat. Adelais danced sideways, expecting to be grabbed by the one who'd touched her, but he was staggering away, both hands covering his face, blood already flowing over his chin. She'd probably caught his nose. Lucky. Sif was indeed with her. She pointed her stave at the other two, glaring at them, crouched and ready to strike. One hung back but the other stepped towards her, and she angled her stave towards his face.

'Take the boys home to their mamas.' Another thing she'd learned in Vriesland. Play the part. Sound as if you're in control, and you will be.

The youth glanced over Adelais's shoulder, and saw something there that persuaded him to flick his hand in a gesture of contempt and back away. Adelais straightened, swallowing, and turned to see a tall, wiry, grey-bearded knight staring at her, ten paces away. He held his hand across his body, ready to draw his sword. Beyond him, a thick-set man-at-arms watched with his arms folded, grinning as if the scene was amusing. Both of them had the look of veterans down on their luck; cast-out retainers of a dead lord, perhaps, but still with the chivalry to come to a woman's defence. The knight straightened, dropped his hand, and inclined his head towards her. That small sign of respect made Adelais swallow again, blinking back tears as reaction hit, and for a moment she bowed against her stave, beginning to tremble, needing its support. When she forced herself upright, all she could see of the knight was the mud-brown hood of his cloak bobbing over the heads of the crowd. Pateras Malory was out of sight.

Adelais pushed forwards, newly fearful of the crowd. She tried to keep the protective knight in view, fearful also that Malory would make contact with Guy without her seeing. By the time they reached the square before the great fire temple, the three prisoners were being pushed up the temple steps onto a wooden scaffold that had been erected in front of the doors. Each step was made of blocks cut from the rune stones that had encircled a sacred grove on this spot before Tanguy brought the faith to Galmandie. Adelais could see carved runes, laid randomly so their meaning was broken, gradually being worn smooth as generations of worshippers trod the old gods into oblivion. Thus were the writings of Tanguy fulfilled: *Evil has many faces, but there is only one Ischyros. Wherever there is a shrine to false gods, it is to be crushed, and its rubble made the foundation of a temple to Him.*

The knight was now only four paces away and Adelais stayed close to him, staring up at the prisoners. One of them had his head bowed, like an ox before an abattoir, passive, stumbling towards his fate. Two stood erect, un-cowed. Soldiers ringed the platform's base, facing outwards, using the flat of their swords to stop any from coming too close, so that those at the front pressed backwards, away from the blades, while the square still filled from the rear. The noise and stink of the crowd was constant, so thick that it might have been the drone of flies over a dung-heap. Into this hum came the insistent boom of the drum, quietening the crowd with each blow as if the drummer were beating the crowd-sounds into the ground. By the time the massive doors of the temple were thrown open, and a procession of nobles and priests emerged, only a few people spoke, and they in whispers: *'Is that the king?' 'No, the chancellor, de Remy.'*

Adelais had never seen an episkopos before, and here there were three, resplendent in their purple – the princes of Ischyros. She watched in awe as they were led to thrones at the back of the scaffold. She hooked her veil more tightly round her face as Ghislain Barthram, the anakritis-general, appeared behind them with Malory. With a final beat of the drum a herald stepped to the edge of the scaffold, holding out a parchment scroll, and the final whispers ceased until the only sound was the soft movement of people brushing against each other as they jostled for a better view. Into this shuffling silence of a thousand bodies, the herald's voice rang clear.

'Know ye that in the twenty-second year of the reign of our most puissant lord, Aloys, King of Galmandie by the grace of Ischyros, reports were made of a bitter thing, a hateful disgrace, most grievous to the faith. Our gracious king had news that the brotherhood of Guardians, spawn of Kakos in the habits of an order of the God, were desecrating the holy texts.'

Murmurs passed through the crowd, and many made the warding sign. In front of Adelais, the elderly knight visibly tensed but kept his head lowered and hooded. His companion rested his hand on his sword's hilt and glared up at the herald as if challenging him to a fight.

'At first our gracious king found it difficult to believe such ominous news, suspecting that those who brought the tidings were acting from malice and envy, moved more by hatred and greed than by any religious fervour. However, so many protested to the king, including persons well worthy of belief, that our lord king met with the most holy high priest, by the grace of Ischyros the ruler of our faith on Earth, and together they agreed upon a full and rigorous investigation to determine the truth of these matters.'

The knight's companion turned his head to one side and spat contemptuously into the dirt. Those around him began to edge away.

'Through the diligence of our lord king, and of the anakritim, this inquiry found that these false brothers committed sins beyond any pardon. When they entered the Order and made their profession, they were confronted with the image of the prophet Salazar, and in their pitiful blindness they were made to spit in his face and upon his holy texts.'

A thousand mouths gasped. The sound spread outwards through the crowd, seemed to break like a wave against the surrounding buildings, and flowed back to the scaffold in a low growl of anger. The herald held up his hand for silence.

'Furthermore, the profane rite of their order was a disgrace to the dignity of the human race. Kakos had so deformed their minds that they were bound to accept the request of another brother that they lie with them carnally in the most horrible, dreadful intercourse.'

The knight clenched his fist amidst the roar of the crowd. Adelais looked around her, studying faces. Some reminded her of spring festival performances, when mummers wore painted masks of devils and the Blessèd Ones. Such onlookers neither believed nor disbelieved, but their exaggerated reactions were part of the entertainment.

'They were found—' The herald waited for silence. '—they were found to be an idolatrous order, worshipping a golden image of a hand as if it were their god. The cords they tied around their waists, over their shirts, were touched to this graven idol, and for this sin above all has the wrath of Ischyros fallen on these sons of infidelity.'

Others wanted to believe. Their faces were pinched or snarling in anger. Some of them stooped to pick stones and dirt to hurl.

'This unclean tribe has abandoned the one true faith of Ischyros as revealed by the Blessèd Salazar, has exchanged its glory for a graven image, and made offerings to idols. Having no hope of crossing the bridge of judgement, they do the will of Kakos on Earth as they shall for eternity in the pit.'

But there were a few, like the knight and the man-at-arms beside him, who watched with a different kind of anger, the disbelieving anger of those who are powerless to stop a great wrong. Carel de la Tour's son would be one of those. There were several grizzled men who might themselves have been Guardians; one leaned on a crutch, trailing a useless foot. Had he, too, been tortured? One of the few who were both visibly affronted and young enough to be Guy stood some distance away, across the space cleared by the swords of the guard. The boy stood beside a muscled man perhaps ten years his senior with the white spark-burn scars of a blacksmith or armourer on his face and neck. Could that be him?

'That you may know these matters to be true, three great officers of the Order have been brought to confess their crimes before the people, and to receive the judgement of the high priest and of our gracious lord, King Aloys. Hear them, and see what becomes of those who deny Ischyros!'

The crowd surged forwards, and the soldiers around the scaffold turned their sword-points outward to keep them at a distance. The first of the Guardian prisoners was pushed to the edge of the scaffold, a balding, white-bearded old man who stood with his shoulders slumped, as if life itself was too great a weight for him to bear. He waited until the crowd was quietened by another beat on the drum.

'I am Fabien d'Erembourc, who was Grand Commander in Delmas.' D'Erembourc spoke quietly, mumbling his words, so that some in the crowd cupped their ears and called for him to speak up. Pateras Malory prodded him as if he were a dancing bear.

'I was admitted into the Order of Guardians fifty-one years ago.' He spoke more strongly, and the crowd quietened as his great age triggered some sense of pity. He looked down towards the knight near Adelais and a flicker of recognition crossed his face, followed by what seemed to be pain as he screwed his eyes shut and spoke towards some point high over the crowd. 'At my admission I was required to spit upon the image of Salazar and the holy texts, and to deny Ischyros. This I did, but with my lips only and not with my heart.' The words seemed wrenched from him, an excruciating litany poorly learned. He opened his eyes, shook his head slightly, and lifted his hands towards the knight as if begging forgiveness.

A moan rose around Adelais like a collective sadness.

'All those I have since received into the Order, I have likewise required to deny Ischyros, for the statutes of the Order required it.'

The moan turned angry.

'Furthermore, we worshipped a hand as our god, in the grievous sin of idolatry.'

Both the knight and the man-at-arms stepped forwards, glaring up at d'Erembourc, but stopped when they met the points of the guards' swords. A clod of earth flew over the heads of the crowd. It burst against the scaffold's railings, showering both d'Erembourc and the ring of soldiers with dirt. The herald moved to stand beside d'Erembourc, held up his hand to quieten the crowd, and read again from his parchment.

'The crimes of Fabien d'Erembourc are grievous, but our

gracious lord King Aloys and the high priest are merciful. Though deserving of the flames of Kakos, Fabien d'Erembourc will spend the remainder of his days in prison, so he may pray that when he crosses the bridge of judgement, he may be shown pardon for a life of sin and be accepted into the company of Ischyros.'

Pateras Malory led d'Erembourc away, and pushed another old Guardian to the rail. At the sight of him, the knight near Adelais swept back his hood, exposing his face, and began to chant in a voice loud enough for the man on the scaffold to hear.

'Ischyros be merciful and shine upon us, and lift *His hand* to bless us!'

The knight had made a strange inflexion as he said 'His hand', giving the words particular meaning. On the scaffold, the old Guardian looked down and smiled in the way a man might greet a good friend after long absence. He nodded once, perhaps in reassurance, and completed the next lines of the chant.

'That the way of truth may be known among all nations.'

The Guardian lifted his head, put his shoulders back, and called to the crowd as if he were a king addressing his knights on the eve of battle.

'I am Bastien Guerin, Grand Master of the Order of Guardians.'

2.4 MALORY

Malory d'Eivet held a scented cloth against his nose to put a sweet smell between him and the multitude below the scaffold. At least the weather was not too warm. The poor always stank more in the heat.

The day was going exceptionally well. Malory had seen Carel de la Tour's son in the crowd, and had lifted a hand in recognition. The hope in the boy's eyes told Malory that he would soon be able to lead him to Montbeauvoir. Moreover, the anakritis-general was well pleased with that first confession. Ghislain Barthram was not a man who showed emotion; he was a black-and-white man, like his habit, without shades in between. Even his mouth was thin and straight as a ruled line on parchment, but Malory had come to know him well. There was a certain set to the shoulders and a look that was not quite a smile, more a hint of satisfaction.

Yet next to Barthram, Othon de Remy – King Aloys's chancellor – was actually beaming, showing so many teeth that his square face had become skull-like. In the matter of the confessions, these political enemies had common cause. De Remy's seneschals, the king's deputies in each region, had orchestrated the arrests to his command. The anakritim had ensured the confessions. De Remy had replenished the treasury while the anakritim had consolidated their grip on the faith. Such public admissions of guilt took away any remaining questions about whether they had been right. De Remy was leaning across the nearest episkopos, trailing the blue velvet of his sleeves across the cleric's purple satin in his eagerness to ensure all three had fully appreciated the Guardians' depravity.

Even the episkopes had made significant looks at each other as Fabien d'Erembourc made his grovelling confession. They were the high priest's men, and the high priest had never been convinced about the Guardians' guilt, despite all the evidence the anakritim had collected. Those episkopes were the real audience for this spectacle, not the rabble below the scaffold. Surely they must now be persuaded?

A notable like Fabien d'Erembourc was an excellent start, and there was not one mark of torture upon his body. Some men, particularly the Guardians' inner circle, seemed immune to pain, though most men had some weakness. D'Erembourc's great fear, they'd found, was being trapped in a confined space. He had been part of that third degree, yet all it had taken to persuade him to tell the truth was to be enclosed in a stone coffin and slid into a low vault that held it shut. And dark. Very dark. They'd left him an airhole, and fed him milk and water through a hollow reed. When they took him out after ten days, he'd confessed to denying Ischyros, but still refused to tell them about the idolatrous hand. He'd screamed and blubbered and fought like a weakling child when they put him back. It only took another day, and by then he was so desperate to stay out of the hole that he'd have told them anything.

This was the art of the anakritim – to know when a sinner has truly told all, and then to grant Ischyros's pardon. It seemed d'Erembourc really didn't know where the hand was hidden, but now he saw his future life in prison, in a cell where he could sit and stand and move his arms, as a vision of paradise.

A clod of earth burst against the rail, and Malory moved forwards to pull d'Erembourc back. He'd done his job, and Malory didn't want the crowd's anger to spill over before they'd heard the others, particularly Guerin. He'd been saving him for last, but perhaps now would be safer, just in case there was a riot. Malory led Guerin forwards, offering the crowd the main dish early in the feast.

'I am Bastien Guerin, Grand Master of the Order of Guardians.'

At least the crowd would have no difficulty in hearing him.

'To say that which is untrue is a crime both in the sight of Ischyros and man.'

Guerin paused, and a quiet tension settled on the crowd. Something in Guerin's bearing had told them that this was not to be a simple admission.

'I tell you, as one who will this day meet his God, that not one of we brothers has betrayed his faith nor his country.'

Malory gasped and took a step forwards, unsure whether to intervene; this was *not* what was agreed. He looked at Ghislain Barthram for guidance as Guerin's voice thundered on from the rail.

'I do confess my guilt, which consists in having, to my shame and dishonour, through the pain of torture and the fear of death, given utterance to falsehoods imputing scandalous sins and iniquities to an illustrious order that has nobly served the cause of Ischyros. I disdain to seek a wretched and disgraceful existence by engrafting another lie upon the original falsehood.'

A sigh spread through the crowd such as Malory heard when a holy relic was revealed. He started forwards to drag Guerin away, but the herald was already ahead of him and had seized Guerin's Guardian surcoat. He tugged at it, but Guerin's hands were locked on the rail so the herald looked foolish. Somebody barged Malory from behind so that he stumbled, dropping to one knee. He looked up to see the Guardian Rahoul Cheyne cuffing the herald around the ear, making him drop the surcoat.

'Crawl away, puppy!' Cheyne kicked the herald in the backside, sending him sprawling. The crowd, which moments before had been throwing clods at the Guardians, now laughed at their captors, rejoicing to see authority humbled. Cheyne stepped up to the rail, clasped Guerin's shoulder in brotherhood, and bellowed at the crowd.

'I am Rahoul Cheyne, who was Grand Commander of Jourdaine. I, too, tell you that the accusations against the Order are false, and born out of King Aloys's greed. My confession, like all such confessions, was wrung from me by the most terrible torture, to my everlasting shame.'

Malory stepped towards the two Guardians, unsure how to stop them without the indignity of a public scuffle. An emphatic hand signal from Barthram stopped him. He too was on his feet, turning to shout at the captain of the guard by the scaffold's steps. 'Provost! Stop them! Seize them!'

One of the soldiers tried to climb the scaffold from the square, but Cheyne drove the heel of his palm into the man's face, sending him tumbling backwards. The rabble cheered as if this was some glorious festival and a tumbler had performed a difficult trick. The mood had changed faster than Malory could say the Prayer of Pardon.

'Know then, and tell all Galmandie,' Cheyne bellowed, 'that Bastien Guerin and Rahoul Cheyne chose a terrible death rather than bring further false dishonour upon our order. We are the Lions of Ischyros. Today we will cross the bridge of judgement and we will do so innocent of the charges brought against us.'

The provost commanding the guard and two of his men

reached the platform, their boots thundering over the wood. A stamp to the back of the knee toppled Cheyne, and the pommel of a sword crashed into his temple. He dropped senseless to the decking, but Guerin took one more breath, and shouted in a battlefield voice that echoed around the square.

'Know your king to be avaricious, and a teller of falsehood. Know your high priest to be weak. And know the Guardians to be innocent!'

A mailed arm hooked around Guerin's throat and dragged him backwards. The old man did not struggle.

A long moment passed when no one on the scaffold seemed to know what to do next, until a swelling roar of applause seemed to spark the dignitaries into action. The episkopes rose, spoke briefly together, and left in flutters of purple, saying they would send word to the high priest. The chancellor, Othon de Remy, smiled a grim, bitter smile at Pateras Ghislain and crossed the platform to face him. The anakritis-general looked away, white-faced, and in that brief exchange Malory saw his superior's royal influence drain away.

De Remy picked at a speck of mud on his glove. He was a short man who refused to look up, so he seemed to be addressing a mole on Barthram's lip. 'We must prevent this contagion spreading.' He had to shout over the crowd's cheering.

'The law is clear,' Barthram answered, loudly enough for his words to carry to Guerin. 'Any man who recants a previous confession of heresy may be considered a relapsed heretic, and may be burned by the secular authorities without further trial.'

Bastien Guerin heard his fate impassively, his face calm, a man reconciled to death, though his body made small jerking movements as a soldier bound his hands behind him. At his feet, Rahoul Cheyne began to stir, groaning.

'Provost!' De Remy called to the captain of the guard. 'Build a stake. In a place the king can see from the palace windows.'

'The Isle of Dogs, my lord?'

'Perfect.'

'I must inform the king.' De Remy lifted an eyebrow at Barthram. 'Perhaps you wish to accompany me, and explain?' The look on the chancellor's face was a foretaste of the meeting to come.

Barthram stepped closer to Guerin and stared into his face. 'Five years, Guerin. Five years' work to come to this point. I never thought you would fail me thus.'

'Was it only five years, Anakratis? You made it seem so much longer. Had I not spoken these truths, I would have failed myself and my immortal soul. One day, you will answer before Ischyros for your foul deeds.'

'I am Ischyros's humble servant and have only done His work. But you must face the fire today, Guerin.'

'And I shall rejoice in that pain, for with Ischyros's grace it will purge me of my earlier weakness.'

'And after your pain, the bridge of judgement awaits you. It will be a long drop into the pit of Kakos.' The anakritis turned his back on Guerin, his jaw tightening. 'Pateras Malory!' His voice rasped like a sword being pulled from its scabbard.

'Pateras Ghislain?'

'I must reach the king before that fox de Remy. Stay with the prisoners. Be my eyes and do what must be done. Make sure the provost waits for a signal from the palace; there will be a meeting of Council but the outcome is inevitable.'

'But our other prisoner, Pateras? Carel de la Tour?'

'Tomorrow. Guerin has bought him another day in comfort. But then you must not fail me; I need to give the king good news, and soon.'

'What of this one, Pateras?' The provost pointed at d'Erembourc, who stood slack-jawed at the rear of the scaffold. 'He has not, er, recanted.'

'Take him to the Black Tower. And as for Guerin and

Cheyne,' the anakritis locked eyes again with Guerin, 'make it slow. The king will want to hear them scream.'

2.5 GUY

'They are the bravest men I ever saw.' Arnaud l'Armurier stared up at the scaffold, where soldiers were milling about the Guardians. Rahoul Cheyne was on his feet again, but white-faced and staggering, holding his head.

'Surely,' Guy answered, 'the high priest will intervene? He must soon know that they are innocent?'

Arnaud spat in the dirt. 'The high priest is in Daija, two hundred leagues away. It would take at least a moon for word to reach him and a messenger to return. Those two will be dead today, before the news has even left Villebénie.'

The prisoners were now at the base of the scaffold and a procession formed around them. Cheyne pushed his shoulders back and forced himself upright, though he winced at barked orders around him. Trickles of blood ran from his ear and nose. The provost, now mounted, led the way westwards out of the square, towards the royal palace. The crowd watched in murmuring quiet, until a voice called 'the prophet Salazar bless you, Brothers!' and a waterfall of applause began in the anonymous depths. As they passed Guy and Arnaud, Guerin called to Cheyne.

'Did you hear, Lord Brother, the king wants to hear us scream. Do you think we can deny him that pleasure?'

Cheyne stretched to his full height, causing fresh blood to fall from his face onto his dirty surcoat. Guy saw that he, too, was old, with perhaps sixty years snowing his beard.

'By the manner of our deaths let us be judged, Master.'

'And let the king be judged, Lord Brother.'

The butt of a spear tapped Guerin on the side, warning him to be silent, but the blow was light, without malice. Most of the soldiers had the pinched faces and hunched shoulders of those no longer enjoying their duty. And at their rear, again mounted on his grey, came Pateras Malory. He seemed to be in shock; he stared at the people around him as if he were unable to comprehend their awe for the two Guardians. No soldiers flanked him, this time, so Guy was able to approach. The grey was fidgeting in the throng, and Guy placed a hand on the horse's shoulder to calm him; Pateras Malory was shaking his head, muttering.

'Fools! Fools! They are heretics!'

'Pateras Malory, it is Guy, son of Carel!'

The cleric looked down, frowning, but his face calmed as he recognised Guy.

'Guy! I have managed to move your father to an infirmary!'

Guy felt a lurch within his chest.

'Where is he? May I see him?'

'He was in failing health when I found him. With the God's help we will save him.'

'Ischyros bless you, Pateras!' Guy swallowed, fearful for a moment that he would weep.

'Come to me outside the Black Tower, tomorrow, after the second office, and I will take you to him.'

Guy gripped the priest's hand and pressed his face to it, but the throng was surging around them and the horse began dancing, sidestepping away. Pateras Malory lifted his hand in benediction and called out loudly enough for all around them to hear.

'Kakos has been at work here today!'

'Aye,' shouted Arnaud, 'and he rides a grey horse.'

The priest's face flushed scarlet as the laughter broke over him, and he spurred after the procession.

'My father lives.' Guy stood still in the seething mass of people, ignoring the jostling shoulders as the crowd swept after the Guardians. 'I will see him!'

'Come, lad.' Arnaud shook his shoulder. 'Let's see today out, and hope for a happier morrow.'

Another hand touched Guy's arm, more gently, and stayed there, insistent. A woman stood beside him, almost tall enough to look him in the eye, respectably but unfashionably dressed in a loose green kirtle. Blue, frowning eyes searched his face as she unhooked her veil to speak.

'You are Guy, son of Carel, the Guardian?'

'Aye.' He was still too dazed to think clearly, or to wonder why a strange woman would stop him in the street, would *know* him even. Without her veil, she was younger than he expected, about his own age, and she had the lean, tanned features of someone who worked much in the open. Beyond her shoulder, Arnaud pushed his way back to them.

'Your father is at the sisterhouse of Montbeauvoir. It is a trap.'

'A trap?'

'This one,' she lifted her chin towards Pateras Malory's back, 'and the anakritim think your father knows where the golden hand of the Guardians is to be found. Go with the priest, and *you* will be tortured until he tells them.'

Guy stared at her, searching her face for signs of falsehood. He saw none. He turned to Arnaud. 'Master, this woman says...'

'I heard. And who are you?' Arnaud moved closer to the woman.

'My name does not matter. I risk much to be here.' Her eyes flicked nervously between Arnaud and Pateras Malory's back.

'How is my father?' Guy faltered.

The woman's gaze steadied on Guy, and compassion softened her features.

'Remember your father as he once must have been. Do not try to reach him now. The anakritim held his feet to the fire, and he will never walk again. More torture will kill him, and his secrets with him. He coughs blood—'

'I must go to him, now!'

'Do you not understand, you fool?' A flash of anger hardened the woman's jaw. 'That is the cruellest thing you could do. There are soldiers with him. You will be taken. They believe he will tell all he knows if he is made to watch them torture you.'

Guy stared at her, his mouth working silently as he struggled to absorb her news. Arnaud touched the woman's shoulder, grim-faced.

'How many soldiers with him?'

'Four, all king's men, all well-armed...' She glanced over Arnaud's shoulder, gasped, and turned away, lifting her veil into place. Guy twisted to see what had alarmed her, and found himself staring after Pateras Malory. The priest had turned in the saddle as the procession left the square, and was looking directly at them with his brow furrowed.

'I must go.' The woman slipped away from them. Arnaud reached out to stop her but she dodged his hand, nimble as an acrobat. Twenty paces away she stooped, leaned on her staff like an old woman, and was lost in the throng. Guy stared after her, numb. In the time it would take to close two links of chainmail, his hopes of seeing his father had been raised, after five years, and then cruelly dashed.

'Remember, lad,' Arnaud rested his hand on Guy's shoulder. 'Trust good steel, and trust the friend beside you, but don't trust priests. I believe her, whoever she is.' Arnaud turned Guy to join the flow of people, and together they walked with the last of the crowd.

'I'll go to my father tonight. Carry him away.'

'By Salazar, you'll take a man who can't walk from under the noses of at least four king's men? On your own? Be sensible, boy. You'll do your father no favours, and I'll lose the best apprentice I've had.'

Arnaud could be brusque when he wanted to hide emotion. Guy let him lead them around the royal palace, following the crowd. His shock was turning to anger, a raw, seething anger that found a focus when they caught sight of the priest in the distance, dismounting on a small, marshy island that trailed downstream from where the Isle tapered into the Gaelle. The causeway of logs onto it was slick with mud and was being trodden ever further into the slime by the throng, but even when Guy stumbled he kept his eyes on Malory d'Eivet's back. If he'd had a sword, he might have pushed his way forwards and run the priest through. Though of course that would earn him the eternal fires of the pit.

But Guy had no sword and Pateras Malory was surrounded by soldiers. Near him, in the middle of the island, Guy could see two men across the heads of the onlookers. They stood on barrels, taking it in turns to beat a stake into the muddy ground with armourers' sledgehammers. For a while the press of people kept Guy and Arnaud on the island's banks, but Arnaud used his muscle to force his way towards the ring of soldiers around the prisoners.

The Guardians knelt facing each other, their hands folded and their lips working in prayer. To one side, stacked baulks of dry timber and faggots of brushwood lay ready. Closer to the stake, a bare-chested executioner blew a head-high heap of charcoal into glowing heat with a blacksmith's bellows. Already those nearest to it in the crowd were backing away, shielding their faces, and those further out protested as they scrambled to keep their footing on the bank. Pateras Malory stood near the prisoners, though they seemed not to need spiritual comfort.

It was unreal. Two men faced a terrible death, and the crowd waited in near-silence. The air crackled with tension as it might before a thunderstorm, though the sky was clear. Afternoon sun slanted over the Gaelle, where boats packed with onlookers rowed steadily to keep pace against the current. Behind Guy, the palace's leaded windows shone in myriad squares of precious glass; behind one of those faceted reflections would be the king.

And still they waited, jostled by those who wanted to stare wide-eyed at the kneeling Guardians. In front of Guy, a fat merchant grabbed at his belt and spun, cursing, but the cut-purse was already gone and the purse backhanded to a waiting accomplice. A hawker pushed through the crowd, selling skewers of charcoaled meat from a tray slung round his neck, until an elderly knight in a dirty cloak shouted at him to show respect, and kicked him into the Gaelle. The laughter that followed was brittle, the nervous release of many breaths that have been held too long.

The executioners climbed off their barrels and shook the stake, now sunk chest-high, to make sure it could not be lifted out of the ground by the victims' writhing. Two lengths of chain, of a size that might hold a bear, were draped over its top and hammered into place with a fist-sized iron staple. It was as matter-of-fact as making armour in the forge. And all the time, the Guardians prayed.

'Salazar's blood, this will be hard.' Arnaud made the sign of the God, touching his head, his heart, and his belly, *mind, soul, and body for Ischyros*. For Arnaud, it was an act so rare that Guy stared at him.

'They are going to use charcoal.' Arnaud pointed at the pile, now whitening with ash. They could feel its heat thirty paces away. 'A merciful executioner will use green wood, so that they choke in the smoke. A cruel one uses dry wood, that they suffer longer in the flame. But charcoal is worst of all; there is no flame, so they roast slowly, like an ox on the spit.'

What had the woman said of his father? 'They held his feet to the fire.' What Guy was about to witness had been done to his father, even if they hadn't held him there long enough to kill him. And it had been done by *that* priest, the anakritis standing so piously above the Guardians.

'I'll kill that damned priest.' Guy felt the rage rise inside him, hot and blind. He hadn't realised he was pressing forwards until Arnaud gripped him by the arm and spun him around.

'Steady, you young fool.' Arnaud stared into his eyes, both hands now on his shoulders. 'There's a better way to help your father. Take a breath. Look around you. How many men do you see who were your father's friends? Men who used to serve the Order? Or those we know to have been Guardians?'

Guy breathed deeply, forcing calm into his body, and scanned the crowd. Again, Arnaud's brother Parsifal would not meet his eye. There were others he recognised. 'Six. Seven.'

'I see ten. They're angry, and they're about to get a whole lot angrier. I'll wager a battle-axe to a cook's knife that by tonight at least half will be willing to strike a blow for the Guardians.' Arnaud shook Guy to emphasise his point. Guy saw that calculating look in his eye often; it was the look Arnaud had when he was moulding sheets of cut leather as a template for another great helm. Guy breathed deeply, calming himself, relieved that his master was considering action.

'Fight with your mind, boy, not your heart. You can't fight the anakritim, and you can't fight the king. Choose a battle you can win, and be satisfied.'

Guy nodded, humbled, and kept his head lowered. The sense of dread around them was almost overpowering. Even if Arnaud had ideas, to do nothing in this moment made Guy feel unworthy, as if he himself were committing the crime.

Guy did not see the signal from the palace, but a gasp like a soft, mass sigh spread through the crowd as the executioners hauled the two Guardians to their feet. They stripped them of their surcoats and shirts until they stood naked apart from their loin cloths. Their old-men's bodies were white and frail; age and years of imprisonment had shrivelled their flesh so that loose skin hung from their warriors' frames. Both shivered. 'We shall be warm enough soon, Brother Rahoul,' Guerin quipped, and Guy could have wept with awe for a man who faced death so lightly. After they were led to the stake, past the searing heat of the charcoal, Guerin even lifted his arms so that the executioner could pass the chain more easily around his body.

'Leave my hands free, I beg you, that I may pray more easily.' Guerin pressed his palms together in the attitude of prayer, and the crowd gasped again. Many made the sign of the God. Surely these were not heretics, but holy men?

Pateras Malory stepped close to them, shielding his face from the charcoal with his sleeve.

'Confess! Admit your crimes, and even now I may unburden you.' When both Guerin and Cheyne shook their heads, Pateras Malory leaned closer to them, speaking too quietly for anyone else to hear. Guy guessed that some final mercy was being offered; strangulation, perhaps, or even a sword thrust, if only they would confess openly. Both shook their heads again.

An obscene quiet settled on the island, where the loudest sound was now the whoosh of bellows and the hiss of charcoal. The executioners were taking it in turns, for none could stand the heat for long. Those resting stood by, shielding their faces or taking draughts of ale from the barrels. Three blacksmiths' rakes, broad and long-handled enough to work a furnace, lay on the ground ready to push the coals around the prisoners' legs.

'Ischyros be merciful and shine upon us.'

A voice rang out in the awful silence, and all heads turned

to look at the old knight who now stood at the edge of the circle around the stake. He faced Guerin, calling out a chant from the Vision of Salazar in a pure, clear voice. He held his sheathed sword flat before him, balanced across his hands in the way a priest would make an offering before the sacred flame. His long, grey beard fluttered away from his face in the breeze. The thick-set veteran they'd seen near the Great Bridge dropped to one knee beside him, also holding his sword in front of him.

'It is the Guardian chant,' muttered Arnaud. 'It was their practice to use it when no priest was present to say the offices.'

'And lift *His hand* to bless us.' At the words 'His hand', the knight took his right hand from his sword and lifted his fingers in blessing, emphasising the words.

'*Amin!*' Guerin lifted his own hand to touch his face, which now seemed suffused with joy, as if he had seen a glimpse of a glory awaiting him. He joined his hands high above his head, making a roof. 'That the way of truth may be known among all nations.'

'They're signing to each other!' Arnaud gripped Guy's arm and pointed. 'Battlefield signs, for when voices cannot be heard.'

Guerin lowered his arms and made a brief, flat movement with his right hand in front of his chest before resuming the attitude of prayer, lifting his steepled hands high in front of his face, with elbows spread as if he was protecting the space between his forearms, where he'd just signed. 'Thy saving health among Thy faithful.'

The knight dropped to one knee, pushing the sword towards Guerin. 'Let all the people praise thee!' The knight also looked radiant; a message had been passed and understood.

'Tanguy's bones, he's taking a risk.' Arnaud glanced around the crowd.

Guerin made one more sign, lifting both arms above his head in a two-handed gripping motion before jerking them downwards. The knight frowned.

Pateras Malory stared at Guerin and the knight, clearly suspicious. He turned to the captain of the soldiers.

'Provost! Finish this, now!'

In the middle of the island, three sweating executioners picked up their rakes and pushed in unison at the mountain of charcoal, sending a fiery avalanche tumbling towards the stake.

A great, collective sigh spread through the crowd as the coals found flesh.

Then silence. An impossible absence of screaming that defied the foul stink of martyrdom.

Until the silence was filled by the rustle of hundreds of people falling to their knees in awe and making the sign of the God.

CHAPTER 3

3.1 ADELAIS

Adelais took the back road to Montbeauvoir, climbing the spine of the ridge, and walking as fast as she could without attracting attention. Had the priest recognised her? She could not be sure, no matter how many times she replayed the scene in her mind. He'd seen her, but at fifty paces, and dressed not as a novice but a merchant's wife. She thought it unlikely that he would come after her until the prisoners were dead, but he might send soldiers. If they found her on the Great North Road, they would know she had been in the city. If they found her at the sister-house, they would never know.

She paused on the brow of the hill where she might look back on the city and watch for pursuit. The afternoon sun spread a weak light over the rooftops, glistened on a loop of the Gaelle, and made the gilded hand atop the great dome of the temple shine as bright as a star. The Guardians were to be burned, she was sure. It was whispered from mouth to mouth in the square outside the temple, and it was written on their faces as they passed her. Yet so many fires burned below her that their smoke merged into a haze over the city, and any one of them could be an execution.

It was the first time she'd been close to a burning. She'd seen criminals hung at Moncrâne, so far away that they looked like tiny, dancing insects. They'd hardly seemed like people at all, although she'd hoped they found peace with their god. Sending men to death by burning, men whose faces she'd seen, was horrible beyond comparison. She found herself holding the *taufr* talisman through her belt bag, taking comfort from it. That might get *her* burned, if it was found, or at least flogged. As she turned back towards Montbeauvoir she remembered something Yrsa had said, years before: *There is no heresy with the old gods. You believe or you don't believe. No priest is going to burn you for believing in the wrong way.*

Adelais paused within sight of the sisterhouse, inhaling the last, heady taste of freedom. She was tempted to keep walking. She could go around the walls, recover the clothes from the cache, and run. They'd search the city, first, if they searched at all. But she remembered the wolf, and the niggling sense that it was a message. Not yet. She was not sure whether it was belief in an omen or cowardice that made her walk dutifully through the gates, hiding her face from the guards behind her veil.

Mitera Chantalle waited for her in the temple, as agreed, kneeling in front of the sanctuary. Above her the blue interior of the dome sparkled faintly as the painted stars caught the light. At the sanctuary's heart the sacred flame burned low.

'I have been praying for you, girl,' the mitera said as she rose. 'Well?' She stared so hard that Adelais had to look away.

Adelais told the eldest daughter of the day's events as she took off her gown. Her mood changed with the clothes. On the road she'd walked tall. Free. Able to look people in the eye. She'd called on Sif and muttered rune song. Ischyros was pulled over her shoulders with her habit, demanding that she shoulder her burden of guilt. Sometimes it seemed that everything under Ischyros was a sin except prayer. The eldest daughter would probably say her sadness at handing back her old clothes was avarice, and she should welcome the mortification of her flesh as her rough habit rubbed her skin.

At least she could keep Yrsa's talisman. A scrip was the only possession a novice was allowed.

'Those Guardians were good men, Mitera,' she finished. 'Two of them chose a terrible death rather than confess.' Adelais paused, wondering if she dared ask a question that might earn her a beating. But then, she and Chantalle now shared a complicity. 'Why would Ischyros kill His own knights?'

Chantalle ignored the question. 'Go to your work, girl. Stay with Adeifi Elodie in the infirmary tonight; it will prevent awkward questions about your absence.'

Adelais hadn't really expected an answer. She paused at the sanctuary door.

'Mitera, I may have been recognised.'

The eldest daughter made a sharp intake of breath.

'I can't be sure, but the priest turned and saw me.'

Mitera Chantalle exhaled, slowly, and closed her eyes.

'Then we are all in the hands of Salazar. If anyone asks, you have spent the whole day in the infirmary. Send Adeifi Elodie to me. Now.'

Thankfully Chantalle did not demand that Adelais return Yrsa's stave. It would be useful on the road, one day soon.

'Tell me again about how you hit the apprentices!'

Elodie sat next to Adelais on one of the empty cots in the infirmary. She seemed to have forgiven Adelais her attempted escape, and her enthusiasm reminded Adelais of exchanging giggly stories and gossip with childhood friends. Elodie had closed the shutters and lit a fire in the central hearth against the night's chill, and homely smoke thickened the air as it found its way out through the thatch. A single tallow candle burned on a shelf, for it was after the evening office and full dark outside.

'I swung it up between his legs,' she demonstrated, 'and he dropped to his knees, holding himself. I swear he went cross-eyed!'

It was good to laugh, and even better to bask in Elodie's admiration. The tensions of the day drained away. They had given both Carel de la Tour and old Perrin more hemlock and henbane for their pain, but Carel stirred at the noise of their laughter and coughed a little blood. They wiped his face and sat silently until he slept. Adelais's habit scratched her skin when she moved, and she missed her old clothes anew. Beside her, Elodie's habit was no finer.

'Why are you here, Elodie?' Adelais whispered when Carel's breathing was deep, with only the faintest rumble in his chest. 'You were born noble. You could have been a lady, with a castle and lands, and fine clothes.'

'And a knight for a husband.' Elodie sounded as if the idea did not appeal. 'My father found me one of those—a great, lumbering ox wrapped up in chain-mail who thought he could win my heart in the tourney. The cooler I was to him, the braver he became until he was the bloody survivor of the melee. The trouble was, he couldn't read without moving his lips, and just the thought of him rutting on me made me ill. I decided a life of prayer and healing was infinitely preferable to lying under a mountain of muscle and raising sons to go off and be killed in the wars. Papa was very upset.'

'But don't you miss the touch of linen on your skin?' Adelais closed her eyes at the memory.

'There are compensations. The company is gentler.' Elodie touched Adelais's hand, letting her fingertips stay long enough for Adelais to know the words had meaning. Not for the first time, Adelais had the sense that Elodie wanted something more from her, something she did not understand or know how to give, although she was honoured by the wanting.

But there were sounds on the road, and the moment was

lost as the terrors of the day returned. Adelais rose to her feet, ears straining.

'Horses. Several horses, coming up the hill.'

They both moved to the infirmary door, holding it slightly ajar so they might see out yet hide within. The guards next door in the travellers' dormitory had also heard; grumbling and the clatter of armour and weapons came through the wall. The square was a paler darkness, bounded by the familiar black outlines of the temple and the eldest daughter's house, until a soldier strode out, holding a flaring torch low until he was clear of the thatch. Adelais gripped her stave more tightly as a pale horse cantered into the square, bearing a dark-cloaked rider. He vaulted to the ground, threw back his hood, and in the flickering flame Adelais recognised Pateras Malory, holding the reins of his grey. He shouted at the soldier with the torch.

'Is the prisoner secure?'

The soldier's answer was lost in the clatter of hooves as two new soldiers rode into the square, their inferior mounts blowing and lathered after the run.

In the door to the eldest daughter's house, another torch was held to a candle, caught, and blazed to show Chantalle, roughly dressed in an unbelted habit and with a cloak thrown around her shoulders. Adelais had never seen her without a cap or hood before; her short hair looked dark and lustrous in the torchlight.

'Pateras Malory.' Chantalle's voice had a forced calm. 'What an unexpected pleasure. Have you come to take away your prisoner?' She tugged the hood of her cloak over her head, holding it closed under her chin to preserve her modesty.

'He is safe?' The cleric's shout was high-pitched with anger. He might even have been frightened.

'Of course. Your instructions were clear. But if you move him, I fear you will kill him. He has a few days in this world at most.'

'What was your novice doing in Villebénie?'

Adelais gasped, and flinched away from the infirmary door until Elodie steadied her with an arm around her back.

Chantalle stood a little taller. 'No novice of mine would be allowed out unsupervised. Which girl do you mean?'

'The thin one with strange eyes and yellow hair.'

'And how do you know she has yellow hair, Pateras?'

'Don't play with me, woman. Was she in Villebénie?'

'Novice Adelais has been in the infirmary all day, Pateras.'

'Bring her to me.'

Adelais did not wait for the eldest daughter to cross the square, but stepped out into the torchlight. She kept her head bowed humbly, and held her hands submissively together across her lower belly. She made a small dip of obeisance in front of the priest.

'I am here, Pateras.'

The anakritis gripped her jaw, hard enough to hurt, and forced her chin upwards until she stared closely into the eyes of a man whose profession was torture. They were dark and narrowed, and he stank of woodsmoke.

'Have you been to Villebénie, girl?'

Adelais took a deep, fearful breath, and nodded. The grip on her face clenched, then lessened until she could speak.

'Tell me what you did.'

'I went to the infirmary at the fire temple, Pateras, with Adeifi Elodie, two days before the feast of the Blessèd Tanguy.'

'Fool of a girl!' Pateras Malory flung her face sideways. 'It is more dangerous than you can imagine to lie to me.'

Adelais stretched her jaw after the wrench. 'But it's true, Pateras. Adeifi Elodie wished to talk to the learned physicians there. I helped to carry back salves and supplies.'

'Today, girl!'

'Today, Pateras?' Adelais let her fear show. She even multiplied it with a snivel. 'No, Pateras. I have been in the infirmary, with Carel de la Tour.' She began to gabble, pouring words out towards the dirt. 'Such a sweet man, Pateras. We all praise your mercy for bringing him to us.'

Pateras Malory made a low growl and flicked his hand upwards in a gesture of exasperation that might have become a blow if Adelais had not flinched away. On her porch, Chantalle made a small sign of dismissal and Adelais began to edge away.

'Who leads among you?' Pateras Malory called over her head at the four soldiers standing by the dormitory. One of them looked at the two new arrivals, still mounted, and raised his hand.

'I do, Pateras.'

'I want two of you awake at all times. One outside, one in the infirmary. In the morning I shall leave for Villebénie, and return with a man who is to be held, but not killed. Do you understand?'

The soldiers nodded. Pateras Malory swung back towards Adelais, his finger stabbing at her face.

'And if you've warned him, girl, you'll find yourself in the darkest hole beneath the Black Tower, begging for death.'

The movement threw Pateras Malory's cloak back from his habit, releasing the sharp, oily smell of charcoaled meat. Adelais stared back at him. And something in the priest's eyes made Adelais wonder if his anger was with her or with himself.

3.2 GUY

'There's a guard.' Guy whispered, pulling his head back into the moon shadow behind Montbeauvoir's temple. The thin, silver light had shown the outline of a soldier outside one of the sister-house's buildings. His silhouette had an impossibly large head, suggesting a chain-mail coif over a bowl helmet, and he wore a sword on his hip. He'd been kicking at stones in the square, bored but very much awake.

Someone swore under his breath. Five men waited against the wall: Arnaud, Parsifal, another former Guardian called Maarten, plus a squire from the Vriesian borders who still sought his Guardian cousin, and a blacksmith friend of Arnaud's who'd served the Order within the citadel. He was probably the one who'd sworn. They all smelt of fire. Six is enough, Parsifal had insisted; six committed men, including two Guardian knights, against four unsuspecting soldiers. Any more and we risk word getting out.

'Then at least we're sure which door's the infirmary.' Arnaud seemed unperturbed. 'The other must be the travellers' dormitory.'

'But I told yer,' the blacksmith hissed. 'Came 'ere once to shoe an 'orse, didn't I?'

Arnaud ignored him, and laid an improvised stretcher on the ground, made of a blanket nailed to two poles. 'No problem. We've planned for a guard.' He turned towards the group. 'Are you all ready?'

Guy swallowed, dry-mouthed. It had all seemed so simple on the Isle of Dogs, amidst the stink and rage of martyrdom. Overpower the guards while they slept. They'd brought rope to bind them. Rescue his father. They'd brought the stretcher to carry him. Simple. Now there was a guard, a real, armoured man that Guy had to knock senseless.

But his father was on the far side of that door. Guy looked around the group. Some of these men he barely knew, but his life now depended on them. Both Guardians wore chain-mail hauberks over quilted gambesons; they could not move fast or quietly and would come last. Neither wore helmets; hauberks could be hidden under a cloak, but it would have been impossible to hide a great helm as they moved through the city. The squire, however, wore a battered bascinet and, like the Guardians, hefted a sword. The blacksmith swung a heavy hammer by his side. These two were lighter on their feet and would run to take advantage of surprise as soon as Guy and Arnaud had done their parts.

The two Guardians risked most; they had tied the red rope belts of their order quite openly around their waists, above their sword belts. They all faced death if caught, but those ropes would earn them expulsion first – the ritual casting-out from the blessings of Ischyros that would place them beyond any pardoning. By the teaching of Salazar they would fall from the bridge of judgement into the pit; to save his father, they risked their souls as well as their lives.

'Guy?' Arnaud touched Guy on the shoulder.

Guy nodded. 'I'm ready, master.'

'Sure? Because you will be seen, and the priest will recognise your description. Once we start, there is no going back for you.'

'I can't leave my father there.'

'So be it.' Arnaud looped a mace over Guy's shoulder so that it hung down his back on a leather thong secured in front to his belt, near the buckle. Guy flexed his arms, testing its movement. He wore a gambeson, a thickly quilted linen and wool tunic, so he felt only the mace's head where it lay against his backside. The gambeson was designed as padding beneath a chain-mail hauberk, but its layers were dense enough to serve as hidden armour. Over it he wore the knee-length, belted cote-hardie tunic worn by men of all classes, although none would mistake his for anything but that of a humble labourer.

'One upwards tug, and it's free. Try it.'

Guy reached over his shoulder, seized the mace's haft, jerked and swung, measuring the distance to the weighted end. The four short, blunted axe blades radiating from the iron-bound haft were designed to crush rather than cut, and it would break a limb even through chain-mail.

'Good.' Arnaud retied the mace and twitched the hood of Guy's cote-hardie into place over the haft. 'Take me as close as you can before you put me down. Hit the helmet hard enough to stun, but try not to kill him.' Arnaud lay flat on the stretcher and held up a leather flask full of pig's blood. 'Spread it all over my face, lad. Make sure I can't be recognised.' As Guy smeared the blood, Arnaud pulled a cloak over himself, hiding a long-bladed dagger in its folds. 'Swords need room to swing,' he'd said, 'and this will be a night for close work.'

'You all know what to do,' Parsifal whispered. 'Now go, and Salazar be with us.'

Guy made the sign of Ischyros, *mind, soul, and body*, lifted the poles, and dragged Arnaud into the square, making no attempt to hide. Arnaud groaned and mumbled on the blanket behind him, with his boots scraping through the dirt. Ahead of them, the guard rose to his feet from the stump where he'd been sitting. Guy knew what the soldier would see, even in this weak moonlight: a youth dragging a bleeding man on a stretcher towards an infirmary.

'Hold, there!' The man's voice was calm, not yet alarmed. Guy kept going, and chose his mark, low on the helmet's side, where the steel would not deflect a swinging blow.

The soldier drew his sword.

'If you please, sir, my father's fallen from the hayloft. He's bleeding bad, sir.'

'Stop right there!' The sword's point lifted, and Guy put the stretcher down. The man was still beyond reach.

'Please, sir, can the good adeifes save him? May I knock?'

The soldier turned away, lowering his guard, his shoulders lifting as he prepared to shout.

Guy hesitated for a heartbeat too long, so that the soldier sensed his charge and the shout became a gasp of surprise as the man turned back, lifting his sword towards Guy's guts. The point ripped through the cote-hardie but slid harmlessly across the gambeson beneath, and then Guy was inside its reach, swinging the mace in a backhanded sweep that caught the man where the chain-mail met the cheekbone. In an instant as brief as lightning Guy saw a mace blade bury itself into the face and the eye burst outwards like an overripe fruit. The soldier screamed and dropped to his knees, his gauntlets clasping at the wound.

Guy stared at him, appalled at what he'd done, until Arnaud grabbed his arm and dragged him forwards, towards the infirmary door. Behind them came the sound of running men as the rest of the group charged into the square.

Another soldier appeared in the infirmary's doorway, sword already raised, and Arnaud stopped, arms spread wide to brace himself, just in time to save himself from running onto the

point. The two crouched in a fighting stance, and for a moment
the soldier grinned, saying, 'come on, then', but at the sight of
armoured knights he changed his mind. He danced back into
the infirmary and tried to slam the door behind him.

Arnaud's shoulder barged it before it could be bolted, and
Guy followed him, shaking off his daze. Arnaud would need
help; leathers and dagger against mail and sword would be an
unequal fight. Besides, his father was in there.

The gloom in the infirmary confused him for a moment.
Beyond Arnaud's shoulder, the soldier backed away, crouching,
making room to swing his sword. Two rows of cots stretched away
into darkness, with too little space in between for Guy to stand
alongside Arnaud. Two beds down, a figure in the robes of a
novice clutched a stave, ready to fight, beside an adeifi whose
hands had lifted to her mouth in shock. In the cot at their feet an
old man held two splinted hands crossed on his chest as if he were
already dead. A single candle burned on a shelf above him. On
the opposite side of the room a priest had risen from one of the
cots and held a dark blanket or cloak against himself as if it were
proof against blows. His white habit was the lightest thing in the
room apart from the candle. Crumpled coverings and straw on the
cots made it difficult to work out which of them was occupied, but
a shadowy figure had raised himself on an elbow in a far corner.
Could that be his father? Guy stepped forwards, climbing over
the first, empty cot. Oaths, cries, and the sounds of blows came
through the wall beside him as the others reached the dormitory.

As Guy came closer the nuns retreated, and the candle's
light fell on the novice's face. Guy gasped as he recognised the
lean woman from the square by the fire temple.

'You!'

The novice grimaced and snarled back at Guy. '*Fjakkinn
hálfviti!*' That sounded like Vriesian, and she wasn't happy.

The soldier chose a good moment to charge; he could hope

to spit Arnaud on his sword's point, and swing to take Guy in the side while he was blocked by the adeifes. His mistake was to broadcast his move with an oath, so the novice had time to turn and see him launch his attack. She closed her eyes and breathed deeply, as if praying, for perhaps one stride of the soldier's charge, until he was level with her shoulder, and in a motion as swift and effortless as a dancer's she swept her stave back-handed across the soldier's shins. The man stumbled to his knees, one hand in the dirt, the other still gripping his sword, with his head now close to Guy's legs. He wore no helmet, just a chain-mail coif, so Guy tapped him on the back of the head with the mace, quite lightly.

It wasn't enough. The man groaned and tried to rise, lashing out wildly with the sword, so Guy hit him again, harder. The man dropped. The mace against chain-mail sounded like a shovel hitting wet gravel.

'I didn't mean you to kill him, you oaf.' The novice sounded furious. Guy looked down at the man he'd just felled, and felt his soul sink towards the pit. *Two*.

'You warned him!' The priest's voice was high-pitched, almost screeching in fury. 'I'll have you expelled! You'll burn!'

Guy looked up, wanting to beg forgiveness, realising for the first time that the dark cloth the priest held was the black cloak of an anakritis and the contorted face above it was Pateras Malory's. Guy let the mace fall from his fingers, knowing that in two blows he had changed his life for ever.

One of the Guardians reached the door and peered into the gloom for long enough to know that no threat remained. He disappeared, joining the cacophony of blows and screams from the dormitory next door. Arnaud bellowed at the wall. 'How fares it, brothers?' The only reply was the sound of a body falling.

'You'll hang, all of you!'

Arnaud pointed at the anakritis with his dagger. 'Sit *down*, Pateras.'

But this had been done for a purpose. Guy looked around, still dazed, until he met the novice's eyes.

'Where is my father?'

The novice seemed suddenly tired. She waved a hand at the cot beside them. 'Here. Do you realise what you've done?'

She kept talking, but Guy did not listen. He knelt beside the cot, unable to believe that this shrunken old man was his father. He remembered a full-bearded giant who towered above him, a man whose laughter rumbled like approaching thunder. This hollow-cheeked, aged wreck could not be him.

'Papa?'

The adeifi knelt on the opposite side of the cot, holding the candle. 'Carel, this must be Guy. Do you not recognise him?'

'Guy?' The old man lifted a splinted hand towards Guy's face, and in the softening of the features Guy finally recognised his father. 'Pateras Malory said he would bring you.' Carel de la Tour began to cough, a deep, bubbling retch that left blood on his chin.

'Papa? What have they done to you?' Guy was only vaguely aware of a silence that told him the fight next door had ended.

The adeifi lifted the blanket over Carel's legs, and held the candle above his feet.

Guy was filled with a rage such as he'd never known, a rage that took form in a snarl as he pushed himself to his feet and grabbed the mace. He'd taken two strides across the room and had raised the mace to strike before Arnaud caught his arm.

'He's a priest!'

'You'll burn in the pit!' Pateras Malory squealed, backing away.

'Burn?' Guy dropped the mace, but pulled Pateras Malory away from the wall and threw him on the ground. 'You think you know all about burning, don't you, *anakritis*? But let me give you a lesson.' Guy dragged him feet-first to the fire in the middle of the room, and held one leg in the embers. Pateras Malory screamed and twisted, kicking ash and charcoal. As new flames flared, Guy caught sight of his father's face, staring at him with such horror that Guy relented and let Arnaud pull him away.

'He's a priest,' Arnaud repeated. 'You'll damn us all. Now go help the others.'

Before Guy could rise, the squire appeared in the doorway, pulling his bascinet from his head.

'You said four. There were six, with these two.'

'Keep your head covered, Brother,' Arnaud called. 'There's one here who would learn your face.'

The squire replaced the helm and hooked the mail gorget over his lower face. He peered into the infirmary's gloom.

'An anakritis! You didn't say anything about a priest, either.'

'Are the guards all secured?' Arnaud asked.

'Trussed like chickens, but the blacksmith has a broken arm. What shall we do with the king's men?'

Arnaud turned to the adeifi. 'Do you have a storeroom? With a lock?'

The novice laid a hand on the adeifi's arm as if protecting her from any involvement.

'The cellar.' The girl's voice was flat, almost despairing. 'The eldest daughter has the key.'

'And where do we find the eldest daughter?'

The novice pointed past the squire's shoulder to where a torch blazed in the square, held by a cloaked adeifi who seemed to be moving in a daze. She knelt beside the guard that Guy had felled in the first rush, and touched his neck beneath his chainmail. She looked up to see the novice watching her from the doorway to the infirmary, and straightened. When she spoke, her voice was soft with shock and disbelief.

'What have you done, girl? What have you done?'

3.3 ADELAIS

Adelais's ejection from the sisterhouse was immediate, and as noisy and public as the eldest daughter could make it.

Adelais understood; Mitera Chantalle needed the anakritis to see her humiliation. Privately, there had been a blessing, and a few coins. 'Go far, go fast,' Chantalle had said. 'The anakritim will have your hide if you're caught, and then we'll both die.' Both of them knew the truth would emerge under torture, so it must not come to that.

Adelais was pushed through the courtyard, driven out with blows across her backside. Mitera Chantalle and Adeifi Fabianne took it in turns to hit her; Chantalle used an adeifi's rope belt, but Adeifi Fabianne had a leather strap, which hurt a lot more. Adelais closed her mind to the imprecations that followed each blow. They'd stripped her of her habit, but given her back her own chemise and kirtle. She was less worried by the pain than she was that the leather would cut the cloth. The only good thing in this whole *fordæmdur* night was that Chantalle had thrown her cloak at her and let her take the staff.

She stumbled through chaos. Pateras Malory had been bound and dumped unceremoniously on the ground; he raved at her incomprehensibly through a gagged mouth as she passed. The raid was disintegrating. Adelais saw five of them. The brigand with blood on his head was arguing with a squire about what to do with the anakritis; it sounded as if the bloodied one wanted to lock him in the cellar with the soldiers, but the squire wanted time to question him about a missing lord. The squire was Vriesian; his accent came to Adelais like a smell of home. A third raider had a broken arm, already splinted by Elodie; two Guardian knights were lifting him into the saddle of a stolen horse. Guy, the oaf with the mace, must still have been in the infirmary.

Adelais was allowed a moment to say farewell to Elodie, who was trying to explain to Guy that his father might die if he was moved. Elodie had tears in her eyes as they embraced, tears she covered with awkward laughter.

'Just when I need you most!' Elodie waved her hand at the groaning wounded before she wrapped her arms around Adelais, pulling her close. 'The Blessèd Salazar preserve you, my friend.' Adelais felt a kiss on her cheek, almost fierce, and a face laid against hers.

'Pray for me, Adeifi,' Adelais spoke into Elodie's ear. She was going to need all the help she could get, and she didn't mind which god it came from.

'Go with Ischyros. I shall miss you.' Elodie sounded choked.

The eldest daughter interrupted their hug, dragging Adelais roughly away. In the square the raiders were still arguing. A Guardian was encouraging bloody-face to go, immediately, while they still had night to hide them. It seemed they all wanted to put as much distance as possible behind them before more soldiers arrived.

A final blow across her rump from Adeifi Fabianne propelled Adelais into the roadway. That hurt enough for Adelais to turn and snarl at her. '*Óhreinn kýr!*' Calling the old bitch a filthy cow felt good. Adelais hauled the skirts of her gown forwards as she walked away, twisting to examine the cloth, and grunting with satisfaction at the absence of rips. Good Vriesian cloth, her father's best. At least she wasn't walking away with her *rass* hanging out. She swung her cloak around her shoulders.

Where now? Adelais looked up at the stars of a clear, cool night. She felt surprisingly good; the decision had been taken for her. Time to go. She had her stave and her scrip –reassuringly hard over the hidden pocket – a pair of sisterhouse boots that might still have a few months' life in them, and enough money to last a week on the road, with care.

Unless she was robbed.

Or raped.

Adelais paused at the crossroads below Montbeauvoir. The road was empty of travellers in the dead of the night, and bordered by ill-defined, vaguely threatening shadows in the moonlight. The horizon was filled, to the south, with the towers of Villebénie's walls. Enough fires burned in the city, even at this time of night, for smoke still to hang in the air, touched with reflected red like the embers of a dying pyre. She could hardly smell the city over the stink of the Pissbourne; the nearby bridge where the Great North Road crossed the stream was one of the points where the ordure carts emptied their barrels into the open sewer beneath. It was not a place to linger. She unpicked the thong from her bag and threaded her sling while she decided her next steps. Soon she'd look for smooth, round stones that would fly true.

There would be a search, and turning north was also what they would expect. Pursuit would follow her down the road, but she could hope to cover two or three leagues before daylight. Then she'd cut across country. Or perhaps she should go another way? She'd heard of counties like Theignault where Galmandie's rule was loose, but knew them only as names and a vague waving of a hand to the east. She hugged herself, rubbing her hands up and down her arms and trying not to breathe the Pissbourne's vapours too deeply while she made up her mind.

East, then, before she turned north. Adelais squeezed the *taufr* for luck. *It's time for me to come home, Amma Yrsa.* She'd walk as far as the Guardian citadel and after that take the next road away from the city.

She paused within twenty paces, only now remembering the men's clothes in their cache in the vineyard wall. It would be worth the risk to climb back up the hill. But as she turned, there were others coming down the road from Montbeauvoir. She could see a helmeted man leading a horse with some kind of baggage tied to its saddle. Three other men followed, two carrying a stretcher between them. Adelais hid behind a roadside elm, realising that these must be four of the attackers. As their voices drew nearer, it seemed that the argument over the priest's fate was still raging. Down here by the foul-smelling marshland there were no dwellings, and they made no attempt to quieten their voices.

'I say we dump him.' That sounded like the bloodied one, who now bore the front of the stretcher. She'd heard that voice before; this one had been with Guy in the square outside the fire temple, the one he'd called 'master'. The bundle thrown over the horse jerked and growled, and she realised they'd tied the priest over the saddle with his backside in the air and his robes flapping in the wind.

'Not till I've asked him a few questions.' The one leading the horse glared over his shoulder towards Pateras Malory, his head moving stiffly within his bascinet and aventail. He spoke in the tones of a Vriesian gentleman, used to authority.

'We should've locked him up with the rest. As soon as he's free he'll run to the nearest city gate and raise the alarm.' That sounded like the bloody-faced master.

'Kill him, I say.' She recognised Guy's voice at the back end of the stretcher.

'Then, by Salazar, you'll burn in the pit for killing a priest.'
This was the tall, gaunt one who walked on his own. He had a
soldier's cloak around his shoulders, probably stolen, with its
hood hiding his face. A scabbard tapped at his leg.

Adelais took a deep breath and stepped into their path,
pushing her kerchief back to show her face. It was a risk, but
these men might have money to help her on her way. They
owed her something, at least.

There was a hiss of alarm and the ring of the Vriesian
drawing his sword before Guy recognised her.

'So, it's the girl who started it all.' The two with the
stretcher laid their burden gently down on the grass by the road.
Carel de la Tour made a slight, bubbling whimper from within.

'And you're the one who made it end in killings. I wanted to
save you from torture, not start a war. Small thanks I get. There
were more of you. What happened to them?'

'One was hurt. Another is helping him home.' De la Tour's
son sounded impatient, as if she was in their way. 'What do you
want, girl?'

Adelais felt anger rising within her. She was cold and she
was tired, with no safe place to go, and it was this oaf's fault. It
wasn't *fair*, though part of her realised she was being irrational.
She'd *wanted* to leave. 'Want? At sunset I had a place to sleep
and food to eat. Now every *fordæmdur* priest in Galmandie will
want my hide.'

The Vriesian snorted at the obscenity. Guy simply
shrugged. That really irritated her.

'I can't do anything about that. Not now.'

'*Fjakkinn hálfviti!*' Adelais swore in gutter Vriesian and
swung her stave at him. He raised his forearms to protect his
face, and the blow thumped into his side with the sound a
broom made when she beat the dirt out of blankets.

'Why couldn't you just stay away?' She wondered why he
showed no sign of hurt. That blow should have broken ribs.

'He's going to die, anyway. Now more men are likely to beat him to the grave and I'm on my own.'

It's what you wanted, came that niggling voice inside.

'Peace! Come with us,' the master said, not unkindly, though his bloody face was frightful in the moonlight. 'At least for tonight. I will give you silver for your journey. But we must move, and soon. The sisterhouse will send word to the city, and by dawn the roads will be awash with king's men.'

Adelais breathed deeply, forcing herself to be calm. Go with them, with the promise of silver, or creep back for the hidden men's clothes? With silver she could buy clothes. She pointed at the trussed cleric with her stave. 'If you let him live, he will show the way for the soldiers to follow.'

'Then it is time for me to ask after my uncle.' The Vriesian hefted his sword and the priest whimpered in fear, but the blade cut no more than a rope under the horse's belly. The man palmed his hand over Pateras Malory's face, and pushed until the anakritis fell backwards into the mud, heavily, with his hands still tied in front of him.

'Name your cousin and you name yourself,' the tall one warned.

The Vriesian unhooked the mail aventail that had hidden his lower face and let it hang loose, revealing the well-favoured face of a man some years Adelais's senior.

'Then know me as Everard, nephew to Brother Sicard de Warelt, who was the first Vriesian to be accepted into the Order of Guardians. Know me also, priest, as one who has sought him for five years, and who is willing to die in that quest.'

'Sicard de Warelt? I do not know the man. I have never—'

The Vriesian grabbed the priest by the robe and dragged him into the middle of the road, where such light as there was fell clear on his face.

'Think again, anakritis.' He rested his sword's tip on the

priest's crotch. 'I may not kill you, but I can spare you from sins of the flesh for the rest of your miserable life.'

Pateras Malory whimpered and tried to back away, but the squire leaned lightly on his sword and the whimper became a terrified scream. The tall one muttered a warning, which the Vriesian ignored.

'What will you do if I tell you?'

'If I believe you tell the truth, I shall let you go.' The squire eased the pressure on the sword. 'You have my word.'

Guy, son of Carel, growled his anger but said nothing.

'De Warelt died four years ago, before I was consecrated. I saw his name in the records.'

'And how did he die, anakritis?' The sword dug deeper into the robe. Pateras Malory twisted away, trying to protect his crotch with his hip.

'He recanted his confession.'

'So you burned him.'

'He was a heretic.'

'I knew him all my life. He was a pious knight, who fought valiantly for Ischyros in Alympos.'

'You gave your word!'

'I did.' The squire stepped back, lifting his sword. 'I shall not have a priest's blood on my soul. But this one,' he pointed the weapon towards Guy, who was tapping his mace against his boot, 'this one has seen what you have done to his father, and I made no promises on his behalf.'

Guy walked towards Pateras Malory, hefting his mace.

'I think we should start with his legs. That'll stop him running for help.'

'Don't, lad.' The older one reached for Guy, but the squire's sword came up, holding him away. The tall one drew his own sword, and the cloak fell back from his face. He was in his middle years, full-bearded, and unkempt. For a moment it seemed the raiders were going to fight among themselves, and

Pateras Malory turned onto his knees and tried to crawl away. He reached Adelais's feet and clung to her, crying.

'There's another way.' Adelais kicked the priest away as she might a dog who tried to hump her leg. She looked to the master for support. 'Strip him.'

'What does that serve?' The master wiped his cheek against his sleeve, freeing a scab of dried blood. Soon he'd be recognisable.

'In his robes, he's an anakritis. He has authority. Soldiers will run to do his bidding. Naked, he's nobody. Naked and stinking, he's a madman. We might all gain a day.'

The tall one began to laugh, a low, rumbling chuckle that grew as he slipped the point inside the cleric's hood and cut. 'This, by Salazar, I'm going to enjoy.' He bent to rip the shredded clothes from Malory's body.

They stood Pateras Malory on the bridge over the Pissbourne, with his hands now tied behind him. The Vriesian and Arnaud pinioned his arms while Guy sliced away the cleric's loin cloth, leaving him totally naked. Adelais sat on the parapet, ignoring the stench from below and feeling strangely light-headed about this madness. Malory's body was white in the moonlight, with the slight belly of one who lived well, and even in the cool air he shone with sweat like some pale slug. It was curious, she thought, that the only pricks she'd seen had belonged to clerics. She tilted her head on one side, comparing. His manhood had shrivelled into the dark mass of his crotch. No comparison.

'Witch! Harlot! Spawn of Kakos! You'll rot in the pit!'

That was unfair. Didn't he realise what Guy had been about to do to him?

'If we ever meet again, Pateras, remember that I've just saved your life.' Adelais looked down at the foul swamp beneath them, where a slow-flowing stream gradually bore away the day's glistening mounds of ordure, and glanced back over her shoulder. 'Shouldn't we untie his hands?'

'Nah.' Guy ran the width of the road to kick the priest so hard on his bare *rass* that he was punched away from the restraining hands and flew from the parapet. Pateras Malory screamed shrilly as he fell, and landed with the sound a bucket makes at the bottom of a well. He disappeared in a spray of filth, staying under for so long Adelais feared that they'd killed him. Convulsions disturbed the surface, then a leg, and finally his head, retching, spitting, gasping.

Adelais leaned against the parapet, enjoying the priest's struggles. As they watched, she and Guy shared a moment that was almost companionable. As the priest sank beneath the surface again she muttered '*fjakkinn prestur*' and straightened.

'You called *me* that.' Guy sounded happy.

'No. "*Prestur*" is Vriesian for "priest". I called you a *fjakkinn hálfviti.*'

'And what does that mean?'

Below them the priest surfaced, gasping. She thought he probably wouldn't drown. 'It means you're a fucking idiot.'

She turned away and left him standing there. Pateras Malory's shouts and curses followed her back to the stretcher and the horse. The men took the priest's robes with them, slashing them into rags that they threw in the stream.

Carel de la Tour was unconscious under the cloak, and breathing in a way that rattled bubbles of phlegm or blood in his chest.

'He needs warmth.' Adelais lightly touched his face. 'And nourishment, if he will take it.'

'We'll go to the citadel.' Arnaud nodded to the east, where the towers of the Guardians' former stronghold showed against the first faint light of dawn, half a league away. The sprawling mass of the city was still one vast shadow, darker than the nearby fields. 'We may hope that they will not think to look for us within their own fortress, and there are still those within who will hide us for a day.'

'Is it not guarded?' Adelais asked.

'The main gates, yes, and the donjon, but it was my home,' Guy replied. 'I know other ways to enter.'

'And I'm for Vriesland.' Everard de Warelt swung into the saddle. 'My family have lands there, beyond Galmandie's new borders. I have heavy news to carry to them.'

'Go with Ischyros,' the tall one called. 'Arnaud and Parsifal l'Armurier will always be at your service.'

So they were brothers, these raiders.

'As will Guy Carelet.'

Van Warelt looked enquiringly at Adelais.

'And Adelais de Vries wishes she'd never set eyes on any of you.'

Everard laughed and lifted his hand in farewell. 'Yet you have done well this day, girl. I hope we meet again. If you reach Vriesland safely, seek me out.'

She watched him canter away, envying his ability to ride north, and perhaps outrun pursuit all the way out of this land of Galmandie.

'Come, girl,' Arnaud called as he and Guy lifted the stretcher. 'We must make haste.'

The sky was lightening fast.

CHAPTER 4

4.1 ADELAIS

The first birdsong of summer's early dawn sprinkled sweetness through the foul air as they made their way east along the bank of the Pissbourne, hurrying as best they could without jolting the stretcher. At the next bridge they turned south, entering the mass of slums that spread outside Villebénie. No birds sang here, though occasionally there would be a cleared square where the chants of the dawn office leaked out of a modest temple. Dilapidated buildings squeezed their path, and there were furtive movements in the shadows, like rats around offal, that made Adelais grip her stave more tightly. From time to time, voices growled at them, demanding their business. Few came close when they said they were taking a man to the infirmary in the citadel compound. 'Fearful sick,' Guy called, 'come not near or you too will die of the contagion.' Only one man pressed closer, demanding money until Arnaud's brother Parsifal let his cloak fall open and the beggar realised he faced an armed knight. After that Adelais took the rear of the stretcher, leaving Guy to walk alongside with his mace over his shoulder.

They paused when the walls of the Guardian citadel rose like another city in front of them, on the opposite side of a more important road. Even this early there was traffic, mainly farmers with barrels of milk or piles of winter vegetables for market.

'So what do we do now?' Adelais craned her neck to look at the wall, perhaps four times her height from the ground to its crenellated top. It leaned inwards as it rose, making it seem even higher. Weeds had found a hold between some of the stones, giving the wall an air of neglect. 'Knock at the gate?'

'Nah.' Guy hid his mace on the stretcher beside his father's comatose body, and led them across the road towards a muddy passageway, running like an earthen moat between the walls of the citadel and the nearest houses. 'There's a backway in.'

'It will be barred,' Parsifal muttered.

'I know a way over.' Guy sounded confident.

'Guards?' Adelais could see four towers before the wall turned out of her sight, although none were manned.

'There are a few king's men at the gate, but not many.' Parsifal was clearly familiar with the citadel. 'They don't stop people going to the temple or the infirmary,' he looked around the group: a woman, three men, and another on a stretcher, 'but we are conspicuous. If Guy knows a quieter way, let us try it.' He waved Guy forwards.

Guy led them beneath the wall until it turned north at a corner tower, now bordering a marshy field where cattle appeared to wade through a knee-high blanket of dawn mist.

'Guardian land, see?' Guy waved at the field. 'Or was. They didn't allow no buildings. And there's a gate. Three towers down.' He seemed proud of his local knowledge.

They rested the stretcher beyond the second tower, at the base of the wall where the grass grew long and soft. Fifty paces away a gate wide enough for a farm cart was barred shut. That did not seem to concern Guy.

'Done this many times,' he joked. 'Just don't tell Papa.' He didn't seem to have grasped how sick Carel de la Tour was. He began to climb, using the angle between the tower and the wall, finding crevices and handholds that Adelais could not see. He paused only once, with his arm through a crenellation, as he watched for movement inside. Adelais gasped as he pushed himself away from the tower, holding on with one hand until he could swing the other arm up and haul himself through.

He was gone long enough for Adelais to worry that he had been caught. She could do nothing more for Carel de la Tour, whose breathing was shallow and strained. The dew on the grass smelt sweet, so she dampened a corner of the cloak that covered him, and bathed his face. He did not wake, though his breathing eased. She looked up to see Arnaud staring at her, his face unreadable under the dried blood.

'Come here, Arnaud l'Armurier.' She stood with the damp cloak in her hand. 'You'll frighten your friends inside.' The face that emerged as she wiped was strong but kindly, and pocked with the white spark-burns of his trade. He watched her steadily, with respect, and she liked that. If he hadn't just wrecked her plans, she might even have warmed to him.

'You're a strange one, Adelais de Vries. Why did you help us?'

She shrugged, backed away, and bent again to the stretcher. She did not want to give him ideas. Besides, he was old enough to have the first silver threads in his hair, maybe even thirty winters.

'The eldest daughter told me to find *him*.' She jerked her head at the wall to indicate the absent Guy.

'But in the fight. You tripped the soldier.'

'Your apprentice had already betrayed me, in front of the priest. My fate was sealed. You had to win.'

'We are in your debt.'

'Which you can repay by helping me on my way. Coin for

my journey. Even a horse.' She looked at him levelly enough to show the extravagant demand was not a joke. L'Armurier's wry smile told her she was dreaming.

The oak gates rumbled as the locking bar was lifted inside, and Guy stepped out beside a man in a rough, homespun cote-hardie, with the tanned, folded face of one who worked in the sun. He bowed to 'Brother Parsifal' and greeted Arnaud like a brother, but barely glanced at Adelais or the stretcher before he led them away, hunched and scuttling as if that made him less visible. 'Talk later. The world is stirring.'

He led them into a vast open space, dominated by the donjon. Its towers flew the king's banner but the battlements were empty. The dome of a temple rose alongside it and there were lower buildings beyond – the infirmary, perhaps. The perimeter wall had clearly enclosed enough land for the Guardian knights to keep and exercise their horses, and to grow herbs and vegetables for their table; it had been divided into three 'fields' by stone walls, though only one was now culti-vated. A cow munched weeds in another; the third was a tangled mess of brambles.

Their escort led them along a choked path to a low, thatched hovel at the junction of the fields. The space inside was so cramped that they had to press against the walls before the peasant could shut the door. Adelais found herself pushed into a corner with her head among hoes and rakes hanging from the rafters; clearly this man was a gardener. The floor was packed earth, and strewn with straw against the damp.

A woman in her middle years had been hunched over the hearth as they entered, stirring an iron pot suspended over a small fire. She rose, pulling a shawl around her, and folded Guy into her arms as if he were her son, until she saw Parsifal, to whom she curtseyed. They all knew each other, and Adelais was ignored on the edges.

'I bring you trouble, old friend.' Guy clasped the gardener

on the shoulder. 'We have found my father, though he is much changed.'

The gardener dropped to his knees beside the stretcher. 'Brother Carel? Can this be you?'

Carel de la Tour did not respond. Adelais pushed through to him and touched her fingers to his neck.

'He is very weak. And beyond any remedy.' She knew her words were harsh, but she still felt the anger tightening her guts at this whole stupid escapade. Their 'care' had hastened the old man's death. 'If this were still the infirmary, we'd call for a priest.'

Guy's eyes widened with the shock of her words. His mouth opened and shut before he spoke. 'But there's an infirmary right here, next to the temple,' he protested, pointing through the wall.

The gardener laid a hand on his arm. 'If you needed to come in the night, by the meadow gate, young Guy, you'll need to stay away from the infirmary. There's king's men in there.'

Parsifal's jaw clenched. 'Are there no physicians still loyal to the Guardians?'

The gardener shrugged. 'You need men of quiet deeds, not tavern swaggerers. And physicians don't talk to the likes of me. I'd ask Pateras Bardolph, but the back door to the temple will be shut until the second office.'

'If Brother Carel lives that long.' Adelais saw the hurt on Guy's face and wished she'd spoken more gently.

'But what can be done *now*?' Guy picked up his father's hand and chafed it between his own, trying to encourage a response.

Adelais lifted her chin towards the corner, where the couple's wooden cot lay under a straw mattress. 'Keep him off the floor. Feed him a little broth, if he will take it. But prepare yourself; I do not think it will be long.'

She settled onto the floor, pulling straw under her kirtle to keep out the damp, and rested her head back against the wall. She had not slept for a day and a night, and her limbs were heavy with tiredness. In time she dozed, but stirred as Arnaud slipped out of the hovel. He nodded at her, saying he'd be back with means to help their escape, and she relaxed, knowing he could be trusted. She slept lightly, lulled by the low murmur of voices around the cot. She overheard enough to know that the couple had sheltered Guy after his father was seized and until Arnaud took him as an apprentice, but apart from brief moments of wakefulness she let exhaustion take her.

She was woken by the bells of the second office, summoning the faithful to morning prayer. In the sisterhouse, the temples of the city had made distant music that rippled outwards from the fire temple on the Isle until a sleepy adeifi would ring a single, tinkling bell to call Montbeauvoir to worship. Here within the citadel the great bells of the Guardian's temple seemed to sound through her body, loud enough to jerk her into gasping wakefulness. Only then did she hear the chimes of the city spreading into the distance.

The gardener's wife lifted a steaming wooden bowl towards Adelais, smiling. After a moment's thought she made the sign of Ischyros in ritual thanks over the food. There was no Mitera Chantalle watching her, but she still needed to play a part. *Mind, soul, and body.* Especially body, and *sætur Sif* she was hungry. It was a thin vegetable broth, flavoured with herbs and a little precious salt, and there was even a crust of coarse bread with which to wipe the bowl. Her belly craved more, but she guessed this couple had little to spare. Adelais smiled her thanks as she handed the bowl back and crossed to Carel's side.

She could see the changes in his face, those signs that Carel's death was close. She rested her hand on Guy's arm when he brought the stretcher to the cot, intending to take his father into the temple, and shook her head. It was time to let de la Tour go gently.

Carel woke shortly afterwards. In the infirmary, Adelais had seen some people slip quietly away, while others had a final rush of energy, as if they knew their end was near and they needed to gasp some final message. A few had wanted to unburden themselves of some great sin. It was a time for a priest, not an unbelieving novice. All a novice could do was hold their hand and soothe their brow. Once, when a priest could not be found in time, she'd eased a man's passing with the words of unburdening, and pretended to press the sacred ash into his forehead. She might follow the old gods in her heart, but that didn't stop her making that simple act of kindness, even if it was heresy for a woman to pretend to pardon anyone. It was one of many things the anakritim would flog or burn her for, if they knew. After they had expelled her from the faith.

At least Carel de la Tour could take comfort in his son's streaming face, and from the presence of another Guardian, for Parsifal also knelt by his side. On his knees, with his hands folded in prayer, Parsifal had the holy, wild-bearded look of the early disciples in the wall paintings. Carel lifted one splinted hand so that the back of his wrist rested against Guy's cheek, and breathed deeply.

'Let the master...' Carel coughed, and a bloody phlegm ran from the corner of his mouth. 'Let the master know I didn't tell them.' He stared wide-eyed at Guy, nodding his head to emphasise his words.

'Tell them what, Papa?' Guy held the hand against his face.

'I told them many things, but not the Hand, not the precious Hand.'

Parsifal made the sign of the God and muttered 'efcharistó ton Ischyros', offering thanks in the High Tongue. He reached to touch Carel on the shoulder, as if to stop him saying more, but a spasm of coughing racked de la Tour's body, curling him over on his side. His final words were mixed with blood so that he seemed to spit them from his mouth in liquid form, one bubbling breath per word that Guy bent to wipe away with a cloth.

'Carel—de la Tour—did—not... Break.'

4.2 MALORY

'Forgive me, Pateras!' Malory d'Eivet staggered away from the anakritis-general's desk, clutching at his belly. He just had time to reach the small stone toilet overhanging the Gaelle before he threw up. Again.

'Your sins?' Pateras Ghislain asked. 'They are indeed grievous.'

Dry sarcasm was the closest Ghislain Barthram came to wit. Malory suspected that, in a small way, his master was enjoying his discomfort. Mostly, Barthram blazed with a cold fury beyond even that he unleashed on Guardian heretics.

'You were saying, Pateras Malory.' The implacable voice came through the toilet's curtains. 'Come, come! Speed is essential to recover the situation.'

Malory sank back on his knees, wiping his face. 'A novice overheard us and warned him.' He groaned as his guts heaved again. This time it was a dry spasm that gripped his whole belly and chest so brutally that he could not breathe. He could only clutch at the stone, face gaping over the void, while his sphincter released a loose trickle into the rags he'd tied between his legs. It was a tiny humiliation in comparison to his journey back from the Pissbourne. He'd staggered through laughter on the road. He'd been pelted with filth, when none would come near him. He'd only made it back through the city after he'd promised silver to the crew of an ordure cart to let him hide among their barrels while they took him to the Black Tower.

'This much I know,' Barthram said. 'The eldest daughter came herself to tell me, weeping with the effort to convince me the girl acted alone. I gather one of the soldiers is dead. At least that will ensure we have Chancellor de Remy's support. But tell me, why were *you* there?'

Malory d'Eivet stood, staggering as his vision spotted. He wiped his backside with the rag, and dropped it through the closet's hole. It floated downwards, folding as it fell, and settled onto the grey circle of the Gaelle, far below. Watching it spin slowly out of his sight made him dizzy and he straightened, struggling to speak around the slush of bile in his mouth.

'I saw the boy with a woman. Outside the fire temple. She seemed familiar.' D'Eivet sat on the closet as his guts boiled again. 'It was only later that I realised it might have been the novice. I took two more men to Montbeauvoir after the burning, just in case the boy went early to his father.' The burning. The memory of it made his mind churn like his belly. He'd seen men burn before, but never like this. There were always contortions and screaming, all so necessary to warn the people of the consequences of heresy. How could those two not scream, even in the slow agony of charcoal, while their own bodies dripped and spat beneath them?

At that thought his guts boiled anew, making him sit again and groan wetly over the hole. All around the stake, men had fallen to their knees, making the sign of Ischyros, convinced they were witnessing a martyrdom. Even Malory himself had begun to doubt. What if the anakritis-general was wrong? He palmed his face in his hands, finding his skin as cold and clammy as the dead cat that had floated beside him in the Piss-bourne. Surely he must soon be empty of filth?

Malory spat, wiped his face again, and tried to stand. 'What will you do with the eldest daughter, Pateras?'

'I invited her to wait below while I contacted her order. I think it unlikely she will return to the sisterhouse. But whether the girl overheard, or was directed, is now immaterial. The important thing is what we do to find de la Tour and his abductors.'

A pitcher of water had been left on a shelf in the closet; Ghislain Barthram was a fastidious man. Malory poured it over his hands in turn, watched the drips fall down to splash into the Gaelle, and wondered if he would ever be free of the stench of the Pissbourne. He'd bathed in lavender water, and had a servant pour more over his hair, but still he stank as if some rot oozed from his body into his clean robe. His newly washed beard still smelt like it was a wick with its roots in filth. Perhaps he should shave.

'The novice is a witch. She helped them.'

'That, too, is irrelevant. She will die in any case. But she is with them, you say?'

'Yes. One Vriesian rode away to the north. He named himself as Everard de Warelt. Three others were walking together towards the east. They carried Carel de la Tour on a stretcher.' Pateras Malory steadied himself against the wall and risked returning to Barthram's office.

'Sit, man, before you fall. We have sent riders towards Vries-land. And since we have no reports of a stretcher being carried on the open road, we can assume the rest are hiding in Ville-bénie. We will guard all roads out of the city and all the bridges until they are caught, but we must give descriptions. Carel de la Tour is easy. What about the novice?'

'Tall for a woman. Lean. Yellow hair, witch's eyes.'

'What does that mean?'

'Pale blue, but dark-rimmed. They seem to look into your soul. She has a small dimple on the point of her chin...'

Ghislain Barthram lifted his nose, just a fraction, and sniffed the air in that rat-like manner of his, smelling sin. Sometimes the sniff was audible. Always, it was disconcerting. Malory looked away.

Barthram's black eyes could bore into you, as well, but like a sword thrust that laid bare the entrails of a soul, judging what they saw. Adelais de Vries's eyes had opened a window, observing, and for a brief, foolish moment he'd wanted her to see good within him.

'She wore a green gown, in the loose style they call a kirtle.'

'And the son?'

'Middle height. Brown hair, with a young man's beard. Well-muscled, as one who works with weighty tools.' Malory paused, remembering two white burn scars on the boy's neck. Like the one with him in the square. 'They were blacksmiths. Or armourers. He and the leader. I'm sure they were together. They had spark-burns...'

'Good.' Ghislain Barthram poured Malory a goblet of wine-and-water. 'Very good. Drink. Keep going. And when we are finished, you will take soldiers and search the armourers' quarter for them, or news of them. I want their names, their families, their fellow craftsmen, anyone who can say where they might hide.'

Soldiers. Malory dreaded the company of soldiers; the memory of their laughter was worse than the stench of the Pissbourne. He'd had to endure the Black Tower's guardroom while his servant was fetched with money for the ordure crew and a cloak for his nakedness. The guards' ribaldry and exaggerated waving of hands under their noses had been humiliating beyond measure. Now they smirked as he passed, and snorted behind his back.

'There were two others. One was a man-at-arms. Could

have been a Guardian. Another had his arm broken. The adeifes were treating him. He spoke with a rough, Villebénie accent.'

'Keep going.'

'Carel de la Tour may be dead. He was fading fast.' Malory gulped watered wine, feeling its sharpness cut through the bile in his mouth and spread uncertain warmth in his belly. He doubted if it would stay there, but it tasted better than vomit.

'Then we will keep all of them alive for as long as it takes to be sure that he did not pass on his secrets. That is our art, is it not?'

Malory closed his eyes and imagined a repertoire of tortures that he could inflict, especially on the girl. He'd make those blue eyes plead for mercy. She would pay, and keep paying.

'And there is so often,' Barthram was saying, 'an urge to tell all at the end, as we have seen.'

Pateras Malory frowned. The anakritis's words had triggered another memory.

'There is one other we must seek. He was at the burning. Dressed as a knight, but his surcoat was plain and his cloak ragged. Old. Long, grey beard. He chanted to Bastien Guerin as the burning began.'

'Let me guess. The sixth book of Salazar, chapter three. "Ischyros be merciful and shine upon us, and lift his hand to bless us."'

'How did you know?'

'It was the Guardian chant. They used it when no priest was present for the offices.'

But *he'd* been there, Malory thought, and they'd refused him. 'The knight and Guerin *signed* to each other.'

'The Hand. Guerin passed on word of the Hand.' Barthram stood, abruptly, and paced the room. 'Would you recognise this knight?'

Malory dropped his eyes. 'He was on the opposite side of the fire. The heat, Pateras... it distorted the air.'

Ghislain Barthram rolled his head back and growled towards the roof timbers. 'I should have had more men there. Who could have thought that a simple burning could go so wrong?'

Even at the risk of further offending his master, Malory blurted out the question that was troubling him so deeply. 'Pateras, how can mortal men stand such pain without a sound? Men always scream. This we know. None can withstand the agony of fire. Yet these men endured a slow burning, in charcoal not flame, in silence. How was that possible?'

'They must have taken a powerful potion, a witches' brew. I have heard of such things. How was *that* possible?'

'I was with them, all day. They had neither food nor water.'

'Then Kakos must really look after his own.'

'The people call them martyrs. Now all are convinced of the Guardians' innocence.'

'It was such a simple thing to ask of you, and you failed.'

'I know not how we could have fared better. The provost is expert in these matters. One of his men was overcome, so great was the heat of the coals.' And Malory d'Eivet's doubts had begun; the Guardians' fortitude had been like the story in the holy texts of disciples martyred in a furnace.

'But Pateras, what if we were *wrong*? What if they were innocent?'

The silence that spread through the room was so profound that Malory became aware of the background noises of Villebénie: the cries of street traders, the rumble of carts over the Great Bridge, and even the flow of water around its stone pillars. Barthram studied a jewelled icon on the wall, a gift from the king, as if he were seeing it for the first time. Slowly, he exhaled a sigh and spoke without turning his head.

'You are young, and I will forgive you that question, but it seems you have failed to understand why we pursue these enquiries so rigorously. The objective is not to discover the truth.' He turned and stared at Malory, showing no more emotion than the iron of a knight's great helm. 'The objective is to gather evidence to prove what we already know to be the truth. And now, more than ever, we need proof of their idolatry. We need that golden hand.'

Malory rose to his feet, clutching at the edge of Barthram's desk as the room spun and coal-black spots swum in his vision. He needed to escape the anakritis-general's stare. And to find a quieter place for his next vomit, for the wine was churning in his stomach.

'I shall take men to the armourer's quarter directly, Pateras.'

'Send whatever you learn to me, so that it may be carried to all posts. Take every man you need, even if you have to strip the Black Tower of guards. Stay out there until you have them. And most importantly...'

Malory turned by the door. 'Yes, Pateras?'

'If you ever question your high priest and your king again, your career and your life may be shorter than you wish. There will be nothing your illustrious uncle could do to save you. Do not fail me.'

4.3 ADELAIS

'Was it worth it?'

Adelais nudged Arnaud l'Armurier with her foot when he didn't answer. He'd returned, via the meadow gate, bent under the weight of a pack of armourer's tools, and clutching a lighter sack of clothing. His purse hung more heavily from his belt; she guessed he'd raided his home and workshop for coin, for the means to live on the road. He now sat on a low, three-legged stool by the gardener's hearth, watching Guy wash his father's body on the cot. Guy was weeping quietly, pausing every now and then to wipe his nose against the sleeve of his cote-hardie. The gardener's wife knelt beside him, helping. The gardener worked his field outside, lest his absence be noticed. Parsifal sat by the door, watching through a crack, his sword across his knees.

'Was what worth it?' Arnaud didn't look up.

Adelais found another stool and sat beside him. 'Two, maybe three men dead. It looks as if you're going to run from whatever you had. He had a life too.' She lifted her chin towards Guy. 'Now all the world will be after us. And for what? A few hours with a man who was dying anyway.'

'We didn't know he was dying.'

'I didn't have time to say.'

'Neither did we know about the anakritis. And you said four soldiers, not six.'

'It was always a risk. Why do it?'

He looked at her directly, and she saw anguish in his eyes. Anguish, guilt, but also something more wonderful. Joyous, even.

'You didn't see Guerin and Cheyne die. They roasted them, slowly, with no flame but from the juices that ran from their own legs. Yet they made no cry. Those who watched fell to their knees in wonder that men could endure such pain in silence.'

'They said nothing?'

'Guerin shouted only once, and that was to curse both king and high priest. At a time when mortal men should be scream- ing, his voice rang out like a commander in battle, calling on them to meet him before Ischyros. The last of the Lions let out a roar that will shake the throne itself. After that, death took them swiftly, and gently, so that we knew them to be holy, innocent men.'

He turned his face away, as if unwilling to let some emotion be seen.

'When they had fallen within their chains, the provost tried to revive them with the point of a spear. When he knew that they could suffer no more, his men piled dry wood around their bodies that they might be wholly consumed. Afterwards people burnt their hands searching for relics in the hot ashes, for all said that they had witnessed a martyrdom.'

'So what made you kill people?'

'We did not mean to kill. We meant to do good. We'd seen a great evil, and rescuing Carel de la Tour was a chance to save one friend from a similar wrong. In this corrupted shit-heap of a kingdom, for once we thought we'd be on the side of Ischyros and His prophet.'

He breathed deeply, his shoulders bunching under his cote-hardie, and she decided that maybe Arnaud l'Armurier was a decent man. Misguided, perhaps, but decent, even if she was still angry with him. He'd taken away her *choice*. She was even tempted to touch his back, to show some understanding, but it would not have been appropriate.

'We meant well, girl, even if little good has come of it.' Arnaud still spoke towards the flickering flame in the hearth. Adelais let the silence stretch and watched the tenderness with which Guy prepared his father's corpse.

'What will you do with his body, Guy Carelet?' she asked, regretting her earlier harsh words.

Guy lifted his head from his task. 'I will lay my father in the temple of his order, among the tombs of the masters. I am sure they will receive him well.'

'And if you are seen?'

'The gardener can take us to the temple. There is a back door into the antechamber that the clerics use for robing. I can ask no more of him, for their lives will be forfeit if we are found here. We will go soon, before the noon office, while the temple is quiet.'

'And then?'

Guy did not answer her question. Eventually Parsifal's looming presence growled from by the door. 'And then we are in Ischyros's hands.'

Guy and Arnaud placed Carel's body back on the stretcher, in the torn, brown gown of his order, and carried him along a field wall to a small gate that opened into a cemetery. Here, in neatly ordered graves beneath the sanctuary wall, lay the bodies of the Guardian knights and sergeants who had died in Ville-bénie. It felt an empty, forgotten corner, though the battle-mented heights of the donjon looked down into it.

The gardener led them to a low oak door in a structure attached to the temple, and knocked. Adelais heard sounds of movement from within, but the door remained shut. The gardener knocked again, and called into the frame.

'Pateras Bardolph! For the love of Ischyros, open!'

The door cracked just wide enough to show an old face, creased like crumpled leather and crowned with a silvered rim of hair.

'It is not convenient, come back later.' The priest's tone was more frightened than unkindly.

Parsifal pushed his way to the front, preventing the priest from closing the door. 'Come, Pateras Bardolph, it is Brother Parsifal. We are all friends here. And we found Brother Carel.'

'Brother Carel?' The gap widened, and the priest came stumbling down the steps. As he knelt beside the body Adelais saw that one sandalled foot was disfigured and missing a small toe; she was beginning to recognise the marks of torture. 'Carel de la Tour was lost to us.'

'Hello, Pateras Bardolph.' Guy smiled down at the old man, who rose hesitantly before embracing him in a rush of recognition.

'Guy Carelet! I did not recognise you.'

'The ones who did this to Papa are seeking us, Pateras.'

Pateras Bardolph looked over their shoulders at the cemetery, and upwards at the donjon's empty battlements, before reaching a decision. 'Then you must come in.' He limped ahead of them into the temple. 'There are others here, but they will not betray you.'

They turned on the threshold to thank the gardener, who seemed relieved to see them go. Adelais began to make the Ischyrian sign of benediction over him but stopped, knowing it to be a sham. Who was she, an unbeliever stripped of her habit, to bless such humble courage?

The room they entered was dark, despite the morning hour; the tall windows in the north wall were almost blinded by the grey walls of a building that Guy said was the infirmary. At first

Adelais was only aware of the stretcher by the door, and of people cramped into a small, ill-lit space, facing each other in the cautious way of fugitives unsure of their welcome. She spun as the bolts were shot home behind her; a man-at-arms had emerged from the shadows and was now between them and the door. Her eyes were still adjusting after the brightness outside, but his thick-set outline and grizzled hair seemed vaguely familiar. He folded his arms and leaned against the door, barring their exit. Adelais turned back into the room, sensing that they were intruding on an important discussion; the space was disordered as if they had interrupted a search. Mighty chests stood opened, with their contents strewn on tables and piled in corners: vestments and silver boxes for sacred ash, and silver tongs to feed a sacred fire.

'I think, Pateras Bardolph, it is time to bolt all the doors.' The voice from the shadows spoke with the gravelly authority of an older man. 'Good morrow, Brother Parsifal. What news?'

They know each other.

'We have brought Brother Carel,' Parsifal answered. 'He died. Peacefully. *Silently.*'

'*Efcharistó ton Ischyros.* May the God welcome him across the bridge.'

Adelais wondered why the shadowed figure had offered thanks for the death of Carel de la Tour.

'What of Brother Maarten?' The shadow was resolving as a man moved towards the light.

'We split up,' Parsifal growled. 'Less conspicuous. There were more than we expected and Marquel the blacksmith was hurt. Brother Maarten is helping him home.'

'You all knew.' Adelais stared from face to half-seen face. 'You planned this together!'

'Ah, the novice.' The grey-bearded knight who had helped her on the bridge stepped fully into view. 'The streets are rife with rumours. All Villebénie is seeking, among others, an armourer and his apprentice, and a lean, yellow-haired novice who now wears a green gown.'

As Adelais's eyes adjusted she also recognised the knight's thick-set companion by the door. Adelais pushed her cap and kerchief back from her head, baring her hair. 'We meet again, messires.'

'You and your friends have a gift of causing trouble. We thought it would be a simple rescue. Now Villebénie burns with stories of a dead soldier, and a young man who kicked an anakritis into the Pissbourne.'

'He was the anakritis-general's assistant,' Guy responded, defensively.

'Then you have my eternal gratitude. And you will be heroes for an hour, which is about as long as you will last when you step outside this temple.'

'But see what he did to my father.' Guy lifted the cloak over Carel's body and pointed at the hands, now clawed across the chest like dead spiders. 'And this!' He pulled it up above the wrecked feet. 'I should have killed him!'

'Your anger is understandable, but it will not save you.'

'I know you, messire.' Arnaud had been watching the knight as he moved around the room. 'You are Humbert Blanc, who was Grand Commander of Arrenicia, and you were at yester-day's burning. I am Arnaud l'Armurier, who was armourer in this citadel until the persecution.'

'I am, and I was.' The knight's voice held a tone of caution, or warning. 'And this is Brother Karlis, who was also a Guardian. Like me, and Brother Parsifal, he still holds his vows to be valid, even though our order is suppressed.'

'Guerin knew you. You signed with him. Battlefield signs. Something about a hand, and a house or a temple.'

Pateras Bardolph gasped, and fluttered his fingers as if he could brush the words away. 'Do not talk of such things!'

'And what does an armourer know of Guardian battle

signs?' Humbert Blanc spoke softly, holding himself very still. The room was newly charged with tension, as if a blade had been drawn.

'When I was an apprentice I followed my master in the holy wars to recover Alympos from the Saradim, messire. I was with Guardian raids down the Berberine coast. Aye, and wielded a sword at times, as well as an armourer's hammer.'

'Did you make your vows?'

'Nay. I had a wife, and she was dear to me.'

The knight's shoulders sagged a little. 'Then I can only beg you never to reveal what you saw between the master and myself.'

'My father died talking about a hand,' Guy added, his eyes locked on the knight.

'And what did he say of this hand?'

Adelais sensed that Humbert Blanc was at his most dangerous when he was quiet.

'He said to tell the master that he told them many things, but not the precious hand, and that Carel de la Tour did not break.'

The old knight closed his eyes and sighed. 'Then he was a prince among men. Pray Ischyros he can now tell the master that himself.'

'How fare *you*, Lord Brother?' Parsifal looked intently at Humbert Blanc, who shook his head slightly.

An awkward silence spread through the room; a priest, five men, and a woman gathered around a corpse. Again, Adelais felt that they were intruding, and that they had interrupted some activity that was important to the Guardians and the priest. The cleric cleared his throat.

'Why did you come here?'

Arnaud spoke for them. 'We hoped to hide. Now, we hope also to lay Carel de la Tour to rest.'

'But why hide here? In a fortress?'

'Sometimes the best way to hide is in plain sight.'

'Soon worshippers may come for the noon office.' Pateras Bardolph paced the room, his fingers fretting at the cord around his waist. 'There will be few, on a working day, but some will come. More will be here at the Lighting of the Lamps. There may be other clerics, and few can be trusted. They must not find you here, either, Lord Brother. It would raise too many... questions.'

Humbert Blanc lifted his head towards an inner door, which Adelais presumed must open into the temple itself. 'Then put us in the crypt during noon office. With Ischyros's help I shall be gone before the Lighting of the Lamps.'

'The crypt. Yes. An excellent idea.' Pateras Bardolph still paced, now limping more noticeably. It must be hard, Adelais thought, to put yourself in danger once you have known such torture. 'And it will be a good place to leave Brother Carel. I will do what I can for him.' He led the way from the antechamber into the temple.

Sunlight streamed into the temple through high, east windows; dust-motes floated in milky yellow beams. Their footsteps echoed in what must once have been a vibrant, holy place. Now it was empty, not so much as if the holiness had left it, but rather that men had left the holiness, leaving a peaceful void behind. The limping priest pulled up a large trapdoor beside the sanctuary. Adelais swallowed her fear as they were led down stone steps, built just wide enough to allow a coffin or a body to be carried into the depths below. The flaming torch that the priest held cast too little light for them to see their way clearly, and yet revealed too much, for some tombs in the crypt's walls lay open, and they walked into a dormitory of the dead. Dusty skeletons, their jawbones hanging open, made silent laughter within their disintegrating robes, and in the guttering light they seemed to move, to shift within their tombs as if curious about their visitors. The place stank of dry mould; Adelais breathed the spores of death.

'By all that is sacred, do not leave us here!' Adelais would not call on the old gods out loud, not in this place.

'Fear not, girl,' Brother Humbert assured her. 'They are all with Ischyros, not here.'

Arnaud bent to heft a cube of broken marble from where the tombs' covering slabs lay resting against the walls. Crumbled mortar lay around them. 'These tombs are newly opened. And so is this coffin.' The lid of a large stone coffin had been lifted off, onto the paving. The body within was no more than bones, powder, and a grinning skull.

'No matter, no matter.' Pateras Bardolph placed his torch in a sconce, knelt by the coffin, and began, reverently, to move the bones into one of the alcoves. He muttered to himself as he worked. 'Move over, Brother Ricard. Your illustrious master would share your bed.'

'For what were you searching, that you would even disturb the dead?' Arnaud sounded incredulous.

'You do not need to know.' Brother Karlis's tone allowed no discussion. 'This, too, must be forgotten.'

They laid Carel de la Tour's body inside the coffin, and stood respectfully back as Pateras Bardolph performed the Office of the Dead. After he had pressed the print of pardon into Carel's forehead, it took three of them to lift the lid back into place.

'I must unbolt the doors for noon office.' Pateras Bardolph turned, looking at the debris around him. 'Now, where can I find mortar?'

He returned, not with mortar but with bread and a skin of wine that Brother Humbert blessed with gentle piety. Afterwards Adelais sat with her back to the west wall, where there were no gaping tombs, and watched the torch burn lower. Guy knelt in prayer beside the coffin. Arnaud and the three Guardians squatted beneath the steps, talking softly.

'So why does a knight need to hide?' Arnaud whispered.

'This, too, you do not need to know.' Brother Karlis's accent was nasal and hard-edged, a hot-stone-and-rough-wine kind of speech, as if his mother tongue was not Galman but the Occan of the south.

'I'd wager my workshop that it has to do with this *hand*.'

'Your workshop will be ransacked by king's men by now.' Karlis seemed to resent the questioning. 'But wager all you wish, armourer, you'll get no answer.'

Exhaustion and wine were making Adelais drowsy, despite the horror of their surroundings. She started into wakefulness at the last guttering of the lamp, and gasped as absolute darkness fell on them. She whimpered a little as she heard movement around her, coming closer, but relaxed as she smelt Arnaud – fire, iron, and sweat, and a maleness that did not threaten. He sat against the wall beside her, and in the terrible darkness she groped for his hand. After a while she allowed her head to fall against his shoulder and, unbelievably, amidst the dead, she slept. She dreamt that the twisted hand of Carel de la Tour, within his stolen coffin, had turned to shining gold, and that the dead masters climbed from their dusty tombs to make obeisance, for the golden hand was lifted in benediction and Carel de la Tour's face was now that of Ischyros's prophet, the Blessèd Salazar.

4.4 MALORY

Malory d'Eivet was pleased with the morning's progress. By the second office they had found a veteran of the wars against the Saradim, now a blacksmith by trade, with a newly broken arm for which he had no adequate explanation. He had served the heretic Guardians. He also had a wife and family living behind his workshop.

They didn't even have to take him to the Black Tower. A soldier simply had to twist the broken arm, and keep twisting until the blacksmith's wife admitted that he had been in a fight the night before. After that they merely had to threaten to break his children's arms and they had a name. Arnaud l'Armurier, who was apparently also Guy's master. Everard de Warelt had revealed his own name, so with Adelais de Vries and Guy, who they learned was called Carelet, they had four names out of the six. The other two were 'brothers' so were probably Guardians.

They were like lice, these Guardians. One never quite eradicated the infestation.

The blacksmith would be hung in due course, but for now d'Eivet had another use for him.

L'Armurier's workshop was productive in a different way.

According to a boy whose role was to bank up the furnace and guard against fire, l'Armurier had returned, taken as many tools as he could carry, and roused his apprentices. He'd given them silver and told them to seek other masters. They were still there, sharing out the remaining tools, when d'Eivet arrived, and he let his men soften them up while he threw up in a quenching bucket. Afterwards he threw the bucket into the furnace. It was the only one of his many vomits that morning in which he took any pleasure.

The apprentices, of course, knew very little, but no matter. They, too, would be useful. By the time the bells for the noon office had rung through Villebénie, every member of the king's army in the city had been given names and descriptions, and he had guards on every gate and bridge. He had confirmation that l'Armurier and Carelet were still hiding nearby, which probably meant that the girl was with them, and he had a growing number of people in his custody who would recognise them. Soon he would have enough to place one on every major route out of Villebénie, and he could put the fear of Ischyros into them to ensure they did his will, with the threat of divine wrath on their families if they didn't.

Then there was the question of the grey-bearded knight. *Think!* But Malory was light-headed. Not even water would stay down.

Carel de la Tour was an easier question. What might they do with a sick man who couldn't walk?

He would personally visit every infirmary within two hours' walk of Montbeauvoir.

Starting with the Guardian's citadel itself.

4.5 GUY

Guy was frightened in the crypt, so frightened that he almost forgot his grief, but at least he hadn't squealed like the girl.

In that impenetrable darkness, his imagination shrank from the unseen corners, and made silent whimpers at every movement. But he wasn't going to show his fear. Not with two Guardian knights and a grand commander in the crypt with him.

Humbert Blanc was agitated, too, though he sounded more excited than fearful. Guy heard a gloved hand striking fist-into-palm, and a muttered oath.

'Heh! By Salazar! The armourer said it!' The knight's low whisper made someone else stir, perhaps Brother Karlis. At least, Guy hoped it was Karlis, not the ghastly bones of some ancient knight.

'Hidden in plain sight!'

There was no way of measuring time, no moving shadows, no changing light. The priest, Pateras Bardolph, was gone so long that Guy feared he had betrayed them. Guy wasn't normally a praying man, but in his mind he begged the Blessèd

Tanguy, whose bones were in the sanctuary above, that there wouldn't be guards waiting for them.

When the oaken trapdoor was eventually lifted and a shaft of light lanced down the steps, Guy had to blink and shut his eyes, but not before he'd seen the girl start and push herself away from Arnaud's shoulder. He found himself resenting that closeness. Not that he wanted the girl, but Arnaud was the nearest thing to family that Guy had left, and on the day his father had been found and lost, he needed him. When Guy half opened his eyes again, the two of them were well apart, looking self-conscious, and at the top of the steps there was only the priest beckoning them upwards.

They were made to wait in the body of the temple while Humbert Blanc ran to the steps to the bell tower, unexpectedly agile for a greybeard, calling for Karlis and Parsifal to follow. Pateras Bardolph limped after them, muttering that they'd find nothing but old vestments, worn beyond use. Guy and Arnaud waited for a while, and then, bored, walked beneath the pillars, talking of ways to escape. As a child, Guy had worshipped here with his father, behind row upon row of kneeling, white-clad knights, all facing the sanctuary and the sacred flame. Now it was an uncertain shelter. Getting out should be easy, if the meadow gate was still unmanned, but he feared they'd only change it for a prison they'd never leave.

'We could split up,' Guy suggested. 'Go separately. Meet again outside Villebénie?'

Arnaud did not reply.

'The girl's the biggest danger.' Guy nodded to where Adelais sat on a stone step. She looked like a lost child. 'It's hard to hide a thin, yellow-haired woman.'

'Who saved you from the anakritim.'

'Yeah, but...' Guy squirmed. He wasn't ungrateful, he just didn't like her. She was too sure of herself; she'd almost taken charge down by the Pissbourne. And too close to Arnaud.

'Lord Brother Humbert is our best hope.' Arnaud glanced at the bell tower door.

'And he has no reason to help us.'

Arnaud stopped, staring at Adelais, who was walking towards them, gripping her staff as if poised to hit them with it.

'Voices carry over stone, you know. Or perhaps all your armourers' hammering has deafened you.' She rapped her staff on the flagstones; the crack echoed around the temple. Guy felt his cheeks burn.

'You say they are seeing a yellow-haired woman.' Adelais glared at them. 'So find me some clothes and I'll leave here as a yellow-headed man.'

Arnaud stared at her. A slow smile spread across his face and he began to chuckle. He led her towards the antechamber. 'We have clothes. You and Guy are almost of a height.'

'*My* clothes?' Guy trailed behind, affronted. He had few enough, and they'd cost much of what Arnaud gave him.

'It is the least you can offer in thanks, lad.' Arnaud closed the door and upended a sack. 'See, here is a loin cloth, a man's shirt, and hose. The sisterhouse boots will serve.'

Adelais stared at the clothes scattered in front of her, then looked up at Arnaud.

'Good. Turn your backs, then. Look at the wall, not me.'

Guy felt Arnaud's hand slide across his shoulders, holding him towards the wall in case he was tempted to sneak a look. In front of Guy's face now hung a small, silvered glass mirror, presumably there so that clerics could adjust their vestments before the offices. Guy swayed a little to one side until an imperfect, smoky image of Adelais's back came into view. She had already pulled off her gown, and was plucking at the sleeve buttons on her chemise, which swelled below a slender waist and hung almost to her knee. As she bent to pull it over her head, the hem rose, and Arnaud reached out and turned the mirror's face to the stone. He made a quiet, disapproving tut.

The rustling of clothes behind them seemed to last a long time.

'I need a man's cote-hardie. This will not work.'

They turned. Adelais stood facing them, her shoulders hunched and rounded. She held one arm protectively across her chest, fingers touching her shoulder. She'd taken off her woman's kerchief and her roughly cropped, boyish hair was the colour of sunburnt straw.

Guy knew she was right; it wouldn't work. Even though the shirt, *his* shirt, hung low enough to cover *his* loin cloth, her hips were too wide, especially when she was hunched like that.

'Stand straight, lass.' Arnaud frowned at her.

She huddled even further into herself, and brought her other arm up so that both arms crossed over her chest.

'Adelais,' it was the first time Guy had heard Arnaud use her name, 'I must make you what you are not: male and ugly. To do that I must see you as you are. Stand straight, like a man. Shoulders back. Good.'

Adelais unfolded her arms and straightened, glaring at them with flush-cheeked defiance. Small, high breasts lifted the shirt; even in man's clothes she was no more male than a bride in her bedchamber. Guy swallowed. In a way he couldn't explain, dressing her as a man made her more of a woman.

'We must hide your waist, and pad out your body.' Arnaud walked around her, critically.

'I am not some cow to be sold at market.' Her face burned apple-red, and what had been defiance now looked like fury.

'No, you are a courageous young woman, and we would keep you alive. We also wish to journey with you without being taken ourselves. Guy, take off your gambeson.'

Journey with them? Guy felt a rush of anger as he pulled off his cote-hardie and unlaced the quilted armour hidden beneath. Arnaud hadn't even discussed that with him.

But the gambeson helped, a lot. It fell from her shoulders to her hips, smoothing her waist and flattening her breasts. A long gash along one side revealed layers of padding, and Guy swallowed as he remembered the sword thrust and the guard he'd disfigured, possibly killed. He bent to pull his feast-day cotehardie from the clothes sack before that too could be given away. The girl could have his ripped one.

Arnaud finished his creation by draping his own, best hood over Adelais's head. It broadened from the neck to cover the shoulders as well as the head, so when Adelais stood, she could indeed pass for a young man. She buckled on her own belt, and put her hand thoughtfully into the bag hanging from it.

'You need a name.' Arnaud seemed proud of his work.

Adelais pulled a piece of leather from her bag. It trailed cords that she wound round her hand as she thought. 'Perrin.' Even her voice seemed to fit the clothes; quite dark for a girl, almost a youth's tenor, though the Vriesian accent was strong.

'Perrin what? You can't use your father's name. It would give us away.'

She paused again. 'Perrin Wilg. It's Vriesian for "willow".'

'I am enchanted to make your acquaintance, Perrin Wilg.'

'*Vilg*,' she corrected him. 'As in victory.'

'Let's see you move around. How does it feel?'

Adelais walked down the room, flexing her shoulders.

'She walks like a girl.' Guy had watched her legs, now visible almost to the knee. He mimicked her, exaggerating her small steps and hands-across-the-stomach posture.

'He's right, *Perrin*.' Arnaud braced his shoulders, demonstrating. 'Shoulders back. Swing the arms. Swagger a little.'

'Walk like you've got something *here*,' Guy clasped his crotch, 'and you're proud of it.'

Adelais threw him a look of pure loathing, though her sharp retort was interrupted as the door to the gardens shook to urgent knocking.

'Pateras Bardolph! An' it please you, Pateras, let me in!'

The gardener brushed past them as Arnaud opened the door. 'Where is Pateras Bardolph? On our lives, I must see him now.'

They found Pateras Bardolph and all three Guardians kneeling at the sanctuary rail in a shaft of early afternoon sun, with the Guardians' cloaks fanned around them on the flag-stones, covering their legs all the way to their spurs. They were singing a praise chant, and even Humbert Blanc's face streamed with tears; they soaked into his beard, touching the curls of grey with the light of sunshine on water. As they entered, Humbert gathered a small package to his body and hid it under his cloak. Guy wondered what they'd found to cause such joy.

The gardener seemed not to notice, but tugged at the priest's sleeve.

'An' it please you, Pateras, there's an anakritis and soldiers searching the infirmary for Brother Carel and his friends. They'll come to the temple next. My poor wife, they'll take her, too. What can we do, Pateras?'

Humbert Blanc closed his eyes in prayer as Pateras Bardolph clutched his arm. 'The crypt?'

'It is too obvious, and we will be trapped.' Brother Humbert spoke quietly, as if disturbed from a dream.

'Then for our sakes,' Pateras Bardolph rose to his feet, 'lock me and the gardener in there. Take the key. Strike me; make it look as if you overpowered us. Now run. Take the meadow gate.'

'They've already posted a guard over the meadow gate, Pateras.' The gardener kneaded his cap. 'An' if it please you, my friend Paget, him what cooks for the infirmary, says they're also looking for a grey-bearded knight.'

A furious hammering sounded through the sanctuary, as of the pommels of swords being beaten against the great doors.

4.6 ADELAIS

Adelais hid in the shadows as the gardener rushed through the robing room, shamed by her man's clothes. She wanted to grab at her old gown and wrap it around her legs, now hidden only by hose below her knees.

She was also angry. So angry that she wanted to hit something. Break a vessel. Even smash the priceless glass in the windows. Carel de la Tour's son had stared at her as if he could see through her shirt, like she was some harlot. Oh, Arnaud had been gentle enough. He'd tried to show her some respect, made her feel that she was a woman rather than some scrawny fowl he was choosing for the pot, but she was aware of his maleness as he walked around her. Guy, though, had been like those boys in Vriesland, undressing her with their eyes; the strutting, pustuled fighting cocks who'd surrounded her on the dyke when she wouldn't let them shaft her. Adelais wound the thongs of her sling around her hand and pulled, as if wrapping them around somebody's neck.

Instead, she went outside, into the cemetery. She was disguised, wasn't she? That meant she could walk around, beneath the empty battlements. Swagger, Arnaud had said.

Imagine you have something between your legs, Guy had
mocked. She growled at the memory, picked up a smooth stone
from between the graves, and rested it in the pouch of her sling.
Twenty paces away, a block near the top of the boundary wall
to the garden had a pointy projection, like a nose, and she imagined it to be Guy Carelet's face. Twenty paces had always been
her best range at pigeons, especially if they thought themselves
safe in the branches. If she shot at twenty-five paces, the bird
would see the stone and fly. At twenty, she could hit it on the
branch or as it lifted its wings for that first, panicked flap.

Sometimes. From deep inside the temple came the sound of
banging, but she ignored it. Concentrate on the quarry. Aim
small, miss small. That's what she'd learned. Aim for the bird
and you'll miss and go hungry. Aim for its eye, and you might
hit the head.

Her first shot went high and right, clicking off the wall's top.
That made her angrier, but now it was a cold, killing anger. She
chose four more stones the size of a child's fist, as many as
would fit in her belt bag, each as smooth and round as she could
find.

The next struck a handspan low-left. Better. Still not good
enough to be sure of the bird.

The third was a finger's width low. Good enough if the bird
was still on the branch. Not perfect.

The sound of running feet interrupted her as she was
loading the fourth stone into the pouch. Guy Carelet leapt
down the steps in one bound, shouted 'Come on!' at her, and
kept running. She let him go. Arnaud came after him, empty
handed, and seized her elbow.

'Come, lass. The anakritim's men are at the door.'

Humbert Blanc ran past in an ungainly lope with his
surcoat flapping at his knees. He held something in both hands,
wrapped in his cloak, whose ends were tangling with his scabbard. Karlis and Parsifal ran after him with swords drawn.

'But my clothes, my stave...' More blows came from within the sanctuary; slower, more regular thumps that sounded like axes being swung against the doors.

'And my tools. No time for any of it.' Arnaud dragged her until she broke into a run beside him. Her squirrel-fur cloak. *Yrsa's stave!*

They paused at the gardener's hovel, hiding behind its wall. The track ran fifty paces beyond to the meadow gate. Above the gate, now firmly barred, a soldier leaned against the battlements, staring out at the fields beyond.

'Why did we come this way, if we knew it was guarded?' Guy asked of Arnaud.

'One would rather,' Humbert Blanc answered for him, 'face one guard here than fight twenty at the main gates, and there is no other way out.' The knight seemed to have taken charge of all of them. He frowned, seeing Adelais's garb for the first time, and nodded, slowly, as if accepting it. He pointed at the sling, still wound around her hand. 'Can you use that, mistress?'

'Against a man? You wish me to kill, sir knight?'

The way Humbert Blanc looked at Adelais reminded her of an old cleric she'd known in Vriesland; Ischyrian but kindly and understanding, with steel-grey eyes that seemed so wise.

'If you have the skill, you can take one life to save six.' The knight spoke calmly, as if she had all the time in the world to make a decision. 'Including yours.'

Guy prodded her in the back. 'Do it. You have nothing to lose.' He looked back over his shoulder, watching for pursuit.

'Except my soul.' She used the Ischyrian word. She just knew she didn't want to kill. And this wasn't her fight. Or was it?

Brother Karlis touched her more gently. 'It is either that, or try and rush him up the steps. We'd lose at least one man.'

Adelais breathed deeply, closing her eyes. *Sætur Sif, sweet Sif, what am I to do?*

'Please, lass,' Arnaud begged her. 'We have no time for debate.'

Perhaps she'd made this her fight when she tripped the soldier in Montbeauvoir. But this would be murder. Adelais exhaled, opened her eyes, and looked levelly at Humbert Blanc. 'Those who murder will burn in hell.' So said his precious Salazar.

Guy swore. 'Tanguy's bones! But you'll let others kill so that you might live.'

Humbert simply nodded, accepting her decision.

'So be it.' He laid the cloak-wrapped bundle in his arm on the ground, as gently as Guy had laid his father in the stone coffin. 'I will try to get close enough to surprise him.' He straightened, and took a single, deep breath. 'Armourer, boy, stay here. Brothers Karlis and Parsifal, come at him from the next tower while he is watching me.' He too shut his eyes, as if in prayer, and made the sign of Ischyros.

'Wait.' That simple action changed Adelais's mind. Or perhaps it had been the piety that settled around the knight as he prepared himself to fight. 'I will do it.'

She too made a sign, though hers was the hammer of Thor. A bit lopsided, perhaps, so they might think it was the *mind, soul, and body* of Ischyros. She looked round the corner of the hovel.

'I must get closer.'

'Look natural, girl,' Guy added as she walked into the open.

'*Look natural*.' Stupid oaf. She was a fugitive novice, dressed in men's clothing, and she was calling on the old gods on her way to murder. *Natural?* If she wasn't so frightened, she'd have sworn at him.

She walked slowly, in plain sight, pushing a stone into the sling's pouch. The man had a chain-mail coif draped around his shoulders, and a leather under-cap still covering his head.

Adelais pushed the edge of her hand against her belt bag,

hoping to feel the reassurance of Yrsa's talisman, but there was only the hardness of the next stone. *Öflugur Sif...* It seemed more appropriate to call on the power of Sif than Salazar.

Forty paces. She clenched the pouch and stone in her left hand, and bundled the cords into her right palm. If he turned, she'd bend and feign interest in the crop growing beside her. *Sif leidtha hændina mína... Guide my hand.*

Thirty-five paces. There were two lengths of iron leaning against the wall beside the guard, one of them with a rope handle. What could that be for?

Was Sif the right deity for this? Yrsa said she was the goddess of young lovers and good harvests.

Rune song, then. *Naudhiz*, the need-rune, for deliverance from distress. She pictured it in her mind's eye, and muttered to herself.

Naudh er thýjar thrá...

Thirty paces. Of course. Iron to beat iron and sound an alarm. If they'd rushed him, they'd have had guards running from all directions. Not one of them would have escaped.

Ok thungr kostr...

Twenty-five paces. Still too far to be sure. The man straightened, reached behind him, and scratched his *rass*. Adelais froze. She was close enough to see his loin cloth as the skirt of his gambeson lifted, and to hear his sigh of pleasure. He relaxed against the battlements, sniffing, and Adelais crept forwards. Aim small, miss small. A seam ran over the crown of the leather cap. *That* stitch. It looked exactly like the *naudhiz* rune.

The stone was heavy in her palm. It would strike like a thrown hammer.

If it hit.

Twenty paces. Two more to allow for his height on the wall, like a pigeon in a tree. She pulled the sling to its full length, feeling the cords unwind in her palm, and swung, knowing that the whir might be heard.

Ok vássamlig verk...

But it would not be instantly understood. The guard straightened, angling his head to catch the unknown noise.

Just like a pigeon.

Sætur Sif, sweet Sif, forgive me.

Adelais let fly.

The stone struck the leather cap with a sound like a wooden bowl being dropped on a table, and bounced high into the air. The guard went rigid, swaying, for long enough for her to think he would turn and raise the alarm, but he began to sway backwards like a felled tree. His arms stayed locked and half-bent, quivering a little, with his legs pointing at the sky as he toppled off the parapet. It was far enough down for him to turn completely over and land on his back with a whump of leather and mail on earth, scattering a brief fog of dust from the dry ground under the gate's arch.

Adelais stared at him, dry-mouthed, with the sling dangling from her hand. She couldn't move, even when Guy and Arnaud ran past her to lift the beam that barred the door. One of the guard's legs started shaking, and lifted ridiculously clear of the ground, like a dreaming dog. She moved forwards, slowly, more to help the man than to escape. His eyes were bulging, as if pushed outwards from within.

'Forgive me,' she muttered.

Arnaud dragged her away. He always seemed to be doing that.

PART TWO

THE HAY MOON

CHAPTER 5

5.1 ADELAIS

Adelais found some comfort in the horses.

Some, but not enough.

Humbert Blanc had led them to a house on the outskirts of the city. The Villebénie home of his distant relatives, with its gardens sloping down to the Gaelle, should have been an island of peace. It was one of a terrace of grand mansions on the north bank, each built of stone at street level with timbered stories stacked above, and all with a gated archway big enough for a wagon to pass from the street into the grounds. Most were occupied by merchants, with the land between the houses and river cluttered by storerooms and workshops. By contrast, the garden of Blanc's cousins, the noble de Molinots, held only stables for the family's horses, a herb and physic plot, and a small orchard of pear and apple trees that softened the stables' smells with the scents of the lush grass beneath the trees.

The horses did not judge her. One day, if she was ever allowed to ride them, they might take her measure and test her, but for now they knew her only as one who fed them, groomed them, and walked them in the little orchard. And sometimes wept into their necks.

Guilt, Amma Yrsa would say, is a very Ischyrian idea; this notion that we were all naughty children who needed to be punished for breaking the priests' rules. Sometimes you make mistakes, she'd say, and have to atone for them; you earn your own fate by your deeds, but you should always walk tall with the gods and live by your word.

But taking a life, in a calculated act of murder? That was hard to live with.

Arnaud often came to sit with her, or to help her tend the horses. Their talk was quiet, lapsing at times into an easy, companionable silence. He asked her once why she'd chosen the name Perrin Wilg, and she told him about the old man Perrin in the infirmary at Montbeauvoir. It was the first name that came into her head. And 'Wilg', she told Arnaud, was Vriesian for 'willow'. Perrin had called her 'Willow' in the bantering, flirtatious way some old men have with maids. 'Slender and supple as a willow switch,' he'd said, 'and you can beat me anytime you like.' It was a joke he repeated daily, laughing until it hurt him. Adelais hadn't objected; the old man was dying, anyway.

Arnaud's presence was a comfort, yet he could not take away her pain. For the first time, Adelais understood the Ischyrian need to unburden and receive pardon.

Yet that morning she was alone, brushing the neck of Humbert Blanc's great destrier, raising a fine dust from its coat. The stallion was dark bay, almost black, yet the sunlight turned the dust into the colour of ripe wheat. The horse liked what she was doing; it had shut its eyes and lowered its head in pleasure. He was called Allier, after a swift-flowing river in Humbert's native Arrenicia, and for a warhorse he was soft as summer butter. She'd thought that any horse big and brave enough to carry an armoured knight into battle would be vicious, but this one was gentle with her, nuzzling her for more when she stopped. If he'd been a cat he'd have been purring.

'You are good with horses.'

Adelais turned at the sound of Humbert Blanc's voice, and dipped her body in deference. She stayed hunched, trying to pull the hem of Guy's cote-hardie further below her knees.

'No, child. Not like a girl. Like a man, thus.' Humbert put his leg forwards and inclined his body, making the gesture look easy and elegant. He was now dressed as a gentleman in a fine damask cote-hardie. Adelais guessed that the thick leather belt at his waist hid the red cord of a Guardian knight. He wore a heraldic badge sewn to his chest, red with three golden flowers, proclaiming him to be a knight in the service of a greater lord. He'd shaved his beard to disguise his appearance; it made him look more regal and less like the wall paintings of Salazar's disciples in a fire temple.

'Now you try, *Perrin Wilg*.' He emphasised her new name. 'These things you must learn.'

Adelais obeyed, blushing with the shame of pushing her leg towards him. Even wearing hose, it felt naked, but as she bowed the destrier nudged her for more attention and she stumbled, her poise broken. Humbert smiled, not unkindly.

'He likes you. Where did you learn to care for horses?'

'My father had three. He was a master weaver, and he had a covered wagon for delivering the finished cloth. Two were big in the chest like this one, but less fine, bred to pull loads. The third was a palfrey that he rode all over Vriesland with samples of his cloth in its saddlebags. He kept a good horse to impress his customers.' She closed her eyes at the thought of home. Even the happy memories were clouded by the pain of her departure.

'Did you ride them?'

'Yes, I rode. For the fun of it.' She found herself smiling at the memory of racing across an open, harvested field with the sound of wind in her ears and her hair streaming behind her. She'd had hair, back then. In the madness of new love she'd even unbraided it. Just the once. She winced away from another painful memory. 'The palfrey was fast, and loved to run. The other two were lumbering great beasts.'

'So how did a rich Vriesian weaver's daughter become a novice in Montbeauvoir?'

Adelais didn't see the point of lying. 'I fell in love with a young cleric, and was sent far away for my sins.'

Strangely, the old knight looked compassionate rather than affronted. 'One imagines that the cleric's penance was somewhat lighter. And your family? Didn't your father speak for you?'

'Ischyrian priests were my father's best customers; over half his business was fine cloth and linen for their robes. It was not in his interest to object.'

Humbert's face clouded. 'A harsh lesson, but not without precedent. It is not the faith that is unjust, child, it is the men within it.'

'This I know, messire.'

'Arnaud l'Armurier has told me of how you helped them. You have courage.'

Yet her courage had damned her. 'I always wanted to escape back to Vriesland, messire. Now I wish I had stayed in the sisterhouse.' Did she really believe that?

'I do not think you would have had a happy life as an adeifi, child. There is too much fire within you. But now you must find another path. Let us walk the horses under the trees. I would talk with you. Come, Allier.' Humbert took his destrier, leaning back to restrain it as it lunged for fresh grass. Adelais untied a gentler palfrey, a sweet-natured mare belonging to one of the de Molinot daughters. The mare, too, was restless with inactivity.

'You are comfortable here?' He waved at the stables with his spare hand. 'We could not lodge you in the house...'

Adelais understood. She did not have the gentle-born manners to pass as a squire or a page, and she could not lodge in the communal menservants' room in the attics. She shrugged.

'It is dry, and the horses keep it warm enough. My duties are light, but I wish I could shed these clothes.' She plucked at Guy's cote-hardie, now mended but still dirty. 'I stink. I doubt if this gambeson has ever been washed.' But it had been soaked in vinegar to kill the lice. It had a sharp smell as well as the sour odour of many men's sweat, and it was laced tight to her body over her shirt. That, too, was now stale.

'I will have fresh hose and linen sent to you, but that padding,' he touched her shoulder though she did not feel his fingers, 'is still your protection against discovery. The de Molinots are loyal, for they have given many sons to the Guardians over the years, but the servants might talk. They are already curious about the boy who sleeps alone in the stables.'

'I understand, messire.' Yet she longed to be clean. Cleansed of dirt, cleansed of the memory of killing.

'I am told you do not eat. It is two days, now, and you pick at your food. Is it not to your liking?'

'Your noble cousins are generous.'

'Without food you will faint upon the road.'

Adelais breathed deeply, lifting her shoulders as if she could shrug off the weight. Yrsa would understand. She'd give her a hug, and those sparkling, mischievous eyes would lift her mood.

'I killed a man.' She formed her thoughts in a way this devout Ischyrian would understand. 'The priests would say that without unburdening and pardon, he would fall from the bridge of judgement into the pit of Kakos.' The mare angled its head into Adelais's chest and rubbed at an itch around its eye. *Horses do not judge.*

'A good man-at-arms is also a devout Ischyrian, for we never know when we will feel a mortal wound. A chivalrous knight must so live that he cannot regret the blow.'

Adelais thought of the soldier in the sisterhouse who'd leered at her and spread his legs. That night he'd been stunned, possibly killed, by Guy with his mace.

'And if that man was not devout?'

'You cannot answer for another's sins, Adelais.' *Adelais*, not Perrin. He was talking to her, not some make-believe boy. 'And do not be troubled. If you look upon a treasure, and covet it, it is not your eyes that sin, it is your heart. If you steal, it is not your hand that sins but your head. If killing that soldier was a sin, it is not yours, but mine, for I sent you to kill as I would couch a lance.' He was close enough to put one hand on her head in benediction. 'Adelais de Vries, I take that sin, if sin it be, on me.'

That sounded and *felt* like a pardoning. More holy in fact than any ash-print with a muttered punishment. But Humbert wasn't a consecrated pardoner, so he couldn't unburden sins, could he? And why did it matter, when she didn't believe in Ischyros?

'Besides,' Humbert continued, 'if you had faltered, I think we would all now be held by the anakritim, and some of us already dead. One believes you have prevented a much greater evil. And courage, in a good cause, is pleasing to Ischyros.'

Adelais tugged at the halter to keep the mare close. It was easier to think with the distraction of a horse beside her; she could avoid Humbert's gaze, even though she knew it to be kindly.

'I did not choose your cause, messire, and I do not know if it is good. In a few short days I have met torturing priests and a man-at-arms who talks like a cleric yet sends me to kill.' She looked him in the eye. 'All my instinct is to trust you, sir Guardian, yet a Guardian charge broke the Vriesian line at Vannemeer and my brother died afterwards. I no longer know what is "good". I do know that I'd like to go home to Vriesland. I'll live with my grandmother if my father won't have me.' Or travel on into the lands towards the Ice Sea where the old gods still ruled.

Humbert rested his hand on his destrier's shoulder, stroking the hide. He seemed troubled.

'You would be taken, and you would be tortured, for you know too much. You would suffer great pain, for you are strong. The strong always suffer most; they fight hardest.'

'I know little enough. I know your names. I believe that both you and the anakritim seek a golden hand that once was the idol of the Guardians. I believe you found something of great value in the Guardians' sanctuary, for you carried away a bundle with reverence, though it was too small and light to have been a golden hand. Beyond that, nothing.'

'You are too sharp, Adelais. Sharp enough to wound those around you. That knowledge is enough to kill us all.'

'I also know that I am kept here. It is a gentle prison, but I may not leave.'

Four men-at-arms now guarded the house, including Parsifal and Karlis, and they all had the broad shoulders and scarred faces of veterans. One of them stood near the wagon gateway at all times, fully armed, and another at the house's doorway onto the street. If she approached, they looked at her in a way that told her to turn back. They spoke little, but their accents were strange and varied; Karlis's nasal tones spoke of Arrenicia, while another was Vriesian, she was sure, and it was said that one was Saxen, though he spoke Galman as well as Parsifal.

'My companions were all Guardian knights until the Order's suspension. Apart from Parsifal, they come from lands that owe little allegiance to Galmandie, so they escaped the persecution. They will be our escorts on our journey, and you can trust them with your life. They must learn that you can be trusted with theirs.'

'*Our* journey?'

'You may have seen my niece Agnès de Molinot in the garden. The mare you hold is hers. She is to be married to Leandre, Lord of Fontenay, and now that the winter rains are over it is time for her to travel to her new husband's lands. Her

father, alas, shattered his hip in a joust last year and may never
ride again, so I shall accompany her in his stead. With de
Fontenay's permission, we will wear his arms.' Humbert
touched the badge on his chest. 'De Fontenay is one of the great
nobles of Galmandie. His name is enough to grant us safe
passage.'

'To where, messire?'

'Château Fontenay is in Jourdaine, south of Moutâne, a
journey of perhaps ten days. Arnaud l'Armurier and Guy
Carelet will come with me, also protected by the badge of de
Fontenay. I would like you to be with us as well.'

'Three days ago, messire, you did not know us. Why are you
being so kind?'

'Carel de la Tour was a Guardian of knightly rank, although
only a lay brother. I will teach Guy Carelet the way of arms, if
he wishes and if he has the aptitude, for his father's sake. In
time, Guy might become my squire. L'Armurier is Parsifal's
brother. He also served the Guardians and will have my protection until we reach safety. After that, there will be many great
lords in need of a master armourer.'

'And me?'

Humbert spread his arms. 'I do not know, child. You remind
me of a young, captive lioness that I saw once in Alympos,
where she had been brought from distant lands. She was beautiful but frightened, and snarled at the world, always ready to
fight. One longed to set her free, as one would like to set you
free, but to free her in Alympos would have meant her death. If
you were a man, you could aspire to the profession of arms and
even to knighthood, for there is a rare strength within you. But
for a woman, without money or father or husband...' He
shrugged again. 'I do not know. I can only offer you my protection, my counsel if you will take it, and silver for your journey if
you want to travel further, once we are free of pursuit. I wish
you to come with us, and not simply because one fears to leave

you behind.' He looked at her with the gentle, unthreatening eyes of an old man.

'I do not understand, messire.'

'You are caught up in great affairs beyond your understanding, but I believe Ischyros has sent you to me, all three of you. I believe you have a purpose in the great mission that lies before us. Will you come?'

Adelais sighed and looked within herself, trying to find that point of calm where the future was clear, but her mind was light with hunger and would not focus. She did know that Jourdaine lay far to the south, away from Vriesland.

'You honour me, messire, whatever your mission. But if you will set me free, I shall take my chances and walk north, to Vriesland, where I may once again be a fair-haired woman.'

Humbert had a way of closing his eyes and breathing deeply when he was troubled, almost as if he were praying.

'I cannot allow you to leave us. If you are taken, before long we will all be captured. We do not fear death, but my companions and I protect something too precious to be lost.'

Humbert's tone made her look at him more closely, and in a moment of intuition she understood.

'You are taking it with you, whatever you found in the sanctuary. The wedding party is just an excuse. Is that your chivalry, messire? To hide behind a bride?'

She expected Humbert to be angry, but he smiled at her gently. 'Agnès de Molinot is another young woman with courage.'

'She *knows*? What of her father? What of her husband-to-be?'

'Agnès is already a widow, despite her tender years, and she needs no man's permission. As for Leandre de Fontenay, I lodged with him on my way to Villebénie, and he himself suggested the idea.'

'The anakritim are looking for a golden idol, a thing of great value, yet what you carried can have weighed no more than a purse.'

Humbert paused before he answered, staring at her. He seemed to be coming to a decision.

'What do you know of the prophet Salazar?' he asked eventually.

'Ischyros revealed himself to the prophet Salazar in Alympos. Salazar wrote His words in the holy texts.'

'True, although most of the holy texts were written later by Salazar's disciples.'

'Like Tanguy, whose relics rest in the fire temple on the Isle.'

'Quite. And where are the relics of Salazar?'

Adelais looked at him, startled. Even to suggest that Salazar was dead was heresy. The Blessèd Ones of Ischyros do not die. 'There are no relics of Salazar. He was wounded when the Saradim captured Alympos, and was borne away on a boat by two disciples. They took him across the sea to the fabled Isle of Elisium.' She repeated the words every Ischyrian novice was taught. 'From thence he will return to lead his faithful in the final battle against Kakos.'

'And how was the prophet wounded?'

'A sword struck off his left hand in the battle. Yet the prophet picked up his own hand and so long as he held it high the forces of Ischyros prevailed. Thus every temple is crowned with a hand, that the God might prevail over evil. It is written.' As Adelais said the words, she understood. 'By all that is holy, you have the Hand of Salazar.' She looked towards the house, half-hidden behind the orchard's leaves. She almost expected to see angels dancing on the roof.

'It was kept in a gold reliquary. The grand master managed to hide the sacred bones as the king's men entered the citadel. There was a final sign that he gave me as he was burned that I did not understand. Now I know it to be the pulling of a bell. He was sending me to the bell tower.'

'And the golden reliquary?'

Humbert shrugged. 'I believe a Guardian knight threw it into the armourer's furnace in the citadel, but I can't be sure. All the knights found in the citadel that day are now dead.'

'But why the secrecy? For two hundred years?'

'The Hand is too sacred for common gaze; not even all the commanders were permitted to view it. That blessing was reserved for the worthiest of the worthy; knights whose love for Ischyros was as great as their prowess in battle. And those who win that holy honour find their lives transformed for the rest of their days. How else do you think that Guerin and Cheyne had the strength to endure the coals in silence?'

'But to keep its very existence secret? Should it not be kept in the fire temple of Daija, with the high priest?' It was like having the real hammer of Thor and not telling anyone.

An image of the anakritim came to her mind, and she understood the answer even as she asked the question.

'There is sanctity within the faith, but the highest levels have lost sight of the God. You have met the torturers. That is but a taste of the corruption at the heart of the faith, where piety is irrelevant in the face of politics, and where men claw and stab and poison their way to the high priest's throne. Priests sell access to relics and forget the teaching of Salazar: "On the day his soul is demanded, the fool in his greed will know that all the gold on Earth will not buy his passage over the bridge".'

Adelais did not respond, but stared at the Gaelle, flowing full enough to swirl against the pilings. A long slingshot offshore, a barge was making slow progress upstream under both sail and oars. Two strokes forwards to one pushed back.

'It would be venerated, but at what cost?' Humbert continued. 'How much gold could be demanded to touch the Hand of Salazar? Kings would go to war for possession of it.'

'How do you know this hand is Salazar's? Any infirmary or graveyard would give you bones.'

'Two brothers fought to defend Salazar that day. Bayard and Jovan de Fontenay...'

'The same family as Lady Agnès's future husband?'

'Precisely. Bayard is Lord Leandre's ancestor. Jovan founded the Order of Guardians. The Hand has been passed from grand master to grand master since the day of the battle. We believe the Guardians have stayed closer than any others to Salazar's teaching. He would never have been so intolerant as Tanguy, never so venal as those who now rule in Daija.'

'Why are you telling me all this, Lord Brother?' She didn't want to know about Ischyrian relics or politics. She just wanted to go home.

'Remember you are no longer just a fugitive novice. You have killed, at my behest, and you are bound up with our cause whether you want or not.' Humbert scratched absent-mindedly at Allier's neck. The horse lifted its head and closed its eyes with pleasure. 'If you left, on your own, you would die, terribly. So would we all, after that, and the Hand would be lost. My brothers and I are now all that are left, and we must take this sacred thing beyond the grasp of King Aloys and the anakritim. Now, will you come with us, willingly, and help us?'

Adelais closed her eyes, reaching for that elusive point of calm within. This was not her fight. *But you're in it, girl,* her own mind replied. *And with this knowledge they won't let you leave alive.* She would continue to let them think she was a devout Ischyrian, and let this fate be woven. The answer rose cleanly within her like a bubble in spring water. 'I will come, messire, and willingly.' *For now.*

'Good.' He turned away, tugging the destrier back towards the stables. 'I will send fresh hose and linen. And we must choose you a horse.'

'What would you have done, messire,' Adelais called towards his back, 'if I had refused?'

Humbert stopped, and rested his forehead against his horse's neck before he looked at her. He did not answer her question directly.

'Carel de la Tour was the last Guardian in captivity who knew of the Hand. Through Parsifal we learned he was to be moved, and one of our number tried to kill him to save that knowledge, before we learned through you where he was to be taken and why. Then Arnaud came to Parsifal with the plan to free Carel from the sisterhouse. If he could not have been rescued, Brothers Parsifal and Maarten would have killed him in your infirmary. Yes, their own brother. Ischyros took Carel de la Tour into his arms to spare them that sin.'

Adelais swallowed. She knew the answer to her question, but she wanted to hear it from Blanc's lips.

'And me? If I had not come?'

'Yes. I would have killed you, child. And for that deed I, too, would have needed pardon.'

Humbert's destrier nuzzled at his shoulder as he led it away and he turned, smiling sadly, to scratch it behind its ear; a gentle old man who would not have hesitated to murder her.

5.2 ADELAIS

When the bells for the noon office were still ringing through the city, Humbert Blanc stood again by the stables, holding a chestnut gelding. He glanced between the horse and Adelais. 'You say you can ride, Perrin Wilg. Try this one. Messire de Molinot says we may take it if we wish.'

Adelais grinned her excitement. She had felt lighter in spirit since her conversation with Humbert that morning, even though his 'pardoning' might be blasphemous. She'd even broken her fast, ravenously. And of all the horses in the de Molinot stables, the gelding was the one she would have chosen for herself: fine-boned, with a spark in its eye that promised intelligence and speed, yet old enough by its teeth to have lost the madness of its first ridden years.

Arnaud and Guy watched her as she fitted the saddle, Arnaud with a smile, Guy with a scowl. Guy had just admitted that he hadn't ridden since childhood and his father's arrest; there had been no need for an armourer's apprentice to learn. Adelais had a frisson of satisfaction that the squire-to-be would drive a cart while she rode.

The gelding had spirit. It danced as soon as Adelais swung

into the saddle, throwing little bucks of excitement. Adelais allowed herself to sit relaxed and heavy until the horse calmed. 'Steady, boy,' Adelais muttered, 'I haven't ridden for a while.'

Not for two years, in fact. Not since the day that she and Jan had ridden far from the prying eyes of their village and become lovers. Adelais sensed that this gelding would love to run, too. She nudged it forwards, starting the process of learning its ways.

Riding must be so much easier for men. Every time she'd ridden before, she'd had great folds of gown or kirtle between her and the horse, swathing her from the ankles upwards. Now, she just had the hose on her legs and Guy's cote-hardie inside her thigh, and the contact was more direct; it was like taking the horse's pulse with her calves. She glimpsed the three men watching her, and wondered if that was why they seemed embarrassed. Humbert had looked away, Guy was wide-eyed and slack-mouthed, and Arnaud had begun a slow smile of appreciation.

She let her joy at riding push aside her modesty. If they didn't like a woman's calves, clad only in hose, they shouldn't have dressed her as a boy. Hadn't Humbert told her to show her leg? Hadn't Guy told her to swagger? Besides, she could talk to the horse with touches from her legs as it curvetted under her; the gelding was learning her as much as she was learning it. She sent it in a slow, controlled canter towards the river, just fifty paces away, and felt its head drop, submitting to her will, accepting the partnership. On the way back towards the stables and the house she showed off, just a little, by making her mount dance sideways in a trot, and the gelding arched its neck proudly, joining in the display. The sun was lighting joy in the orchard, and she had found the beginnings of a new friendship, so why didn't the men look happy for her?

She had to swing her leg high over the cantle to dismount. The sound of Arnaud sucking air through his teeth should have warned her, but she turned to look at them, laughing with happiness.

'I think we'll get on well. What's the matter?'

Guy swallowed, still staring at her. 'She'll betray us. Soon as she gets on a horse, she'll betray us.'

'What?'

Arnaud dropped his eyes. 'We'll have to find you some other clothes, lass.'

'But you put me in this thing.' She tugged the chest of the cote-hardie away from the gambeson beneath.

'When you ride—' she could swear that Arnaud was blushing '—it lifts.'

Guy cleared his throat. 'And there's nothing underneath but a woman's arse and an empty loin cloth.'

Adelais felt the colour rising to her cheeks, but gasped as Humbert uncoiled, swinging his arm up and sideways until the back of his gauntleted fist struck Guy in the face. The blow sent Guy stumbling backwards until he hit the stable wall and slid to the ground. He lifted a hand to one eye, slowly, as if in shock, and stared at Humbert with the other. Blood began to pour from his nose, flowing over his chin onto his chest.

'Why...?' Already, his lips were sticky with gore.

Humbert flexed his fingers.

'If you aspire to be a man-at-arms,' he spoke quietly, but as tightly as a crossbow cord, 'you will learn to treat damsels with respect.'

Damsel. A high-born virgin. He did her too much honour.

'But...'

If Adelais hadn't been so ashamed, she might almost have felt sorry for Guy.

'You will ask Adelais's forgiveness. Now. On your knees.' Humbert pointed at the ground by Adelais's feet, and kept his finger indicating the spot through the long silence that followed.

Slowly, with visible reluctance, Guy rolled away from the stable wall and crawled to the spot.

'I humbly—' A clot of blood swung from Guy's upper lip, and he paused to wipe his mouth on his sleeve. '—I humbly beg your pardon, *lady*.'

Adelais wasn't sure how to respond. She was flushed with humiliation, trying to tug her cote-hardie further down her thigh, but she straightened and responded formally, forcing herself to sound gracious. 'Adelais de Vries accepts wholeheartedly.' Then, after a moment's thought, she extended her leg as Humbert had taught her, and held out her hand. 'And Perrin Wilg would value your friendship.'

Guy put his hand in hers and rose to his feet, his eyes locked on the hem of her cote-hardie. *Sætur Sif, what had he seen?*

Humbert nodded his approval. 'I will find you some more appropriate clothing, and agree a price for the gelding with Messire de Molinot.' He paused, as if unsure what words to use. 'You ride well, young woman, but you may want to consider a little padding.' He coughed, and waved his hand vaguely in the area of his crotch. 'Around here.' He walked away, leaving Adelais hunched over, clasping her hands in front of her belly, her face burning.

Beside her, Arnaud clapped Guy on the shoulder. 'By Salazar, you had that coming, lad. But look on the bright side. You might get your cote-hardie back.' He waved at the blood streaking Guy's chest. 'Looks like you need it.'

Adelais hid in the gelding's stall while she made her preparations. She'd found a bradawl and thread among the horses' tack, but she was shaking so much with anger and humiliation that she had to steady the spike with her spare hand. She breathed deeply, several times, then made small holes in the edges of the leather pouch of her sling. She still had one stone, chosen for weight and smoothness, and she sewed this into the pouch. She could break the threads with a single tug, if necessary, but they'd hold the stone in place. She tied the thongs of the sling around her waist, adjusting their length until the pouch hung just above her sex, where it could be held to her body by her loin cloth. She had no mirror, and couldn't ask, but she hoped Arnaud would tell her if it looked wrong.

Humbert returned soon after she'd finished, bearing a garment over his arm.

'This, Master Perrin, belonged to Messire de Molinot.' Humbert held out a calf-length, hooded robe of a style called a herigaut. 'It will mark you as a *man* of quality, so you must behave as a gentle. There is also fresh linen and hose. When you are ready, we shall walk out together and scout the route we must take out of the city. I wish to test your disguise before we risk the whole party.'

There was more. In the bundle Humbert left, Adelais found a bone comb and a small piece of soap wrapped in a coarse cloth. She drew water from the well, stationed Arnaud outside the stables to guard against visitors, and shut herself in an empty stall. For the time it might take the sisterhouse to say a whole office she scrubbed away the days of grime, and when she once again felt a clean woman she held the bucket in front of her, two-handed.

'I name you Perrin Wilg!' She aped the Ischyrian Office of Naming and upended the bucket over her head, gasping as the cold water cascaded down her naked body.

The herigaut gave her confidence, even more than her new cleanliness. It was a heavy outer garment with long, trailing sleeves, and it hung loose to below her knees. It showed signs of wear and mending, but the green cloth was a fine quality that caught the light so well that she wondered if threads of silk had been woven into the wool. The skirts were slit to the crotch to allow for riding, and she experimented with swinging her leg over a trestle to be sure that she could mount decently. Perhaps a single stitch would be needed.

When she emerged, Arnaud made a leg, bowing as he would to a noble.

'Master Wilg.'

She repeated the gesture, smiling as if they shared a private joke. 'Master l'Armurier.'

'Give me your comb. If you will permit?' Arnaud teased her hair into better order, and she warmed to that intimacy. He stood back, looking at her critically. 'Good, but blonde hair might attract attention, even on a youth. We should hide your glory under your linen cap, perhaps.'

When the cap was in place, and stray curls tucked inside, Arnaud offered her his arm. She tilted her head to one side, lifted one eyebrow in gentle reproof, and let his arm hang there until he realised.

'Of course. Forgive me, *master*.' Arnaud bowed and waved her forwards. 'Brother Humbert awaits.'

Humbert Blanc nodded qualified approval. 'You have the herigaut of a gentle, and the boots of a peasant, but no matter.' Humbert walked around her. 'The most important thing now is your bearing. Imagine you are a lordling. Put your shoulders back. Stare at people as if you are their superior. Come! And if you wish to address me, in the street, call me Sir Galfrid, not Brother Humbert.'

Arnaud made to follow, but Humbert stopped him. 'No. Just Perrin. I would like a new edge on all weapons, Master Armourer, ready for a departure tomorrow, and all mail cleaned and mended. There is much to do. You will find tools, whetstone, and rivets in the house.'

As Arnaud nodded his obedience, Humbert led Adelais through the gate out into the mass of carts and people flowing between the city's East Gate and the Great Bridge. He walked with an assurance that made the crowds part for him, as if he were a rock and they the river. He wore no armour, and carried no weapons save the sword on his hip, though Brother Karlis followed them about ten paces behind. Was he protecting them or watching her? Perhaps to calm her, Humbert muttered advice. 'Take longer steps. Don't be so dainty. Head up, shoulders back. Swagger. Good.'

Humbert kept a steady pace; a knight with somewhere to go, but in no hurry to get there. The sling with its stone tapped against her as she walked, gently pleasing in the way that cold, clean water on her breasts had been pleasing, like the first pangs of appetite. Adelais watched the crowds, at first nervously, and then with growing confidence as she began to feel invisible. Always, as a woman, there had been the eyes of men travelling her body, even when she wore the habit of a novice. Now, men ignored her. She felt liberated, and lengthened her stride, until a passing maiden glanced at her from under lowered lashes, and smiled, swaying her hips. That was... confusing, and a little uncomfortable.

She only faltered once, when they reached the Black Tower and turned onto the Great Bridge towards the Isle. Here there were more soldiers, and the closer they came to the royal palace and the fire temple, more clerics. She shied at the sight of an anakritis the way a horse might shy at a sudden noise.

'Keep calm, *Master Perrin*.' Humbert steadied her. 'Look ahead. Act as if you are their benefactor.'

It was easy for him to say. Any one of these cowled clerics could turn and she'd find herself staring at Pateras Malory. *He* would not be fooled by a gentle's herigaut. Adelais fingered the edge of her linen cap, making sure no stray hair was showing.

All horses, and anything drawn by horses, came to a halt in a seething mass on the southern side of the Isle, where a crowd waited to cross the Little Bridge to the south bank. The three of them pushed their way through a complaining press of merchants until they could see onto the bridge.

Soldiers wearing the king's badge were searching every cart; they pulled a blonde merchant's wife out of the throng and thrust her in front of a Daughter of Salazar, who sat tiredly on a stool at the entrance to the bridge. The adeifi shook her head and the woman was released, shouting abuse at the soldiers.

'I can go no further, messire.' Adelais tugged at Humbert's sleeve and they stepped into a sheltered doorway. 'That is Mitera Chantalle, who was eldest daughter at my sisterhouse.'

'And she would betray you?'

Adelais shrugged. 'Unlikely, but who knows what threats have been made?'

'I like this not, Lord Brother.' Brother Karlis stared at the choked bridge. 'Whoever is directing this has the power to keep an eldest daughter here, and with more soldiers than we could fight.'

Humbert touched his face thoughtfully and frowned, as if surprised to find his beard gone. 'And if we were discovered, we would be trapped on the Isle with the garrison of the Black Tower at our backs.'

'Perhaps they are only searching for the girl?' Brother Karlis spoke as if she wasn't there.

'Unlikely. We'll try another gate.'

Adelais was more subdued as she followed Humbert back to the north bank, remembering his words: 'You know too much to be left alone and alive.' What would they do if they decided she was too much of a risk? The sling tapping her body became an irritation rather than a pleasure.

There was similar chaos at the eastern gate, where Adeifi Elodie could be seen, watching like Mitera Chantalle. She too looked tired.

'This one will not betray me.' Of that she was sure. Adelais walked forwards, watching and waiting for a reaction.

Elodie's eyes passed over her, and snapped back before she looked away. She pretended to touch the embroidered healer's badge on her chest, and made a subtle, waving motion with her fingers in front of her body. *Pass. Don't talk.*

Adelais waited until she was almost level with Elodie before speaking.

'Will you bless me, Adeifi?'

'Of course, young master.' Elodie's eyes darted left and right before she waved at a stool beside her. 'Come, kneel. Don't soil your fine clothes in the mud.'

As Adelais knelt in front of her, Elodie placed both hands on her head and leaned forwards so she could talk quietly.

'It does my heart good to see you, Adelais. Do not linger. We are watched.'

'And if I should come this way again, Adeifi?'

'For my part, it will always be a joy. But if you come with friends, watch for the pox-faced youth on the other side of the road. He will be well rewarded if he sees his former master, an armourer.'

'Are all gates so guarded?'

'All. Now go with Ischyros.' She straightened, making the sign of the God, *mind, soul, and body*, over Adelais's head.

Adelais turned as she rose, and looked for the boy with the pox-marked face. He was lifting his head from time to time to watch the traffic, but the flow was slow and he seemed bored. He was a youth of perhaps fifteen summers, and seemed more concerned with pushing a finger into a nostril. He examined the results, flicked, and looked up at the sky as if measuring the time until his watch was over.

Elodie could be trusted, but if they were to leave by this gate, they would also need to silence the boy somehow. Adelais wondered if she would soon have another soul on her conscience.

5.3 MALORY

'We found Carel de la Tour's body, Pateras Ghislain. It had begun to leak.' Malory d'Eivet stood in the anakritis-general's office, swaying a little, next to one of the narrow windows overlooking the Great Bridge. The cool air helped him to keep the bile in his stomach. Now he understood only too well why stone coffins had drain holes.

He still couldn't eat. At least, he couldn't eat and keep the food down. He'd broken his fast with a little bread and honey, thinking he was past the worst, then lost it again at the sight of de la Tour. Now he was dizzy for lack of nourishment. Usually the anakritim's tormentors cleared away the mess after interrogations. Malory had never had to endure the milky-eyed, accusing stare of a man several days dead.

'So, Pateras Bardolph was not telling us the whole truth.'

Malory nodded and rested his forehead against the cool stone, even though the sunlight hurt his eyes. Beyond the dazzle, the daily life of Villebénie flowed across the bridge as continuously as the river beneath it, appearing and disappearing between the artisans' booths that lined the way. Carts. Merchants. A young noble in a green herigaut escorted by two men-at-arms. A waft of river-smell reached his nostrils, laced with sewage, and his stomach heaved again.

Malory turned back towards the anakritis' desk, and the whole chamber seemed to dance. He blinked, swallowing thin saliva.

'The priest was complicit. There was ash on de la Tour's forehead. He'd been given the Office of the Dead.'

Ghislain Barthram opened his hand towards a chair, for which Malory was grateful.

'Perhaps we should question him more closely?' Barthram continued.

There were times when Malory d'Eivet did not enjoy working for the anakritim. Pateras Bardolph might once have been a Guardian, but he was still a priest, and had been reconciled to the faith. He was one of their own. It went against the grain.

Malory shook his head. 'He is one of their third degree, I am sure. Putting him to the torture would yield nothing in time to help us.' Malory could tell by looking at Pateras Bardolph's eyes when he'd questioned him in the Guardians' temple. There was a calmness there, the same withdrawal from life that he'd seen in the faces of Guerin and Cheyne. Pateras Bardolph had been tested once, and had not broken. Now he seemed even stronger, in some strange way; a man reconciled with Ischyros, sure of his passage across the bridge of judgement.

But Malory knew himself also to be devout. Tempted, of course, and sometimes failing, but still a man of the God. He wished Pateras Ghislain was more open to a theological discussion on the rectitude of their work.

'And has the gardener more to tell us?'

Malory shook his head again, more emphatically this time. 'He speaks the truth, I am sure. Guy Carelet came to him with the armourer and the novice, carrying de la Tour. He took them to the priest. They were overpowered by a knight who had been searching the temple.' Malory had only to show the gardener and his wife the instruments of torture before they fell over themselves to tell all they knew. He'd been merciful. They were people of little consequence and he had bigger fish to fry.

'You are sure the gardener did not know the knight?'

'I am sure, Pateras, but he described him well, even to the Guardian cord beneath his belt and the courtly accent, with a hint of the south. Maycea, perhaps, or Arrenicia. He is also sure that the knight's search had been successful. He spoke of tears of joy, as if the knight had seen the prophet Salazar himself.'

'Or their damned idol. We searched the temple, but never thought to open the tombs.'

'Naturally.'

'They all left together?'

'The gardener did not see the girl. We found her cloak and gown, so she must have found or bought clothes.'

'They are being helped.' Ghislain Barthram steepled his hands. 'I thought we had rooted out the whole Guardian heresy.'

'Surely the king arrested every Guardian in Galmandie?'

'Of course!' Pateras Ghislain jumped to his feet, striking his fist into his palm. 'Bring me the records. All the depositions sent to the high priest's enquiry. He will be an officer, of commander rank, old, who was out of the country when the arrests were made. Go!'

The bands of sunlight had swung across the chamber and narrowed into faint lines when Pateras Ghislain hit his desk in triumph.

'I have him! Lord Brother Humbert Blanc, Grand Commander of Arrenicia.' Barthram drew his finger down the scroll, reading. 'Arrested in Saxenheim.' He tapped the scroll in irritation. 'The Saxens were strangely fastidious about the use of torture, and he never confessed, but he was imprisoned there after six Arrenician brothers were brought to the Black Tower and attested that he used heretical practices at their admissions.'

'One imagines that the six brothers *were* tortured, Pateras?'

'Of course. How else were we to learn the truth?' Pateras Ghislain seemed not to notice Malory's irony. 'The Saxens must have released him.'

'I hear the Saxens are still too lax in their faith, too close to the heathen realms to the north.'

'He also refused to abjure heresies he claimed not to have committed. Such arrogance.' Ghislain Barthram steepled his fingers, tapping his fingertips against each other. 'I should like to meet Brother Humbert. Send word of his name to the captains. The gates and bridges are all guarded?'

'Every one, Pateras. With watchers that know either the novice or the armourers by sight. And watchers for the watchers, lest they try to betray us.'

'They are searching all wagons?'

'Not all. The ordure carts...' Malory swallowed again at the memory. The Black Tower's guards were still laughing and pretending there was a smell when he walked past.

'And for what are they searching? How have you described the hand?'

Malory pulled the documents to him, more to give himself time to think than out of need; his vision had begun to dance with little black spots, like flying soot.

'The king's own arrest warrant describes it as "a golden idol in the form of a man's hand which they kiss and worship".'

'Yes, yes, but what do the confessions say? Again.'

'The Guardians' own descriptions are inconsistent. One describes it as having the form of a man's hand, but large, like a giant's golden glove. Another said it was borne into private meetings of the commanders on the shoulders of four priests.'

'So it is heavy. And made of gold.'

Surely that couldn't be a touch of avarice in the anakritis-general?

'When we let Fabien d'Erembourc out of his coffin he said the idol was hidden from the sight of the uninitiated beneath a linen cloth until only third-degree initiates were present...'

'And this they worshipped as their god.'

'It seems to have inspired terror and adulation in equal measure.'

Malory blinked away his near-delirium. He wanted to find a comfortable feather bed and sleep until his guts would accept meat and wine. The last thin lines of sunlight faded, plunging the chamber into a comfortable shadow...

He jerked awake to find Barthram staring at him through narrowed, calculating eyes.

'Are you losing heart, Pateras Malory?'

'Never, Pateras.' Malory sat straighter in his chair.

'Good. Tomorrow morning I wish you to take me on a tour of all the gates of Villebénie, and show me your preparations. In the meantime, set your clerks to discover if Brother Humbert has relatives in Villebénie. Find every branch of his family, even the distant cadet lines. And Pateras?'

Malory paused on his way to the door.

'Go gently. We want to take them all, not scare them away.'

5.4 GUY

Guy had to bend until he was almost crawling to push the barrel up the slight incline from the riverbank. A complete suit of mail – hauberk, leggings, and coif – had been buried inside in vinegar-soaked sand so that the churn of sand against mail would clean it of rust. He stopped when he reached Arnaud, breathing heavily. Arnaud had found a blacksmith's portable anvil and was sitting on a stool, repairing the rivets on newly cleaned mail. It always seemed to be the leggings – the chausses – that went first, chafed between stirrups and spurs. Guy upended the barrel and pulled out the coif for inspection.

Arnaud barely looked up. 'Again.'

Guy swore inaudibly and almost threw the barrel onto its side. Going downhill was not too bad, and he'd laid a log to stop the barrel rolling all the way into the river, but pushing it back up again was hard work. And this was only the second suit of mail. He had three more to do. Guy allowed his mind to drift, savouring the memory of Adelais riding over this track, so pleased with herself for mastering the horse, and so blissfully unaware of how *bare* she'd become below the hem of her cote-hardie. *His* cote-hardie. It had ridden up until he could see naked flesh, and even the lacings that led so enticingly upwards to secure her hose. As for when she'd dismounted, why, men's loin cloths weren't cut to go round a woman's arse.

Humbert's blow had surprised him. By Tanguy's bones, if she was going to dress as a man, then she should be able to take jokes like a man. Guy rubbed his nose on his sleeve, pushing at the itch inside, and felt crusted blood crumble in his nostrils. *Damned woman.*

The cart he'd have to drive had been rolled through the gate, and now stood by the house, slowly filling with supplies. It was a small, four-wheel affair, about the width of a man's height and twice as long, which probably meant two horses. No problem. He'd done that sort of thing many times for Arnaud, but he'd wanted to ride out with the men-at-arms. Soon he would be a squire. Almost one of them.

A dark-haired, full-figured woman was coming through the orchard from the house, dressed in the rich gown of a lady. She took big, confident strides, and the servant girl following her had to trot to keep up. The lady was young, perhaps twenty summers, and carried a crossbow slung over her shoulder while the servant staggered under the weight of a hunting spear and other equipment. Arnaud stood as she approached, and Guy made a small, courtly bow. 'My lady.'

'Hullo. I'm Agnès de Molinot. This is Mathilde.' Agnès had the unforced, breezy accent of a gentlewoman who doesn't have to prove her class. Her voice was loud and jolly, as if she'd just come back from a good hunt. 'We're going to be travelling together. By the God!' She stared at Guy, grinning. 'How did you get that shiner?'

Guy touched his face. He hadn't realised he had a black eye. 'Brother Humbert saw fit to chastise me.'

'Hah! Then I'm sure you deserved it. I brought some things to pack.'

Guy suspected that Agnès de Molinot would always talk in

short, clipped sentences. Arnaud held out his hand. 'That's a fine crossbow. May I look?' He cradled it with professional interest, testing the tension of the cord. To Guy, the tapering wooden stock suggested a noble's hunting weapon rather than the heavier, windlass crossbows of war.

'One needs the lever to span it.' Lady Agnès pulled a steel contraption from her servant's arms. 'Here, I'll show you.'

Arnaud handed the weapon back, smiling quietly in a way that said he'd been spanning crossbows since before Lady Agnès had her first pony.

She rested the crossbow's stirrup on the ground, fitted the steel lever to two metal lugs on the stock, engaged the cord to the lever, and heaved upwards, grimacing at the weight. There was a loud click as the cord engaged with the nut.

'A goat's-foot lever.' Arnaud was clearly impressed. 'Less power than a windlass, but much faster to load.'

'That doesn't really matter if one's hunting, of course. One only gets one shot. Try it.' She pulled a bolt from her quiver, and Arnaud sighted along its flights, which looked as if they were made of copper.

'A *vireton*,' Arnaud remarked. 'The flights are twisted to make the bolt spin in flight. It will hold its line well.'

'It's fearfully accurate. I once brought down a hind at more than forty paces!'

'You have the very latest in weaponry, my lady, but this head,' Arnaud fingered the bolt, which had a broad, barbed point to strike deep and hold in flesh, 'won't penetrate mail at that range. If you ever have to shoot at a man, I suggest you wait until he's very close.'

'You'd be surprised, armourer. Mathilde, put one of those shields against a tree.'

'Allow me.' Guy moved to help the servant, who was struggling with the weight of a war shield, a thumb's thickness of solid oak. It had been covered with leather that had been boiled until it was hard as metal, and it bore the freshly painted retainer's badge of de Fontenay.

Mathilde followed Guy through the orchard, becoming more animated away from her mistress.

'Will you come to the feast tonight?' She seemed breathy with excitement.

'Didn't know there was one.' Guy turned at a tree, and was told to go further by Agnès.

'It's for Messire an' Madame de Molinot to say goodbye to Lady Agnès. There'll be dancin' after, an' minstrels, an' wine...'

'That'll do,' Agnès called.

Guy looked back. Thirty paces. The shield was a small target at that range.

'I think your mistress is going to lose a bolt.'

It seemed that Arnaud had the same idea, for as Guy and Mathilde returned he handed the crossbow back to Agnès.

She grinned, challenging him. 'Fancy a wager?'

'If you can hit that, my lady, I'll sharpen your bolt-heads and hunting spear for you.' Arnaud winked at Guy; he'd have to do that anyway. 'And if you miss?'

'A flagon of wine for you and your apprentice.'

'Done.'

Agnès slotted a bolt onto the stock and breathed deeply, nestling the stock into her cheek. She aimed slightly high at first, bringing the weapon slowly downwards as she exhaled.

The snap of the bow was followed, two heartbeats later, by a crack as the bolt struck the shield, which rocked against the tree and fell sideways.

It had not only hit the shield, it had punched a handspan of point through to the inner side. Arnaud crouched and tugged at the shaft, which was firmly stuck.

'Two handspans off centre, but not bad, my lady.'

Agnès glared at him until she realised he was teasing. She handed him a belt with a quiver and a pouch for the lever.

'Eight bolts. A dozen more up there. And would you be awfully kind and get that out for me?'

Guy watched Agnès and Mathilde walk back to the house until Arnaud tapped him on the belly with a pair of armourer's pliers. 'You wanted a break from cleaning mail, didn't you? Don't damage the flights.'

Guy grabbed the pliers and swore. 'Bloody gentles.'

Arnaud grinned at him and imitated Agnès de Molinot's accent. '*Awfully* good of you.'

5.5 ADELAIS

Adelais stumbled from embarrassment to humiliation as she served at the high table, knowing nothing of the rituals of nobles' feasting. Worse, she'd been made to wear Guy's cote-hardie again, lest the 'servant boy' should arouse comment by appearing in Messire de Molinot's old clothes. 'Just don't swing your leg over any benches' was Guy's comment, and Adelais wished she could blacken his other eye.

She'd managed the hand-washing formalities reasonably well, she thought, kneeling beside Agnès de Molinot's chair with a bowl of lavender water and a cloth. It was the closest Adelais had ever been to a lady, and perhaps she stared too long at this richly robed vision with the dark, lustrous, gold-netted hair. Agnès de Molinot was beautiful, in the long-cheeked, small-mouthed way of Galman women, and she had the poise to talk to a purple-robed episkopos as easily as Adelais talked to Adeifi Elodie.

'I think your page is in love with you.' The episkopos nodded across Lady Agnès, and Adelais felt herself blush.

'Hullo. Who are you?' Lady Agnès looked down to where Adelais knelt beside her. She sounded curious, not superior.

'P-Perrin Wilg,' Adelais stuttered. Agnès's green, smiling eyes matched the emeralds around her neck. 'I serve Sir Galfrid.'

Agnès lifted Adelais's chin. 'Well, Perrin Wilg, one day those fine looks will win many a girl's heart, but not mine. Messire de Fontenay might object. Now off with you.'

Agnès's amiable smile became a frown as Adelais spilt the lavender water on the boards. *Sætur Sif, steady my hand before I spill the soup.* Adelais cringed at the thought of oysters in almond milk splashed over that velvet gown. She tried to catch Humbert Blanc's eye, hoping he would see her discomfort and find her some other duties, but Humbert was busy making pleasantries with Lady Agnès's mother. Arnaud could be no help; he was seated below the men-at-arms and above the household servants, at one of the messes where the lesser guests ate from communal dishes. He could not be seen to direct a page boy.

Adelais's attempts at carving the swan earned her a cuff round the ear from the de Molinot's steward, who cursed her as an unmannered Vriesian who should have stayed in the stables. She consoled herself with a goblet of wine behind the servers' curtain, watching, learning, irritated that Guy was doing so much better. He was even allowed to help the steward carry a vast pie around the hall on a board; it was said to contain the meat of a whole roast deer and numerous capons and goslings. The pie paused at each mess so that all might admire its gilded crust, painted with the intertwined arms of de Molinot and de Fontenay.

Adelais didn't know which was worse: her awkwardness as a serving boy or her fears for what must come in the morning. Here, all was jollity, the greasy laughter of rich food and wine, yet at dawn they must emerge to brazen their way through the city gates. Brother Karlis, sitting at the nearest of the messes with the men she knew to be Guardians, caught her eye and winked at her. He was one of the few who knew Perrin Wilg was an impostor. He was also someone she'd heard calmly discussing whether to kill Arnaud's boy at the East Gate. He and Humbert Blanc had decided to try bribery; if they killed him, he'd be missed, and the road would be flooded with soldiers within an hour.

Then they'd given her a part to play. *By the gods, why can't we just stay here?*

Adelais swigged again, drowning her trepidation. She might be dead within a day, or, worse, in the hands of the anakritim. Karlis lifted his goblet to her, signalling for more wine, and she took over a jug.

'Steady, boy. You're doing fine.' Karlis had to half shout over the music of a trio of troubadours. The other three Guardians looked at her levelly; they seemed the only sober men in the hall. She was learning to tell them apart. The one giving her a half-smile of encouragement was Brother Maarten. He came from Vriesland's southern, Ischyrian borders and was fair-haired like her. He seemed the kindest of them all. Arnaud's brother Parsifal was quiet, almost withdrawn, while Paget from Saxenheim wore a look of perpetual boredom. None of them spoke much to the other gentles at the table.

Adelais smiled wryly to herself as she returned to the serving table, hearing the troubadours singing with exquisite melancholy of a knight's devotion to his lady; a low, slow tenor line interplayed with faster, higher, counter-tenors. She sipped more wine and giggled at the thought of a woman pretending to be a man listening to men singing love songs in women's voices.

Love. Would she die without knowing a man's love again?

More immediately, would she succeed at the East Gate? Adelais could not believe that they would risk their lives, *all* their lives, and a sacred relic, on the hope of buying the silence of an apprentice.

That, and prayer.

'We are in Ischyros's hands,' Humbert had said, quite calmly, as they walked back from the East Gate. 'If it is His will, we will pass through safely. If it is not, then we shall endure martyrdom with no less courage than Guerin and Cheyne.'

Adelais wasn't ready for martyrdom. She wanted to live, to find a good life in Vriesland, and perhaps a man who'd share it.

At least her duties were lighter after Humbert led the Guardians out to say the evening office, the Lighting of the Lamps. Adelais had time to quaff wine and pull a piece off the cooling breast of the swan. If this was to be her last night of freedom, perhaps even her last night alive, she was going to enjoy herself. She cheered with the rest when, after four courses had been served and cleared, the steward carried in a marzipan confection of a knight and his lady, also painted with the arms of the two families, and surrounded by sugared plums. More musicians followed, humbler minstrels now, playing festive songs on lute and drum and rebec. At the sight of them the guests cheered and pushed the trestle tables back against the walls to clear space for dancing.

Adelais had always loved dancing, even as a child; her father took a cart to Siltehafn for the fairs and there would be minstrels in the streets. She loved it not for the way it brought boys and girls together, but for the way the music made her body sway with the beat, unlocking happiness. She took a last gulp of spiced hippocras and joined the crowd, flushed with wine and the heat of the room. Without thinking, she tugged Arnaud towards the ronde that was forming.

'No, silly!' Agnès de Molinot's servant girl came between them, a pretty little thing in a tight-laced dress. 'It goes boy-girl-boy-girl.'

'Oops!' Adelais giggled at Arnaud's frown. It made him look old. Really, really old. 'I'm Vriesian, you see.' She made a loose, flapping motion with her hand to dismiss her mistake. 'We do things differently there. Boys and girls all mixed up.' She giggled again, starting to sway her body with the beat of the drum, imagining skirts brushing her legs, something soft and fine.

Arnaud's hands gripped her shoulders from behind, stilling her. 'Go to bed, *Perrin Wilg*.' He leaned forwards to speak into her ear. 'Before you betray us all.'

But there was dancing, and wine, and on the eve of the unknown she felt so alive that she could have climbed to the rooftops and shouted her name, her real name, at every boring, hard-faced priest in Villebénie. *I'm Adelais de fjakkinn Vries, and I'm a woman!*

But she'd be good. Very good. Especially with Arnaud's hand in the small of her back, pushing her into the garden. He could push a little lower if he wanted. She wouldn't complain.

The night air in the garden was summer-soft and rose-scented, though her shirt felt clammy where it was pressed against her body beneath the gambeson. She longed to throw off that crushing heaviness, perhaps even to dance under the trees in just her shirt and hose. Music spilled through the open shutters above as a minstrel sang the first line of an earthy, ribald song, starting the ronde:

> *When flowers bloom in spring-o, the maidens*
> *start to sing-o—*

And the dancers called out the response:

> *For love not money, come sip my honey.*

Stamp!

They'd be holding hands, circling, laughing, with more jugs of wine waiting.

'Dance with me!' Adelais held both Arnaud's hands, leaning backwards for balance as they circled, swinging her hips, and the sling pouch with its stone rolled from side to side over her body, under her loin cloth, teasing her. Beyond the outline of Arnaud's head, a patchwork of apple trees swayed with her, their leaves dark against a velvet sky that held the first, fine shaving of the hay moon and constellations of stars. The stars spun with them until a new and unexpected hunger grew within her, deep in her belly, and she stumbled.

'Are you well?'

'A little too much wine, I think.' But it wasn't just the wine. There'd been a flutter of something deliciously wicked within her, a momentary spasm beneath the rolling slingshot. It was enough to fold her over for a moment.

'Time for bed.' Arnaud helped her stand. 'We have an early start.'

Adelais found she was too breathless to speak, but she didn't want him to go. She wanted to find another jug of wine, sit in the orchard, and talk. Talk about anything that lengthened the night and staved off the morning. She wanted to sit with Arnaud, dear, gentle, safe Arnaud, and talk the night away. Too-safe Arnaud, for tomorrow they might be dead and tonight she wanted to feed the hunger within her and be touched, even kissed, but Arnaud was pulling away, leaving her, dropping her hands, his face unreadable in the darkness.

'Sleep well, *old man*.' That was cheeky, she knew, but she'd drunk enough wine to make light of the years between them.

'Good night, *youngling*.' The word for 'little youngster' turned the moment into a flirtation. For a moment he stepped closer and she closed her eyes, tilting her head back, hoping he was going to kiss her, but he merely drew his thumb slowly along the line of her lips.

When she opened her eyes he was gone.

'*As gonatisoume!*'

The cry of 'let us kneel' in the High Tongue cut through the fog of Adelais's sleep, and for an instant she thought she was in the temple by the sisterhouse, shamefully dozing through an office, but her eyes flew open and registered the rafters of the saddle store, cobweb-grey in the dawn. She threw aside the horse blankets that covered her, rolled onto her knees, and groaned as the movement sent pain pulsing behind her eyes. She rose slowly to her feet, holding the wall for support, and put her eye to a crack in the door. Outside, Humbert Blanc and the four Guardians knelt facing away from her, towards the east and Alympos, holding their sheathed swords flat in front of them in the manner of an offering at a sacred flame. Each wore the red cord of the Guardians around his waist, and in their midst Humbert said the litany of the dawn office.

Or perhaps it was already second office. Her mind wouldn't work.

And she needed to piss. Badly. But she was still only wearing a shirt. Just a shirt. Adelais opened the store's door, wincing at its creaks, and slid along the wall into the first stall of the stables. 'Her' gelding watched her over its shoulder as she squatted.

'Don't look so disapproving. You piss here too.'

Adelais's voice seemed to have dropped to truly masculine depths. Outside the litany stopped and she tensed, hoping she wouldn't be trapped away from her clothes. But the silence was broken by a new chant – a hopeful song of praise at a time of swelling crops. Adelais put her hands in the gelding's trough and splashed water over her face, groaning at the memory of the previous evening. Had she really flirted with Arnaud? While dressed as a man?

By the time Humbert ended the office by calling '*as sikothoúme*' – let us stand – she was dressed, in hose, gambeson, and herigaut. Already there was more movement outside. Servants packed final stores and provisions into the cart. She stumbled to help and was roundly cursed for her slowness in backing two heavy horses between the shafts. Mathilde, the servant girl, brought her a breakfast of yesterday's bread and leftover venison. She offered Adelais a jug of small ale, smiling as if they shared a secret, but Adelais waved the ale away. She preferred to put her face into the horses' trough.

Three of the Guardians waited by the cart, fully armed for war in coats of mail, with their shins and knees protected by greaves and poleyns of boiled, hardened leather. Red linen surcoats emblazoned with the de Fontenay badge now hid the rope belts of their former order. When Humbert Blanc and Brother Karlis appeared from the house, with Humbert bearing a roll of linen reverently across his arms, the three fell to their knees. Parsifal called out the opening words of a chant in praise of Salazar. 'Who brought the light of Ischyros to the world...' and all five called the response: 'of whom shall I fear?' They might be dressed in de Fontenay livery, but they were still the Lions of Ischyros, with swords by their sides.

Humbert laid the roll in the cart the way a mother might lay an infant in its bed. It looked no more than a bolt of cloth such as one might buy in any marketplace, wrapped for the journey in coarser, oiled cloth to guard it from rain. Adelais stared at it, knowing that this was as close as she had ever been to a holy relic, and wondering if she should feel its power. Or did relics only have power for those who believed in Ischyros?

Humbert straightened, ending the chant: 'Give me not up to mine enemies; for false witnesses have spoken against me, breathing out violence.'

He stepped back as the Guardians turned the final response into a triumphal shout.

'Attend upon Ischyros; be strong, take courage; yea, follow His path for ever!'

They all made the sign of the God, *mind, soul, and body*, as Humbert called, 'Lord Brothers, to horse!'

Adelais, Guy, and Arnaud helped them mount, holding the destriers' heads before passing up shields and lances. Parsifal angrily demanded to know who had put a hole through his shield, but Adelais could only shake her head in bewilderment. Arnaud smiled and hid his face by tightening Humbert Blanc's girth. At least he was smiling, and didn't seem angry about her foolishness last night.

Adelais waited until the last minute before mounting; the de Molinot's yard was milling with horses. Each of the five Guardians rode a destrier and led a riding horse. Two calmer beasts waited between the traces of the baggage cart, now with Guy and Mathilde on the seat, and Arnaud sat astride a steady nag. Her own gelding was spirited, fidgeting against its bridle and feeding off the excitement. The de Molinots' steward held Agnès de Molinot's palfrey; if she didn't come soon there'd be chaos, but the family farewells were happening inside, privately.

Agnès emerged with tear-streaked face, and was helped into the saddle while the episkopos made the sign of benediction over them. He was pasty-faced with indulgence, and as Adelais mounted he dropped his hand to his purple-wrapped belly and belched.

Humbert touched his spurs to his destrier's side and dipped his lance to pass through the gates.

'Forward, in the name of Ischyros!'

CHAPTER 6

6.1 ADELAIS

Adelais knew her job at the East Gate would be all about bravado. Even in the early morning the queue of people and wagons waiting to be examined stretched over a hundred paces. In the afternoon, as merchants left the city, she'd heard it would be much longer and the gate itself would be angry chaos. When they slowed to a halt she tied her gelding's reins to the rear of their cart and pushed her way to the gate on foot. She swallowed, and forced herself to put her shoulders back. *Swagger, girl.* It was time to play the lordling.

She hadn't expected the soldiers to be laughing. The searches had set loose a cage of chickens that were now running free among the horses' legs, and a buxom farmer's wife was chasing after them, bent over, arms outstretched, her body bouncing heavily beneath a loose, homespun gown. She screamed imprecations until she recovered one squawking bird and stood to cuff a soldier round the head with her spare hand, and the laughter started again when she grazed her hand on his helmet. On the far side of the road a young noblewoman had been forced to remove her head dress, spilling blonde curls, and was almost spitting her fury as she was pulled in front of Adeifi

Elodie. Elodie shook her head and lifted her hand in an apologetic little benediction. She hadn't yet noticed Adelais.

The pox-marked apprentice boy stood at the roadside, sniggering at the way the farmer's wife was trying to stuff the bird back in its cage and sucking her knuckles at the same time. Adelais turned to look back down the road. The queue was edging forwards, and the pennon of Humbert's lance fluttered perhaps eighty paces away. Soon their faces would be visible. Time to move. She touched the boy on the shoulder.

'What's going on?'

He was shorter than her, which made it easier to sound like a lordling. The boy turned a pointy, pitted face towards her. Arnaud had recognised her description, and called him 'a weasel who'd sell his own mother if the price was right'.

'Searching for a gang what stole treasure from the Guardians' temple,' his eyes flicked over her herigaut. 'Messire. Was my cursed master led 'em an' killed a king's man.'

'I'll wager they'll pay you well if you see him.' *Sætur Sif*, her voice sounded like gravel in a barrel after the previous night's wine. And this morning she felt closer to the old gods, who loved and drank, than she did to the Blessèd Ones of Ischyros.

'A silver mark if they catch him!'

Adelais pulled a gold coin from her belt bag, made sure the boy had seen it, and dropped it in the mud. He gasped and reached downwards, but her boot covered the coin and he straightened, looking at her warily.

'That's a crown. Good Saxen gold, not King Aloys's base metal.' *Play the part. Act tough.* 'And it's time for you to take a piss. A long piss.'

'Yeah. Yeah, sure.' He started to bend again but Adelais put her hand under his face and straightened him. Over his back, their conversation had not yet been seen. Half the soldiers were chasing chickens, making *pock-pock* noises and laughing like drunkards, and the rest were searching the next cart in line.

'Let's be sure we understand one another, Jesper, son of Hugues.' His eyes widened as Adelais used his name. 'Do you see the man behind me?' She glanced towards Brother Karlis, standing ten paces away, sword on hip. Of all their escort he alone wore little armour, for his part would require fast riding later, but he toyed with a rondel dagger, a vicious weapon with a long, triangular blade. It had no cutting edge but a very sharp point, and Karlis said it was useless for anything except battle, when a strong blow at close quarters could punch it through chain-mail or the sights of a great helm. It was a killer's weapon, and this armourer's apprentice would know that.

The boy nodded, and Brother Karlis smiled at him like a wolf who'd been shown a lamb.

'If you betray us, he will kill you. When the sun is a handspan higher you will find him there.' She lifted her chin towards a wayfarer's inn outside the gate. 'He will give you another crown for your continued silence. And remember, Jesper, son of Hugues, our friends know who you are and where you lodge. Now, when I've gone, you'll go take a piss, won't you?'

'Yes, messire.' The boy sounded terrified. Good. Adelais lifted her foot off the coin.

Humbert's group were now only twenty paces away, and they all seemed to be watching her, except Guy, who was hunched over on the seat of the cart beside Mathilde with his hood pulled over his face. Arnaud, riding behind the cart alongside one of the Guardians, had also covered his head, though his eyes glinted within his hood. She reassured them with a nod.

The crowd beyond them was giving way, yielding passage to two men wearing the black and white of the anakritim. One pushed his way through the queue astride a lordly, chestnut destrier, while the other, riding a fine grey, angled his body deferentially towards him. Adelais knew those horses. She spun around so she was facing away from them, eastwards through the gate, and breathed deeply, forcing away the panic that rose within her. Across the road, Adeifi Elodie stared at her, eyes wide with recognition and alarm. She raised her fingers in benediction before folding her hands in prayer.

Adelais angled out into the road, keeping her back to the queue and dawdling until Humbert's horse was alongside her. He did not look down so she tugged at his spur and tried to keep the terror from her voice.

'The anakritis-general is come. Here. Now.'

6.2 MALORY

Malory d'Eivet had broken his fast with a single egg, and though his belly was grumbling he felt strong enough to notice Pateras Ghislain looking from side to side, sniffing for heresies on the wind as they rode.

'What progress are you making with Humbert Blanc's family?' Barthram tended to bark questions, so it was impossible to relax.

'Since last night, Pateras? Little enough, I fear.' Malory thought the suggestion had been impracticable. The noble families had so many interconnections by marriage that they were like spiderwebs laid upon spiderwebs. 'And some of them are people we can ill afford to offend.'

'The king will pardon anything if you bring him proof of the Guardians' idolatry.'

So what was Malory supposed to do? They could not send soldiers to search every noble house in Villebénie. Questioning such people required a more sensitive approach, and Malory felt less than his usual commitment. Perhaps it was sickness and exhaustion that had him waking in the black hours of the night, thinking *what if we were wrong?*

'We must also consider,' Malory added, with some irony, 'those who would help the fugitives out of a sense of grievance, even though they are not related to Blanc.' Which made the scale of that task overwhelming. So many great families had given generations of their sons to be Guardian knights. A grieving mother or brother might never believe that their loved one could have committed such sins, whatever the evidence. So many. Malory needed to be progressing inquiries, not taking Pateras Ghislain on an inspection of the Villebénie gates.

'Such as?'

By the bones of Tanguy, did Barthram really not understand how many they'd hurt?

'The Guerins or the Cheynes, perhaps? Then there are the families of the fifty-four...'

Ahead of them, a noblewoman's party, an important one judging by the men-at-arms around her, was being inspected at the East Gate. An elderly knight beside her carried a pennon with the golden flowers of de Fontenay, one of the noblest families of Jourdaine, and Malory winced as soldiers tipped open chests in their cart, spilling fabrics. A youth on the driving board stayed hunched into his cote-hardie with the hood up, holding the cart's reins, but a servant girl turned to kneel on the seat, shouting back at the soldiers to take their filthy hands off her lady's finery. The girl was wearing a gown laced tight to the waist in the new, almost indecent fashion that squeezed the breasts together and upwards until they appeared ready to burst out of the open V of her chemise. Malory's view as she leaned over the seat, gesticulating, was enough to make him rein in, flushed with guilty pleasure. He must be feeling better to notice such things. *Salazar, save me from this desire.* He was only vaguely aware of movement around them: the noblewoman arguing with the gate's captain, the knight at her side, a man leading a chestnut gelding to the front.

'But what are you looking for?' The noblewoman sounded

outraged.

'Thieves and murderers, m'lady,' the captain replied. He must have seen too many angry people in recent days to be concerned by this one.

'I am Agnès de Molinot. What have I stolen? And whom have I killed?'

Every noble he stopped must have shouted variations on 'do you know who I am?'

Pateras Ghislain nudged his horse towards the knight, and Malory looked up. He'd learned to take notice when Barthram moved.

'Do you travel far, sir knight?'

'To my lord's lands in Jourdaine.' The knight glanced at the anakritim robes, and added, 'Pateras.'

'And who is your lord?'

'Leandre, Lord de Fontenay. I am escorting his future wife, the Lady Agnès. And you are?'

'Ghislain Barthram, the high priest's anakritis-general for Galmandie.'

If Barthram expected fear or deference, he was disappointed. The knight replied with tight-lipped, barely controlled hostility.

'And King Aloys's personal pardoner. Which role do you serve today, Pateras?'

'I serve Ischyros, sir knight.' Pateras Ghislain pointed at a youth who had mounted a chestnut gelding and was riding slowly away from them, beyond the barrier. The drapes of a herigaut's hood around the boy's shoulders concealed all but a white linen cap. 'Who is that?'

'That is my page. I have sent him forward to secure tonight's lodging.'

'I would speak with him.'

The knight locked eyes with Barthram, a battle of wills that set the knight's almost-black destrier circling Barthram's chestnut. 'Then ride after him. *Pateras*.' The knight nudged his destrier until its rump was towards Pateras Ghislain, and Malory knew enough about horsemanship to suspect that the over-the-shoulder rebuff was deliberate; the destrier was a living weapon, trained for war, and if the anakritis tried to ride past, an imperceptible signal would unleash a mighty kick from both hind legs directly into the belly of Barthram's horse. There could be apologies, afterwards, but it would be deliberate. And lethal. Barthram's horse knew this, and spun away, almost unseating him.

'Oh, well *sat*, Pateras.' Now the knight was mocking them. By the wounds of Salazar, he had balls to take on the anakritis-general. 'It is so unsettling for the horses, is it not, to be held still in this press of people?'

Malory watched the knight's legs as they moved against his horse's side, controlling it with flawless ease despite the chain-mail and greaves. Something was not quite right.

'Why,' Malory looked up, 'would a knight not wear the golden spurs?'

There was a tense pause before he answered. 'I am but a poor knight in a greater lord's service. Gold is beyond my purse.'

Barthram's eyes narrowed. 'The Guardian rule prohibited such signs of wealth, did they not?'

Agnès de Molinot nudged her horse between the two men.

'Come, there are no Guardians now, as you know better than any, Pateras.'

'But were you ever admitted to the Order, *Brother*?'

'I believe Sir Galfrid has been a loyal man-at-arms to the de Fontenays for many years.' Behind them, the queue was growing restive, with shouts of 'Get on with it' echoing between the houses. 'If this,' Agnès de Molinot swept her arm around the scene at the gate, 'is your doing, Pateras Ghislain, for what are you seeking?'

'A golden idol that the heretic Guardians worshipped, in

the form of a giant's hand.'

'Then finish your search for this giant's hand and let us be gone, for we have far to go.'

One of the soldiers searching the cart pulled out a tightly bound roll of cloth about as long as a man. The servant girl in the scandalous gown made a grab for it but the soldier knocked her arm away.

'What's this?'

'Finest linen for my lady's clothes.'

'Open it.'

The noise of the crowd was now a steady, seething hum of resentment. A moulded lump of mud and horse shit arced over their heads and burst in the roadway at the gate. Soon the soldiers would have to start breaking heads to keep order. Barthram was looking steadily at Malory, watching him watching the girl.

'Enough!' Malory motioned with his hand for the girl to roll up the linen and waved to the captain to let them through. He could not resist glancing back at the girl. Of all the burdens of priesthood, this attraction was the heaviest. Her lacing was so close to unravelling, and there would be a jolt as the cart moved...

'Show me your watchers, Pateras Malory.' Barthram was still staring at him. Malory closed his eyes to help himself think. *East Gate. Who had he put at East Gate?*

'The adeifi is there.' He pointed towards Adeifi Elodie, who seemed lost in prayer. 'And the boy...'

By Tanguy's bones, where was the boy?

Barthram seemed to have forgotten his own question. He was watching the departing entourage of Agnès de Molinot: a page and servant girl on the cart, a knight, a manservant, and three men-at-arms, all well-mounted, all bearing the de Fontenay arms. He lifted his face and sniffed. 'I smell Guardians, Pateras Malory. I have a nose for them.'

6.3 ADELAIS

It had taken all of Adelais's concentration to ride forwards without looking back or breaking into a gallop. Her hands shook, sending quivers down her reins, until she grasped the pommel of her saddle, white-knuckled; it was easier to ride with a loose rein, controlling her gelding with her legs and weight. She spoke to him constantly, calming him, calming them both, fearing some skittish buck would dump her in the roadway in sight of the gate.

She'd spoken to the anakritis-general. Actually spoken to him. She'd been standing next to Humbert's horse, bracing herself for discovery, and Ghislain Barthram had reined in beside her, staring down with those eyes that seemed to see through her. She'd returned his stare, and she was proud of that, but she'd had to swallow before she could speak, and then it was only to say 'good morning, Pateras' in her wine-gravelled voice. If she'd had to suffer that stare for a heartbeat longer, her knees would have folded, but Arnaud had come between them holding her gelding's reins, saying 'your horse, Master Perrin' as if he were her servant, and steadying her with his eyes until Humbert had waved her forwards, alone.

She'd mounted, sat tall in the saddle, and ridden forwards, making no eye contact with the soldiers. *Sætur Sif*, make them see that she was a man, nobly dressed, carrying no baggage, no possible reason for them to stop her when the crowd was so restive. Pace after plodding pace she'd nudged her mount forwards, dreading a bellowed summons from behind, and despite all Yrsa's warnings about using rune song she muttered the song of *bjarkan* as repetitively, as obsessively, as any Ischyrian priest with a chant of Salazar.

'*Bjarkan er laufgat lim...*'

Bjarkan, the rune of the earth mother.
'*Ok lítit tré...*'
The rune of protection, of nurturing.
'*Ok ungsamligr vidhr...*'
The rune of concealment.

Adelais stopped at the edge of the slums encircling Ville-bénie, letting her breath out in a great sigh that felt as if she'd held it in all the way from the East Gate. She climbed off in what was more a controlled collapse than a dismount. Her legs would hardly hold her, but she forced herself to stand calmly, stroking her horse's muzzle as she stared back along the road. What if the rest had all been stopped? What if a mounted troop was sent after her? When the de Fontenay pennon appeared over the heads of the people on the road, her relief made her weak again and she had to cling to the horse for support.

Humbert said nothing as he passed, merely nodded. Guy was ashen, staring forwards, slack-jawed, while Mathilde berated him on the cart's seat in the grumpy tones of one who had already said the same words several times. 'Fine help you turned out to be. Them soldiers might have had their way with me...' Only Arnaud reined in to wait as she mounted, and they fell into position together at the rear of the little column.

'How are you?' His eyes were gentle and caring. None of the Guardians were close enough to hear.

'Just wonderful.' The slight quaver in her voice denied the words and she pulled a little half-smile. 'I was worried about you. Worried about everyone, I mean.'

'And I about you. Well done, youngling.'

She'd never heard that word said with such respect. If they'd been alone, and on foot, she'd have hugged him. She needed a hug.

They pushed on as fast as the cart and the road would allow. When Villebénie still filled a quarter of the horizon behind them like a smoking dung-heap, the road bridged a great river that Arnaud said was the Fauve. The men-at-arms breathed a little more easily after that, as if a boundary had been crossed. When the sun was at its highest, and Villebénie was but a smell on the wind, Humbert called a halt in the square of a small town; here they would rest the horses and wait for Brother Karlis. Adelais dismounted stiffly, her legs and backside already protesting after half a day in the saddle. It had, after all, been over two years. Townspeople watched from their doorways, hanging back in the shadows, wary of armed men. Humbert walked down the line and called to the Guardians.

'Light armour only, from now. Switch to riding horses to rest your destriers.' He pulled his bascinet and aventail over his head. 'L'Armurier, Guy Carelet, help us disarm. Perrin Wilg, watch the road behind.'

At this peaceful sign an innkeeper approached cautiously, wiping his hands on a filthy apron and offering meat and ale. 'The finest quality, messires, and much cheaper than Villebénie!'

Adelais was pacing the road at the edge of the village, easing her legs, when Mathilde brought her a bowl of pottage and a mug of small ale, and stayed to talk.

'I reckon them's all Guardians, like that anakritis said.' Mathilde spoke breathily, like a gossip, and watched Adelais for a reaction. 'They was all wearing that red rope thing around their waists, under their armour. Jus' imagine, the Lions of Ischyros!'

Adelais shrugged. 'If they were Guardians, they'd probably not like it shouted around.'

Mathilde pouted her disappointment at Adelais's answer. ''Ave you known Guy and Arnaud long?'

Adelais shook her head.

'Only, you an' Arnaud seem real friendly.' Mathilde nudged at a stone with her foot.

'He's a good man.'

'In Villebénie the justices found a man who lay with other men.' She flicked a glance at Adelais.

'Why do you say that?' Had she done something else wrong, besides flirting with Arnaud?

Mathilde shrugged. 'Dunno. You seem safe, somehow. For a man, I mean. All the menservants at Messire de Molinot's house tried to grab my tits at some time. But I think I could just talk to you.'

'Thanks, I think. And no, I'm not a man who likes men.' Adelais wondered what Mathilde might want to talk about. 'What did they do to him, that man who loved other men?'

'They cut off his balls,' Mathilde said matter-of-factly.

'Ouch.' Adelais wondered what they'd do with women who loved other women. Had Adeifi Elodie been like that? She'd sometimes thought that Elodie wanted more than friendship. How would that work, without a prick? And was it as much a sin as it was for men, to the Ischyrians?

'Sometimes girls like to talk.' Mathilde looked down,

blushing a little, but with both arms behind her back so her figure strained at the lacing across her chest.

By the gods, this is getting complicated. Adelais didn't know what to say. She smiled in a way that she hoped was not too encouraging, and cleared her throat as a single rider appeared where the road crested a hill, a thousand paces away. 'Is that Messire Karlis?' Adelais hoped the relief hadn't sounded in her voice.

Mathilde stood on tiptoes to kiss her on the cheek, her arms still held behind her.

'It's nice when men are shy.' She smiled over her shoulder as she left.

Adelais watched Brother Karlis approach. He slowed beside her, letting his exhausted horse drop its head. Adelais walked alongside and reached up to touch its sweat-lathered neck.

'All well, Brother?'

'When I left.' Brother Karlis would say no more until he was with Humbert Blanc in the square. He accepted a leather tankard of ale and drank deeply as the others gathered around him: Humbert, Paget the sneering Saxen, Maarten the kindly Vriesian, Parsifal the tall, quiet one. They all looked as if they could pray over their swords or kill with them with equal ease.

'"Tis done, though I trust him not.' Brother Karlis swigged again. 'I put the fear of Ischyros into him, and then watched until a new apprentice replaced him. He left fingering the coins in his purse.'

'Do you need to rest?' Humbert handed him bread and a piece of cold fowl.

Karlis shook his head. 'I'll rest this horse, though, and ride my destrier.'

'Then we push on, now.' Humbert lifted his head and called to Arnaud. 'L'Armurier, you stay here for a while, with Perrin Wilg. Wait on that rise where you can watch the road. Try and keep half a league behind us. Wilg has the fastest horse, and it carries the lightest weight. He is your messenger. If we turn off the Orval road, I will leave a man to warn you.'

'Understood, messire.'

Adelais stood a little taller at the realisation that she was being trusted with a soldier's role. She smiled at Arnaud in a way that even Mathilde could only see as masculine cama-raderie.

'It seems we are a team, old man.'

6.4 MALORY

Malory d'Eivet touched the willow switch across the boy's bare backside quite gently, almost as if he was caressing the welts, but the wretch still whimpered and clenched his buttocks. The trick was to let the 'informant' know *exactly* where the blow would fall, to within the width of a woman's finger. The expectation was so important.

'Now, Jesper, son of Hugues, let us try again.'

The whimpering rose into high-pitched begging, almost as if the boy's voice hadn't broken. 'No-no... please... no.'

Malory kilted the skirts of his robe more securely through his belt, the better to run, and backed to the far side of the room. The boy was bent over, spreadeagled with ankles and wrists strapped to the legs of a table, and he was bare from the waist down. A fine cote-hardie and a new pair of boots lay on the floor, beneath the boy's nose, where they'd catch any puke or snot. Pateras Ghislain was quite fastidious about his personal chamber. He was watching from a far corner with his elbows resting on the arms of a throne-like chair, his hands joined and his fingertips touching his lips. Thin morning light through an unshuttered window put that corner in shadow and made his expression unreadable, but he was utterly still, as if a statue had been draped in the black-and-white robes of the anakritim. The draught from the window carried the smell of rain as well as the pervasive stink of the Gaelle.

Malory started his run from the same point each time, a particular crack in the flagstones. It helped with accuracy. And the sound of four running paces was like a drum roll before a hanging.

It was all about expectation.

'Please-please-please.'

Perfect. The willow landed exactly along the line of an existing welt. Malory flicked the wand in the air while he waited for the scream to subside into blubbering.

'Remember, young Jesper, this is not torture.' By Tanguy, he felt dizzy. His body wasn't ready for such exercise. 'A priest does not apply torture, though if you do not tell us the truth, there are masters of the craft waiting for you downstairs. This, boy, is merely *chastisement*. Now, yesterday you wore cast-off rags, so where did an apprentice without a denier to his name acquire a new cote-hardie? And boots that could grace a gentle?'

'I told yer, me uncle gave me them.'

'Lying child, you have no uncle. That, it seems, was Arnaud l'Armurier's way; to take in the waifs and strays.'

Jesper pulled against his restraints, making a high whining noise as Malory touched the welt with the wand, again. He'd drawn blood with that last blow; small red spots were welling through the skin. He backed away once more, ignoring the sounds from the table. Priests were not supposed to shed blood, but this was not a time to be fastidious in front of the anakritis-general.

'And there's still silver in your purse. Lots of silver. You have been bribed, boy. Admit it or we'll have you hung as a thief.'

The buttocks always clenched that little bit more during the run.

'Nooo...'

Right on the mark. Malory dabbed at his face with a cloth as he circled back to the table. This was getting messy.

'Now, tell us who gave you the money, boy.' This time Malory angled the switch so that its tip went between the boy's legs, across the balls. They'd retreated into a tight little walnut but they were still there, and *that* was where the next blow would land. It was all about expectation. The screaming started while Malory was still backing across the room.

He was two steps into his run before the boy finally blurted out something useful.

'Yellow hair. He had yellow hair.'

Malory sighed and stopped by the table, breathing heavily, steadying himself. For the first time, Pateras Ghislain had reacted, leaning forwards. Malory held the wand against the balls again, just to remind him, and spoke very quietly.

'Tell me more, boy.'

'He had yellow hair. Linen cap, but some had fallen out around the neck. He gave me gold to look away.'

'Describe him, boy.'

'Lean. Young. A beardless youth. Clear skin. Blue eyes. A handspan taller than me. Green herigaut.' Jesper, son of Hugues, was babbling. Anything to stop the wand striking where it now rested. Malory knew that this was truth. And he knew who this 'youth' had been.

'And was there anyone with him?'

'A man-at-arms. He'll kill me.'

'Talk or I'll do the job for him. Describe him.'

'Old, maybe fifty. Greying. Not fat, but stocky, you know?'

'Go on.'

'Middle height. Surcoat with a badge.'

'What sort of badge?'

'I dunno...'

Malory moved the switch a little, enough to press against the walnut.

'Like a shield. Red. It was red. Red shield with three yellow flowers.'

The anakritis-general stood.

'So I was correct. Red with three golden flowers. De Fontenay's blazon. Malory, ask Chancellor de Remy if he would be kind enough see us. Immediately.'

Malory left the boy sobbing into the tabletop.

6.5 ADELAIS

Adelais could see rain showers drifting towards them across gently undulating countryside; cobwebs of rain hung from dark clouds, touching fields that were patterned in alternating strips of crops. Adelais didn't mind the wet. Arnaud had laid a horse blanket on the ground and spread his cloak around them, and she liked that shared warmth.

She also liked this routine that Humbert had set for them, following the main party. His light horse, he called them, his scouts. Keep half a league behind, pause on any high ground, trot fast through any valleys but don't over-tire the horses. Above all, keep looking back.

The party had slept in an inn the night before, or rather Agnès de Molinot and Mathilde had slept in the inn. The rest of them had the stables. Humbert and the Guardians had chanted the Lighting of the Lamps before they slept, kneeling before a candle to symbolise a sacred flame. Humbert had claimed the cart for his bed, lying on leather-wrapped chain-mail with his drawn sword beside him and his head near the roll of linen.

Adelais had washed her face and hands in the horse trough,

night and morning, wishing she could take off the foul gambeson and change her shirt. Under the cloak, in their second vantage point of the morning, she and Arnaud both smelt of horses and unwashed bodies, but this was a good place from which to watch. A tree-crowned hill off the road gave them a view of almost a league to the east, and here they lingered, exchanging life stories, relaxed in each other's company.

'Was she beautiful?' Adelais didn't know why it was uncomfortable to know Arnaud had been married. He had loved, and been loved.

'The greatest beauty comes from within, lass. She would have been about your age now, when she died. She had all the care the citadel could provide, even the Guardians' own priests to pray over her when the baby would not come. I begged Ischyros to take the child and spare her, but He took them both. I've never been one for prayer, since.'

'Before Vriesland was conquered we had wise women, *seidhkonur*, to help with birthing. Sometimes women died just the same. People didn't blame the gods, they just said it was fated.' Adelais looked down, drawing a twig through the grass. 'Do you still miss her?'

He stretched out his hand, baring a scar on the back of his wrist. 'The hurt fades with time. It becomes like a wound that has healed, though you carry the mark always. I mainly miss the companionship now. That sense of wholeness. Talking. Do you miss your man in Vriesland?'

'Actually, no. Not any more.' Adelais had told him about her first love, the trainee Ischyrian cleric, Jan. These days Jan wasn't even a scar, more a wistful memory, the sweet ache of being close but not touching. He'd made her feel beautiful, though; she who'd always been ashamed of her small breasts and wide shoulders. Milkmaid's shoulders, her father had called them.

'Looking back,' she continued, 'I think I wanted to escape

the old merchant that my father had chosen for me more than I wanted Jan. I was rebellious, and Jan was weak. I thought we could run away together.'

She wished in a way that there had been more joy in their coupling; it would have made it more worthwhile. Their one time had been a snatched, breathless hour; a fumbling urgency that turned too quickly to pain. She certainly didn't miss that. More hurtful still was the way he'd told her afterwards that they could never marry. That was before the Ischyrian guilt took over and he ran off to tell his priest how he'd sinned.

'And your father brought you to the sisterhouse.'

'I was damaged goods.' She managed to keep bitterness out of her voice. 'No, I don't miss Jan. I miss my grandmother, Yrsa, more. Much more. She brought me up after my mother died.' Adelais paused, wondering how much to say. 'She never converted, even when the old gods were banned. Amma Yrsa was a *seidhkona*.' She felt safe with Arnaud. He would not betray her. 'She and my father hated each other!'

They were silent, staring back down the road. A slight, steady traffic flowed past in both directions: merchants in carts, a striding cleric and, once, a knight with his squire and train of horses. Nothing that might threaten their group.

'You never thought to marry again?' she asked after a while.

'My wife set a high standard to follow, and Guy has been as good as a son to me, these last few years.'

'I think Guy's jealous of me.'

'Jealous? Why, lass?'

'Because you and I are easy together.'

Adelais wondered at this ease she felt with Arnaud. Would it have worked with Jan if they'd ever found such companionable quiet? Probably not. They'd both been too young.

But Arnaud was awakening an appetite within her like the first pangs of hunger; stirrings that she had not felt for two years. He treated her with respect and did not flaunt his strength. She liked that. She even caught herself wondering what it would be like to be covered by him and see those shoulders spread above her.

Adelais shifted on the blanket, suddenly aware of new heat within her and how close their legs had become.

'The rain is easing. Time to go, lass.' Arnaud put his hand on her knee, then took it away swiftly, as if he'd changed his mind.

'But which way?' She let the question hang. They had two good horses grazing the grass under the trees, and Arnaud had silver in his purse. They could ride away, just the two of them, be in Vriesland before the hay moon was over.

'With our friends.' Said with firmness, not reproof.

'Of course.' She stood up, scattering raindrops from Arnaud's cloak. Her legs had stiffened as they sat, and ached in protest at the second day in the saddle. 'Do you know,' she said, as she flexed her shoulders and arched her back, cat-like, 'I'm glad this happened.'

Arnaud grinned at her, his eyes sparkling. 'The sisterhouse would never have held you, Adelais.'

'Humbert said something like that. What do you mean?'

'You wear your beauty lightly, as if you are unaware of it, but one day it would have become a burden. You are a woman who needs to love, and to be loved.'

Adelais hid her smile by bending to stretch the ache out of a leg. She might be tender and saddle-bruised, she might be dirty and stink, but she'd never felt quite so alive as in that moment.

6.6 MALORY

Malory d'Eivet had never been admitted to the office of the chancellor before. Othon de Remy had added a new wing to the royal palace, using money borrowed from the Guardians that would not now be repaid. Within it, de Remy's private office had windows in the latest, mullioned style, for this was a palace, not a fortress, and the windows were glazed with real glass that kept out the smell of the Gaelle. The chancellor immersed himself in this professional domain the way a great noble wrapped himself in armour; it was a statement of invincible power. When they'd been admitted to his sanctum, de Remy was already with the provost of Villebénie, the commander of the capital's guards, and he stared across the table at Barthram as if the anakritis-general was a petitioner rather than a prelate. Malory sat a respectful distance down the table. At least he'd been allowed to sit.

'Either the Guardians' idol is with them, or they have hidden it again in Villebénie.' Barthram kept his voice level, presenting facts without implying guilt, and showing no outward sign of discomfort at meeting in de Remy's office rather than in the tapestried neutrality of the court. 'The de Molinot house is being searched as we speak.' Pateras Ghislain glared down the table at Malory, as if to say, *if you had done your job, we'd have searched it before they left.*

'The de Molinots and the de Fontenays are powerful, and have the ear of the king,' de Remy mused. 'Leandre de Fontenay's father and grandfather were both seneschals of Jourdaine. Could it be that they are being used and are innocent of collaboration?' De Remy, ever the politician, wanted to be sure of his facts before moving against such families.

'The marriage is genuine, and has been long planned.' Barthram made his steepled-hands motion, and spoke into his fingertips.

'So why does the father not escort his own daughter? Why would de Molinot send Humbert Blanc?' De Remy did not sound angry, but then he was not the one who had failed the king.

Barthram tapped his fingertips, a sign of irritation. He wanted to finish the talk and take action, but he needed de Remy's support. Only the chancellor could order soldiers on the scale they needed for pursuit and search. 'Blanc and de Molinot are related. Seigneur de Molinot broke his hip in a joust last year and can no longer ride. The journey, with escort, is also long planned. We gather Blanc is known to de Fontenay and is trusted by both families.'

After a tap on the door, a clerk on the anakritis-general's staff was permitted to enter. He bent to Malory's ear and whispered until Malory nodded his dismissal. The three at the end of the table waited, expectantly.

'Humbert Blanc has been staying with the de Molinots for ten days, and as far as they are aware did not spent a night elsewhere. Four men-at-arms have since joined him. The ones we believe are the armourer, his apprentice, and the novice appeared four days ago, which would be the morning after the incident at the sisterhouse.' Malory prided himself on presenting information clearly.

'So they and Humbert Blanc were in league.' De Remy sighed. 'How does a sisterhouse novice know a Guardian grand commander?'

'This we have yet to discover,' Malory replied. 'You should be aware that Seigneur de Molinot has requested to see the king to protest; his house is being searched most rigorously, so far with no result. I personally believe the golden hand is on the road, with Brother Humbert.'

'And are we sure they have it?'

'They have something, either an idol or a relic.' Barthram's candour surprised Malory. But then, de Remy had orchestrated the fall of the Guardians from the beginning. His soldiers had made the arrests and seized their wealth for the king. 'Either way, it is of such value to the Guardians that men will die for it and count their lives well spent.'

'There have been rumours, through the years, of the existence of the real Hand of Salazar.' De Remy spoke quietly, probing, his eyes on Barthram.

'Which every Guardian grand master has denied. And why would the Guardians hide a relic of such value?' Barthram stared levelly back at de Remy.

Chancellor de Remy pushed back his chair and crossed to the window, staring out across the Gaelle towards the massive walls of the Black Tower. He held both hands behind him, and curled his fingers repetitively into his palm as he thought. 'The first step is to find them, and to discover what they have. They will pass through Compeigne to Orval, and then on into Jourdaine towards Moutâne. We must persuade the local authorities to join the search.'

Barthram made a small, courtier's cough. 'Remember that de Fontenay is the authority in northern Jourdaine.'

'Quite. So we must try to seize them before they cross into

the duchy. The seneschals would probably tell us to find our own damned idol, but if we were pursuing the desecrators of a temple who had stolen a relic...' De Remy left his words unfinished, and turned to face them.

Barthram nodded, almost imperceptibly. 'Then it must be sufficient to call it a stolen relic. That is enough to win the support of pious men.'

'Agreed.' De Remy looked at Malory. 'But they were searched at the gate?'

'We had them, messire, and we knew it not. Pateras Ghislain and I watched their cart being searched, and saw nothing, yet I am sure it was there to be found. I think this novice is a witch, and used dark arts to conceal it.'

'Or perhaps there was no golden idol to be found, but something more easily concealed.' De Remy returned to his chair. 'A woman dressed as a man, you say.' He seemed to find the idea intriguing.

'She is a most unnatural woman. She dresses as a man, and can lower her voice to sound like one. She is a witch.'

De Remy looked unconvinced. He picked a goblet of wine off the table and swirled it, staring into its surface as if seeking inspiration. 'So how many of them are there?'

'Humbert Blanc,' Malory began, ticking the party on his fingers.

'One.'

'Four other men-at-arms, who may also be Guardians.'

'Five.'

'Agnès de Molinot and her maidservant.'

'Who must not be harmed. Seven.'

'Arnaud l'Armurier and Guy Carelet.'

'Nine.'

'And the unnatural woman, Adelais de Vries.' Malory almost spat her name.

'Who may be the most dangerous of all. Ten.'

'Plus spare horses for all the men-at-arms, and a baggage cart.'

'So they will move slowly. Six leagues a day on good roads, usually five or less.' De Remy still stared into his goblet, thinking.

'And by the time we organise pursuit, they will have a day and a half on us.' Malory leaned forwards, his impatience for a moment conquering his deference.

De Remy put his goblet back on the table so gently that it made no sound. He locked eyes with Malory, making him flinch. The king's chancellor clearly did not like to be pressured.

'But we know where they are going, don't we, *young man*?' The absence of 'Pateras' was a calculated insult.

Malory dropped his eyes. 'Yes, messire. To Château Fontenay, in Jourdaine.'

'A journey of at least ten days. So all is not lost, despite your incompetence.'

Ghislain Barthram cleared his throat, intervening. 'How many troops can you muster, de Remy?'

'Provost?'

The provost of Villebénie shifted on his seat. 'We must still protect the king and his officers. Eighty, perhaps.'

'And if an enemy was at the gates of Villebénie, how many could you send to the walls? If our lives depended upon it?'

The provost shrugged. 'Two hundred.'

De Remy relaxed into his chair. 'Better. Two hundred it is, then. Send messengers on the fastest horses to every seneschal on their route. I will give you letters. If they pass the fugitives on the road, they are to take no action but are to alert the nearest force capable of overwhelming them. His Majesty requests the Count of Compeigne to man every bridge and river crossing between the Fauve to the north and the Gaelle to the south. Agnès de Molinot is not to be harmed, and the others only if they fight; they may have information that the anakritim would be only too happy to extract. All of them to be held, with all baggage unopened. Do you understand?' •

'Yes, messire.'

'Your own forces will push down the roads until they make contact. Send men in light armour ahead for speed, heavy armour to follow. Clear?'

'Yes, messire.' The provost stood.

'And I want you to lead this personally, Provost, in the field. Now go.'

Barthram coughed again as the provost left. 'Impressive, de Remy. I would like Pateras Malory to accompany him.'

The chancellor and the anakritis-general glared at each other. Malory understood why; if this Hand was a treasure beyond price, presenting it to the king would make the giver's standing unassailable.

De Remy nodded, slowly. 'As you wish. But let's find it before we fight over it. Just now His Majesty is mightily displeased with us all over this lingering Guardian question.'

The anakritis-general stood. 'I think it is time for me to pay a visit to the high priest in Daija.'

De Remy thought for a moment. 'Let me guess. You will travel, perhaps, via Orval and Moutâne?'

Ghislain Barthram's smile tightened his face without touching his eyes.

6.7 ADELAIS

Dusk would come early that evening, pushed down by lowering skies, and Adelais wondered whether she and Arnaud might find the others before dark. Traffic on the Orval road thinned out as travellers sought shelter in the few wayside inns, and as the afternoon wore on the two of them often trotted alone, with the wind pushing them forwards and fluttering Arnaud's cloak around his horse's neck. Both horses were tired, and Arnaud's slightly lame, by the time they saw Brother Karlis sitting astride his destrier, his lance pointing at the sky. He growled his greeting.

'You two took your time.'

Arnaud grinned. 'Good to see you, too, Brother.'

'We took the lesser road.' Karlis inclined his lance towards a track forking away from the road through thick woodland. 'An old soldier's instinct. Too many people to tell of our passing on the Orval road. And too easy to be trapped.'

Adelais glanced down; the chosen path was wide enough for a single cart and looked as if it might lead to a hamlet and no further. Waterlogged wheel-ruts ran either side of a grassy strip, newly printed with the hooves of many horses. Their horses, presumably.

'Where does it lead?' Arnaud sounded unconvinced.

Karlis shrugged. 'Brother Parsifal scouted it for a half a league. Lots of nice forest to hide in, he says, and it seems to keep going. So long as it points east and away from any garrisons, I'm happy.' He wheeled his horse and Arnaud fell in beside him. Adelais followed, sighing at being left to bring up the rear. Her whole body ached, and she was so tired she was almost asleep in the saddle. She began to dream of her cot in the sisterhouse, or the horse-warm stables in the de Molinot mansion.

She was dozing in the saddle when Karlis held up his fist, halting them, and pulled off his bascinet, angling his head to listen. At the edge of hearing was the sound of a cantering horse, a noise Adelais had been too tired to truly notice. Karlis edged his horse forwards to where the trees thinned. Ahead of them, open fields stretched to a forested horizon so far away that the trees looked like three-day stubble on the face of the land. To their south, the main road was only a few bowshots away, steadily diverging from their new path. A lone horseman in the blue tabard of a royal servant hurried his horse towards Orval. It was hard to tell at that distance, but he seemed to Adelais to be a small man on a lean, wiry horse. He wore no armour.

Karlis scratched his cheek, waiting until the rider was out of sight. 'Now, why's a king's messenger in such a hurry?'

Arnaud rode into the open, turning to watch for more riders as they left the shelter of the trees. 'I'll wager he carries no good news as far as we are concerned.'

The messenger unsettled them, sharpening their exhaustion, and they kicked their horses into a final trot towards the forest, constantly looking over their shoulders to see if they were watched from the main road.

Brother Paget greeted them from the edge of the forest, where there was a view of perhaps half a league back down the track. A bowshot beyond him, Humbert had made camp; horse lines had been stretched between the trees, and a fire blazed in a clearing, set with an old campaigner's skill to leave only the lightest trail of smoke. Guy and Mathilde knelt beside it, turning a small deer on a makeshift spit. Agnès de Molinot watched them, still cradling her crossbow with the pride of a successful hunter. She looked up as Adelais and Arnaud arrived.

'Well, this is all very companionable!'

She made it sound like some glorious adventure, staged for her benefit; there might be silken pavilions and servants to care for her, rather than a small fire and a covering of cloaks under the stars. Adelais stared back, too tired even to dismount until Arnaud came and held her bridle.

'Come on, lass. Give the poor beast a rest and some feed.'

Lass. Adelais dropped to the ground, realising that this was the first time since the attack on the sisterhouse that she could actually be herself, not Perrin Wilg, the boy who slept in the stables. She pulled the linen cap off her head and ran her fingers through her hair, teasing it away from her scalp.

'Lass?' Agnès stared at her. 'By the God, you're a woman!'

Adelais began to make a foot-forward bow but stopped herself in time and dropped as feminine a curtsey as the herigaut would allow. 'Adelais de Vries at your service, my lady.'

By the fire, Mathilde stared at her, open-mouthed. It seemed she was a girl who blushed easily.

'Blessèd Salazar, I thought you and him—' Agnès glanced at Arnaud, then turned away, flapping her hand in confusion. '—I thought... Shit, I'm sorry.'

So she too had thought they were men who liked men. Adelais led her gelding towards the horse lines, too tired to react. Her whole body was stiff and aching, and she remembered how, at home in Vriesland, they'd sometimes been allowed the luxury of washing in a barrel of water that had been heated over the fire. Below the track lay a shallow, tree-fringed lake, one of many scattered across the countryside where it had never been cleared and drained for the plough, and she knelt at its edge to splash cold, clear water on her face. It tasted rich and peaty on her tongue.

'Don't be upset, lass.' Arnaud stood nearby, holding a bucket for the horses.

Adelais wiped her face and flicked water, scattering raindrop ripples on the surface. 'And we haven't even sinned in the conventional way.'

She was too tired. She wasn't thinking straight, and now a silence full of meaning stretched between them. She felt her own blood pumping in her veins.

'Lass...' He swallowed.

Brother Paget's call, summoning Humbert to the edge of the forest, broke the moment. They followed, never touching but close enough for her to be aware of each of his strides, and joined a small group forming where the underbrush would screen them from view. It seemed lighter here at the edge of the forest; the cloud was clearing, now streaked with red in the west, casting a sharp, sunset light across the fields. They could see the main road in the distance, an intermittent line through folds of the countryside, and on one of those stretches rode a large body of horsemen. Perhaps thirty lances were bunched together, keeping a steady league-eating trot so that they moved across the land in an inaudible mass like a monstrous caterpillar. They all watched until the soldiers passed out of sight towards Orval.

'A messenger, then cavalry,' Humbert muttered. 'I think the boy must have talked.'

'They might not be looking for us.'

No one answered Guy.

'Let's talk as we eat.' Humbert led the way back to the fire, leaving Brother Paget at his post, and sending Parsifal to find a place to watch further east, down the track. They stood in a circle around the fire while Humbert gave thanks, a ring of eight: three Guardians, two armourers, three women. They sat on saddle blankets to eat scorched and bloody venison on stale bread. Humbert broached a small keg of wine, but there were too few leather tankards to go round so they were passed from hand to hand, lady to servant, knight to master-craftsman, Guardian to... Adelais wondered how to describe herself. Novice? Page boy? Or an outcast woman, a she-wolf of the forest?

Humbert cleared his throat. 'If you were the king, Brothers, or his man de Remy, what would you be doing? What do you read from the messenger and the cavalry?' He passed a tankard to Brother Karlis as if passing on the authority to speak.

Brother Karlis sipped. 'I'd alert all garrisons ahead of us. Every town will be watching. I'd put a ring of steel around us, then mounted troops behind to flush us out. Trap us between the two.'

'And how long before they know we are not on the road?'

Karlis poked at the fire, sending sparks spiralling upwards, and for an instant the faces became visible in the darkness. Mathilde was staring at Adelais. She looked lost and frightened. 'If they do not find us soon,' Karlis spoke slowly, measuring his words, 'maybe even by first light, they will loop back and search the lesser roads.'

Adelais shivered, chilling as her sweat dried. She missed her squirrel-fur cloak, left in the Guardians' temple. Arnaud shifted a little closer and put his own around her shoulders. That tenderness was as warming as the wool.

'Will they stay together?' Humbert asked the group.

Arnaud received the mug and lifted it to his lips. She felt his voice rumble where their shoulders touched. 'There are too many possible paths. They will divide into scouting groups. First find us, then bring enough men to be sure of defeating us.'

'You learned well in Alympos, armourer.' Karlis's chuckle was crusty, like logs falling together in the fire.

'Then if they find us, *when* they find us, we must make sure that none of them live to tell.' Humbert stood. 'Tomorrow, we ride in armour, for by Ischyros's grace we will find battle. Come, Brothers, let us eat. Afterwards we will chant the Lighting of the Lamps.'

Soon Adelais and Arnaud were the only ones by the fire. Guy had been sent to relieve Parsifal; Mathilde and Agnès had laid their bedrolls in the cart, and were whispering beneath its covering; the Guardians had chosen the lakeside as their place to pray. The rise and fall of their chanting came through the trees. Adelais pulled Arnaud's cloak a little tighter round her shoulders. Behind them were campaigners' beds of dry fronds, mainly firs, to soften the ground, and saddle blankets to cushion them, but she didn't want to move; Arnaud's presence was too comforting. He was strong, he was gentle, and he made her feel safe even though life was falling apart around them. And this evening might be her last night alive.

'Frightened?'

She nodded. Down by the water a fine tenor voice lifted into the Guardian chant. *'Ischyros be merciful and shine upon us, and lift his hand to bless us.'* Soon they would finish. Then she would have to give back the cloak, curl into more horse blankets, and try to rest.

Arnaud's arm rose across her shoulders, squeezed, and dropped; an ending, not a beginning. 'Best get some sleep, youngling.'

She woke, shaking with cold, when the night was still fully
dark. She could see a few stars through the branches, but not
enough to tell the hour. She lay hunched into herself, shivering,
until there was movement beside her and she tensed, lifting her
head and pushing back her hood.

'My cloak is big enough for two.'

She curled into Arnaud's warmth as he pulled the cloak
around them both. It had a smoky, masculine smell that was
uniquely his, and she slept easily.

When she next woke he had gone, though his cloak was still
over her, and the sky was lightening in the east. The camp
stirred around her; the Guardians were already saddling their
destriers. Mathilde was boiling the deer's bones to make a
breakfast soup. Humbert was slowly, patiently teaching Guy
the sequence of arming a knight while Guy fumbled at the
points that tied the chausses of each leg to the gambeson. It
seemed that although the faith banned all superstition, every
knight had a 'lucky' sequence for being armed, steps that must
be meticulously observed. Guy nodded a greeting when he saw
Adelais watching, but stared hard at the cloak.

She found Arnaud at the lookout place, rubbing his own
shoulders for warmth.

'It was my turn to watch.' Arnaud straightened, conquering
his shivering.

'I brought your cloak.' She held it out, embarrassed and not
sure what to say now she'd slept beside him and shared his heat.
'Thank you.'

The field beyond was a slab of grey that faded into the
ghost-light of dawn. The perfect curve of the hay moon, so new
it might have been drawn with a fine quill, hung low and faint
in a lightening sky; only a few stars remained. The wind had
dropped overnight, and the scent of fresh-cut pine filled the
lookout place; someone, in the night, had made a nest of fronds
beneath a spread of saddlecloths.

Adelais heard Humbert coming before she could see him, the rippling of thousands of chain-mail rings moving against each other. He handed them bread and tankards of soup.

'I've left you my riding horse, l'Armurier. He is old but safe, and yours is lame. This is an excellent vantage point, so let us be a league ahead before you follow. Then ride fast until you find another. We'll be off as soon as we can see the path.'

'Understood. Salazar speed you.'

Daylight was growing rapidly. Now she could see the woods half a league away across the fields; before it had all been a dark blur. The first birds were about; a dawn chorus began and, high above, a great bird of prey soared with its wingtips splayed like fingers.

'Would you take over here for a while, lass?' Arnaud picked up a saddlecloth and nodded down the hill, where the lake was a sheet of lighter grey between the trees, reflecting the sky beyond. 'If I'm going to die today, I'll die clean.'

'In a lake? At dawn?'

'It's like quenching steel, lass. Makes you harder.'

Did he realise that could have two meanings?

Adelais heard him gasp as he entered the water, even forty paces away, and looked over her shoulder. A mass of undergrowth screened the shore and, flushing with guilt at what she was doing, she backed downhill until clothing came into view, draped over a bush. She walked further, slowly, until she could see him silhouetted against the water. He stood thigh-deep, broad-shouldered, narrow-hipped, and naked. He was blowing heavily, puffing out the shock of the water, even as he splashed more over himself. Adelais felt a need stirring within her that she did not fully understand. Was this love or lust? Or simply affection for a man who made her feel warm and respected? And did it matter, on the day they both might die?

She ducked out of sight as he started to turn. When he returned, dressed and drying his hair on the saddlecloth, he grinned at her in a way that might have been a challenge. Adelais stood and took another cloth.

'My turn.'

She wondered if he'd watch, and she behaved as if he was, walking down the hillside with her shoulders back and her hips swaying with each step. The appetite within her was confusing and deliciously sinful, an appetite that was fed and yet made worse by the way the stone and sling tapped against her body beneath her loin cloth.

Adelais undressed by the same bush, not looking back, and waded in. She paused when the water reached her thighs, almost regretting her impulse, but kept going. She would *not* squeal. When the cold reached her backside, she lifted her arms over her head and allowed her body to topple forwards. She would *not* thrash around, either. She was proving something, to him, or to herself, so she rolled onto her back and floated, letting the water lap over her breasts, tightening her skin. Only when her body was still, right to its core, did she allow herself to climb out, walking tall, palms out, just in case. She didn't look up, but drew a left-pointing arrow in the foreshore mud with her toe; the *kaunaz* rune of deep, carnal passion.

Kaun er barna böl...

She was playing with fire. Delicious, deep-belly fire.

The air was icy against her skin, and the saddlecloth seemed to smear the water rather than absorb it, so Adelais donned her shirt but carried her herigaut and gambeson until she could dry. She walked up the hill with the hunger growing within her, *tap, tap*, and a sense that she was moving towards something she didn't know how to start but probably couldn't stop. She could feel Yrsa's talisman through the belt bag, gripped in one hand, and knew that her grandmother would give her a knowing, mischievous smile at this moment. This was a morning for the old gods whose symbols were carved into the *taufr*: for sweet Sif, lover of Thor, or for Freyja. Ischyros would definitely not approve.

Ok bardaga för...

The main road was empty except for the first, innocent travellers, ambling their distant horses towards Villebénie.

Ok holdfúa hús...

'All clear, still?'

Arnaud didn't answer. She didn't mind that look, not from him, not at that moment, for she knew her shirt was sticking to her body. Adelais looked up as the circling birds made a high, mewling scream.

'What are they?'

Arnaud stood behind her, close enough for her to feel the warmth of his breath on her neck. 'Eagles? Kites? I don't know. I'm a city boy.' He put one hand on her breast, cupping it so gently that he might have expected her to brush it away, but she leaned back into him, holding his hand there before she turned to kiss him, and an urgency overcame them both. He peeled her shirt over her head, wrapped his cloak around them, and held her against his heat. As his lips tasted her face, her neck, her breasts, she realised that this, too, was a form of worship.

Adelais gasped as he entered her; she'd thought there might be pain, for there had been pain that time with Jan. She had not foreseen this instant, blissful union. While her mind could still think, she realised that this man knew more about loving than any youthful cleric would ever know. Either that, or she had been possessed by some wanton spirit, for this pulsing beast was not her; it *could* not be her, hollowing her stomach to take him. *She* had never learned such things. *She* could never show this wild abandon, this clawing for the body held so lightly above her. A dizziness filled her, rich as strong wine and pure as snowmelt. And as the world faded, some echo of her former self was able to wonder how it could be, when his weight was covering her, ploughing her, *impaling* her, that she could still soar and scream with the eagles.

Afterwards she lay against his side, filled with a dreamy lassitude, snug beneath the cloak against his naked warmth. From time to time he'd twist his head to watch the road, and the movement tugged at the cloak, until a cool line spread down her back that became sharp and chill between her legs. She rolled on top of him, twitching the cloak back into place, and cradled his face in her hands. She wanted to absorb every detail of him, to savour the joy of a lover's skin, to explore this man who'd unlocked wonder. Being naked with Arnaud felt as natural as puppies tumbling over each other in a litter.

'You have stars on your face.' She stroked his stubble, parting the hairs to expose a pattern of small white burn marks. 'And more on your chest.' She lifted off him to look, and his face rose to kiss her breasts.

'Sparks,' he mumbled. 'How's the road?'

'*Fjakk* the road.' She looked, anyway, but closed her eyes as his tongue traced the curve under a nipple. The hunger began again when he nuzzled her, tongue working, and she felt him swell. His hands dropped to her backside, stroking the skin between her legs, and she groaned, moving against him.

'Who's a greedy youngling, then?'

Adelais grinned, enjoying the wonder on his face as she reached around to guide him, making her body his sheath.

It was his turn to gasp. She was learning fast.

She, they, must have slept. Adelais jerked awake, still lying over him, and stared down the track. She sat upright, frowning, as lights sparkled among the woods in the distance. Arnaud reached up for her, but she lifted his hands away, kissing his fingers, full of regret at the ending of a moment. She knew that the dancing lights were reflections of the rising sun on soldiers' lances.

'We have company, my love.'

CHAPTER 7

7.1 GUY

Guy looked nervously over his shoulder, glancing down the string of horses tied to the back of the cart. Beyond them three of the Guardians rode their destriers, fully armed, unencumbered by their spare mounts. Any attack would likely come from behind, so Humbert had changed their order of march; just Parsifal went ahead as scout, staying within call of a small hunting horn. Even with three knights behind him, Guy felt vulnerable driving the cart. He couldn't outrun a charging cavalryman and he couldn't fight. He didn't even have a sword. Beside him on the seat Mathilde was still muttering about Adelais. Yesterday Mathilde had spent half the journey looking backwards, wondering if 'Perrin' was safe. Now she was all prim hostility. 'A woman dressed as a man. 'Tain't natural.' He wished she'd shut up.

Humbert rode with Agnès de Molinot just ahead of the cart. Lady Agnès rode one-handed, straight-backed, waspwaisted, with the skirts of her gown fanned over her horse's rump. One day he would be a knight and he would be able to woo a lady like that. She'd tie her favour round his lance before

a tourney and he'd win her heart with his courage and prowess.
He should be learning how to fight, not driving a cart.

It was mid-morning when sounds of a cantering horse
reached them, and both Guy and Mathilde twisted to look backwards again. They both heard before any of the Guardians, and
by the time the knights had wheeled their mounts and readied
their lances Guy had absorbed new learning: a helmet and
aventail of mail deadens hearing. He also wondered why a
single horse was coming; surely there should have been two?
But just Arnaud came into view on Humbert's riding horse,
which arrived rapidly enough to send the unridden horses
pirouetting.

'They're coming,' Arnaud shouted, even before he'd
stopped.

'How many, how armed?' Humbert sounded too calm. 'And
where is the girl?'

'They were half a league behind, in the woods beyond the
fields. They stopped to hail another group on the road.' Arnaud
was breathless from the ride. 'Adelais said she'd wait until she
could count the lances behind us. She has sharper eyes and the
faster horse.'

Humbert waved a mailed arm at Guy, gesturing him and
the cart onwards. 'Keep going. As fast as you can without
breaking a wheel. Brother Karlis!'

'Lord Brother?'

'Ride forwards with Brother Parsifal. Find a place to fight
where none can turn off the path to encircle us. We need a
battleground where a few brothers in armour might hold the
way against many.'

'Just like old times, Lord Brother!'

As Brother Karlis cantered away, Guy had the curious
notion that the ageing Guardian was enjoying himself.

Humbert joined Maarten and Paget behind the cart. 'Half a

league or less, probably at trot, against us at cart speed.' He was
thinking out loud. 'They will be on us soon. Come, l'Armurier!'

Arnaud was hanging back, staring down the empty track.
His clothing was dishevelled as if thrown on in a hurry.

'L'Armurier!' Humbert had to call again. 'You can help her
most by preparing for battle, not getting in her way.'

Karlis and Parsifal had stopped about a thousand paces
further on, where the track passed between another shallow
lake and a steep, curving, scrub-covered slope. An abandoned
hovel that might once have been a swineherd's cot nestled
deeply into the bank, its sagging roof on the point of collapse.
They gathered beside it, waiting while Humbert rode his
destrier backwards and forwards, looking at sight lines,
thinking.

'We do not have long,' Karlis prompted. 'We might hide two
riders in the thicket up there,' he pointed above the track, 'but
not if they're keeping a good eye open.'

'Then we must make sure they are looking forwards, not up
the slope.' Humbert seemed to come to a decision; he sat
straighter in the saddle, and began giving orders in a crisp,
urgent voice.

'Guy Carelet, take the cart and all spare horses to the
furthest point you can see on the track, where it bends out of
sight. Run horse lines, and make them visible from here. Stay
there, on the ground. Let them see you.'

'I can fight,' Guy protested.

'Don't argue.' Humbert spoke sharply, then more gently.
'You have no weapons and no armour, boy. You would die. This
is what pages do; you hold the horses while the knights fight.
Now wait to hear the whole plan.'

'I too have no weapon, but...' Arnaud gestured at Agnès's
hunting spear in the cart.

'No, l'Armurier, I have a different task for you. Take one of
the ropes we use for horse lines. Find a strong tree up on that

bank, and another between the track and the lake. Run the rope along the ground over the track, and hide as best you can where you can see me. When I lift my lance, count to five and heave on the rope so that you trip their horses as they ride past. Understood?'

Arnaud grinned, and took the spear as well as the rope.

'Such deceit is not chivalrous,' the Saxen, Brother Paget, complained.

'It is no less chivalrous than digging pits against cavalry in front of the lines,' Humbert snapped. 'Both bring down the horses before their lances can strike. Now take the rear with Brother Maarten. Both of you hide in the thicket until they are past.'

'And you?' Paget seemed disposed to argue.

'Brothers Parsifal and Paget and I will be by the horse lines. We want them to think they have caught us unprepared. We want them to charge, then when l'Armurier creates chaos in the middle we'll hit them from both sides. Let none escape.'

'And what if they are more than a scouting party?' Paget's tone often sounded a little superior, the edge of a sneer in his voice.

'Then, Brother, we shall perform such a deed of arms as will remind King Aloys of the prowess of the Guardians.' This was the Parsifal that Guy remembered from before the persecution – the bright-eyed hero.

'That which we carry has a way of defending those who serve it with a pure heart,' Humbert added, quietly.

Guy heard, and frowned at Arnaud. What did Humbert mean by that?

'What about the girl,' Agnès de Molinot asked. 'Perrin, or Adelais, or whatever her name is?'

'Probably halfway to Vriesland by now,' Brother Paget muttered under his breath.

'Hold your tongue, Saxen,' Arnaud snapped, 'or an armourer will teach you chivalry. She will come.'

Humbert turned to Agnès. 'My lady, would your servant have a spare gown? I have a role in mind for young Adelais.'

As Mathilde rummaged in the baggage, Agnès swung out of the saddle.

'And I have a role for this.' She pulled her crossbow from the cart and strapped on the quiver and spanning lever.

'My lady, please stay with the horses.' Humbert sounded cross. 'Until now, you could be innocent...'

'Then I'd best stay out of sight, hadn't I? Here would be good.' She looked through the door of the ruined cottage.

'Lady Agnès, I must insist. We cannot protect you there.' For the first time, Humbert's voice rose.

'Fear not, I shall have a good friend with me.' Agnès put her foot in the crossbow's stirrup, engaged the lever, and strained to span it. 'Now go, uncle, unless you and your brothers are going to waste time carrying me bodily from the field.' She reached behind her for a bolt, and fitted it to the groove.

Humbert glared at her, and she smiled back at him in a battle of wills.

'Time is running out, uncle.'

Humbert let out a low, exasperated snarl. 'Then stay inside, whatever happens. Now, Brothers, go to it, and Ischyros be with us all!'

Guy flicked the reins to move the carthorses forwards, his own anger a match for the fury blazing on Humbert's face. Horse lines. How was he going to learn the profession of arms in the horse lines?

7.2 ADELAIS

Adelais found it hard to believe she was threatened. The horsemen trotting towards her across the fields looked pretty, even at a distance; they were an entertainment, like the grand parade before a joust she'd once seen in Vriesland. They couldn't possibly mean her harm, not when she was so wonderfully alive. Each part of her body sang in sweet harmony with another, like minstrels at a feast; her head with her heart, her fingers with her toes, her belly with her breasts... For today she had breasts; she was Adelais, not Perrin Wilg, despite the gambeson and lordly herigaut she'd donned as Arnaud left. She wanted to whirl and dance at the edge of the forest as if this were all some wonderful game, or a tourney, and she a spectator cheering for the other side.

Even her horse wanted to play. Left alone, without the rest of the herd, he was restive and keen to run, so Adelais only had to give him the rein and let him fly while she whooped into the wind.

She should have paced him. The little gelding was blown long before she found the others, but she forced him on, hating herself for what she was asking. By the time she saw Humbert

waiting alone astride his destrier, the beast was almost staggering, and her euphoria had long since bled away with his energy.
Now she feared the pursuit. The lances behind were coming for
her personally. *So move, my sweet, tired boy*.

Humbert wasted no time with pleasantries.

'How many?'

'Eight.'

He said something quietly that could have been an oath, but
was probably a prayer.

'How armed?'

'Lances? One of them flies a pennon.'

'No. What armour were they wearing?'

She shrugged. She hadn't let them get *that* close. 'None
wore a great helm.' Their heads would have looked bigger and
squarer, even at a distance. 'Where is Arnaud?'

'Then probably light armour only. How far behind?'

'A thousand paces when I left.'

'Did they see you?'

'No. Where is everyone? Is Arnaud safe?'

'I am here, youngling.' Arnaud stood beside a tree near the
lake shore, grinning at her, and she felt her soul lift.

Humbert threw her a servant's dress that was lying across
his saddle. 'Take off your herigaut and put this on. Give your
gambeson to Arnaud. I'll take your horse. Hurry.'

He rode two paces down the track, giving her the illusion of
privacy. Adelais kept her eyes on Arnaud as she pulled off her
outer clothing until she stood in hose and shirt. Her man's loin
cloth felt strange, a denial of what had happened. Yet even in
the tension of the moment she had the urge to put her shoulders
back, to display to her lover, just as he was talking to her with
his body as he ripped off his cote-hardie, ready for the
gambeson.

'Paget! Maarten! Eight!' She looked over her shoulder at
Humbert's battlefield shout, in time to see Humbert open his

fingers twice: five then three. Brother Paget acknowledged from the edge of a thicket on the hillside.

Adelais made a moue of disappointment as Arnaud shrugged into the gambeson. The next time she wore that it would be fragrant with *his* sweat. At least the dress was fresh as she pulled it over her head.

'It is too short, messire.' The hem dropped only to her shins.

'No matter. They are looking for a yellow-haired woman, and we will show them a yellow-haired woman. There's a bucket by the road. Pretend to be filling it. When they come, drop it and run towards the cart. Scream if you like. That's all you have to do. Understand?'

'But where are the rest?' She could see Arnaud, and Guy with the cart and the spare horses. She'd seen Paget, but no one else.

Humbert wheeled his horse towards the cart. 'At my command plus five, l'Armurier. Not before.' He trotted away, dragging her gelding towards the horse lines.

Silence. A solitary robin sang somewhere, but otherwise silence. Arnaud smiled reassurance at her. He held a rope in one hand, and she followed it with her eyes where it ran across the track, hidden with mud and turf. The other end was tied head-high in a tree. A tripwire. She began to tie her sling around her middle, outside the gown, turning it into a simple belt. If they expected a woman, she'd give them a woman's waist.

'Why "plus five"?' she whispered to Arnaud.

'He will charge. He cannot signal once he is charging.'

Adelais inflated her chest to speak more but Arnaud lifted his finger to his lips. The distant jingling of harness was softer than the birdsong, at first. Adelais began to breathe heavily, and kept her eyes locked on Arnaud. In Vriesland she'd heard that a *seidhkona* would sing rune song before battle was joined: *thurs* for defence. Remember the point, Yrsa had said; it protects the warrior the way the thorn protects the rose:

Thurs er kvenna kvöl...

Or *tiwaz* for victory. *Týr er einhendr áss...* She couldn't think. *Sætur Sif, I am frightened.* As the sound of the troop rose to a steady rumble she mouthed 'I love you' at him and began to back away, holding the bucket. He mouthed something back. The sound of the troop was now a drum roll, growing ever louder.

She didn't have to act; she was truly terrified. She stood in the middle of the track, staring at the soldiers as they trotted into view a hundred paces away. They were led by the one with a blue pennon on his lance, riding a better horse than the rest. A squire to lead the troop. He had a fine bascinet on his head with a chain-mail aventail, while the others had mail cowls over simple bowl helmets. No hauberks. No mail leggings. Just gambesons. They were strung out along the path; only five were in view by the time the leader had covered half the distance to her.

The squire shouted in a light, 'what do we have here' tone, though the words were lost in the noise of the horses. Adelais dropped the bucket and backed away as he kicked his horse into a canter. She understood Humbert's plan. They had to charge, had to commit. She squealed, gathered up her skirts, and ran.

There were shouts behind her as the troop saw what she could see: a cart and horse lines, a lad carrying a saddle near a servant girl, who was starting to scream; signs of a camp unguarded save for a single knight on his destrier. *Easy pickings.* The drumming of hooves changed pitch; now it was heavier, faster, more urgent. Had they committed to a charge? She cursed the folds of the dress that hampered her legs, slowing her. Two other Guardians rode out of the bushes behind Humbert, who lifted his lance, both signal and challenge, and with a touch of his spurs sent his destrier from stand to canter. Without knowing why, she began to count, so much more slowly than her heart.

One.

'Get out of the way, girl!' Humbert's voice, muffled inside his helmet.

She'd been lost in the unreality of the moment; two fully armed knights, their great helms peering over their shields, coming at her stirrup-to-stirrup, one in each rut of the track so they filled its width. She only knew them to be Humbert and Parsifal by their horses. And as they came, they lowered their lances together, quite slowly, as if they were a pair of dancers acting in unison. Twenty paces behind came Brother Karlis with his lance still upright, his destrier's iron-shod hooves striking sparks from stones in the path.

Two.

Adelais threw herself sideways towards the lake, grabbing at a sapling to spin herself round. One of the king's men had closed up alongside his leader, and both were hunched behind their shields, their lances almost level; the others were scattered behind, all coming fast. Too fast. The leaders would be past the rope before Arnaud lifted it. Or was that what Humbert wanted?

Three.

'Now!' Humbert's shout was to Parsifal, not Arnaud.

Adelais had never seen trained destriers in action. They both surged from canter to gallop, hurling themselves at the oncoming horses without the slightest flinch to spoil their masters' aims, and the sound of their hooves was like being outdoors in a thunderstorm. Their assailants' faces peered over their shields, and in the widening eyes of the squire she saw a man who has seen his own death hurtling towards him and can do nothing about it.

Four.

The collision of the four horses was the thunderclap at the heart of the storm, and the crashes that followed might have been trees felled by the blast. Humbert's lance struck the squire squarely in the face, snapping him backwards out of the saddle as loosely and as heavily as an empty hauberk. The squire hit the ground at almost the same instant as Parsifal, in another mighty double-drumbeat of sound. A terrible, wordless cry came from Arnaud in the bushes as his brother fell.

Five.

The squire's riderless mount had been barged into the undergrowth between the track and the lake. There its bridle caught on a branch and it spun, squealing, bucking at the restraint. Between Adelais and Humbert, the squire's companion galloped over Parsifal's body, throwing away a shattered lance. He was still reaching to draw his sword when Karlis's lance point ripped into his unshielded shoulder.

Parsifal had not moved.

Adelais stopped counting. In that almighty collision, and in less time than it took to pour a mug of water, two men had died and one was swaying in his saddle, about to drop. She looked frantically for Arnaud, but he was screened from her view, so she stepped onto the path. More king's men were charging towards them. Humbert and Brother Karlis had reined in, and held their horses level with the ruined hovel. Both horses danced underneath them in their urgency to attack the nearest man, now only a few paces beyond with his lance already couched, hurtling towards Humbert.

Arnaud's rope came up like a bow string and the charging horse cartwheeled, throwing its rider forwards so that his lance speared the earth and his face smashed into the turf. He bounced along the ground towards Adelais and lay still, but his horse thrashed on its side, screaming. A tree by the hovel was dragged half out of the ground and came crashing onto the track. Beyond it, the mounts of five more king's men shied and milled, blocked by the tree and the flailing legs of the horse. At their rear, two Guardians eased their destriers clear of a thicket, launching into the charge as eagerly as fighting stags in the rut.

She heard herself scream 'Arnaud!' and ran forwards, because one of the king's men was at the edge of the track, unable to ride into the undergrowth but stabbing his lance towards Arnaud's hiding place.

Weapon. She needed a weapon. She picked up Parsifal's fallen lance and swung towards the fight, wishing she had a lighter, less unwieldy weapon.

Between her and the rider attacking Arnaud, the unhorsed king's man now stood, swaying slightly, but holding a drawn sword in his right hand. In that moment Adelais knew the only thing keeping her alive was her womanhood. He stared at her, frowning away his concussion, a man of about Arnaud's age with open, farm-hand features beneath the stubble on one side of his face. The other had been scraped into a mess of blood and mud by his fall. One eye was watering and he blinked, rapidly.

'Drop it, girl!' He did not sound threatened. Was not threatened; the lance was twice her height and useless on foot against a sword. A trickle of blood and goo dripped from his nose and he sniffed. 'I said drop it!' He lifted his sword towards her, and in a sharp *snap-thump* was thrown sideways as if kicked by a horse. He sprawled on the path, lifted his head to look at the copper flower that had bloomed on his side, then stared up at Adelais as if she could explain what had happened.

'I think you're supposed to hit him with the pointy end, not wave it about.'

Agnès de Molinot leaned back against the doorway of the hovel, fitting the spanning lever to her crossbow with a shaking hand. She looked pale; her smile, like her humour, was forced. The man on the ground slowly folded double, making a high-pitched whine of agony. The bolt was probably in his guts, low down, near the hip. Adelais kicked his sword away and looked for Arnaud.

He lived! He was holding off a rider with Agnès's hunting spear, though he kept glancing up the path towards Parsifal's body, his face stricken. Neither he nor his attacker could press their attack through the undergrowth, in the same way that the tree and the injured horse prevented Humbert and Karlis reaching the soldiers beyond. Here, the fight was at an impasse. To the rear, a melee had formed around Maarten and Paget. Adelais saw a king's man dismount and run up the hill beyond the hovel, drawing his sword, and she knew that he was trying to work his way round to take Humbert and Maarten from behind.

'Man coming round!' she shouted at Agnès, but Agnès was still fumbling for another bolt, so Adelais stood by the doorway with the lance pointing up the slope, its heel grounded near her foot, hoping to hold the man off until Agnès could reload. *Mighty Thor, máttugur Thor, help me.* Perhaps she should sing rune song. *Thurs er kvenna kvöl...* She couldn't think. What were the *fjakkinn* words?

The soldier came round the sagging roof in a rush, and for a mad instant Adelais though he was too young to be carrying a sword; he had creamy skin with spots of bright colour on his cheeks and just the faintest darkening on his upper lip. A helmeted angel. She wanted to tell him to wait, they didn't have to kill each other, but his momentum was unstoppable, and he slid feet-first down the bank towards her, slashing at the lance with his sword. The blow knocked the shaft downwards, so the point slid up the inside of his thigh, under his shield, under his quilted gambeson. The lance shaft slammed backwards in Adelais's hand until its butt was driven into the earth.

Liquid gushed down the shaft and impossibly, horribly, it became shorter in her hand as the boy slid down it, screaming. He dropped his sword and shield and tried to grip the lance with both hands, but still he came closer. Adelais let go of the shaft as blood and piss reached her hands, but the lance fell no further, wedged now between the earth at her feet and some point high on the bank, beyond the boy's back. She stared at him, her mouth working, unable to believe what she had just done, and still the boy screamed.

'By the God, remind me never to upset you.' Agnès finally fitted a bolt onto her crossbow. It took her several rattling attempts to engage it.

Adelais turned away from the boy, lifting her palms to stop her ears against the screams, but she smelt the sticky mess on her hands. She shook them uselessly in front of her and ran, sobbing, towards the lake. Nearby there were the blows and oaths and groans of combat, the snap of the crossbow, and hammering of weapons against shields, metal, flesh, but Adelais didn't want any part of it. She wanted an end to it all. She wanted peace. She wanted to be clean.

Agnès found her kneeling in the water, her borrowed dress soaked to the thighs and elbows. She was crying and scooping up handfuls of silt, rubbing the slime over her fingers as if it were fragrant oil, scrubbing them, rinsing them, and doing it over again. Anything to rid herself of the smells and stains. Agnès stood beside her with her fine boots in the mud. She lifted Adelais under the arms, and turned her towards the road.

'It's over, lambkin. Come away, now.'

Agnès put an arm around Adelais's waist to steady her. Perhaps she needed steadying too, for they walked through carnage. She had her crossbow slung around her neck and the man she'd shot with it still squirmed in the road, moaning, smearing a bloody slug-trail along the ground behind him. A horse stood near him on three legs, quivering in agony. The young soldier Adelais had spitted on Parsifal's lance was still now, leaking, mouth agape, staring at the sky with unseeing eyes. Adelais turned her head away as if she'd been struck.

Humbert stood in the roadway, his head bent in prayer. It took Adelais a moment to realise the armoured bundle at his feet was Parsifal. Arnaud knelt by his brother's body, rocking backwards and forwards on his knees, weeping silently. Adelais strained towards him, but Agnès held her back.

'Don't, Adelais. If you go to him now, he will break, and be shamed. Hold him later, privately.' Agnès tugged her towards the cart. 'Come, lambkin. I need wine.'

7.3 GUY

When the noise of battle ceased, and the horses had calmed a little, Guy walked slowly down the track. Mathilde had clung to him, whimpering, but he put her aside gently, saying he must help. Too few of their friends still walked amidst the carnage.

So much blood. It made him think of the wall paintings in the fire temple on the Isle that showed sinners falling from the bridge of judgement; in the fiery pit below they were impaled or torn apart by ravenous beasts in a hell of running blood, but this was worse. These were real people, so newly dead their bodies were still oozing.

He passed Lady Agnès with her arm around Adelais, who was soaking wet and holding both hands clawed before her. Neither of them seemed hurt, but Adelais's face was slack and pale, and her eyes red and swollen.

'Come, lambkin, I need wine.' Agnès sounded numb.

Guy stared open-mouthed. Lady Agnès de Molinot was calling Adelais *lambkin*?

He could not tell who lived. Humbert, yes. Standing, head bowed, holding the trailing reins of his destrier. Arnaud, at his feet, moving. Wounded? And a hunched bundle of chain-mail on the ground.

Parsifal?

Arnaud had taken off Parsifal's great helm, and the mail-framed face was angled towards them, eyes half-closed. If it had not been for the broken lance beneath him he would have looked peaceful, a knight awakening, not dead. Parsifal couldn't die, not the base-born hero who'd earned knighthood in battle. But the lance was not beneath him, it was through him, through shield, hauberk, gambeson, arm, chest, pinning him forever in the hunched position of the charge.

'His shield split.' Humbert sounded flat, disbelieving. 'It must have struck a point of weakness, some flaw in the wood.' His voice softened into something close to tenderness. 'We were in Alympos together. Twenty years I have known him.'

'I could have helped.' Guy stared at Arnaud's rocking back, wondering if and how to support him, until a sudden groan and sigh came from a tangled mass of bodies further down the road. Brother Karlis had been kneeling in their midst; he now pushed himself to his feet, blood dripping from the dagger in his hand. Humbert did not react.

'You did help. You calmed the horses.' Exhaustion dragged at Humbert's face. 'The first lesson of chivalry is discipline. Obedience to orders. You are alive because you obeyed. And now you can help more. There is much to do.'

Another Guardian lived. Paget pushed himself away from the support of the ruined hut's wall and walked towards them, visibly fighting to stay upright. The Saxen had slung his shield over his back and held his left arm close to his body, trying to stem a flow of blood from near the armpit. Karlis followed, close enough to catch his brother if he collapsed.

'That was indeed...' Paget seemed to have difficulty breathing. '... a mighty deed of arms.'

'You are badly wounded?' Humbert asked.

'It was a skilful blow. Inside my guard.'

'Go to Adelais. She will bind it. How fares Brother Maarten?'

'He lives now.' Brother Karlis grimaced. 'But he'll not see sunset.'

Humbert closed his eyes. 'So half our strength is gone.'

Karlis nodded at the soldier still squirming on the track. 'And none must know our weakened state.' He crouched and pulled the chain-mail coif off the man's head. His movement was gentle, almost kindly, the way a father might prepare a child for bed.

'No, please.' The soldier pushed his shoulders up, trying to rise, though he stayed balanced between his palms and one knee, trailing the leg on his wounded side. A new flow of blood trickled from under his gambeson. 'I won't tell. Please.' His eyes darted between each of their faces until Humbert squatted in front of him.

'Your wound is mortal.'

'No, no...'

'It is in your belly, man. Will you make your unburdening?'

'You are a priest?' Hope blazed in the soldier's face.

'I am simply a Guardian. Come, make your peace with Ischyros. A battlefield unburdening.'

'Please...'

'Say after me. *Evlogiménos Ischyros, Pateras ólon...*' Humbert began the Prayer of Unburdening in the High Tongue of the prophet.

'*Evlogiménos Ischyros...*' The man mumbled the words, his eyes darting between the Guardians.

'*Dóste chári ston amartoló...*'

'*Dóste chári...*' He began to cry.

'*Párte to város mould apó tin amartía...*'

'*Parte...*' The mumbling became inaudible.

'*Parakaló mou.*' Humbert spoke strongly, more command than supplication. 'Grant me pardon...'

'Please...'

'Say it!'

'*Parakaló mou.*'

'*Ópos syncharó állous.*' Humbert stood and backed away from the man, his hand on his sword hilt.

'No!' The soldier shook his head.

'Say it!'

The soldier's eyes were locked on Humbert's hand, away from Brother Karlis, who had drawn his sword behind him.

'*Ópos... ópos...*'

'*Me óli mou tin kardiá.*' With my whole heart.

The soldier's lips moved, though Guy heard no sound until Brother Karlis's sword fell, striking off the man's head with a single blow. Karlis rested his point and made the sign of the God.

Guy could not tear his eyes from the gushing corpse. He'd never seen a man killed like that. Helpless, pleading.

Humbert also made the sign of Ischyros, and sighed.

'We must now conceal as much as we can. L'Armurier, we grieve with you, but we must erase what traces we can. You and Carelet unload the cart and repack onto horses. The soldiers' bodies can go in the lake. Brother Karlis and I will help you when we have cared for Brother Maarten.'

Maarten lay on the ground, ashen-faced, with one leg at an impossible angle. An axe had bitten clear through his mail and into his side, shattering his hip. His blood streamed across the path, trickling towards the lake. By the time Guy and Arnaud returned with an empty cart, Karlis knelt at Maarten's side and Paget stood at his feet, his bandaged arm in a sling. Humbert held the roll of linen towards him, opening it to show something hidden inside.

'*Efcharistó ton Ischyros.*' Brother Maarten let out a single, joyous cry of thanks, as Karlis opened another vein. He stayed on his knees to hold Maarten's hand as he died.

'Giving a friend peace is always the hardest life to take.' Karlis stood, making the sign of the God. 'No matter how near they are to death. Maarten and Parsifal gave thanks that they never had to do that for your father.'

Guy only half-heard, and was too shocked to understand. Yes, Maarten's wound was mortal, but Karlis had just killed a dying friend.

They managed to coax the injured horse into the hovel, where Guy covered its eyes while Arnaud put it out of its misery with a single blow of a war hammer. A few strokes of an axe brought the remains of the roof down over it. They buried Parsifal and Maarten together in a clearing, prayerfully, with stones to protect their bodies from foxes and wolves, then scattered leaf-mulch over the shallow grave to hide the spot. The soldiers' bodies they loaded onto the cart, which they pushed into the lake at a point where the track met the shore. When the wheels could be dragged no deeper into the mud they slid the bodies into the water. To Guy, that felt like a second murder, a further desecration that denied the dead proper rites. It was also a sinful waste; they had saved only enough armour to equip Guy and Arnaud. The rest went into the water to weigh down the bodies. Its value would have fed a large village for several moons. At Humbert's insistence they toppled the cart over until only the rims of its wheels showed above the surface, and these they smashed off with axes and the war hammer.

'Why?' Guy asked. Like Arnaud he was stripped to his loin cloth and soaking wet. He could understand the pause to bury the Guardians, and at least throwing the soldiers in the water spared the time to bury them, but why waste time hiding the cart when they should be fleeing? 'We can't hide all the signs of the fight!'

'More rain is coming. It might wash away enough blood for

them to ride on by.' It was the first time Arnaud had spoken. It didn't sound like him at all, but like a man whose vital years are long gone. 'But we can confuse them. They won't know if any of their men still live, and they won't know if any of us died.' Guy looked back at the water from the shoreline, making sure that nothing could be seen above the surface.

When they had dressed, Humbert waited for them on the road, holding two swords flat across his arms.

'Arnaud l'Armurier, this was Brother Parsifal's. I know you will bear it with honour, in his memory.'

Arnaud accepted the sword flat in his hands, like an offering. His shoulders shook as he lifted it to his forehead.

'And Guy Carelet, Brother Maarten bore this in many deeds of arms worthy of song, though he himself gave all the glory to Ischyros. Bear it well. When there is time I will teach you to wield it skilfully.'

Guy received it with equal reverence, his wonder momentarily blanking the horror of the morning. The sword was of an old style with a round pommel, a thick cross guard, and a fat, leather-bound grip that filled his hand. He drew it a forearm's length from its scabbard, exposing fine steel stained by much combat, and with the slightly uneven edge of frequent re-sharpening. Guy slowly slid the blade back into its scabbard and lifted it to his face as he had seen Arnaud do.

'I shall strive to be worthy of it.'

'Good.' Humbert flexed his shoulders as if he could shed his exhaustion like a cloak. 'Now arm up, choose a horse, and let us be out of here.'

'But I cannot ride...'

'You are about to learn.'

7.4 ADELAIS

Adelais was allowed to gather up some loose horses and to bandage Brother Paget, that was all. She was able to help Arnaud and Guy unload the cart into the road, and managed to put her arm briefly around Arnaud's shoulder, but he was not yet ready to be held. When she tried to help the others near the hovel, Paget held out his good arm, barring the way and insisting there was nothing more she could do. 'You and Lady Agnès have already seen and done enough.' At first she was cross. She wanted to show she was strong, after her weakness in the fight, but then she glimpsed them pulling the boy off the lance and turned away, nauseated and ashamed.

Agnès couldn't look, either, so they sat on baggage, facing each other. They had one mug of wine that they passed between them, and neither of them had thought to look for another. A bond had grown between them in front of that hovel; not quite a sisterhood, but something harder, iron-forged. Agnès flinched at each thump of a body into the cart and drank deeply, her eyes locked with Adelais's. At least one of those bodies would be her kill. Mathilde sat at a little distance, pale-faced, watching the men with round-eyed, morbid fascination.

'I'm sorry.' Adelais's shame was for more than the killing.

'What for?'

'I lost control. Went mad when you needed me. Won't happen again.'

'You stopped him. I was shaking so much I couldn't reload.' Agnès passed over the mug, two-handed, but still Adelais managed to spill some onto her wrist. She drank, stared at the trickle of red running down the back of her hand, and hardened herself to lick it away. She was surprised that it only tasted of wine.

A splash made them both look up, before they could stop themselves. The cart had been backed into the lake so that water lapped into it, and Guy had just pulled a body off the top of the pile into the water. It didn't sink straight away; air trapped in the gambeson kept it afloat, with a rosy stain spreading around it, while Arnaud, *her* Arnaud, pushed it into deeper water with a lance.

'*Sætur Sif!*' Adelais stood up and paced among the baggage, walking an urgent, aimless little path like a wandering insect. She'd made a couple of stumbling turns before she realised she'd called aloud on the wife of Thor. Thank the gods Agnès didn't speak Vriesian.

'Steady, lambkin.' Agnès stood in front of her, holding both her shoulders, forcing Adelais to make eye contact again. She had green eyes that hid their own shock. Which she masked with brittle humour. 'You'll spill the wine.'

'You saved me, too. With the crossbow.'

'It's not the same as killing a hind.' Agnès took the mug and gulped wine. 'One doesn't feel good about it.'

'Will you teach me to use it? Not today, but...?' It was an almost trivial request, the words tumbling into a void where normal life had been, but Adelais knew that if they had to fight again, she didn't want to be close enough to feel the mess on her hands.

'Awfully easy. Hardest bit is the spanning.'

They were both filling time with sound. Anything to distract them from the splashes, until Agnès glanced at the lake and sighed.

'It's all right now, they've finished with the bodies.'

Adelais turned. The men had overturned the cart so that only the tops of its wheels showed above the water. Arnaud climbed onto its base, standing knee-deep and stripped to his loin cloth in a strange echo of the dawn. He hadn't even worn a loin cloth then, and for the first time since Vriesland she'd known the delicious sin of lust. Except only the Ischyrians called it a sin. The goddess Freyja was worshipped for it. Now, Arnaud was smashing the wheels with great blows of a war hammer. He was swinging wildly, too heavily, purging grief with violence. He was all lean muscle, shining wet, Thor himself in living flesh, and yet she felt no fire in her belly. Affection, yes. Pity, yes. Love, probably. Lust, no. She'd rather crawl away on her own, find a lonely hut with a blaze in its hearth, and drink herself into oblivion. Perhaps Agnès felt the same. Perhaps they could drink together, like ribald soldiers. 'Did yer see the look on that bastard's face? Didn't 'e squeal!'

'Is Arnaud your man, then?' Agnès had to tilt the cask to refill the mug. She looked flushed and fumbled a little.

Adelais didn't reply straight away, but watched Arnaud wading to the shore, pink water breaking over his thighs. Her mind had drifted not to the morning's coupling but to her panic when she thought he was going to die, and she knew that if another troop came down the track, she'd feel the same.

'Yes, he's my man.' On reflection, she'd let Arnaud into her imagined drinking hut; strong, safe, and gentle enough to pick up the pieces.

'He's a good man. You're lucky to be able to choose.' Agnès de Molinot swayed a little and kicked at a saddle as if it had caused her to stumble.

'You didn't choose Lord de Fontenay?'

'It's all about lands with families like mine, and de Fontenay has *big* estates.' Agnès breathed 'big' as though the estates were part of de Fontenay's anatomy. 'Papa says you can ride for three days in any direction from Château Fontenay and still be on his land. I had more say with him than I did with my first husband. My father arranged that one, to a lonely old man with a very big title and a very small prick.' Agnès held her finger and thumb close together in front of her eye, rather unsteadily, and let out a short, manic giggle. 'But I hope Leandre will keep me happy. He looks vigorous. Like your man. More wine?'

Adelais thought Agnès would crumble into tears at the first sign of tenderness. What she needed – what they both needed – was a hug, but that was absolutely not what Agnès would want; she needed to be the lady, in control of herself, even if slightly drunk. In control of Adelais, if only by calling her 'lambkin'.

Sometimes Adelais didn't understand Ischyrians. If even a gentle like Agnès felt lust, how could it be a such sin? Only because the priests said it was. Hunger couldn't be a sin, for if it was, the most sinful soul would be a starving beggar. Greed was just as bad as lust, they said, though she'd watched an episkopos gorge himself at the de Molinot's feast. The old gods were easier to understand; they fought and *fjakked* and feasted like mortals. And as Yrsa said, you honoured the gods by your actions; you didn't grovel for your failings.

That still didn't make her feel good about killing.

She watched Arnaud walk up the road to her. He'd found himself a jack-of-plates from one of the dead soldiers – a jacket of armoured tiles sewn onto quilted, padded linen. He paused long enough for her to hug him, murmuring her sympathy. That morning she'd moulded her body into his; her fingers had traced the muscled valley of his spine. Now he felt like a walking statue, hard-edged and awkward in her arms. He set her aside, not unkindly, and she guessed he was struggling to hold himself together, resisting the tenderness that would tip him over the edge.

CHAPTER 8

8.1 ADELAIS

Adelais feared the horses would give them away. They could not take them all, even with each of them leading a baggage-laden spare. Yet no one suggested that they should be slaughtered; these men who killed so effectively could not bring themselves to such murder, and the unused horses followed them in a loose, uncontrollable herd. Where the forest had been cleared for farmland, peasants would run from their fields, gathering children into their hovels at the sight of them all. Horses riding loose in the company of men could only mean violence or robbery. Near the second such clearing they paused to swap a lame animal for a sound one, and tethered the rest to trees, leaving wealth beyond a peasant's imagining for the taking.

At the next fork of the path they turned south, riding hunched forwards in their saddles like robbers. Humbert set a regular pattern of five hundred paces fast trot, then five hundred in walk to stave off the horses' exhaustion. In the late afternoon Humbert halted them at the edge of the trees where a vista of open fields stretched to the horizon. A village large enough to have its own temple lay in a shallow valley below, and he chose to wait until dark before riding through.

Even the Guardians eased themselves out of the saddle stiffly. Mathilde's calves had been chafed raw by her stirrup leathers. Humbert let Adelais open the roll of linen, just enough to tear bandages from its edge, which she used to bind Mathilde's legs and to replace the dressing around Brother Paget's wound. Humbert watched closely, gathering the roll to himself as soon as she was done.

Adelais also bound Guy's legs beneath hose that had been rubbed into bloody holes. He accepted her help in silence. After the fight she'd tried to caution him against taking Brother Maarten's destrier, but he'd brushed her words aside and climbed into the saddle, with Maarten's sword at his side. Perhaps in his mind he had already become a knight, in his looted gambeson and hauberk, but the beast had promptly thrown him. Humbert had assigned him a gentler mount, saying that highly trained horses need highly trained riders, and both Parsifal's and Maarten's valuable warhorses must be led, carrying armour.

Adelais tended their injuries in a state of exhaustion, as if she hadn't slept for two nights. Her whole mind might have been wrapped in a gambeson, shielding her from all touch, all sensation. Somewhere inside was the Adelais of the morning, soft and warm and wanting to be loved, but the evening's reality was a numb fumbling at linen, a slack-minded inability to remember infirmary basics like knotting a bandage.

She glanced at Arnaud as she worked. He'd taken himself a little apart to sit on a fallen tree, staring away from the group, and when the bandaging was done she went to sit by his side. He was like a man stunned by a blow to the head. In front of him, on the leaf mould, lay the fine bascinet from the squire Humbert had killed. Arnaud had rinsed out the gore but she could not look at it without remembering the instant Humbert's lance had struck home, when the de Fontenay pennon below the point had streamed into the squire's eye. She reached for his hand and their fingers twined, naturally, gently, but his grip slowly strengthened until he held her as tightly as a drowning man might clasp a rescuer. There were no words.

'L'Armurier! Wilg!' Humbert's call seemed to come from far away. 'Let me show you all something.'

He gathered them in a circle, insisting that even Mathilde join them.

'This morning was but the beginning. In the coming days I will ask much of you, and I want you to understand my purpose. Here is Villebénie.' He put Arnaud's bascinet on the ground with its chain-mail aventail fanning out over the leaf litter. Fortunately the open, empty face was pointing away from Adelais. 'And this is Orval.' He took four paces and dumped another helmet on the ground. 'Three more days' riding, well-mounted, if the roads are good. It might have taken us five with the cart, had we remained undiscovered. Now, along the back roads...' Humbert shrugged. 'The Gaelle runs between the two towns, thus.' He drew a great, moon-shaped arc between the helmets with the butt of Agnès's hunting spear.

'And where are we?' Agnès asked.

Humbert tapped the spear on the ground, about a third of the way from the bascinet to the helmet. 'About here, north of the Gaelle. We must be close to the border of Compeigne. The Count of Compeigne is King Aloys's son, Prince Lancelin, so we can expect no help until we have crossed the river into Jourdaine.'

'And Château Fontenay?'

'South of Moutâne, about as far beyond Orval as Orval is from Villebénie.'

Guy blew out his cheeks. 'We have food for two more days.' He stood at the edge of the group, gripping the hilt of the sword on his hip. Despite the indignity of being thrown that morning, Guy had more of a swagger about him in his borrowed armour and knight's sword.

'I am more concerned about the men hunting us. I plan to find a way across the Gaelle, and press on south and east into Jourdaine, where the golden flowers of Fontenay are held in as much esteem as the king's own banner.'

'The bridges will be watched.' Brother Paget lowered himself, sighing, onto his shield. He looked pale; his wound was still bleeding into its fresh bandage.

'I rode this way when I came to Villebénie. The Orval road runs close to the river.' Humbert used the spear as a pointer. 'There are towns with bridges here, and here.'

'All with garrisons,' Brother Karlis growled.

'All the more reason to reach Jourdaine. That duchy may be a fief of Galmandie, but the duke's allegiance to King Aloys is more tenuous. Around here,' Humbert drew the butt of the spear across the river, 'the Gaelle divides and merges around islands. A road leads south, and I met a merchant who had come that way from Genilly, and before that Arrenicia. With Salazar's help, this is where we will cross.'

'And then?' Arnaud spoke for the first time. Even without the bascinet, he looked a different man from Adelais's lover of that morning. He now wore Parsifal's sword on his hip, and his torso was bulked out by the jack-of-plates. In the dying light of the day, Adelais noticed that its former owner's blood still crusted the plates below his throat.

'First, let us cross the Gaelle. We may have to fight.' Humbert's brief reply showed a reluctance to say more. Adelais guessed that was in case anyone was captured and forced to talk.

'And why are we so important, Lord Brother?' Arnaud persisted. 'I thought you had offered us your protection to get us out of the city, and now the whole country is raised against us. All this for a few broken heads at a sisterhouse?'

Silence spread around the group. The Guardians and Agnès looked at their feet. Only Arnaud, Guy and Mathilde waited for an answer to the question. Humbert breathed deeply and closed his eyes before he spoke.

'They believe we carry a precious holy relic.'

'The golden idol of the Guardians.' Arnaud made that a statement, not a question.

Humbert inclined his head. 'That is what they think.'

'And do we?'

'We carry no gold.'

'But we do carry a relic,' Arnaud insisted.

'I believe Ischyros will see us safely through. He has a way of defending those who serve Him with a pure heart.' Humbert looked at the sky, and spoke again, cutting off discussion, as Arnaud began to press for an answer. 'Let us rest until dark. We will then ride on for as long as the moon lights our way.'

Adelais wondered what would happen if they did win through. Jourdaine might see itself as a separate duchy, but the duke would be unlikely to defy the king openly. Instinct told her that the king's men would be waiting for them at Château Fontenay, if they did not find them before.

And Humbert hadn't told Arnaud, Guy, and Mathilde about the Hand of Salazar. Adelais guessed why; the Guardians would kill anyone who knew rather than let them be taken by the anakritim, and Brother Humbert had only told her to keep her with them willingly.

Such knowledge might prove costly.

8.2 MALORY

In terms of his personal wellbeing, life was looking up for Malory d'Eivet. After two days' hard riding he had slept well, in a feather bed, at this manor on the borders of Compeigne. Better still, he had broken his fast with bread and a little cold fowl, and so far he felt no signs of throwing it up; he'd vomited the previous day's breakfast over his horse's neck within a league of setting out. The local seneschal, alerted by a galloping messenger, had ridden here to greet them, but since the pursuit was now a secular matter, Malory could allow himself to ease his aching limbs in a corner while the seneschal argued with the provost of Villebénie.

The seneschal was one of those warrior lords who can dominate a room without trying; he had the body and face of a man who had been wielding a sword while Malory was still learning his letters, and Malory was very content to let the provost lead the discussions. They were not going well. With the greatest respect to Chancellor de Remy, the seneschal was saying, His Highness the Count of Compeigne did not maintain a standing army. There were enough soldiers to keep order in the larger towns, though few were mounted. The seneschal's tone implied that unlike the king, the Count did not have the money to keep men sitting around on their fat arses. Of course, their host added, some lords maintained men-at-arms on their estates when they were not away at the wars, but such domains were scattered, and one could scarcely command a lord to search the countryside for thieves running from Villebénie. The seneschal spread his hands. So sorry.

The provost tapped the document on the table between them. 'Othon de Remy writes with the king's authority.'

'I don't care if he speaks with the authority of Salazar himself, I can't create men who don't exist.'

Malory coughed.

'Sorry, Pateras. And can I ask why a priest is so interested in capturing these thieves?'

'They desecrated the temple in the former Guardian citadel, and stole a holy relic.' He was coming to believe that it might *be* a relic. Surely they'd have found an idol in that cart. Either that, or Kakos had blinded them. 'The men are Guardian heretics, and we believe that a witch rides with them, one who can change her form at will to be man or woman.' Malory watched for a reaction, and was satisfied when the seneschal made the sign of the God and sent up a cry to the Blessèd Salazar. His attitude visibly changed.

'What makes you sure they are coming this way?'

'They are escorting another woman into Jourdaine, a lady who is to marry Leandre de Fontenay.'

'Then you must be very sure of your facts to risk de Fontenay's wrath. He is the noblest lord in Jourdaine, after the duke.'

'Quite.' The provost's manner had also softened; he was now explaining, not demanding. 'The lady may be wholly innocent of their evil, and she must not be harmed. So large a party as hers is remembered, and they were ahead of us on the road for our first day. Then nothing, so they must have turned aside.

We also have reports this morning that a patrol did not return from the area where they were last seen.'

The seneschal thought for a moment. 'If they go south, they must cross the Gaelle west of Satine. East of there, they would also have to cross the Nineve, which flows southwards into the Gaelle, or take a very long road to the north.'

'They will go south,' Malory offered from his corner. 'Whether by deceit or not, they wear the badge of de Fontenay, which would not be challenged in the duchy. It is also a more direct route.'

The seneschal inclined his head. 'Then we must concentrate what forces we have at the Gaelle bridges.'

His 'we', not 'you', was most satisfactory.

'And where are those?'

'At Searle, three hours' ride away.' The seneschal set a goblet on the table. 'Gallbridge, perhaps two hours further.' Another goblet. 'Satine, half a day beyond Gallbridge. There are enough men at Searle to place ten at each bridge. That would deny them passage.'

'Any other bridges?' the provost challenged.

'There is a lesser road that runs south towards Genilly, about here.' The seneschal laid his dagger on the table, to the west of the goblets. 'Though it is little-used while the river is full. The road tends to flood, and a wagon would sink into the mud. We had heavy rains in the last moon. The bridge's spans are of wood not stone, and can be washed away, but I believe it still stands after the floods.'

Malory d'Eivet stood, ignoring the stiffness in his legs. 'Is it guarded?'

The seneschal looked at Malory as if the question was particularly stupid. 'In Compeigne, we have no need to guard bridges, nor the men to do it, Pateras.' He said 'Pateras' as if he meant 'child'.

The provost intervened, restoring secular control of the

conversation. 'That is where they will cross. I feel it in my bones. How far is it from here?'

'Two hours' hard ride at most.'

'If we were to ride now, how many men could you spare?'

The seneschal nodded towards the open shutters. In the courtyard outside, his escort stood at their horses' heads, eyeing the provost's men warily; this was Compeigne, where even the king's men rode by permission of the count.

'I have just six men-at-arms with me. Two I will send back with orders for the men at Searle. I will come with you myself, with the remaining four, lest anyone thinks that Chancellor de Remy is assaulting Jourdaine through the county.

'And we have thirty with us.' Malory d'Eivet pushed himself as upright as any warrior. 'Let us see if we can beat them to the bridge.'

Finding the relic, or idol, would delight the king and restore Malory to the good graces of the anakritis-general, but in a way that was only Malory's duty. That was business. The girl, though, was another matter. He would make her pay for every ache, every puke, every humiliation, and his retribution would be an utter pleasure.

8.3 GUY

A damp mist blew up the valley of the Gaelle, half rain, half cloud. It seemed to suck the wet from the flooded water meadows and spray it in their faces; their horses' manes were beaded with moisture. When Humbert finally allowed a rest, in a copse that Karlis had found, Guy almost fell out of the saddle. This was their second attempt to find a bivouac where they could hide from sight. They'd ridden through much of the previous night by moonlight, with their passage marked by barking dogs and shouted challenges as they dropped ever lower into the fertile lands nearer the river. With moonset came cloud, and with the cloud came the rain, until they blundered in a starless darkness that forced a halt.

Their first camp had been at the edge of a wood, where their flint and kindling found little to burn and they lay shivering on saddle blankets, wrapped in their cloaks. Nothing in Guy's apprentice years had taught him the practicalities of wearing armour on campaign, as opposed to merely making it, and his first lesson was that it was cold. The chill of Brother Maarten's hauberk seeped through the padded gambeson beneath into his body, and he felt as if he were trying to sleep in a drift of snow. And this was the hay moon, for the God's sake; it was supposed to be warm. His second lesson had been the importance of fit. He'd also taken Maarten's chausses – his chain-mail leggings – but discarded them at the first rest after loose mail rasped at the sores on his legs. He'd retied the bandages as best he could in the dark, unwilling to ask Adelais. The three women lay huddled together under Agnès de Molinot's fine cloak; lady, servant, and novice together.

They'd abandoned that first camp when the grey light of dawn showed a village nearby, close enough to make discovery probable. Guy had to be roused, though he had no memory of sleeping. They mounted once more, stumbling onwards until Karlis, scouting ahead, found them this patch of woodland on the last, long slope into the valley. They looked out over a broad swathe of fields towards a road that seemed to mark the edge of firm ground; no tilled land lay beyond it, only floodplain pasture that gleamed wetly in the morning light.

Guy groaned as Humbert ordered, 'No fires.' He began to cut himself a rough bed of thin branches.

'Not you, Guy Carelet.' Humbert handed Guy a hunk of stale bread and a piece of cold meat. 'You and I are going to look for the bridge. Leave your hauberk; it bears the marks of recent battle.'

'Now? But sire...' If Guy closed his eyes, he'd fall over with exhaustion.

'Come, boy,' Humbert's voice hardened. 'If you would learn to be a knight, then you must be merciless with your body. Sloth and indolence are the enemies of prowess.'

Guy's rage stung him into wakefulness. He'd ridden through most of the night, with barely any sleep. His backside was sore and his legs chafed raw, and a man three times his age called him idle. He ate furiously, on his feet, glaring at Humbert. The old knight ignored him while he and Brother Karlis lifted the linen roll reverently off the back of Humbert's destrier. Whatever they were carrying that was so important must be in that roll. The Guardians would let no one else touch it.

'You are angry,' Humbert said as they rode from the camp. He didn't sound as if that mattered to him.

'Sloth and indolence are harsh words, messire, and ill deserved.'

'You must learn to obey, without question, whatever your lord commands. Discipline was at the heart of our order; we fought as one, not as a loose company of knights that sought individual glory. Discipline, and a willingness to die in the performance of a great deed of arms, rather than accept the dishonour of retreat.' Humbert paused where a slight rise gave a view of the valley. The Gaelle gleamed intermittently through the trees, but there was no sign of a bridge in the stretches they could see.

'All I said was "now?" messire.' Besides, Guy didn't aspire to being a Guardian. The Order had been banned, on pain of expulsion for any who still professed to be members.

'You questioned my order. But you are young, and have much to learn, so this time I will explain. I chose you to accompany me because it is likely that, through the grace of Ischyros, we will find battle this day. Our success, and our lives, will depend on the swords of Brother Karlis and Brother Paget. Therefore, I let them rest, and appointed l'Armurier to watch the camp. Furthermore, you are now armed as a squire; a knight with his squire will attract little attention.'

They had reached the road, which was empty at this early hour. Humbert stood in his stirrups, and looked up and down the valley.

'Southeast, I think.' He turned his horse.

'Why, messire, do you say we might find battle "through the grace of Ischyros"? Should we not seek to avoid it?'

'In many ways, boy, the life of a man-at-arms is akin to the life of a holy man. A chivalrous knight will eschew ease and bodily comforts as a good cleric mortifies his flesh to strengthen his soul. Discipline is as much denial as it is striving for some great end.' Humbert caught sight of Guy's face and laughed. 'Did you really think the golden spurs would come easily, boy? Just because you now wear a knight's sword on your hip? The honour of knighthood only comes through prowess, and prowess comes through discipline.'

'But to welcome battle?'

'Some holy men and women are called to martyrdom. They do not seek it, but neither do they flinch from their path, and so they achieve grace in the sight of Ischyros. In the same way, if a knight is blessed with the opportunity of a great deed of arms in a noble cause, he should thank Ischyros that he has been given the chance to win lasting honour.'

Guy shifted in the saddle, uncomfortable with Humbert's words. If they saw a troop of the king's men, the last thing he'd want to do was thank Ischyros.

They rode in silence until Guy summoned the courage to challenge the ageing Guardian.

'Do you think the Lady Agnès seeks martyrdom? Or Mathilde?' Guy certainly didn't.

Humbert laughed. 'Of course not! No true knight would harm a lady.'

'And that which you protect, this relic of which you will not speak. Would that be best served by our deaths?'

'Our deaths may be demanded by the God at any time. Perhaps your father's death served the God.'

'*What?*'

'Do you remember the anakritim's plans? To torture you to make him speak? He had already endured more than can be expected of any man, even though he was not of the third degree, but I do not think any man could watch his son suffer agony if he had the power to end it.'

'But we rescued him!'

'And if you had not succeeded, either Parsifal or Maarten would have given him peace to spare him that test.'

'You *ordered* them to kill my father?' Guy was incredulous. If they had not been mounted, he might have struck the Guardian. 'They would have killed him?'

'Aye, and died willingly in the attempt, if necessary.'

Guy felt his control slip. 'What knowledge can be worth murder, for Tanguy's fucking sake!'

'You are tired. I shall forgive you the blasphemy. Think, boy! How much would your life be worth if you knew what the anakritim so desperately want to know? I tell you only so you know that if you follow the path towards knighthood, I will expect absolute obedience. Absolute, *unquestioning* obedience, even if it means sacrificing your own life, or a brother's. Or going without rest.'

'But he was my father!'

'You may as well know,' Humbert sighed. 'I would rather you heard it from me. One brother had already died trying to end his life. We had thought your father dead, you see. When we learned through you and Parsifal that he was alive and was to be moved, there was no time for plans. We only knew that he could not be left alive and in captivity. The watcher at the gates of the Black Tower that morning did what he thought was right and attempted to take your father's life. He died trying. I did not order that, though I honour his courage. But yes, I did authorise Parsifal and Maarten to end your father's life if he could not be saved.'

Guy remembered how Parsifal would not meet his eye. Parsifal the hero. Parsifal who would have carried out the order to kill his father.

'You're no better than the anakritim! They torture, and you murder.'

Humbert stayed infuriatingly calm, as if Guy were merely an infant in a tantrum.

'I think,' he said, 'that if one of the brothers had had to take his life, your father would have accepted the blow willingly, with grace. He lived by the same code. Obedience unto death.'

'*Fuck* your code. I want no part of it.'

Humbert was silent for several strides of their horses, watching the road ahead. The first traveller of the morning, a cleric in the brown habit of a wandering preacher, had appeared around a bend.

'If the anakritim capture you, boy,' Humbert spoke quietly, his eyes on the cleric, 'it won't matter which code you live by. You'll scream and die like everyone else. Hola, brother!' Humbert reined in. 'We seek the road to Genilly.'

The man leaned on his stave, looking up at them. His eyes lingered on Guy, who wanted to hit something. Shout. Scream. Anything but exchange pleasantries with a passing cleric, who now turned his attention to Humbert.

'That is an interesting blazon, sir knight. Red with three golden flowers. And all the countryside is searching for thieves and murderers wearing the arms of de Fontenay. If you plan to rob me, I have nothing but my robe and staff.' He spread his hands wide to emphasise his point.

Guy's hand went to his sword, ready to unleash his fury, but Humbert merely smiled and leaned forwards in the saddle. 'If you can read my face as well as you read heraldry, sir cleric, then you will know I mean you no harm. I too am a man of Ischyros, although on this journey my order permits me to wear the blazon of Fontenay. Now, will you show us the way?'

The cleric stared hard at Humbert, and began to chant. It seemed to be a test.

'If Ischyros is my light, I need fear no darkness. If Ischyros is the citadel of my soul, of whom shall I be afraid?'

Humbert responded immediately, smiling in recognition.

'When foes and adversaries assail me, uttering falsehoods against me, they shall stumble and fall!'

A grin spread across the cleric's face. 'Guardian?'

'There are no Guardians now, brother. Perhaps you might want to consider a later verse from the same chant: "Teach me Thy path, sweet God, let it be plain before me amongst mine enemies. Let not my foes seize me, for they make false witness against me, and they breathe out violence."'

The cleric reached up to clasp Humbert's hand. 'Go with Ischyros, Guardian. Travel this road to a crossroads half a league upriver. Take the road to the south. The bridge lies a league beyond, but the way is heavy.' The man lifted his sandalled foot to show the mud caking his legs.

'And is the bridge guarded?'

'Not when I crossed, at dawn.'

'Ischyros bless you, Brother. The faith has too few men who truly serve Him, and today you are His messenger.'

'*Amín.* There are many devout men who know that a great evil was done to your order.' The cleric raised his fingers in the sign of benediction, and showed no surprise when Humbert wheeled his horse to ride back the way they had come. Guy followed, fists clenched in his reins, glaring at Humbert's back the same murderous way he had once glared at Pateras Malory.

'You trust him? An unknown cleric?' Guy was incredulous enough to speak, almost spitting the words at Humbert's back.

'Not all clerics are anakritim. We each saw the truth in the other, and he did not lie. We must move now, before the king's men reach that bridge.'

8.4 ADELAIS

Adelais may have slept a little in the copse, on a brushwood mat that Arnaud had cut to keep her clear of the wet, but she was soon awake and shaking with cold. She rose and walked beyond the camp, hugging her herigaut close to her body, knowing that Arnaud would follow. She was worried for him; he was like a stone statue in a temple that might topple and shatter at any moment. Several hundred paces from the camp she waited for him, looking out through dripping leaves at a vast, lush valley. The air was laced with smells of leaf mould and mushrooms, almost autumnal in the wet.

The last time they'd been alone together she'd been naked, but it might have been a different woman who'd felt the heat of his body and, deep in her belly, a different, softening warmth that was also a hunger. A day and a night before, she'd flexed her shoulders to push her breasts more closely against his chest; now her gambeson met his jack-of-plates and she felt nothing but the pressure of his arms. The only skin she could touch was his face, and his three-day beard was rough as a boar's hide under her fingers. But his lips were soft, and it was good to be held.

To be held, and to hold, as Arnaud's shoulders shook and he finally began to weep, heaving great sobs into her neck. With the layers of armour between them all she could do was to stroke the back of his head and make gentle shushing sounds as she might to a child. Perhaps this was how lasting unions were made – forged in ecstasy and hardened in sorrow, when a proud man allows a woman to be the stronger partner.

When he was quiet she dropped her hand to the top of his leg, to find a place beneath the skirts of his jack-of-plates where she might feel his warmth. Hesitantly, his hand mirrored hers, tightening as he crushed her to him. For a moment the memory of their ploughing was like the scent of a rose in a midden; it had flowered, had been real, out there beyond the shit. Would flower again. But not on a dripping morning when they were both bone-cold, leaden with exhaustion, and reeling with memories too brutal to comprehend.

'He was always the strong one.' Arnaud had to swallow before he could say more. 'Better than everyone else at whatever he did. Sword or anvil. In the saddle or on his knees.'

'You're a good man, too.'

'It's like the God has taken away one of my legs and I don't know how to stand up any more.'

'Then lean on me, my love.'

That earned her another squeeze, and a brush of his stubble against her cheek.

'He kept his faith. After all they did to his order, he kept his faith. I lost mine when the God took my family.'

'Then his God will have welcomed him home.'

He breathed so deeply it was almost another sob. 'I need you, Adelais.'

This was a time when they needed a place alone, not to couple but to comfort; to feel each other's warmth, skin to nurturing skin.

'They're coming back.' Arnaud nodded over her shoulder.

His voice was thick and he had to clear his throat. Adelais turned and recognised Guy and Humbert's horses on the distant road. They let each other go, though their hands touched, squeezed, and affirmed.

Humbert and Guy did not dismount.

'There is a bridge, two leagues away, and it is unguarded.' Despite his years, Humbert showed little sign of tiredness. 'We ride now, all together. Brother Karlis, take the lead. No rearguard.'

Adelais found it threatening to be on the open road, in plain sight. They rode in the trot-walk-trot pace that spared the horses but ate the leagues, forcing their way past merchants' and farmers' wagons on the way. Adelais kept looking over her shoulder, searching the road behind them for signs of pursuit.

Soon after turning south at a crossroads, the road disintegrated into a morass of mud, and their pace slowed to an unsteady walk. Some attempt had been made to create a causeway with rubble trodden into the mud, but recent rains had washed much of this away. In some places the trail was lifted on a dyke above the surrounding floodplains, in others it could be seen only by the tracks of other travellers, or by poles marking the route through reed beds to firmer ground.

They were half a league into the wetlands when Adelais saw the lances waving over the reeds behind them. At first, she thought they were bare trees, all bunched together like a thicket, but then the path straightened and she saw the men-at-arms beneath. She was ashamed of her squeal of alarm. She told herself it was the shock of seeing the priest on the grey horse at their head.

When she was a child, she'd had nightmares after seeing wall paintings of the fiends of Kakos devouring sinners in an Ischyrian temple. The worst dreams were when she was running away from Kakos but was so mired in mud that she struggled to lift one foot in front of the other, and all the time this obscene evil was coming after her, gross and unstoppable and ever closer. She'd scream as his claws gripped her shoulder, and she'd wake into a moment of utter terror until the shape in the darkness spoke soothing words in her grandmother's voice. *Hush, hush, mynn litla Sif.* No loving hand would wake her now. They forced their horses forwards, but the lances were catching up. Then the lances, too, hit the thickest mud and gained no more.

Brother Paget's destrier was the first to go lame. It slipped in some unseen hole beneath the mire, stumbled, and came up limping on a foreleg. Paget began to fall behind, shouting at them to go on, not to wait for him, while he switched to his riding horse. Brother Karlis stayed with him to help him remount, their boots slithering and sucking at the mud.

Finally, the ground began to rise, almost imperceptibly. As they approached the bridge the causeway was better made, even bounded with baulks of timber. From this slight elevation Adelais looked back again. The spears were perhaps a thousand paces behind.

The bridge was formed of wooden spans between pairs of stone pillars that lifted the roadway far enough above the water to allow barges to pass underneath, and it was narrow, with barely the width for a single cart to pass; little balconies had been built out over the water at the pillars to allow a traveller on foot to step out of the way. On the far side it dropped to a small island that divided the river's flow; a further, single-span bridge reached from the island to the next shore.

Humbert and Adelais waited on the central span for Paget and Karlis to catch up. Paget was hunched in his saddle, his shield arm trailing and the bandage bloody beneath his armpit. He paused with them, looked at the further bridge, and dismounted.

'I shall go no further. Here is where I make my stand. Shall I hold them while you wreck that next bridge, Lord Brother?'

'I like this plan, Brother Paget.' Karlis also dismounted. 'You'll need some help.'

Paget clasped his hand. 'I could wish for no better company.'

They both sounded cheerful, as if they were about to enter a friendly joust with blunted weapons.

'This is a noble deed, Brothers.' Humbert stared at them.

'By Ischyros's grace, we will have a mighty passage of arms.' Paget turned to stroke his lame destrier's neck, his face now tight with emotion. 'Old friend, we have seen much together, but I have one last service to ask of you.'

He positioned his horse carefully across the road at the first stone support where the incline levelled, and tore a strip off his surcoat to cover the beast's eyes. His own eyes were full as he took a war hammer from Karlis and swung the heavy spike hard into his horse's forehead. It fell as if some supporting cord had been cut, and rolled on its side, its legs twitching. Paget bent to open an artery in its neck with his dagger, and stood clear of the gushing blood.

'Farewell, old friend.'

Adelais had never seen a knight weep before.

'Brothers, it has been an honour to serve with you.' Humbert was also visibly moved.

'Go swiftly, Lord Brother.' Karlis was readying his own horse, whispering softly into its ear to calm it amidst the smell of blood. 'The God is blessing us with the chance to die as Lions. Make best use of the time we buy for you.'

Adelais looked over her shoulder as Humbert led her away. The king's men were now two or three bowshots away, still stumbling in the mud.

'Why?' She was just realising the enormity of what had

happened. If they succeeded in destroying the bridge, there could be no escape for Paget and Karlis.

'The horses block the road, like a parapet, so the enemy can only attack on foot. The blood will make the approaches slick.'

'But *destriers*?' Such horses were of immense value.

'The destrier is a knight's true companion. It is a bond beyond love.' Humbert's face was stricken, and she realised he too was weeping. 'Four friends will now die together. Let us profit from their sacrifice.'

They gathered on the far shore while Arnaud and Guy set to with axes on the supporting beams, one each side, and Humbert formed the horses into a team ready to drag the weakened timbers from their bases. Guy was attacking the timbers with unsustainable violence, as if murdering the bridge; his blows were ill-aimed but sank deep, sending chips spinning through the air. Adelais, Agnès, and Mathilde were compelled to watch; there were only two axes. The two Guardians were silhouetted against the sky, and seemed to be fitting a cloth to the end of a lance. They tied the lance to the bridge's parapet, and the cloth became a Guardian banner: a rearing, clawing, red lion on a white and black field. The column of soldiers, at least twenty strong, was now a single bowshot beyond them. Adelais felt useless; a spectator when she should be helping.

'To Kakos with this.' Agnès pulled her crossbow from its leather case and strapped the belt around her.

Humbert had seen. 'Please don't, Lady Agnès.'

'But I've got to do something to help.'

'Until now, you could be an innocent victim of abducting Guardians. As soon as you are seen to fire that weapon, you will be as guilty as the rest of us. I cannot allow that. Nor would Leandre de Fontenay.'

'But I could use it.' Adelais held out her hand. 'Please?'

Agnès swore under her breath before she unbuckled the belt.

'Adelais, don't!' Arnaud stood waist-deep in water, axe in hand, his eyes pleading. At his shoulder, a notch of paler wood showed in the black timbers of the bridge support.

'That is what you can do,' Adelais nodded at the bridge as she strapped the belt around her, 'and this is what I can do.' She took the crossbow from Agnès.

'Foot in stirrup.' Agnès showed her the readying position. 'Spanning lever onto those two lugs, then hooked onto the cord. Good. Now heave until it clicks.'

It took a lot more effort than Adelais expected.

'Engage the bolt, like this. Point and shoot. Told you it was easy. Take the spear as well, in case you don't have time to reload.' Agnès squeezed Adelais's arm, real concern in her eyes. 'Don't get stuck over there, will you?'

Adelais's mouth was dry as she crossed the island, trailing the spear in one hand and the spanned crossbow in the other. An air of unreality settled on her, like a fever. Silly, inconsequential thoughts filled her mind. *I should have taken a swig of water from a skin. Is Adeifi Elodie still sitting at the East Gate?*

The brothers turned at the sound of her footsteps on the bridge's wooden roadbed.

'May I stand with you, Brothers, beneath that illustrious banner?'

'You are welcome, Mistress Adelais.' Karlis grinned up at the flag. 'I've been carrying that secretly for five years. Today is a good day for it to fly again. Do you know the first rule of our order?'

Adelais shook her head.

'No brother may leave the field of battle while a lion banner flies. There is no surrender, no retreat. Please do not think you are bound by such an oath. You do not need to die today.'

Brother Karlis stared at her with a sad intensity, and she knew he would have to kill her rather than let her be taken. She took a deep breath, and showed that she understood.

'If things go badly for us, Brothers, you would do me a great service if I died here rather than in the hands of the anakritim.'

At that, Brother Paget lifted his sword to his face in salute. 'It is an honour to fight alongside you, Mistress Adelais.' He stood lopsided, hunched into his wound.

They did not have long to wait. The men who had come to kill them halted where the firmer ground was broader and the front ranks could spread out, five horsemen wide. The rear ranks waited in twos, stretching way back along the road. *So many.* Sheets of blood flowed down the incline towards them from the carcasses of the horses. From behind Adelais came the steady drumbeat of axes on wood. How long would it take?

Pateras Malory was in front of all of them, riding backwards and forwards, apparently making some kind of speech, although the words were indistinct. When he caught sight of Adelais his voice rose to an audible scream.

'It's her! The yellow-haired witch! Five gold crowns to the man who brings her to me alive!'

'He's awfully cross, isn't he?' Brother Paget seemed more amused than concerned.

'I don't think he likes you, mistress.' Karlis began to chuckle.

Adelais didn't intend to kill. Loosing the crossbow at Pateras Malory was an act of defiance, like an obscene gesture. For a moment the bolt seemed to hang in the air, shrinking, before it dropped. *By the gods, what have I done?*

Her line was good, but she'd underestimated the drop. As Malory pirouetted in front of his troops, the bolt struck his grey in the rump and the beast leapt, squealing, into the air. The anakritis was still in the saddle after that first buck. And the second. By the third he was sprawling in the mud at the edge of the road, and a ripple of laughter spread through the king's men.

Karlis clapped Adelais on the back, hard enough to hurt even through her gambeson.

'Perfect shot!'

'I didn't mean to wound the horse...'

'It doesn't matter what you intended. You've shown them we have a crossbow, so they'll come cautiously. You haven't killed a priest, which would make them angry, you've just made him look a fool.'

She seemed to have a talent for that. Adelais hid her smile by bending to span the crossbow. Foot into stirrup. Engage lever, lugs, and cord. Heave. She was glad of the opportunity to practise before the fight began.

In front of them a richly dressed man-at-arms dismounted, handed his reins to the man beside him, and walked slowly up the slope towards them. He wore light, padded armour only, plus a bascinet and aventail, and he held his hands away from the weapons on his hips. He picked his way fastidiously between the streams of blood as if unwilling to dirty the golden spurs of knighthood on his boots.

'Don't shoot him, lass.' Karlis laid his hand on her wrist. 'He's coming to talk.'

It hadn't occurred to Adelais to shoot him.

The knight stopped near the dead horses' hooves.

'Ranier de Searle, Seneschal of Western Compeigne.'

'Brother Paget FitzMaurice of the Knights Guardian.'

'And Brother Karlis Forcalquier.'

The seneschal did not look at Adelais, and she did not offer an introduction.

'Brothers, there can be only one end to this.'

Paget and Karlis merely smiled.

'In Compeigne,' the seneschal continued, 'the king's men operate by my permission. If you surrender now, I will take you into my custody. The priest and provost can go home empty handed. But you appreciate I cannot allow you time to consider.' He lifted his chin towards the further bridge and the sound of axes *thunk*ing into wood.

Paget made a slight bow. 'You are too kind, but we must decline.'

A loud splash and a cheer came from behind them. Adelais turned to see a heavy timber floating downstream.

'So be it. May Ischyros have mercy on you.' The seneschal turned, slid slightly in the blood slicking the road, and retraced his steps with his arms spread wide for balance. When he was beyond hearing, Karlis began issuing orders.

'Brother Paget, take the left. Adelais, stand beyond him, over there.' He pointed to the small balcony over the water. 'Keep behind the swing of our swords, and see if you can keep them away from Brother Paget's wounded arm. How many bolts do you have?'

'Six more.' Adelais wedged herself in place, watching down the road. She would be slightly behind the Guardians but able to fire across their front.

'Wait until they are close. From there you may be able to shoot towards their sword arms. If they are well shielded, shoot for their legs. See if you can bring one down in front of the horses. After you shoot, they will try to rush us. Stay calm, just focus on reloading.' Karlis laid a lance across the body of a horse.

Adelais wedged herself into the angle of the balcony, and rested the spear against the rail. Below her, the river flowed fast enough for the stone support to leave a wake, like a boat. She wondered if this was her dying-day. Yrsa would say that their fates are already woven, so the only choice is to face what comes with courage.

Another timber shot out from the side channel, spinning away downstream.

A group of about a dozen soldiers had been ordered to dismount and were preparing. It all seemed so ridiculously calm; they were tightening harness and testing the swing of their sword arms as if they were preparing for a parade.

An image came to her of Yrsa working galdrar-magic, seated with her knees spread man-wide, her shoulders back, strong, as she lifted her staff and let its butt fall onto the wooden floor, beating the rhythm to her song. Adelais looked down at the crossbow, lying in her arms like the *tiwaz* rune.

Tiwaz, the rune of honourable victory. The rune of the god Týr who sacrificed his own hand to bind the great wolf Fenrir. Before the old gods were banned, Vriesian warriors had carved *tiwaz* into their sword hilts for protection. She'd promised Yrsa that she wouldn't use rune song until she had the lore to wield it well, but she'd already broken that promise. And if ever they needed rune song it was now, on what might be her dying-day. Adelais missed Yrsa's staff that she'd had to abandon in the fire temple; would a hunting spear do as well? She picked it up, stood tall, and began to thump its butt into the boards of the bridge.

'*Týr er einhendr áss...*'

Below them, the soldiers drew their swords and were formed into ranks of three, enough to fill the width of the track. It still might have been a practice. They came with their shields held in the centre of their bodies so that their rims almost met their neighbours', and held high so that just their helmeted eyes peered over the tops.

Adelais stood taller and punched her defiance into the decking as she sang.

'*Ok ulfs leifar...*'

Paget looked at her.

'Vriesian?'

'It's an old song my grandmother taught me.'

He nodded, made the sign of Ischyros, pulled his great helm

over his head, and began his own chant. Karlis joined in. 'Ischyros be merciful and shine upon us...'

Another drumbeat began as the soldiers' boots left bare soil and tramped onto the bridge. It was time to put down the spear.

'*Ok hofa hilmir...*' Had she missed some words? Yrsa would repeat the chants endlessly when she was working *seidhr*. Adelais swallowed. *Skit*, her mouth was dry.

'... and lift His hand to bless us...' The Guardians' voices sounded muffled and a little hollow inside their helmets.

A soldier in the front rank slipped on the blood and fell onto all fours with his weight on his shield, his body now exposed. He stared at Adelais, expecting the shot.

She couldn't do it. She could not look a man in the eye and take his life. He scrambled to his feet and the moment was lost.

'Steady, girl. Nice and calm.' Karlis's voice.

'... that the way of truth may be known among all nations.'

The men were almost upon them. Karlis stepped back from the horses' carcasses, holding the lance, and ran forwards, thrusting it between the shields.

Adelais fired into their legs. She missed the man she'd been aiming at, but the soldier behind went down with a bolt through his calf. His fall sent another man tumbling.

'Don't watch! Reload!' Karlis again.

'*Týr er einhendr áss...*' Foot in stirrup, lever on lugs, hooks on cord. '*Ok ulfs leifar...*' Heave. *By Thor, it was hard.*

'*Ok hofa hilmir...*' Her hands were shaking so much she couldn't fit the bolt into the groove. *Breathe!*

'*Týr er einhendr áss...*' *Done.* Now she could look up.

Two men were climbing the barrier of horses in front of Paget; they'd seen he was already wounded. Their shields were towards him, exposing their sides. The nearest one had already climbed onto the horse's flank and raised his sword to cut downwards.

Her bolt buried itself under his armpit and he fell back. She didn't hear him shout.

'*Ok ulfs leifar...*' Stirrup. Lever. *The fjakkinn lever!* She'd dropped it. Again. Heave. Fumble for bolt. Ignore the sounds. Look up.

Paget was on his knees, head bowed. Another soldier climbed onto the belly of the horse, reversing his sword for a two-handed downwards killing stroke, and Adelais shot from her hip. The bolt lifted the man and dropped him on his backside in the roadway. He raised a hand to the flights protruding from his chest, frowned, and toppled sideways.

Stirrup. Lever. Heave. Engage bolt. Look up.

And there was no near target. Four men lay dead in front of them. Three more were wounded and were being helped down the road, one with his sword arm awkwardly lifted, clasping his helmet, exposing a bloody mess around the copper flights under his arm.

'We did it!' Adelais felt as if she'd drunk a whole flask of wine. What was it that made *this* killing acceptable? Because they'd been trying to kill her? Because she'd prayed to the old gods? Because she'd saved Paget's life?

'That was just the beginning, girl.' Karlis pulled off his great helm and sat heavily on his dead horse's side. The chain-mail down his right forearm hung in tatters, and blood was dripping from his fingers. 'By the wounds of Salazar, I am getting too old for this!'

'Shall I bind your wound?'

'See to Brother Paget first.'

The mail of Paget's hauberk showed the bright new metal of a blow, and he was hunched over, breathing shallowly. When Adelais eased his great helm from his head, his eyes were wide and staring. He took shallow, panting breaths in between words.

'Axe. Think. It. Broke. Ribs.' He tried to stand the way a drunkard would try, arm flailing until he grabbed her shoulder to steady himself. 'Must. Show. Still here.' He squeezed her shoulder. 'Good girl.'

'Help me lift them, mistress.' Karlis pointed at the bodies. 'We can use them to build our barrier.'

Adelais found it hard to swallow. As she helped Karlis heap the dead soldiers onto the impromptu barricade, her thirst was so great that her mouth might have been carved from stone. Thirty paces behind her there were skins of water, and she glanced back, wondering if there was time to fetch one. On the bank, Humbert had harnessed four horses to a single line and was dragging at a bridge support.

But another group of soldiers was already forming in the roadway below. No time for water.

Behind her, there was a loud crack of splitting timbers as a support gave way. When she glanced over her shoulder, the downstream side of the bridge had sagged. Two more timbers fell from its surface into the water. Humbert was moving the team to the other side.

'Time for you to go, Adelais.' Karlis might have been telling a child it was time for bed.

'Time for us all to go.'

'The banner still flies.'

'Then bring it!'

'They will rush us if we leave. They wouldn't get horses across now, but they might still repair it and be after us. You go. Tell the lord brother to finish the job. Tell him we did not shame our brethren. By the time they cross this earthly bridge, two Lions will have crossed another, together.'

Karlis pulled his arm from the straps of his shield, and nudged her away. She stood, undecided, until Paget put his sword arm around her, and hugged. 'Brave. Girl. Go. Take spear. Leave crossbow.'

She wept as she left them, filled with a sense of betrayal.

The sounds of battle started again as Adelais sidestepped

along the bridge's remaining parapet. She had to hurl the spear ahead of her. Below her, taut, dripping ropes stretched to the horse team, where Humbert watched her over his shoulder. He spurred his horses forwards as Arnaud grasped her hand, pulling her to the shore. She was still scrambling for a foothold when the splitting timbers screamed behind her, louder than the fight on the bridge.

Adelais was expecting Arnaud to hug her when they found firm ground. Instead, he seized her by the shoulders and shook her, hard.

'You little fool!'

Hurt, she broke away, turning her back on him. Further down the bank, Humbert sat astride his destrier, offering her the reins of her gelding, and she crossed to him.

'Well done, girl.' He spoke quietly, his praise dropping from a weight of sadness. 'Our lioness has claws.'

Adelais mounted and stayed with him on the bank while the others rode on, away from the river. They sat quietly, side by side, with streaming faces turned towards the wrecked bridge, honouring the brothers. At first, both Guardians fought shoulder to shoulder behind their barricade, though Paget sagged, visibly wounded. By the time Humbert had drawn his sword, only Karlis was on his feet. As Karlis fell, Humbert raised his sword to his face in salute, only lowering it when the melee of blows over Karlis's body quietened and the seneschal himself climbed over the barrier. He stood with his fists on his hips, staring at them. Behind him, the silhouette of Pateras Malory wrenched at the lance holding the Guardian flag.

Only when Malory had thrown the banner to the ground did Humbert wheel his horse to leave.

8.5 MALORY

It was almost twilight when the provost's men crossed the river at Searle, the nearest bridge over the Gaelle to the fight, and by then Malory d'Eivet was heartily sick of the bickering.

The provost, with seven dead men, and another four who would be lucky to fight again, had rounded on the seneschal for not joining the battle at the bridge. The seneschal had shrugged, saying it wasn't his battle; did they really expect him to send his lightly armed men against fully armed Guardians, just because Chancellor de Remy requested his cooperation? What's more, the Guardians had flown the lion banner. On a hundred battlefields that banner had flown for no surrender, no retreat. Win or die. Hadn't the provost heard the whispered awe from the men he sent up the road? *The lion banner.*

Then there'd been the whole bloody mess to clear up. More time lost while the seneschal's men scoured the countryside for a cart they could requisition for the wounded. Eight graves to be dug at some dingy village temple for seven provost's men and one Guardian, for the only good thing to come out of the day was that one of the Guardians lived. Malory had pulled off the man's great helm out of curiosity, wanting to see the face of someone who'd caused such trouble. The helm had been creased by an axe whose owner was now telling the story to anyone who would listen, while conveniently forgetting to mention that his opponent was already twice wounded.

Apart from the blood crusted around the Guardian's nose and one ear, he looked surprisingly peaceful. Malory had taken out his silver box of sacred ash and, in a show of compassion, started to give him the Offices of the Dead. There'd been a faint breath on the back of his fingers as he went to press the print of pardon into his forehead. Now the Guardian lay in the bottom of the cart with the rest of the wounded, and all the men had been told to keep him alive so he could be questioned.

Worst of all, Malory had had to leave his beloved grey to heal at a manor on the road. They'd managed to pull the bolt out of its rump, at the cost of a kick that broke another man's leg. The horse had even bitten Malory, sinking its teeth into his shoulder when Malory had tried to hold its head and soothe it. Now Malory rode a dead trooper's horse, an evil-eyed beast that threatened to dump him if he lost concentration.

The last thing Malory wanted to hear, as the dejected column rode over the Gaelle into Searle, was that the anakritis-general awaited him at the keep.

Malory supposed it was not too surprising. Searle, after all, lay on Pateras Ghislain's planned route from Villebénie to Orval, and thence to Moutâne. He guessed that news of the morning's skirmish would have preceded them, so it would not be an easy meeting. Malory invited both the seneschal and the provost to join him. It had, after all, been an entirely secular operation in which Malory was merely an observer.

The seneschal declined.

'I am a chivalrous man, Pateras. I heard what the anakritim did to the Guardians and it was not worthy of chivalry. This man fought bravely, and I want no part of what the Angel of Death will do to him now. It will not be honourable.'

It took a while for Ghislain Barthram to accept that the county of Compeigne would not be assisting the pursuit south of the Gaelle. The provost relayed the seneschal's reasoning that the fugitives would now have a day's lead, and the border with Jourdaine was less than a day's ride south. The Duke of Jourdaine would be understandably hostile to armed incursions into his duchy, as the seneschal was sure the anakritis-general was about to discover. And northern Jourdaine had a lot of empty country for the Guardians to hide in. Furthermore, Humbert Blanc wore the blazon of de Fontenay, whose family had been seneschals of Jourdaine for generations. Jourdainian lords would instinctively side with that badge against any Compeignois, or even royal troops.

The provost did not relay the seneschal's distaste for torture. Ghislain Barthram listened to his report in silence, warming his hands at the fire that had been set for him in the keep's solar against the unseasonal damp. The blaze was modest enough to be contained within an iron fire basket, though it lay within a fireplace large enough to roast an ox.

Or a Guardian.

'Agnès de Molinot is still with them, is she not?'

'Assuredly, Pateras,' the provost answered. 'She was seen from the bridge.'

'Then they must, eventually, come to Château Fontenay. We will ensure that they are appropriately received. But first, you say one of the Guardians survives.'

'He was knocked senseless in the fighting,' the provost answered, 'but has since recovered his wits.'

Barthram picked up an iron poker and prodded the burning wood. 'Provost, do you have two men who can help us? Perhaps those with a sense of grievance after today?'

'I am sure they can be found, Pateras.' The provost rose to his feet. 'But the man fought well. Surely a swift execution would be more appropriate?'

'Remember this man is a heretic and despoiler of temples. We must know if the idol or relic they stole is still with them, and, if not, where on the route they have hidden it. Besides, an anakritis may not order an execution. Nor may you, in Compeigne. That power lies with the secular authorities. So find me those men, and leave us if you do not have the stomach for it. We will need more firewood, rope, and a board the size of a man. That is all.'

Malory closed his eyes as the provost left. He hated this part of his role – the screaming before pardon could be given.

'Tomorrow I shall go to Moutâne and thence to Château Fontenay,' Barthram said. He was very calm; the imminent torture was as much a part of his life as the dawn office. 'From there I shall travel to Daija. It is time I briefed the high priest on events.' Which was probably Pateras Ghislain's way of saying his reputation with the king was declining, and he needed to rebuild his standing with the higher echelons of the faith. 'When you have finished here, you and the provost will continue the pursuit.'

'And if I capture them, Pateras? Do I take them to the king in Villebénie or to you in Daija?' From Moutâne, the distances would be about equal.

'To me. Extracting truth from Humbert Blanc will require particular skills.'

Malory sipped wine and waited, feeling nauseated at the thought of what was to come.

Two men brought the basic paraphernalia of torture: a board that they laid upon a bench, ropes to strap a man to it so that his feet could be held in the fire, and a bucket of water with which to revive him. They left and returned with the prisoner between them, supporting him under both arms.

Malory knew at once that Brother Paget was of the Guardians' inner circle, that third degree that was so hard to break. He had been stripped to his loin cloth and shirt, which was brown with blood down the shield arm, yet even in that degradation there was a serenity about him; not so much an absence of fear but the palpable strength to conquer it. He was already white-faced with pain and taking short, panting breaths from a rib-crushing blow to the side, but he returned Barthram's stare without flinching.

This, too, was part of Pateras Ghislain's method for breaking down a prisoner – to watch and drink wine while the victim quaked in the presence of the instruments that would cause such pain. Many would collapse at this point. They'd beg, they'd blubber, they'd say anything and promise anything to avoid the coming agony. But Paget FitzMaurice broke the leaden silence by speaking calmly, as if he was in control.

'So, Anakritis, there is a dance we must make together.' The Guardian's voice was breathless from his wound, but clear. He sounded more tired than afraid. 'You must inflict hurt, and I must endure it until I die, but I do so willingly because when all the pain is done, I will cross the bridge of judgement into the arms of Ischyros.' He sat down on the board and swung his legs up onto it, though he grimaced and touched his side as he lay back. There was just the slightest shake to his hands as he composed them on his chest in an attitude of prayer. 'Now, shall we begin?'

CHAPTER 9

9.1 ADELAIS

In the days after the fight, Humbert withdrew into himself; to Adelais he seemed less vigorous, heavy with regret, and even older. 'A lion banner still flew, and I could not go to them,' he'd said, revealing distress that went to the core of his being. No reasoning of hers could talk him out of it. The group travelled quietly, nursing their own thoughts as though they rode through some vast temple. Guy trailed behind, sullen and uncommunicative, until even Arnaud gave up and left him to his own gloom. Arnaud and Adelais rode side by side, when the path would allow. His back grew a little straighter with each day, but Agnès was the first to recover when her horse lifted its tail and farted, spectacularly. Agnès's rich laughter seemed mildly shocking at first, but it broke the ice.

On the fifth day from the bridges, Humbert brought them to a halt at the edge of a stand of trees. He bade them dismount and rest while he watched for signs of movement in a fortified manor two fields away. He sat still, the way a cat might hide unmoving beneath a bush, waiting for the right moment to strike. When he'd been there long enough for the rest of them to eat a frugal meal, Adelais went to squat beside him. Before the fight at the bridges she would not have dared to intrude, but now he seemed to welcome her presence more than he did the others'. Perhaps it was because she shared the same sense of dereliction of duty in leaving Paget and Karlis to their fate, or maybe it was simply that she had fought beside them. She handed him the last of a pheasant she'd brought down with her sling the day before; scavenging enough for five was proving hard without the crossbow.

She nodded at the manor. 'Why the interest, messire?'

It was a modest place, as lords' dwellings went. Stone-built with a single tower, it was too small to be called a castle, though a curtain wall enclosed barns and outbuildings. A line of peasants worked their way along field strips, stabbing at weeds. A small village lay some distance beyond the manor, and the smoke of Orval smudged the horizon to the north.

'I know the family. We need supplies, we need rest, and I would send word to Leandre de Fontenay.'

A bell tolled for the afternoon office from the temple of the distant village, and the peasants shouldered their hoes.

'So why do we wait?'

The peasants trudged back towards the village with the weary, round-shouldered air of people who spent their lives toiling in the fields. None of them went to the manor.

'The family are known to have links to the Guardians, and might be watched. There could be a troop of soldiers within that curtain wall, and we would not know about them until we were within the gates.'

'Then let me ride on alone and see. What is the lord's name?'

Humbert considered for a moment, and nodded. 'Very well. Ask for Thebault Cheyne or his son Dreux.'

Adelais rose to her feet. 'Cheyne? I saw the Guardian Rahoul Cheyne proclaim his innocence in front of the fire temple of Villebénie.'

'Rahoul was Thebault Cheyne's brother. I do not think they will betray us.'

Adelais touched Arnaud briefly on the shoulder as she passed, and he reached for her hand, a trailing fingertip caress. He'd forgiven her the madness at the bridges. Perhaps he envied her the chance to fight rather than hew away at wood. Arnaud's eyes would shine when he looked at her, so maybe they'd make love again, when they had a chance; he seemed stronger now, less bowed by grief.

Riding ahead to scout alone came naturally these days, though Adelais knew that Arnaud did not like it. After eight days in the saddle, she'd learned to trust the little gelding's senses; he seemed alert to dangers before she could perceive them. Sometimes, they were simply the irrelevances that alarm a horse on its own – a rag caught on a twig, or a figure made of sticks and sacking to scare the birds from a field. At other times, he'd hear approaching riders long before her own ears picked up the sound. Once, he'd stood quivering at the sight of a lone wolf, but he hadn't bolted. The wolf had stared back at them, grey, white-bibbed, and magnificent, and Adelais had felt her spirits lift. Her grandmother Yrsa was of the Wolf People, and Adelais decided that wolves were good omens. Without the wolf at the sisterhouse she would have escaped a day earlier and never met Arnaud.

Though perhaps she would have been closer to Vriesland.

She was reassured by the ease with which she nudged the gelding towards the manor; he'd never yet let her be surprised. She saw no movement beyond the manor's gates, and heard no sound except the soft thud of his hooves on the turf.

Adelais paused at the open gates, scanning the run-down, slightly impoverished courtyard beyond. A line of lean-to stables resting against the curtain wall were largely empty, and the wall itself was more of a barrier against thieves than a protection against assault; it had no battlements or walkway. She was starting to notice such things.

'And what might you want, young man?'

The grey-haired man in the doorway to one of the outbuildings was dressed in a clean, good-quality cote-hardie, with the broad leather belt and fine boots of a man of standing. A badge on his chest proclaimed him to be a senior retainer rather than the lord.

'I have a message for Thebault Cheyne, the seigneur.' Adelais no longer thought it strange to be called 'young man'.

'Then you have a long ride ahead. He is with His Grace the Duke, fighting on the borders of Alympos.'

'Or his son Dreux.'

'With his father. I am their steward. What is your message?'

Adelais began to wheel her gelding. She would have trusted a Cheyne, with Humbert's encouragement, but not a retainer.

'Who sent you, boy?' A woman's voice made Adelais pause. The lady emerging from one of the stables had the accent and dress of a noble, yet she carried a currying brush and her gown was dusted with horse hairs. She was plain, big-boned, and wore her hair in maiden's braids although she was of an age when most women were wed. She seemed vaguely familiar. So did the boy of about twelve summers who appeared behind her, and Adelais remembered a moment outside the Black Tower when this lady was knocked to the ground by soldiers. The boy and a steward had stood over her while a doomed Guardian had cried 'Courage, Isabeau'.

'You will not remember me, my lady, but I too was in front of the fire temple on the day your illustrious uncle was martyred.'

Isabeau Cheyne swallowed before replying. 'Martyrdom is a word that few would dare use.'

'Though deserved, I understand.'

'You were there? I took my brother away. We could not watch...' Isabeau pulled the boy closer.

Adelais shook her head. 'No, but the one who sent me prayed with them to the end on the Isle of Dogs.'

'And he is?'

'Humbert Blanc, who was Grand Commander of Arrenicia.'

The steward let out a sigh that was almost a hiss, but Isabeau raised a hand to silence him.

'He is nearby?'

'Yes, my lady.'

'Then bring him, and all with him.'

'Take care, my lady!' The steward's protest was a low, warning growl. 'All Galmandie is seeking them. Your father's lands will be forfeit!'

'Then we must be sure that all Galmandie remains in ignorance. Go, young sirrah, and bring them here, for my beloved uncle's sake.'

The tension of the journey fell away in the warmth of Isabeau Cheyne's welcome. For Agnès de Molinot there was an empty chamber with a feather bed in the tower, servants to carry her baggage, and great jugs of warmed water in which to bathe away the dirt of the road. Isabeau Cheyne looked surprised when Agnès pulled 'Perrin Wilg' into the chamber as well as her own servant Mathilde, but made no comment.

A little later the yellow-haired youth in the travel-stained herigaut was transformed. For Agnès and Mathilde, dressing her became a game. She was their creation, from the silken hose and borrowed gown to the caul headdress that, with a little padding, could have held a lady's full head of hair. To be sure, the gown was somewhat loose around the chest, but there was a fine linen chemise to go beneath it. There were even soft leather house-shoes that almost fitted, and that stayed on perfectly well when stuffed with scraps of linen.

Adelais and Agnès entered the hall of the manor arm in arm, with Mathilde following behind, and all three enjoying the shock of her appearance. Arnaud gazed at her in a way that made her want to pirouette, just for him. Guy was wide-eyed and slack-jawed, while the steward seemed affronted. Humbert came forwards, taking her by the hand as if she were indeed a gentlewoman, and presented her anew to Isabeau Cheyne and her young brother Ordric.

An impromptu feast had been arranged, using whatever materials where already to hand in the manor: new bread; soups of dried pulses; a freshly slaughtered chicken and a suckling pig flavoured with dried herbs; cheeses, and fine Jourdainian wine. Isabeau Cheyne made a pretty speech of welcome, which carefully avoided any matters that gossiping servants might carry to the village, and which invited them to stay until they were fully rested. The seating caused the steward some confusion; should Adelais join the family on the high table, or sit with the base-born in the body of the hall?

Adelais solved the problem for him by sitting in the hall, opposite Arnaud, but above Guy and Mathilde. To her right, on the high table, Isabeau presided, flanked by Humbert and Agnès. Next to Agnès, young Ordric Cheyne looked along the high table to Humbert with hero-worship already shining in his face. The boy wanted to hear words that would make his uncle a hero too, not a heretic who'd defied a king. He was offering questions to be rebutted.

'... surely a king is always deserving of the loyalty of his subjects?'

Adelais only half-listened, feeling light-headed even before the first sip of wine. There was a fire at her back, hot food in front of her, and Arnaud looking at her as if she were the sweetest dish on the table. He too had shed the cares of the road, and even set aside his grief; she had not seen his face shine like this since the morning she had lain with him.

'Not all princes are worthy,' Humbert answered.

Arnaud kicked off his boot beneath the table, worked his foot under the hem of her gown, and began to caress the inside of her calves with his toes. Adelais glared at him and pretended interest in Humbert's discourse as the toes stroked upwards...

'A prince's true authority is grounded in a sense of duty. A prince who uses his authority for his private enrichment has empty mastery.'

Adelais crumbled bread as Arnaud's toes reached the inside of her thigh. She mouthed 'stop it' at him, but he only lifted an eyebrow at her, somewhere between seduction and challenge.

'Kings, and all chivalrous knights, should fix their minds on honour, not lands or wealth.' Humbert could expound on chivalry the way a priest could thunder in a fire temple. Beside Adelais, Guy stabbed his knife into his meat hard enough to turn heads, but she was growing used to his moods and ignored him. Her mind was filling with earthier thoughts.

Arnaud leaned backwards, the better to lift his foot, and Adelais hurriedly adjusted the tablecloth to conceal the tent that appeared in her dress, between her legs.

'A knight whose heart is set on wealth will fear to die,' Humbert declaimed, 'for his wealth will die with him and be given to those who come after, but an honourable knight does not fear to die, for his honour will last forever.'

Adelais eased her body forwards, enough to make contact, grateful that this night she was dressed as a woman, without the need for a loin cloth. Arnaud's foot was warm inside his hose and filled the space between her thighs. She closed her legs around it, smiling innocently across the table.

'To oppose a king, or even a high priest, who wages war for dishonourable reasons is not treachery, but the chivalric duty of those who have higher ideals.'

Adelais gasped as Arnaud began a slow, repeated curling of his toes.

'What's the matter with you?' Guy scowled at her.

'Nothing.' She dropped her hands into her lap, hard enough to push Arnaud's toes off the edge of the bench.

'But do not vassals swear allegiance?' Ordric was clearly enthralled. 'If they rebel, is that not faithlessness to their sworn word?'

'The Knights Guardian owed allegiance to the high priest, not to any earthly power. The Order was formed to defend the borders of Ischyrendom against the Saradim infidels, not to enrich kings.'

Arnaud leaned over the table once more, and whispered to her. 'They have given me a chamber to myself.'

Adelais bit her lip. It was going to be a long feast.

Adelais waited until the manor was quiet before she slipped out of the canvas trestle bed that had been set up for her in Agnès's chamber, and pulled on her chemise. Arnaud's chamber, she knew, was directly above, and she felt her way up the staircase in the dark. The stones were cold and coarse under her feet, a spiral stairway to enchantment. His door stood ajar, waiting, and a thin band of moonlight came through a narrow window slit in the outer wall, showing, of all impossible luxuries, a feather bed with an indistinct form lying within it.

'I thought you must have fallen asleep.'

She sighed, relieved to hear his voice. Walking into the wrong chamber would have been too embarrassing. She pulled the chemise over her head and stood naked in the moonlight, letting him look at her.

'By Salazar, thou art beautiful.' He lifted the covers. 'Come.'

· · ·

Adelais had never woken to see a lover's face on her pillow, in any bed, let alone in one that held her body as softly as a kiss. She lay facing him, close enough for them to be breathing each other's air. She blew a little harder until Arnaud's nose wrinkled, and again until he woke. The transformation of his face as he saw her, that lightening, that spreading smile, was pure as the dawn and more honest than any words. It compelled her to reach out to touch him, letting her fingertips read his cheeks, his stubble, his lips, his body, and wonder at the languorous, sensual awareness of warm skin.

That morning there was no urgency to their coupling. In the night he'd put his hand over her mouth to stifle her cries, saying 'hush, youngling', and in the soft light of morning she kissed the bruises her teeth had made on the edge of his palm. It was slow now, as tender as touch, eye to shining eye on the pillow, until the moment he moaned and found a shuddering release.

She slipped from his bed while he slept, and pulled on her chemise. The manor was stirring, and she wasn't sure if their hostess would approve.

A low, throaty chuckle came from Agnès's bed as Adelais eased back into their room, wincing as the door creaked.

'Was it good?' Agnès patted the bed beside her. 'Come, tell me everything!'

Adelais slid under the covers. Agnès was bristling with excitement, her eyes flicking over Adelais's face.

Adelais rolled on her back. She wasn't sure where to begin, or how much she wanted to share.

'I don't think I'd have made a very good adeifi.'

'You certainly sounded as if you were enjoying yourselves.'

'What?'

Agnès pointed upwards to the beams supporting the floor of Arnaud's room, and made a low, repetitive creaking noise. '*Crr-ikk, crr-ikk, crr-ikk!*'

'Oh, by all that's sacred!'

Agnès threw herself back on the pillows, dropping her hands palm-upwards by her head, and switched from creaking noises to high, half-stifled whimpers as if in the throes of ecstasy. 'Hmm... hmm... hmm... *ooh.*'

'Stop it!' Adelais pushed Agnès's shoulder, giggling.

'You made me want to see Leandre de Fontenay even more.' Agnès sighed as the laughter faded.

'Have you ever...?'

'With de Fontenay? No.' Agnès stared upwards, frowning a little as if thinking deeply. 'What do adeifes do?' she asked after a while. 'I mean, when they want to, need to, er... take comfort?'

Adelais took a moment to organise her thoughts.

'In the infirmary, we learned how the four humours must be in balance, so an excess of lust, which comes from the hot, sanguine humour, must always be countered by cold. We were encouraged to conquer our feelings by soaking ourselves in buckets of cold water from the well.' But Adelais remembered the opposite effect on the day she swam in a lake, letting cold water lap around her breasts while she hoped that Arnaud was watching. 'It didn't always work.'

'I think I'd rather hang on to the lust.'

'One of the older adeifes said she spoke to a learned doctor at the Villebénie university. Apparently it is written that women's wombs can become congested when they are not warmed by a man. He encouraged her to find a midwife who should dip her finger in oil and "move it about vigorously".'

Agnès giggled. 'Interesting.' She didn't sound at all offended by the idea.

'I've always wondered if that old adeifi was volunteering her services as a midwife.' Adelais remembered the relish with which the whiskery Adeifi Fabianne had relayed the advice. 'Some of the girls did that to themselves.' Sometimes there had been furtive rustlings on their straw dormitory mattresses, like dancing mice, that ended with a stifled gasp into a pillow.

She also remembered the way the culprits had been teased. *'Eleanor finger-fucked herself last night.' 'Did not!' 'Did too. I heard you.'*

'Did no one take a lover?'

'Only the eldest daughter.'

But there had been one or two special friendships in the novice's dormitory, girls who shared a cot for warmth when the nights became cold. They'd all slept naked, as was the custom, as Agnès was now on the far side of the bed. When did innocent friendships become 'special'? Had Adeifi Elodie wanted a friendship like that? She'd never know.

Agnès flung back the covers and cracked open the shutter on the window, spilling a gentle light over her body. It touched her hair with auburn where it tumbled over her breasts; Leandre de Fontenay would be a lucky man. Agnès looked out at the day and sniffed the air. 'Personally, I find the best cure is a good gallop.'

Adelais groaned and shut her eyes. The last thing she wanted to do that day was ride a horse.

9.2 MALORY

Brother Paget FitzMaurice endured for five days in Searle's small castle. The morning after Paget died, Malory d'Eivet climbed into the saddle as tiredly as if he had already ridden ten leagues. Around him the troop's survivors sat on their mounts with their heads down. Their depleted numbers had been replenished by the arrival of another patrol, but none of them would meet his eye. They'd all been shamed by the torture, even if they had not been the ones inflicting it.

The last time Malory had felt this bad about himself was after a visit to the stews. There had been a girl there, probably newly culled from the waifs that seemed to wash up on the south bank. He hadn't asked her history – recently orphaned, perhaps, or a servant girl who'd caught the roving eye of a master and been thrown out by his wife. Who knew? Who cared? She'd been so innocent, so deliciously vulnerable, so frightened, and so very young. He hadn't meant to hurt her, but afterwards he'd felt this same wave of guilt, this same feeling of being soiled that no amount of unburdening could assuage.

He'd gone back, some days later, with gold in his purse and a vague idea that he could offer the girl his protection. 'Alas, messire,' the mistress of the stews had said, and it was always *messire* in the stews, where he was never seen in priestly robes, 'alas, she didn't last, but I have another, just as fresh...'

Now, in the same way, an old Guardian had made him feel fouled beyond redemption.

For most of those days, since Pateras Ghislain had left for Moutâne, Malory had been in charge of the interrogation. Before then, throughout his years with the anakritim, Malory had been able to intercede for a prisoner; he'd done Ischyros's work by begging for their suffering to stop. He could see himself as doing the work of the Blessèd Ones, imploring the Angel of Death to desist. But without the anakritis-general, it was Malory inflicting the pain.

Or rather his men. No priest could hold a man's feet in the fire himself, but he could order others to do so. Even the soldiers had become tired of it, for they were not the usual crew of hardened tormentors from the Black Tower. They'd become awkward, unwilling, and then angry. It had been one of their blows that had killed the Guardian, a frustrated 'talk, damn you', and a fist into the chest that must have punched an already-broken rib into a lung. As he coughed blood, the prisoner had tried to speak, so Malory bent low and put his ear to Brother Paget's gory mouth. All Paget had said was 'I forgive you.' He'd looked so peaceful, afterwards. Almost *grateful*.

And Pateras Malory had learned nothing. Not even confirmation that the idol or relic existed.

He'd given Paget the Office of the Dead, administering the holy signs and the sacred ash as tenderly as he might to his own father. '*Apó ti chári tou Ischyros, sas xefortónomai tis amartíes sas.*' By the grace of Ischyros, I unburden you of your sins. He yearned for a truly holy man to say the same words over him.

'*Anapáfsou en eiríni.*' Rest in peace.

By Salazar, he needed pardon.

9.3 ADELAIS

'Shall we turn?' Adelais and Agnès had ridden beyond the little village near the Cheyne manor, crossed a stream that wound its way northwards towards Orval, and taken a farm track as far as the edge of the forest rimming the shallow valley. Adelais felt guilty for taking the horses on an unnecessary ride; they too deserved some rest. Besides, Adelais had a slight discomfort between her legs, something between remembered pleasure and present tenderness, and she wanted to enjoy the coming night.

Agnès grinned as she wheeled her mare, putting her shoulders back in a way that issued a challenge without any words being spoken. Both horses knew what was coming, and began to dance, their tiredness forgotten. Their riders, after all, were turning them towards home, or at least a stable with dry bedding and feed.

'Race you to the stream.' Agnès raked her heels back without waiting for a reply, and launched her horse into a canter that became a full-out gallop as she lifted out of the saddle.

Adelais's gelding needed no command. Adelais gave him his head, already needing to angle her face and half close her eyes

against the mud that Agnès's mare was kicking into the air.
Agnès was a fine horsewoman, but she had a slightly heavier
build, and Adelais's gelding was fast, gradually narrowing the
gap until they were side by side, both women whooping into the
wind at the madness of the moment, with neither horse and
neither woman willing to yield. They hit the ford across the
stream in a single sheet of spray, and let the water bring the
horses to a bouncing, bounding, snorting halt.

'Feeling better?' Adelais grinned at Agnès, whose face
glowed behind spatters of mud. Her bosom was rising and
falling as if she had only just remembered to breathe.

'Almost as good as a man. Almost. Here.' Agnès pulled a
scrap of linen from her cuff, kicked her horse alongside Adelais,
and leaned out of the saddle to dab at her face.

'I spoilt your gown.' Adelais looked down at her borrowed
dress, whose rich wool was now caked with starbursts of soil.

'Let it dry, it will brush off,' Agnès said airily, handing
Adelais the linen. Adelais reached over to wipe mud from
Agnès's cheek.

'What do Vriesian girls call each other when they're
friends?' Agnès's green eyes watched her closely.

'*Vinkona myn* is Vriesian for "my friend".'

'And if they're best friends?'

Adelais turned Agnès's chin and daubed at the other side. It
was hard to reach from the saddle. '*Kjúkling*, perhaps. It means
"chick".'

'*Kjúkling*. I like that.'

Adelais sat back, laughing. Agnès's accent was terrible. 'K-
yoo-kling,' she corrected.

'*Kjúkling*. So what will you do after all this is over,
kjúkling? Will it be l'Armurier and babies?'

'I suppose so, if Arnaud will have me.' She handed back the
scrap of linen. 'That'll have to do, until we have water. You'll
need to brush it out of your hair.' *Babies*. That prompted her to

try and remember the phase of the moon; her courses were well due, although she felt none of the usual signs. No tension, no spasms, no irritability. In fact, she felt gloriously well.

'You may need to hide for a while, all of you,' Agnès continued, 'somewhere beyond the reach of the king.'

Adelais had realised that. 'King Aloys only holds the southern half of Vriesland. The lands beyond the Schilde are still free. Yellow hair is less remarkable there.' And Yrsa's home was on the way, if she hadn't already been driven north by Ischyrian repression. She could let Yrsa know she was alive. Return the bind-rune *taufr* still hidden in her belt bag, once it had done its job. Fulfilled its destiny, Yrsa would say.

'Come back to me, when it is safe.' Agnès sounded a little embarrassed as she turned her horse towards the shore. 'True friends are hard to find.'

'I'd like that.' It was the first time Adelais had truly realised that their journey might soon come to an end. She would miss Agnès de Molinot a great deal. 'Maybe I could creep back as Perrin Wilg to feast at your wedding.' Adelais nudged her gelding towards the bank. It trotted through the water in a high-stepping, prancing motion; the splashing around its knees sounded like pitchers being emptied into a barrel.

'Take care. What would you do if the future wasn't to be a man and babies?'

Adelais had thought of that, too. 'I'd like to be a healer. If I had the money, I'd learn to read so I could study the physicians' texts.' She could recognise her name, that was all, and only in Galman, not the High Tongue. Ischyrian healing couldn't all be prayers and the herbs she already knew; there must be good wisdom to find in their books.

'Are women allowed to be physicians in Vriesland?'

'Before the conquest, *only* women were allowed to be healers. The lore was passed from mother to daughter, by word of mouth. Now they're called witches and they're burned alive if they are caught.' Adelais was dangerously close to saying too much. It was so easy to be relaxed with Agnès.

'In Galmandie you have to be a cleric to be a physician. Even if you dressed up, I can't see you taking vows.' Agnès's knowing smile hinted at the night before.

'There's no law against women reading, is there?' Adelais could 'read' all the runes – the *staves*, Yrsa would say – but they were quite different from letters. They were pictures that hinted at a mystery. *Fehu* ᚠ could mean wealth, or power, or the start of a cycle. The Galmans had a letter like *fehu*. It even sounded a bit like it. 'F'. But it wasn't the same. She could sing *fehu* – *fé er frænda róg* – but you couldn't sing a letter. You had to put it with other letters before it meant anything.

'No, no law against women reading.' Agnès looked almost shy for a moment. 'Stay with me in Fontenay, when it's safe. I'd teach you to read.'

'Would you?' Adelais stared at Agnès. The enormity of the offer was humbling.

'We could read your learned texts together. By the God, if Leandre de Fontenay does his duty by me, I'll need something to take my mind off babies and servants.'

Adelais reached over and grasped Agnès's hand. 'Thank you.'

'Don't get too excited. We need to reach Château Fontenay first. Keep the king's thieving fingers off the Hand. I gather Humbert told you about that?'

'Sometimes I forget what we are carrying.'

'De Fontenay must be rather upset by now. He thought it was going to be so easy. "Let Humbert Blanc bring it home in secret," he wrote. Hide it on a cart with my trousseau. Who would interfere with a de Fontenay bride and an escort of six knights?'

'Six?'

'There was to have been another. I'm not sure what happened.'

'Have you seen it?' Adelais wasn't sure she liked the idea of a long-dead hand wrapped up in their baggage, however sacred.

Agnès shook her head. '"Too holy for common gaze," says Humbert.'

'But you're Agnès de Molinot!'

'Different sort of common, *kjúkling*.' Agnès was practising the word. 'Most of them only saw the gold reliquary, and even then under a cover. Humbert says the only Guardians who were allowed to see the Hand itself were the worthiest of the worthy. Valiant knights who loved Ischyros more than life itself, and whose purity had never been defiled by a woman.'

'That's sad.' Adelais should not have been surprised; after all, their priests vowed celibacy, but the Guardians had all seemed so muscular that she couldn't imagine they had never known a woman.

'No gold, no women, and unbreakable obedience to their rule. The best of them took their vows very seriously.'

'*Sætur...*' Adelais only just stopped herself exclaiming the name of Sif. Now Adelais knew the joys a lover could bring, she felt sad for their dead companions. Karlis, Paget, Marquel, and Maarten had died never knowing that wonder. Even Humbert, though he was now old enough to be a grandfather, had never raised a child. Did their god really demand such denial?

'What will Lord de Fontenay do with the Hand, if we reach him?'

Agnès shrugged. 'One imagines that he shares the Guardians' view that it should remain hidden until the faith would treat it with proper reverence.'

'It still seems strange, though, to be chased across Galmandie for a few old bones that will end up hidden in a crypt somewhere.'

'My friend, you and I are insignificant.' Agnès gave a self-deprecating shrug. 'We're like peasants caught between armies when the knights charge. We just have to keep running or be crushed.'

Adelais eased her seat in the saddle, lifting her weight off the ache between her legs, and found Agnès looking at her with a slow-spreading, intimate smile.

'Though you seem to be having a lot of fun as we go.'

9.4 GUY

In a way, Guy had preferred Arnaud when he was quiet. Arnaud couldn't sing but that didn't stop him making a quiet, tuneless noise to himself as he put an edge back on a blade. The scrape of metal over the whetstone had more melody.

'When flowers bloom in spring-o, the maidens start to sing-o...'

Guy could guess what had lifted his spirits. He'd seen the glances between Arnaud and Adelais; those bright-eyed looks they thought were secret and which hinted at a private knowledge; the fluttering of fingers as they passed each other, and by Tanguy, they found many times to pass. He just wished Arnaud would stop the wailing.

'For love not money, come sip my honey.'

Guy would have gone elsewhere, but it would take two men to move the borrowed anvil that lay between his knees, so he stayed sitting on his stump and tried to drown out the noise with hammering as he repaired chain-mail.

'Are you going to tell me what's the matter?' Arnaud sighted along the edge of the sword, turning it in his wrist.

'Nothing.'

'So much "nothing" that you've hardly spoken a word for six days. And if looks were knives, the lord brother would be dead of a thousand wounds. *When flowers bloom...*'

Guy relented. Anything to stop that noise. 'It's Parsifal.'

'What about Parsifal?'

'And Humbert. All of them. Humbert ordered them to kill my father and they'd have done it. That man we were told tried to kill him on the road, before we rescued him, he was a Guardian, too.'

Arnaud ran a blade of grass down the edge of the sword. Satisfied, he sheathed it and looked at Guy.

'Makes sense.'

'What do you mean?'

'There's more at stake here than us. Why do you think king's men and anakritim are after us? Your father knew something that I don't want to know and neither should you. Otherwise, they'd have to kill us, too. Whatever it is, it ain't for the likes of us.'

Guy hit a rivet into a link. Too hard. He swore and reached for the pliers to prise open the buckled join.

'I always wanted to be a knight. I wanted people to look up to me, like they did to my father. Now I'm not so sure.'

'Fine.' Arnaud reached for another sword from the pile beside him. 'Nothing wrong with being an apprentice. You do the messy tasks for me while you learn to be an armourer, or you do the messy tasks for Humbert while you learn to be a man-at-arms. Whichever way you go, you've got a few years of shovelling shit. You could be a master armourer one day for sure, but you might never win the golden spurs.'

'But...' Guy thought he'd get more understanding. Maybe even sympathy.

'But what? And do that link again.'

'L'Armurier! Carelet!' Humbert's call interrupted them. He

beckoned them inside. 'Now Lady Agnès and Adelais have returned, I have news to share with you in the hall.'

Isabeau Cheyne and the boy, Ordric, smiled a greeting even though they sat alone at the high table with their steward, Clovis, standing protectively behind them. They might have been waiting to hear petitions at a manorial court. Clovis was the only Cheyne servant in the room and his manner was cool. Agnès perched on the edge of their table in a way that managed to establish her nobility without undermining their authority. Adelais sat where she had the night before, scratching at mud on a borrowed gown. She'd left off her linen cap, so her short yellow hair fell forwards in a way that was disturbingly boyish; she'd developed a mannerism of pushing it back out of her eyes. Those lean features didn't help, even though her skin was freshly washed and glowing; she looked like a boy-mummer at the plays, a handsome, dressed-up youth on the verge of manhood. Guy turned away, even though Adelais looked up and smiled. She was, well, *confusing.*

'Come close; I don't want to shout. Sit if you wish.' Humbert stood below the dais where his voice would reach everyone. Arnaud took the bench next to Adelais, who smiled at him under her lashes and dropped her hand beneath the table. Sweet Ischyros, they made it obvious.

'As you know, we must soon deliver Lady Agnès to her future husband. It is likely that those who have pursued us will be waiting in Jourdaine.' Humbert spoke quietly, so his voice would not carry beyond the group. 'I had hoped to send private word to Leandre de Fontenay, so that he could escort us through whatever safe passage he thought appropriate.'

Humbert paused, looking at the Cheynes and their steward. 'It is four days' riding to Château Fontenay; eight days for a messenger to reach Lord Leandre and return. I believe it would be asking too much of Lady Isabeau to host us for that long. The risk of discovery is too great.'

Clovis nodded his approval. Adelais pouted her disappointment at Arnaud.

'Lady Isabeau has, however, offered us the services of her steward, Master Clovis, who will lead us via little-used roads and will act as our messenger when we are close to Château Fontenay.'

'And once Mathilde and I are safely with de Fontenay,' Agnès asked, 'what will happen to the rest of you?'

Humbert turned to look at her. 'I plan to take a boat down the Naeva and then strike west, through the hills of Maycea and on into Arrenicia. The count is an old friend, and will hide me until the king gives up the hunt. I am sure he will extend that protection to l'Armurier, Carelet, and Adelais if I ask it. However, our horses need rest,' Humbert glanced at Agnès, 'so with Lady Isabeau's permission we will stay two more nights here.'

Guy wondered why Agnès de Molinot rolled her eyes at Adelais.

Clovis held Guy's arm as they were leaving the hall, and looked hard into his face.

'The king must want you very badly to pursue you across Compeigne and Jourdaine.'

'We have left reason enough on the road behind us.'

'They say you desecrated a temple and stole a precious relic.'

Arnaud appeared beside them, standing close to Clovis. Arnaud had a way of broadening his blacksmith's shoulders that could intimidate opposition; Guy had seen him stop a tavern fight just by standing up. 'We have stolen nothing. And is it not enough that your mistress finds us worthy of her support?'

The silence stretched until the man dropped Guy's arm. 'Of course.' He backed away.

Arnaud scratched reflectively at an old wound on his wrist and watched Clovis go. 'That one makes me nervous.'

9.5 ADELAIS

'It's been too easy.' Arnaud sat on his cloak, looking down into a gorge where a narrow, overgrown track wound through trees, bordering a stream. At the mouth of the valley, Clovis had said, the track met a larger road that led to Moutâne.

Except that they didn't want to go through Moutâne. They needed a quiet route to skirt the city and reach Château Fontenay, just half a day's ride to the south from where they waited, but beyond the River Naeva.

'Can't you believe in good fortune?' Adelais shuffled closer to him until their hips touched, and pulled the hood of her herigaut forwards to shield her face from the fine, misty rain blowing across the valley. It was enough to dew the grass with moisture, but she chose to be out in the open, sharing the first watch of the morning with Arnaud as he would later share hers. 'Just keep your eyes on the road,' Humbert had said. Sometimes the lord brother behaved like her father had, back in the days when boys began sniffing at their door.

'One of us should have gone with him. I don't trust him.'

'But that young anakritis knows all our faces except his.'

'Even so...' Arnaud scratched at his wrist scar. 'Until the

bridges they were on our heels. We had to fight them twice. In the five days since we left the Cheyne manor, we haven't seen one king's man. Not one. It makes me nervous.'

'Maybe Master Clovis knew the quiet roads.' Like the one below them, which ran through empty, forested country, too folded to have ever known a plough. They'd passed through villages, but no towns, bivouacking at night in places like this – a hilltop clearing as bald as an old man's pate with a clear view of the road below and an escape route behind.

'Do you trust him, then?' Arnaud challenged.

Adelais pushed hair out of her eyes. It was growing; long enough be an irritant but it would be moons before she could tie it behind. 'I trust the Cheynes. He is their servant.'

'He has been gone a day.'

'He said it would be at least that.'

This hilltop was as far as Humbert would allow without sending word ahead. They could not blunder into Château Fontenay without knowing what awaited them.

'And if he was taken?'

Adelais nudged him with her shoulder. It wasn't like Arnaud to be this nervous. 'Then we'd see a troop coming in time to fade into the woods. This isn't such a bad life.'

'I think Lady Agnès is tiring of it.'

Adelais looked behind them. Agnès sat on her own on a log under the trees, huddled into her cloak. From time to time she'd throw pieces of twig onto the grass in the way of someone who has nothing else to do; she missed her crossbow and the ability to hunt for the group. She said she felt useless, and, no, she didn't want to learn how to use a sling, even if Adelais could bring down a couple of pigeons on some days. Mathilde sat on another log, stirring a pot over the fire. She was becoming good at scavenging for herbs. Humbert and Guy seemed finally to have made their peace; Humbert was teaching him swordcraft about fifty paces away with slow swings and exaggerated paces.

'I'll go to her.' Adelais touched Arnaud's leg as she rose, a light caress in lieu of a kiss. She missed the Cheynes' feather bed; it had been hard to be intimate on the road. They'd snatched just one moment, on a day when the stone-filled sling tapped insistently against her body and she'd welcomed the coarse bark of a tree against her back rather than soft linen. It had lessened that particular hunger in a mildly unsatisfying way, like cold waybread in the days after a feast.

Agnès looked up at her and smiled in a wan, bored way.

'Did you tell him?'

Adelais shook her head. 'Not yet. I'm only a few days late.'

But she was sure. Her whole body sung with the life within her. There was a new tightness to her breasts, a heightened sensitivity as they brushed her shirt. She even imagined they might already be a little fuller, a little weightier.

'You're with child. I see it in your skin. It shines.' Agnès wiped a thumb across Adelais's cheek as she sat beside her. 'Under the dirt.'

'It feels...' Adelais struggled for words. 'Like sunshine on snow.'

'Why don't you tell him?' Agnès nodded towards Arnaud, who was climbing to his feet where the hill dropped away into the valley.

Adelais found it hard to explain. She watched him stride over the grass towards Humbert and Guy, broad-shouldered and physical even under a damp cloak, and she knew that it would change things between them. Arnaud would become more protective, more careful, and she wanted still to wrap her legs around him while there wasn't a bump in the way.

He called to them as he passed. 'The steward's coming back. Alone.'

.   .   .

Clovis dismounted stiffly at the edge of the camp and let Guy take his horse. He seemed tired even beyond his years and did not speak until Agnès tapped her foot impatiently.

'Did you see de Fontenay?'

He nodded. 'Lord Leandre sends greetings, my lady. He is relieved that you are safe, but cautions you against crossing the Naeva until he can provide his own escort. The river lies across your way and there are king's men on the bridge. There are more in the town.'

'In strength?' Humbert asked.

'I sat for some time at an inn before I made myself known to Lord Leandre. The innkeeper said the anakritis-general himself had been at Château Fontenay three days before, and yesterday the provost of Villebénie arrived with more men, and another anakritis.'

'Malory d'Eivet,' Arnaud muttered. 'Now we know why we haven't seen them on the road. They're waiting for us here.'

'If Lord Leandre leaves Château Fontenay with armed men,' Clovis continued, 'he will be followed. He bids me lead you to a small château on this side of the river; it is now a hunting lodge and empty save for a castellan and his family. His lordship will leave Château Fontenay privately and will greet you all there. He is eager to see the lord brother, but regrets that only Lady Agnès and her servant can be escorted openly through his lands. He will, however, provide a boat for the rest of you; the Naeva is navigable here and flows southwards. It will take you beyond Jourdaine.'

'I understand.' Humbert nodded as if this was only to be expected. 'He cannot be seen to shelter those who are sought by the king. The boat is most generous. When should we arrive at this château?'

'He awaits his future wife eagerly, and bids you come with all haste.'

Agnès turned away immediately and gathered her cloak

from beside the fire, but Humbert looked long and hard at Clovis until the man dropped his eyes.

'There is no trickery?'

Clovis looked him in the eye. 'On my word, my lord, I have served both you and my master well.'

'And who is your master, man?'

'Seigneur Thebault Cheyne, my lord, as you know.' The man seemed affronted, and Adelais wondered what Humbert had seen in Clovis's face to cause him unease. For the first time since leaving the Cheyne manor, Humbert summoned Guy to help him don full armour, and insisted that Guy and Arnaud wear the red de Fontenay surcoats.

Agnès de Molinot whooped with excitement at their first view of the château across the water meadows. 'De Fontenay is there!' She pointed at the banner flying from the tower – three golden flowers on a red field.

'Wait, *kjúkling*.' Adelais had to reach across and catch Agnès's bridle to stop her cantering forwards. 'Let us be sure.'

It looked peaceful enough, at this distance. Here in the lowlands the rain had stopped and the cloud seemed higher and broken, yet there was enough wind to blow slanting drips from the trees and stir the de Fontenay banner. From this angle, it seemed a relatively small château with one round donjon tower. Two smaller towers framed a gatehouse in the curtain wall. It stood on a slight rise above a stream, and, if not for the flag, it might have been deserted; the only signs of movement were the cattle in the meadow beneath its walls, and a pair of ravens flying near the gates. They tumbled on the wind like scraps of black cloth.

Ravens. Yrsa used to say that ravens were the messengers of Odhinn. Adelais fingered her scrip, feeling for the hard reassurance of the bind-rune *taufr* within.

'Shall I see what welcome awaits us?' Clovis began to edge his mount forwards.

'Not alone.' Humbert looked around the group, now bunching behind them on the road. 'Adelais? You have a talent for scouting.'

'Take this.' Agnès handed her the hunting spear. Adelais wished she'd salvaged a shield and a helmet after the fight in the woods.

Her gelding was nervous, from the moment they left the rest. That was a bad sign. He pirouetted at a fork in the road where a lesser track branched off to ford the stream on its way to the château, and she had to kick him onwards. Blank arrow slits looked down at them, and Adelais stared back, fearing a crossbow in the darkness beyond. She'd seen what a crossbow could do, even to an armoured man, and she wore no armour but her padded gambeson. They paused at the gate, staring through the opening into an apparently empty courtyard beyond. The ravens cawed a raucous protest between the gate-house towers above them. One flew almost into her face, so close that she saw the oily shine of its wing feathers as it swerved away. Protest or warning? And why did she suddenly think of the wolf who'd barred her escape from the sisterhouse? Adelais watched it land in a window slit above them. Beneath its claws the sharpened beams of a portcullis hung down into the archway like a row of blackened teeth. The great, iron-bound oaken doors stood open, and had been open for long enough for weeds to grow around them. That was more encouraging.

Clovis shrugged and rode into the courtyard beyond. He turned his horse and lifted his arms from his sides.

'Nothing.'

Adelais nudged her horse's sides but again he spun, refusing to go forwards until she tapped him on the flank with the butt of the spear. A bloom of sweat spread across his neck and he quivered as he obeyed. He was making her nervous; riding under that portcullis felt like riding into the jaws of a beast.

The courtyard spread around them, its battlements devoid of life, and she rode a circuit around it, bending to peer into the doors of the towers. The ground floor of the great tower would be the guard room. Empty. Silent, with wooden steps leading upwards. A stone-built hall spread along the wall from the tower, its windows blank. The smaller doors to the gatehouse tower were shut. A line of stables against the curtain wall held only two shaggy-maned workhorses that would be unfit for any warfare. There was a fourth tower on the south side, and from this came an old man in a dirty cote-hardie, hunched over and wringing his hat ingratiatingly in his hands.

'Welcome, gentles.'

'Where is Lord Leandre?' Clovis shouted at him.

'There is just me and my son, messire. But my lord will be here anon. He sent word to welcome you.'

The silence stretched. A shaft of sunlight broke through the cloud, strong enough to make the old man squint, and Adelais's gelding danced sideways at nothing more than a damp leaf flipping over in a corner. She stroked his neck.

'I feel it too, boy.'

The steward seemed less concerned. 'Shall we call the others?'

Adelais did not answer, but stared hard at the tower behind the man. She thought she saw movement beyond its door. Clovis showed his irritation.

'By Tanguy, will you search the whole castle?'

A boy of about fifteen came into the light, swallowing nervously.

'My son, gentles. Shall he hold your horses?'

Adelais ignored him but wheeled and rode out through the gatehouse. One of the ravens swooped low enough for her horse to dance sideways. Outside she spread her arms wide and waited for the others to come. Humbert led the way with the wrapped roll of linen tied to the back of his saddle. The red skirts of his surcoat flapped against the almost-black coat of his destrier. Red flag above, red livery below, red pennon on the lance; all should be well. Why did it feel so wrong?

'I do not like this, messire,' she greeted him. 'Just a man and a boy, but it doesn't feel right. I would keep your sword to hand and watch your back.'

'Yet they fly the banner of de Fontenay. Lord Leandre is an honourable man.' Humbert dipped his lance to pass under the portcullis and led the way into the courtyard.

Adelais hung back as they rode past her: Arnaud, half smiling but scratching nervously at his wrist; Agnès, lifting an eyebrow at Adelais's face; Mathilde, with half the packhorses behind her on a line; and Guy bringing up the rear with the rest. She followed them in, finding it easier to push her horse through the gate than it had been the first time.

Adelais dismounted in the courtyard, still not quite trusting the empty battlements. She looked up, watching for movement beneath the conical roof of the great tower, and put out her hand to stop the old castellan as he passed, leading a horse.

'If de Fontenay is not here, why do you fly his banner?'

'He bid us fly it to make you welcome, mistress.'

Mistress. Adelais began to turn. She was dressed in a noble-man's herigaut, with her hair trimmed to a man's style. She carried a spear. Why had he called her 'mistress'? Her heart began to pound.

'Trap!' Her voice came out as a reedy squeal and she swallowed to force moisture into her mouth. 'It's a trap!'

They were all on the ground, turning to look at her, all except Clovis. The Cheynes' steward was still mounted, and edging his horse towards the gatehouse. She began to run towards him, but he jabbed his heels backwards, kicking his horse into a canter. *Too far.* She hefted the spear into an overarm hold and trailed it, preparing to hurl, judging speed and movement the way she'd lead a bird with her sling.

But Guy was in the way, running into her line as he angled to intercept the rider. She abandoned the throw as he grabbed the steward's stirrup. From within a gatehouse tower came a mighty, clanging blow, as of a sledgehammer knocking out a wedge, and the portcullis began to drop, thundering downwards behind the horse. Adelais glimpsed Guy being dragged along, with Clovis punching downwards at his face, just before the portcullis's iron teeth bit the roadway behind Guy's heels.

Now there was noise around the courtyard. The snap of an iron bolt as the old man dragged his son back into the small tower and slammed the door, the rumble of heavy boots on wooden stairs within the great tower. The group backed into a defensive circle, weapons drawn, as armed men streamed out of the towers onto the battlements. King's men, with the yellow-on-blue, sunburst-on sky royal badge on their chests. More were coming out of the great tower into the courtyard, encircling them. They moved swiftly but without running, confident that Humbert's party had nowhere to go, stopping only when they had them surrounded.

Pateras Malory and a captain emerged from the great tower. The anakritis held both hands over his belly, with each buried inside the opposing cuff of his habit. He looked as if he were hugging himself with joy.

Adelais circled, looking for a way to escape, starting to mutter the rune song of *tiwaz*. It had worked on the bridge, hadn't it? *Tiwaz,* the rune of victory. '*Týr er einhendr áss...*' but she couldn't think. '*Ok ulfs... ulfs leifar...*' It was hopeless. Arnaud's sword, Humbert's sword, and her spear faced a dozen men, and there were more on the walls. The soldiers were all crouching, hefting their weapons, peering over their shields, waiting for the word. Only one of the king's men stood upright, a man who'd sought a position directly opposite Adelais, cradling Agnès's crossbow. The quiver at his side was almost empty, but a bolt lay on the groove and the weapon was spanned.

'You recognise this, don't you, witch?' The soldier was sneering, enjoying himself. 'This is for my brother, and all the others who died at the bridge.'

He levelled the crossbow at her guts. Adelais stared at it, unable to believe that this was actually happening. The world around her sharpened and narrowed into shining focus on the point of the bolt; so sharp, so deadly. It had been honed, *by Arnaud*, so that the steel gleamed brighter along its edge in the sunlight. Behind that point she saw each tiny fold in the man's skin where his left palm cradled the stock. Nothing else, though she smelt the friends around her: Arnaud's furnace-and-sweat, Mathilde's soap-and-bread, Agnès's last traces of scent. She thought she heard three separate cries of '*no*': Arnaud, Agnès, and, unbelievably, Malory d'Eivet, but in that final moment she was aware only of two things – Arnaud, lunging forwards even though he had no chance of preventing the shot, and the whitening of the soldier's knuckles as he squeezed the trigger lever.

The snap of the weapon's release and the blinding kick of the bolt's impact came at exactly the same instant.

9.6 GUY

Guy wasn't going to let go. He had hold of Clovis's stirrup leather with one hand and was being dragged along as the horse charged down the track, but he was too angry to even think about releasing his hold. A blow to his side, probably from the horse's knee, drove the breath from his body but even that could not shake him off. The punches to his head didn't matter. He was too low for them to land with any force, and he still wore a helmet. He managed to reach Clovis's sword hilt with his other hand, taking enough of a grip to stop it being drawn, and for perhaps fifty paces they were locked together while the horse cantered sideways, unbalanced, and Guy's feet bounced brutally over the ground.

The horse slowed in the waters of the ford, enough for Guy to get his legs under him and reach upwards, abandoning the sword hilt for Clovis's belt. He swung there, using his whole weight to drag the man sideways out of the saddle. Guy kept his grip on the belt even as chill water closed over his head. His ears filled with the sound of hooves thrashing stones in the stream bed, a ringing hoof-kick to his helmet, and, even under water, the bubbling groan of an injured man.

The fight went out of Clovis. Guy felt him sag, even though Guy had not landed a blow. He struggled to his feet, gasping, but still stubbornly holding the belt. Clovis was slumped through it, retching, and Guy dragged him towards the shore, where the horse waited, watching, snorting. The steward showed no signs of injury but was pale as death, and Guy guessed that he'd been trampled.

'Why?' He dropped the man where it was shallow enough for his face to be clear of the water, even though his hair streamed away like grey weed. 'Why?'

Clovis was conscious, though his eyes were unnaturally wide and his mouth gaped. He took shallow breaths as he spoke.

'I swore to my lord Cheyne... that I'd protect his family... and lands while he was at the wars.' He coughed briefly, painfully.

'So how does this betrayal serve your lord?' Guy grabbed the sodden cote-hardie and shook him. A wince of pain creased the man's face.

'You are thieves, murderers, and... desecrators of temples. All Galmandie knows this.'

'Lies!' Guy let him drop back into the water. But were they lies? 'Lady Isabeau ordered you to help us.'

'She is a only woman, a weak woman... I had to protect her from herself.'

Shouts from the battlements made Guy turn and look up. Two soldiers were pointing down at them and calling back into the courtyard.

'And that banner.' Guy waved at the red and gold of de Fontenay flying over the tower. 'Does de Fontenay know what is being done in his name?'

A creaking of ropes and wooden machinery came from the gatehouse, followed by the steady click of a windlass. Guy stood. It was time to go before they raised the portcullis. But where?

'I never reached de Fontenay.' Clovis coughed again and clutched at Guy's legs. He seemed desperate to be understood. 'They would have taken my lord's lands...'

Guy shook one leg free and kicked the man hard in the guts. Clovis folded around Guy's boot, eyes wide, mouth gaping in a silent scream. Guy wrenched free and staggered towards Clovis's horse. It stared at him from the bank, trailing its reins, nostrils flared.

'Steady, boy.' Guy knew now what he had to do. Find de Fontenay. Before he was caught by the king's men in the hunting lodge behind him or on the road ahead of him.

9.7 ADELAIS

The impact punched Adelais backwards so brutally that even after she hit the ground she continued to slide backwards, folded over as if sitting, with her legs trailing. Some buried, silent corner of her mind screamed '*not fair*', like a beaten child, but there was no pain, not yet, just an appalling, breath-stopping violence. Nearby there were sounds of fighting; the crunching *whump* of steel against mail, then groans, but she couldn't lift her head. Couldn't even lift her arms, which lay palms-up beside her legs, twitching. And low in her belly the shaft of a bolt thrust upwards, offering the dull copper flower of its flights towards her face.

The effort to breathe straightened her body just enough for her to topple sideways, until her cheek fell into a trampled mass of mud, old straw, and new weeds.

Fragments. Impressions.

A nearby voice shouting. 'Stop, I want them alive!'

Someone kneeling by her body. Green gown. Must be Agnès, touching her shoulder, calling her name in desperate, loving tones. Where was Arnaud?

Then Humbert, sword gone, shield gone, sliding his arms

under her shoulders and knees, turning her gently and lifting her. She tried to look around, but her head lolled back and the circle of soldiers appeared, upside down, staring at her, parting for them; their image swayed as Humbert walked.

The first pain. Not the sharp, slicing pain of a stab, but a spreading, whole-belly ache like a kick from a horse.

Humbert laying her on a pile of straw in a stable, where he shouted at Mathilde to bring linen '*and run, girl*'.

Where had she heard that before?

Then a different pain. A sharp, rending agony from her sex to her navel as if something had torn within her, a pain that creased her over within Humbert's arms.

And a thick stickiness between her legs that dribbled downwards over the cheeks of her backside, so much of it that she might have pissed herself.

But gauntleted hands seized Humbert, pulling his arms behind him, binding him.

Adelais doubled over in the straw, instinctively drawing her knees up to protect the life within her. *Gods, the pain!* She sank her teeth into her own lip, biting down to contain the scream, and clutched at green velvet as Agnès knelt beside her, holding her, stroking her face too softly to touch the agony.

She took a great, shuddering gasp. Was that the first breath since she was hit? If she could breathe, she could speak. 'Where's Arnaud?' Now the breaths were coming in short, urgent pants to compensate for all the air she hadn't taken.

The welling compassion in Agnès's eyes frightened Adelais. Agnès only made hushing noises, while she reached under the skirts of Adelais's herigaut, working upwards towards the point of impact. Gentle fingers parted a loin cloth that was already saturated and plastered to her body. Adelais saw Agnès frown, not understanding what she touched, and withdraw a bloodied hand. Agnès then reached for the small eating knife that hung from her belt. In anyone else's hands, the cold touch of the blade against her sex would have been terrifying, but Adelais waited, trusting, as Agnès sawed near the wound and pulled out a leather pouch.

'By Tanguy, what is that?' It grated as Agnès held it in front of Adelais's face with blood-smeared fingers, and a large, broken chunk of stone fell out of a rip.

Adelais groaned. 'Sling.' She was frightened to ask about Arnaud again, frightened of the answer.

'Well it hung in the right place.' Agnès rolled Adelais onto her back and pushed up the hem of the herigaut, more confidently now. 'That, and a gambeson, and maybe a rain-wet crossbow cord.' Agnès cut away at the sodden loin cloth. 'The bolt punched the stone deep into your belly, but did not break the skin. By the God, that must hurt.'

'But... blood?' It was harder to breathe on her back. She tried to draw up her knees, curving around the pain, but that hurt even more.

'Comes from your womb, lambkin, and there is much more than from a late bleed. I fear you are sorely hurt, inside. Where *is* that girl?'

Adelais's mouth gaped wide, unbreathing, her whole body clamped rigid. She needed to suck in air to fuel the heaving sob that rose inside her as the reality of *blood* and *womb* hit home. Finally, a shuddering gasp. And a groan, not a howl. Her ruptured belly would allow no more. Where was Arnaud?

Soldiers arrived, dragging a body. Agnès pulled the herigaut over the bloody mess between Adelais's legs, and shouted at them.

'Give the woman some privacy!' She sounded like Lady Agnès again, Agnès the noblewoman, not Agnès of *kjúkling* and the bloody fingers.

'Sorry, m'lady.' The soldiers dropped the body unceremoniously on the straw. A jack-of-plates rattled as it fell. 'The anakritis wants us to keep him alive, but he's done for, short of a miracle.'

'Arnaud!' Adelais tried to rise, but her legs wouldn't work and she crumpled back into the straw.

Agnès put her arms around her shoulders, and tried to stop her. 'Don't look, lambkin.'

But she had to look. She had to touch him. And she could just about crawl, using her elbows, dragging her body. More sticky wetness gushed between her legs.

Arnaud had taken two great wounds that she could see: a slashing blow to one leg that must have brought him down, and a sword thrust that would have struck upwards while he was on the ground, for it had lifted the overlapping armour squares on Arnaud's jack-of-plates and gone into the chest. He was conscious, but coughing blood, and his eyes darted from side to side like a frightened animal until he saw Adelais.

Then he smiled. He turned his head towards her on the straw and actually smiled, the way he had on the Cheynes' pillows. He lifted a hand to touch her face with the back of his fingers, and tried to speak but could only cough.

Adelais crawled a little closer as more blood ran from the corner of his mouth. She put her ear next to his face.

'Young... ling.'

'Hold... on... old man.' Adelais looked up as Mathilde staggered in under the weight of the great, wrapped roll of linen. 'Please hurry.'

Another cough.

'My. Youngling.'

Agnès's cry of alarm made Adelais turn. Mathilde had picked up Agnès's eating knife and severed the bindings around the linen, pushing at it so it unrolled over the stable floor. There was a slight slope, and the roll had run on for at least two paces before stopping against a post. A package no bigger than a child's forearm lay under the last of the roll, wrapped in stained, neatly folded, ancient silk. Tumbling out of a corner was the edge of a mummified hand; it looked like an old glove, long-discarded and dry.

Adelais rolled onto her back, one hand still gripping Arnaud's, throwing the other sideways towards the Hand. Ischyrians believed relics could work miracles. This was their most sacred relic on Earth and Arnaud was born Ischyrian. If only she could reach it and bring it to him, he might be healed. Her fingertips touched it at the limit of her stretch, a fleeting sense of dryness, but Agnès snatched it away so Adelais was looking at her friend, not her lover, when Arnaud coughed one more time, and gripped her hand the way a drowning man might grasp a rope. She even let his hand go, despite the great, bubbling sigh behind her, in her attempt to grab the Hand of Salazar. This time she touched only the wrapping, smearing bright-red blood on ivory-yellow silk.

'Bring it to him. Let him see it.' Her voice was weak, more in her head than her ears, and she dropped her hands, folding with pain as a spasm gripped her. With her cheek in the straw she could see the world beyond the stables: soldiers binding Brother Humbert, and others shouting towards the battlements. Malory d'Eivet opening their baggage. No one was watching. *'Please!'* She managed to lift her face. Agnès had placed the package back in the linen and was rolling it. Mathilde was bent over the roll's loose end, ripping the edge into bandage strips between her fists. She didn't seem to be aware of Agnès's panic.

'It will heal him,' Adelais begged.

Agnès paused long enough to make the sign of the God. 'It is too late, *kjúkling*. Look.'

Arnaud's eyes were half-closed, staring across the straw at her, but they did not move when she turned. When she reached him they were still fixed on some point beyond her shoulder.

The bellow that filled the stables could not have been hers. It was low, visceral, the cry of a mortally wounded animal. Only the pain it brought to her stomach told her it came from her own body.

She wasn't sure how she managed to stand. She had no recollection of climbing to her feet. She only knew she had to plant her feet wide to stay upright, but that opened a new flood of blood and she doubled over, pushing her knees together to try and stop it. The bolt still hung from her herigaut, snagged on the padded gambeson beneath. She wrestled with it and wrenched it out, staring at it stupidly; its point had buckled backwards, making an eagle's beak.

Eagles. Arnaud and eagles. Arnaud and eagles and screaming. Everything was connected and nothing was making sense.

Now they were all looking at her. Four soldiers backed away, making the sign of the God. Why did they look so frightened?

'Why?' Adelais staggered as the courtyard began to spin. 'Why did you have to kill him?'

All around her, people were watching. Soldiers had stopped ransacking the baggage to stare. Humbert was on his knees, arms tied behind him, looking at her the way her father once had when she was a sick child. And all of them, except Humbert, looked terrified of her.

Especially Pateras Malory, who backed away, also making the sign of the God.

Adelais dropped to her knees as she felt the darkness swallowing her, even though Agnès, *sætur* Agnès, was holding her under her arm, trying to lift her. She tried to fling the bolt towards the priest, but she was weak and it skittered ineffectually along the ground.

'Why did you kill him?' she asked one more time, quietly, and slumped sideways into Agnès.

CHAPTER 10

10.1 GUY

Half a moon before, Guy couldn't ride. He'd still never ridden on his own before, only with others from Lady Agnès's party, and he didn't know the Cheyne steward's horse. He gripped it tightly with his calves, as he'd been taught, and flicked its shoulders with the end of the reins to make it run. Then he passed their attackers' mounts – about twenty of them tied up in horse lines at least five hundred paces from the little château. They were all unsaddled, so he let his horse drop back into the walk-trot routine that covered the leagues without blowing the beast. It would be a while before they could follow. He had no idea how far he had to go, but that filthy steward had been to Fontenay and back in a day and a night.

Or had he?

And he had no idea what was going on inside the château, or hunting lodge, or whatever it was. They might all be dead by now; he'd heard shouting and the sound of many boots as he was dragged away. Fontenay. He had to get to Château Fontenay and he hoped it wasn't far; the horse would tire quickly with his sodden weight. His gambeson was shedding water down the inside of his legs, and the red surcoat was plastered to his hauberk so that each ring of mail showed through the cloth.

Two leagues to the south the track emerged from the forest and joined a larger road, with a steady flow of traffic in each direction. He turned towards a five-span stone bridge he could see crossing a great river in the distance; he knew he had to cross a river.

There were soldiers at the bridge, with the yellow sunburst on blue of the king on their chests, and they were alert. A travelling group of merchants was being questioned and their cart searched. Guy put his nose in the air and trotted forwards as if he had more right to be there than they did. He was, after all, wearing the de Fontenay badge.

They let him through. A hard-faced veteran called 'go for a swim, lad?' in a rough, Villebénie accent, but he ignored it. Laughter followed him down the road.

Walk, trot, walk, trot. His hose squelched inside his boots. After two more leagues on the road his horse was tiring, and Guy paused at a fork in the road, unsure. To the east, a city that must be Moutâne lay smudged across the horizon; the other way led south, into hills. Guy paused. Most of the traffic was going to or from the city. Coming from the south was a knight with his squire, both well-mounted and equipped, though wearing no armour. Guy took a risk and hailed him.

'Messire, can you tell me the way to Château Fontenay?'

The knight looked Guy up and down, his lip curling with amusement.

'A man-at-arms in the de Fontenay livery, wet as a newly caught carp, asks the way to Fontenay?'

Man-at-arms. Guy sat a little straighter. 'I was part of the escort for Lady Agnès Molinot, Lord Leandre's future bride. We were attacked upon the road, messire.'

The knight stared for barely two breaths. 'Take my squire's horse. Yours is blown. Come with me.'

The last time Guy had tried to ride a horse of this quality it had thrown him. This one was more forgiving, but the speed was still terrifying. He found himself praying for the brief respites of trot that the knight allowed in between canters. Within a league the road had curved into a valley that divided around a long, central hill. Crowning the hill was a château large enough to encompass a small town. Its bone-white towers stretched into the distance, and from the largest of these flew the golden flowers of de Fontenay. At the hunting lodge, that had been a trick. This time he knew it meant the lord was at home.

People stared at Guy as he followed the knight up the road to the gate and down the central road within the walls, a bedraggled, saturated, unknown man in familiar livery. A stable boy took their horses in front of a great hall, and Guy was shown into an antechamber where his boots left wet prints upon the flagstones. Servants watched him from the door, whispering among themselves.

The noble who strode into the room could only be Leandre de Fontenay, even if the servants had not parted and bowed; he wore his authority like a great, invisible cloak. He was of middle height, so Guy looked into his eyes as he rose from his obeisance. Penetrating grey eyes, he noticed; they seemed to look into him as well as at him. He seemed to be about Arnaud's age, say thirty summers, with the first threads of grey in dark hair, and Guy wondered why this great lord had not married before.

'And you are?'

'Guy, son of Carel, my lord.'

'You wear my livery, yet you are not of my service.'

'I was in the escort for Lady Agnès de Molinot, my lord. We have been attacked on the road.'

Leandre turned and gestured to the men and women who had followed him into the room.

'Go! All of you.' He turned back to Guy.

'Where?'

Guy told him, as best he could. Leandre de Fontenay lifted his hand to pause him, and opened the door. He issued swift instructions for a troop to be prepared immediately; they should bear weapons but should not delay to don armour. Choose those with fast mounts. And send for my squire. Oh, and bread, meat, and wine for this man. He turned back to Guy.

'How?'

'We were betrayed by our guide, the Cheyne steward. Your banner flew from the tower. It was a trap.'

'How many against you?'

'I was trying to bring down the traitor and could not count, but there were twenty horses nearby. They are king's men.'

'And with Lady Agnès?'

'Just Lord Brother Humbert, an armourer, and two women.'

'There were to be more.' Leandre spoke through a clenched jaw. Guy would not want to cross this man.

'We were attacked before. Twice. Four Guardians have died.' Guy felt suddenly emotional, on the verge of weeping. He swallowed, mastering himself.

Leandre de Fontenay closed his eyes and breathed deeply.

'And how fares Lady Agnès?' Almost as an afterthought.

'She was unharmed when I left.'

'You were with Lord Brother Humbert, but you are too young to be a Guardian.'

'I am the armourer's apprentice, messire. The lord brother took us into his party.'

The door opened and a squire entered, bearing armour across his arms.

'Just greaves, poleyns, and gambeson. They are light and we need speed,' Leandre told him, keeping his eyes on Guy. 'And an armourer's apprentice survived where Guardians died.' It was said levelly, with respect.

'The Guardians did the fighting. And a woman with us.'

Guy dropped his head, hoping he did not sound bitter. 'I held the horses.' The squire was buckling greaves around his lord's legs; the hardened leather covered the shins from knee to ankle and had been painted the de Fontenay red. Poleyns for the knees lay ready. Guy found himself envying the kneeling man, able to arm his lord for war and to ride beside him into battle.

'So how were you soaked?' Leandre pulled his gambeson over his head and lifted his arms while the squire tugged at laces to tighten it to his body.

'I brought down the traitor in the stream outside the walls, and took his horse.'

Leandre nodded his approval. 'You have done well.'

'Shall I come with you, my lord?' Guy asked.

'No, you will stay here. My scope against king's men is limited, even on my lands. They may insist on arresting you. Besides, you are tired. You would slow us.'

De Fontenay took his surcoat from his squire – bright red with the three golden flowers front and back. His face when it emerged through the neck was surprisingly kindly. No one had looked at Guy with that much respect for years.

'So you will stay here. When I return we will discuss whether you wish to continue to wear that livery, in my service.'

Guy dropped to his knee, humbled, and kept his head bowed as Lord Leandre left. He did not want anyone to see his face at that moment. One more kindly look and he would be shamed.

And he'd just glimpsed a muscular kind of chivalry that was so much more appealing than the murderous piety of the Guardians.

He could imagine himself serving this lord.

10.2 MALORY

Now, even the provost's soldiers knew that she must have been a witch. Have been? Still was – for now – since she clung to life. Like Malory, the troop had seen her go down with a crossbow bolt in her belly, and such a wound must be mortal. Slow and exquisitely painful, but mortal. You don't get up from a wound like that; you writhe on the ground and pray for it to end. Yet she'd come out of those stables on her own feet, and screamed at them. Not so much screamed as snarled, like some beast from Kakos's pit, crouching there knock-kneed with blood streaming down her legs and smeared across her face. They'd even seen her rip the bolt out of her own body.

Now, none of the men would go near her. They'd had to untie the Guardian and order him to carry her back into the stables. Humbert Blanc and Lady Agnès had made a great show of praying over her, and even said that by the grace of Ischyros her death was not certain.

Impossible. But if she did live, by Tanguy he'd have some questions for her.

The day wasn't going how Malory had planned. He hadn't wanted any of them killed, not yet. The dead feel no pain and

can give no information. One idiot soldier with a grudge, and it
had all gone wrong. What had persuaded that fool armourer to
rush forwards in her defence? Of course he was cut down. So
unnecessary. True, the armourer mattered less than the witch or
the Guardian; Malory hadn't expected him to have much information, but now he'd never know. And Carel de la Tour's son
had got away. It had seemed such a clever idea to hide their
horses in the forest to make the castle look empty. Very clever,
until they needed their horses to chase the boy.

Worst of all, they still had not found the golden hand, or
idol, or whatever it was. He'd personally watched the men
unpack every bag, every package. They'd unwrapped every roll
of chain-mail and found nothing. Weapons, yes. Armour, yes. A
lady's gowns and trousseau. Hairbrushes and tiny, stoppered
glass bottles of oils and lotions now lay scattered in the mud.
But nothing that could not be part of the baggage train of a
noblewoman and her escort.

At least Malory had the Guardian. He hadn't tried to question him yet, and he wouldn't, not here. Malory recognised the
calm acceptance of a man of the Guardians' third degree, and
he knew that whatever pain and pressure he could apply, it
would be to no avail. Malory would take Humbert Blanc to the
anakritis-general at Daija, with the girl, if she lived. Pateras
Ghislain was so much more experienced at these matters.

It was late afternoon, and they were on their third search of
the baggage, when an armoured knight rode into the courtyard.
Malory would have known it was de Fontenay, even without the
three golden flowers emblazoned on the red surcoat. He looked
no more than thirty summers, yet the squire at his heels bore a
lance with the square banner of a war leader – a captain of
battles – in the same colours. They had clearly ridden hard;
their destriers' necks were streaked white with sweat, and the
red-painted greaves and poleyns armouring de Fontenay's legs
were spattered with mud. A troop in the de Fontenay livery

began filing through the archway, still mounted, silent and menacing. More waited on the meadow beyond. The king's men began to back into the middle of the courtyard, just as the witch's group had earlier in the day.

De Fontenay rode one circuit of the courtyard in silence, staring at the debris of the search. The soldiers backed away from him nervously, like thieves caught in the act. He ignored Malory but stopped in front of the provost.

'I am Lord Leandre de Fontenay.' He pointed upwards at the tower as emphatically as a sword thrust. 'By whose authority does my banner fly here? And where is Lady Agnès?'

'I am here, my lord, and it lifts my heart to see you.'

De Fontenay stared at the woman by the stables for so long that Malory wondered if he recognised his future wife. She'd folded the sleeves of her gown back to the elbows, exposing the loose, bloodied cuffs of her chemise, and she was wiping her hands on a scrap of linen. Her skirts were brown with mud and had wisps of straw hanging from them, and only her bearing distinguished her from the maid at her back.

'You are injured, my lady?'

'No, my lord. I am merely tending the wounded.'

De Fontenay dismounted, and his squire rushed to take his reins. He greeted his future wife with a courtly bow, but no touch or kiss, and her face fell as she dipped her body in response.

Humbert Blanc had been tied with his hands behind his back to a post of the stables, and pushed himself upright against it.

'And Brother Humbert. How fare you, Lord Brother?'

'Well enough, my lord. Better than these souls behind me.' He jerked his head towards the stables, where three bodies lay in a row: the dead armourer; the trampled Cheyne steward, coughing his last like a drowning rat; and the witch. A roll of linen lay near them with strips torn from it for bandages.

'What happened?' Leandre de Fontenay spoke quietly, but in a voice heavy with menace. Pateras Ghislain had the same skill.

'We were betrayed by that man.' The Guardian lifted his chin towards the steward. 'Lured into your castle by your banner and a false message.'

'Where we were set upon by these thieves,' added Agnès de Molinot.

Fool-born wench! Malory stepped forwards. 'My lord de Fontenay, I must protest.'

The knight could move astoundingly quickly. Before Malory could utter another word, de Fontenay's fist gripped Malory's robe at the throat, tight enough for the gauntleted knuckles to push into Malory's windpipe.

'At this moment, priest, only your robe is keeping you alive. You will *not* interrupt the Lady Agnès. Do you understand?' De Fontenay lifted his grip until Malory's sandals were scrabbling at the ground. He couldn't speak, but he could nod. With all the strength of a man trained for war from childhood, de Fontenay threw him backwards. Malory landed heavily, rolled over onto his knees, and retched.

'You were saying, my lady?' De Fontenay spoke with excessive courtesy. He wasn't even breathing heavily.

'The thieving you can see around you. They believe we carry a golden idol, but have found nothing. They have just killed one of my escort, and grievously wounded my friend.' She pointed at the witch, who lay unconscious, pale as death. Her blood had begun to darken on the straw beneath her, and Malory realised, with mild surprise, that his life would be emptier if she died. His desire to bring her to justice had been as all-embracing as a pilgrimage.

'The boy is your friend?'

'*She* has been my companion, my lord, since we left Villebénie.'

'She is a witch.' Malory struggled to his feet. He was a consecrated priest. He would *not* be cowed. 'A novice adeifi, ejected by her order.'

'Be *quiet*, priest.'

'She has proved herself a valiant woman,' Humbert Blanc added, 'and worthy of honour.'

'Then you can tell me her story later. Where is my castellan?'

Malory backed away as they brought the old man to him. This was, after all, a secular matter, led by the provost, who'd so far been silent. The old castellan dropped to his knees in front of his lord, wringing his hands and weeping.

'Forgive me, my lord, they made me do it. They took my wife. Said they'd throw her from the battlements unless I raised your banner.'

'Who, castellan? Who made that threat?'

The castellan twisted, and pointed at the provost.

'And who are you, sirrah?'

'The provost of Villebénie, my lord.' His voice was almost steady. 'These are my men.'

'They attacked us twice on the road, de Fontenay,' Humbert Blanc said. 'They killed four men-at-arms. We thought they were brigands.'

The provost's anger erupted. 'By the wounds of Salazar! We wore the king's badge!'

'And you would never fight under a false blazon, would you?' De Fontenay's voice was tight as a bowstring. He lifted his eyes to the banner over the tower to emphasise his point.

The provost ignored the comment. 'The Guardian and the witch are sought by Othon de Remy. They are wanted for murder, the desecration of temples, and theft. They are now prisoners of the king. One other fugitive escaped.'

De Fontenay walked a few paces out into the courtyard, lightly punching one fist into the palm of his other hand. In front of him a soldier dropped a lady's gown onto a loose pile of clothing the way a boy would drop a stolen apple.

De Fontenay turned to face the provost.

'There are no charges against my future wife, one presumes?'

'None, my lord.' The provost kept his eyes lowered, his manner sullen.

Malory stiffened. They couldn't just let her go. He had to swallow before he could speak. 'Though we would like to question her about events on the road from Villebénie.' He realised his voice was a little shrill.

De Fontenay stared at him as if he were a pot-boy rather than an anakritis, and turned to look at Lady Agnès's bloodied hands. 'I think you have done enough to her already.' He straightened, as if he had come to a decision. 'You will repack all that belongs to Lady Agnès. She will identify what is hers, and when she is rested I shall ride with her to Château Fontenay. For now, your men may hold only the baggage, horses, and armour that belonged to her escort. Am I understood?'

'And the Guardian? Or the witch, if she lives?' The provost seemed ready to argue.

'For tonight, you will release Messire Humbert Blanc into my parole. Lady Agnès and I would dine with him. The girl,' de Fontenay glanced at the witch's body, sounding as if he wasn't sure if she was a boy or a girl, 'is going nowhere, save perhaps the bridge of judgement, but we will tend to her needs as best we can in the castle.'

The provost breathed deeply. 'Beware, de Fontenay. Obstruct us and you obstruct the king.'

And, Malory thought, the anakritim.

10.3 ADELAIS

Arnaud came to Adelais in that dream-fever state when everything is real but nothing obeys the rules the gods set for the world, for Arnaud was dead, and yet he smiled at her and called her his brave little youngling. He had blood trickling down his chin, and an armourer's hammer resting over his shoulder like Thor, the thunder-god lover of Sif. Adelais called his name and reached for him, but cried and closed her eyes at the pain in her belly, while Amma Yrsa pushed her back into her pillows with gentle hands, saying 'hush, my sweeting'.

Yet Yrsa's face was younger, the mother Adelais had never known, perhaps. Gentle, healing hands would hold an earthenware bowl to Adelais's lips, tilting infirmary tastes of henbane, hemlock, and opium into her mouth. Afterwards Adelais would sleep, but in the sleep came pain as material was tugged from within her that had crusted and turned scratchy at its edges. The pain would wake her long enough to see those hands twist linen into a candle shape, and there'd be more pain as it was pushed into place and bound with linen strips around her hips and belly. All the time Yrsa would say she was being gentle as she could, my sweeting, not in Vriesian but in the earthy vowels of Jourdaine.

Yet as Adelais slipped back into sleep she'd hear the drumbeat of rune song in the Old Tongue. *Úr er skýja grátr, ok skára thverrir...* Sometimes she'd imagine a wolf watching over her, nodding its head in time with the rune song, and Adelais would smile in her sleep, for Yrsa's sigil was the wolf, and who but Yrsa would know the song of *úruz*, the rune of healing? In response Adelais traced the rune upon her own belly.

ᚢ

Úruz, the sign of soft rain; *úr is the weeping of the clouds...*

One time, when sleep lay lightly upon her, she began to weave her own voice with the song: 'Ok hirdhis hatr...' but a hand was placed softly over her mouth and the same voice said the same words: 'hush, sweeting'. There had been a time when Arnaud had done that to silence her, and in her ecstasy she'd sunk her teeth into his hand. Now she contented herself with a kiss, up into a palm that smelt of herbs and fresh bread. It was too soft to be Arnaud's; his had forge-made callouses, and his touch, his caresses, had been like silk-wrapped iron.

She couldn't imagine anyone loving her like that again; it would hurt too much.

Once, the prophet Salazar came to see her, standing at the foot of her bed with a bloodied hand, and she tried to rise to show respect, but that hurt too much. When she opened her eyes after the scream it was only Humbert, standing there with bandaged fingers. He looked down at her with his two-week beard and the tenderness of a suffering prophet in his eyes.

One of them was always there; Agnès, Mathilde, and Amma Yrsa. Or was it the goddess Eir? She heard them call her something like that. Their faces became blurred; the servant,

the friend, and the healing goddess, but only Yrsa, or Eir, sang
rune song.

A pigeon woke her on a morning of golden light, making its
hoo-hoo, ho-ho call outside an unshuttered window. Adeifi
Elodie used to keep the shutters open in the infirmary, saying
cool breezes blow away the bad airs of sickness. Adelais turned
her head to see a woman's face that was both familiar and
unknown beside her on the pillow. Eir, perhaps. This woman
lay above the covers in an undyed, homespun gown and apron,
while Adelais was naked beneath them. Eir snoring, she awake,
but so light-headed she might be floating next to the ceiling
timbers; everything so sharp, so clear, each swirl of the grain,
each cobweb. Definitely awake. And perhaps a little hungry.

Adelais tried to move, just a bit, and stopped. Anything that
involved tensing her stomach was a mistake. She lifted the
covers, and looked down, surprised at the hollow beneath her
ribs. She'd never been fat, but the ends of her pelvis now stuck
out like a calf's horns. There was a bandage around her waist
and between her legs that held a pad of linen in place, and from
this angle the linen showed only a small half-moon of dried
blood. Above the bandage, her whole belly was bruised purple,
fading to livid reds and browns at her waist. She pushed her
fingers under the bandage, tentatively, exploring, and found a
tiny square of wood between the wrapping and her belly. She
pulled it out, and found herself staring at runes that she had not
seen since she was sent away from Vriesland.x

ᚢ ᚠ ᛒ

Uruz for healing, *ansuz* the god-rune for the gift of life, and
bjarkan for the gentle nurture of the earth mother. Someone
had cared for her who knew the forbidden lore.

'You're awake, are you? That's good.' The woman stirred,

and pushed herself off the bed. She was short, broad, and had strong, bare forearms that Adelais could imagine dusted with flour and kneading dough. 'I'll fetch my lady.'

'Who are you?' The goddess Eir wouldn't call anyone 'my lady'.

'I'm Elyse, the castellan's wife.' Her face dimpled when she smiled. 'And I'd say you're going to live, thanks be. They're calling it a miracle.'

No miracle, just a stone the size of a child's fist.

'Arnaud's dead, isn't he?'

She couldn't quite separate dreams from reality, but of that miserable fact she was certain. As the dreams faded, the soul-crushing loss was settling on her.

Elyse sat on the edge of the bed and took her hand.

'He was your man, wasn't he? Well yes, my sweeting, he's dead. That anakritis gave him the Offices of the Dead and we laid 'im to rest outside the castle walls, 'im and the other one —'im what betrayed you. There used to be a village and a temple there, so he's in sacred ground, if that was important to him. It was nicely done, though my husband will carry the weight of obeying those murderers until his dying-day.'

Adelais found she was too numb to cry, but it was a comfort to watch the woman's gentle face and feel her hand being stroked.

'You sang rune song.'

'We'll let that be our secret. Please?' Elyse's eyes blazed a warning.

Of course. Adelais understood the enormity of the risk Elyse had taken. 'And you gave me herbs. I tasted henbane.' Here at least was something of this world. Talking about herbs would keep her mind from Arnaud's death.

'Henbane and betony, hemlock and lettuce, honey and vinegar. Plus a few secrets of my own.'

One of which was precious opium. 'Will you tell me your measures? Too much hemlock or henbane would have put me to sleep for ever.'

'You have healer's skills? Then I'll tell you later. First let me fetch my lady, and bring a little broth.' Elyse squeezed Adelais's hand one more time. 'Do not try to move. You are not yet whole. Besides, there are guards below who would be rough, out of fear.'

She couldn't move anyway, but why should soldiers be afraid of her?

'I need to...' There was no polite word for 'piss'.

'Make water? Good. Then Mathilde and I will lift you onto a pot. You must suffer being treated like a baby for a few days.'

Agnès came while Adelais was propped up on cushions in a fresh chemise, finishing her second bowl of broth – a transformed Agnès in a cleaned gown and spotless linen, a noble Agnès with a caul of golden net restraining brushed and shining hair.

'She is alert, my lady, and so much stronger, and her water runs clear...' Elyse clearly took personal pride in Adelais's recovery, but Agnès stopped her with a gentle lifting of the hand.

'Elyse, I would talk with Mistress Adelais before I leave with my lord de Fontenay.'

They looked at each other while Elyse left, each suppressing a smile that had no obvious cause.

'You look beautiful, *my lady*.' Adelais smiled and tried to bow her head in a way that robbed the words of all formality, but winced at the movement.

'I must impress my future husband, *kjúkling*. He is not best pleased by recent events.'

'He blames you? Brother Humbert said it was his idea!'

'It was supposed to be so easy. Bring the Hand of Salazar in my baggage, wrapped up in a roll of linen. Now four brothers are dead, plus Arnaud. I'm told there are fifteen king's men dead or missing, and more wounded, so my future husband has a lot of explaining to do at court. And don't be fooled by this chamber; you and Humbert are prisoners. You will have poorer hospitality when you leave de Fontenay's protection.'

'We will be given over to the anakritim?' A wave of weakness flooded over Adelais, and the broth spoon slipped from her fingers. Agnès rescued the bowl and sat on the bed beside her, resting against the pillows with one arm around Adelais's shoulders.

'Once you were captured, it limited de Fontenay's choices. He cannot oppose the king, not openly, even here in Jourdaine. He cannot pretend that you are elsewhere. When you can travel, the priest will take you both to the anakritis-general at Daija. Only my rank stops me from being bound and taken with you.'

Adelais let herself be pulled sideways into Agnès's chest. The way Agnès lay her cheek onto Adelais's head was comforting, yet brought no comfort, in the way Elyse's stroking hand had comforted her for the death of Arnaud, yet could not bring him back.

'Agnès, I'm frightened.' She was being kept alive to be tortured.

'All is not lost.' Agnès kissed her head. 'De Fontenay will write to the high priest himself asking him to intervene. He will say that we thought we were attacked by brigands. They have no evidence of theft. No golden idol.'

'They did not find the Hand?'

'It stayed hidden in the linen when we were searched, and is now guarded by de Fontenay. It seems to have a way of protecting itself.'

'But not always those who serve it.' An image of Arnaud's bloody face came to Adelais's mind. 'What happened to Guy?'

'He pulled the steward from his horse, and used it to find de Fontenay. The guards on the bridge over the Naeva did not stop a lone youth. He is safe, and the provost does not know. Leandre is minded to offer him a position.'

'That ride must have taken courage.' Adelais was revising her opinion of Guy.

'Adelais, I must warn you that the priest may accuse you of witchcraft. You pulled an arrow from your belly yet have no visible wound, just bruises. If so, you must argue that it was a miracle, not witchcraft.'

'But the sling and the stone?'

'Only Elyse and I know about that, and I suggest you tell no one else, not even Brother Humbert. He thinks you live because you are protected by Ischyros. He even thinks that you may be one of the Blessèd Ones. It is important to let him think that.'

'Why? Why not just tell them about the stone?'

'Think, Adelais. De Fontenay and I can no longer save you from the anakritim, but the high priest in Daija might. He would not intervene to save a sorceress or a thief, but he would if he thought you were proof of a miracle, and especially if he thought you were sent by the God.'

Adelais began to laugh, very gently. Agnès wanted her to play the part of one of the Blessèd Ones that protect the Earth from Kakos, and she didn't even believe in Ischyros. She stopped, quickly. Laughing was painful.

'Seriously, *kjúkling*, you must be a messenger of the God. Make them fear you.'

'In blasphemy lies my salvation?' She must be delirious to make such jokes.

Agnès squeezed her shoulder. She wasn't laughing. 'Just don't let them persuade the high priest you're a sorceress.'

Adelais nodded, though her face was still cushioned in the softness of Agnès's velvet-covered chest. She tried to sit straighter, and groaned. All movement, except turning her head, seemed to go through her belly.

'How long before we travel?' The prospect of sitting on horseback was as frightening as the thought of the anakritim waiting in Daija. She'd die.

'The priest has agreed to wait for two days after all bleeding stops. He wants to deliver a live prisoner for questioning, not a corpse. You will then be carried by litter to a boat. After that, it should be a gentle journey. The Naeva flows all the way to Daija.'

'It is the priest that worries me most. The thought of being in his control is almost more than I can bear.'

'He hates you with a vengeance. He's like a spurned lover, bent on revenge. What did you do to him?'

'I kicked him in the shit. Well, Guy did, but it was my idea...'

'You did *what?*'

So Adelais told Agnès the story of the Pissbourne, and together they began to laugh. It was a mad, hysterical laughter that bubbled up through all the fears and the loss, and it hurt. A lot.

'Stop, Agnès.' The laughter was cleansing but each spasm pulled at the muscles in her belly, and Adelais doubled over, trying to stifle them. 'Please stop.'

'Oh, *kjúkling*, I shall miss you.'

They lay together until they could breathe normally, with Adelais's face again against Agnès's breast. It still shook a little with the aftermath of their mirth.

'Agnès, my friend, I have a great favour to ask.' She looked up. Agnès had tears in her eyes, but they were happy tears.

'Anything within my power.'

'I fear torture. I fear I will not be strong enough to resist, and if I was forced to tell them about the Hand, it would hurt you and de Fontenay badly.'

'This we know. It is why de Fontenay will petition the high priest.'

'De Fontenay is an honourable man to let me live. The Guardians would have killed me rather than let me be captured.' Adelais felt a new stillness within Agnès's body; perhaps de Fontenay too would have let her die without Agnès's protection. She reached for Agnès's hand, and took a deep breath. 'Elyse is a wise woman, a healer. She knows the secrets of the herbs.'

'I have seen her work, these past few days. She has saved you as much as the stone against your belly.'

'She has a potion, with hemlock and henbane. Even, I think, a little opium. I would like to take some with me, secretly.'

Agnès tensed. 'I will not be complicit in your death.'

'But if I reach a time when all hope is lost, and there is only pain, will you be complicit in my silence? For your sake?'

Three days later, Adelais could stand. She could even take a few, faltering steps in the chamber, though she had to hold the corner-post of the bed while Elyse knelt at her feet and adjusted the hem of a gown, a farewell gift from Agnès. In front of her, in a window, Elyse's half-tame ravens fed on corn that she'd scattered. They'd arrive flapping, strut into the embrasure as if they owned the castle, and tilt their heads on one side to watch Elyse work.

'They tried to warn me, aunty.' She was growing to love the castellan's wife, and 'aunty' seemed to show the right mixture of respect and affection. 'The ravens. They tried to stop us at the gate.'

'Doesn't surprise me. They're sharp as a cook's knife, them birds,' Elyse mumbled around the pins held between her lips.

'My grandmother had ravens, too. She said they were messengers.'

'Is she the one what taught you the runes?'

Adelais looked down; neither of them had mentioned the songs of healing since Adelais woke. Elyse's mop of mouse-brown, silver-streaked hair bobbed at Adelais's knees.

'My grandmother was a staff-woman, a *seidhkona*. Still is, if she lives.' If anyone could be trusted with such knowledge, it was Elyse.

'Don't ever let that anakritis know. He'll burn you, for sure.'

'And you took a risk, singing over me and putting healing runes over the wound.'

Elyse rocked back on her heels, and looked up, taking the pins from her mouth. 'I sang for one who carries a *taufr*.'

Adelais looked quickly at her scrip, lying on the bed with her belt, as panic rose within her.

'Don't worry, it's still there. And I did not have to search you. I felt its presence. A *taufr* is a living thing. It too has a destiny, and yours was never to die that day.'

'You know the ways of *seidhr*?'

'What is *seidhr*, but listening to the warp and weft of fate? Or rather knowing *how* to listen?' Elyse climbed to her feet, pushing against her own knees. 'You are just beginning, sweeting. You hear the warning of the raven, but you are not yet listening. And like runes, what we see and hear is like the shadow of a greater truth. Show me your *taufr*.'

Adelais picked up her scrip, slid out Yrsa's talisman, and gave it to her. She hadn't realised how short Elyse was until she stood beside her.

'This was carved by one well versed in *seidhr*.' Elyse bent to examine the pattern of incised lines. 'The bind-rune is many runes laid on top of each other,' Elyse turned it in her palm, 'and the shape of every rune, its *stave*, is only a shadow thrown by a much greater secret, which is forever hidden from our sight but held within the threads of fate.'

'You sang the song of *úruz*.'

'*Úruz*, and others. The song of each rune is its voice within the web, like a stream over a waterfall. And, like a stream, each rune flows on beyond our understanding. Together, many runes can make such music that the web itself can change. You know some rune song?'

It was a statement, not a question. In her delirium, Adelais had tried to join her voice with Elyse's.

'I have heard my grandmother sing.'

'Beware. To sing rune song without knowledge of the craft is like giving a child a sword. There is small chance of a good outcome, and great risk.'

'My grandmother warned me.'

Elyse lifted the *taufr* to her face, peering closely at the carving. 'One rune is carved more deeply than all others. See?' She handed back the talisman.

Adelais hadn't noticed before. She had to twist the *taufr* against the light to see.

'*Thurs*.' It had been the first rune she'd learned from Yrsa. *Thurs*, the giant-rune, the rune of Thor, the warrior – mate of Sif. *Mynn litla Sif.*

'You know its song?'

Adelais breathed deeply, but Elyse reached up to put her hand over her mouth to stop her. 'Hush, child, not now. You have power you do not understand. Only ever sing that if you are in great peril. Then sing as if you are calling on Thor himself.'

Elyse took her hand away slowly, looking up into Adelais's eyes.

'My grandmother said I had power. I didn't understand her.'

'The threads of fate connect us all. Your grandmother would call them the *urlogthættir*. I cast the runes for you, quietly, when all were sleeping. It does not work so well if I choose for you, rather than you choosing for yourself, but I saw that you are at the centre of many threads, holding many destinies in your hands. Until you know what you are doing, you will be like wildfire that destroys the good wood with the bad.'

Elyse spoke with an intensity that stunned Adelais.

'The last thing my grandmother said to me was that I am like the tall tree that draws people to its shelter, but also draws the lightning, and lightning kills.' Was Arnaud part of that prophecy? And the Guardians?

'That is a heavy destiny.' Elyse squeezed her arm. 'Come back to me, if ever you can, my sweeting. Mayhap it is my fate to pass on my learning to you.'

'If I live, aunty.'

At that Elyse pulled Adelais into a hug. When they broke, Elyse had tears in her eyes.

'Which reminds me, I have one more gift for you, from me and from my lady, and the gods grant that you never use it.' Elyse took a tiny glass phial from the scrip at her own belt and clasped it as if she was unwilling to hand it over. 'One drop in wine will ease pain, two and you will sleep for half a day. Five and you will never wake, but it would be a gentler death than any the anakritim would give.'

Adelais took it out of Elyse's hands and pulled her close. Elyse fretted against her, covering her distress with words.

'I'll sew a pocket for it, high inside the skirts where no man should ever search you...'

Adelais rubbed Elyse's back with one hand, thinking it strange that she should be the one to offer comfort. The other hand held the phial. Its cork had been sealed with hard wax, and the wax incised with the *thurs* rune. In her mind, and only in her mind, Adelais rehearsed the never-to-be-sung rune song of Thor:

> Thurs er kvenna kvöl, ok kletta búi...
> *Thurs is the agony of women, the cliff-dweller...*

PART THREE

THE BARLEY MOON

CHAPTER 11

11.1 ADELAIS

To Adelais, it was a pleasure-voyage towards the pit of Kakos, or the Hel of the old gods. The broad-beamed, shallow-draught trading vessel that Malory d'Eivet had hired rode the Naeva's meandering waters smoothly, and the hay moon had brought good weather. A steady south wind brought not the stink of a city but the sweeter smells of lush Jourdainian countryside. On the first day, on longer reaches where it blew on the beam, the crew hoisted the single, angled sail, but on the second day the Naeva swung south and joined another river, flowing fast and full from mountains to the east. Now the wind was in their faces and the crew allowed the river to do the work for them, rowing just enough to let the helmsman steer. It became a passage of gentle idleness, but if ever Adelais began to enjoy the moment, she only had to look at Malory d'Eivet's face; the loathing she saw there promised agony to come.

Yet in the priest's unguarded moments she imagined she saw doubt, as if he could not quite decide whether she was a witch or an angel.

The river men had placed Adelais and Humbert in the bow, not unkindly; they'd given them a pile of sacking to cushion the deck, and a canvas awning to screen Adelais when she needed to use the bucket. Even so, Adelais could not understand Humbert's contentment. He prayed regularly, singing praise chants as if his heart truly sang. At other times Humbert sat with his neck resting against the bulwark, smiling up into the sun. He might have been sailing to the arms of Ischyros rather than to the anakritim and their tormentors, but in the crowded boat she had no opportunity to question him.

The chains around their ankles were Malory d'Eivet's idea. Adelais found it hard to think of him as *Pateras* Malory; it implied too much respect. But the chains, as heavy and deadly as armour if they sank, now bound her and Humbert to each other and to a bench seat that the sailors called a thwart. Perhaps d'Eivet felt more nervous, now he had only six soldiers with him – five ruffians and an older one they called 'the sergeant', who kept himself apart. The provost, apparently, had sent two on ahead to Daija, to alert the anakritis-general, and had returned to Villebénie with the rest, bearing news of their capture to Chancellor de Remy.

One of the soldiers was sick. Adelais could see him shivering, despite the sun, and he had a dazed, half-sensible, fevered look. He carried his sword arm in a sling; apparently Arnaud had managed to land one blow before he was killed. Adelais beckoned him to her, though he was reluctant to approach until she pointed at his arm. He sat on the thwart by the mast, which was as far as her chain would let her move, and took off his gambeson stiffly, staring at her all the while. She had to gentle him as if he was a horse as she peeled back his shirt.

The wound was a deep stab, rather than a shallower slash, and it was infected, oozing humours that had crusted on the red, inflamed skin around its lips, but Adelais was more concerned about the man's fever. He let her touch her hand to his brow, which was hot, and his pulse and breathing were too fast to be explained by his scramble through the boat.

The realisation that she was concerned surprised Adelais; for a moment she might have been back in the infirmary. She had forgotten that this man was one of those who had killed her Arnaud. For about five deep breaths she stared at the soldier, wondering whether to let him die, and the man stared back, nervous of her witchcraft. The deadliest thing she could do now was nothing. Yet Arnaud had been Ischyrian, at least in name, and by that faith his soul would have another burden if the man died; an unpardoned sin to pull him from the bridge of judgement.

'Pateras Malory!' Adelais called the priest. He, too, seemed reluctant to approach, and came no further than the same bench on the other side of the mast. He made the warding sign against Kakos as he sat.

'Well?'

'Your man has wound fever. It starts with infection in the wound, then the fiery humours spread throughout the body. He may die, and die swiftly.'

'I shall pray for him.'

'He needs an apothecary as well as prayer, and the town on the shore over there will sell the means to keep him alive.'

'I will have no witchcraft.'

'I am no witch, but I learned some healing craft in the sister-house's infirmary. You can save his body with herbs that will cost a few deniers, or you can save his soul with prayers that will cost nothing. You must choose.'

Malory d'Eivet shook his head. 'Prayer must suffice. I wish to reach Daija swiftly.'

'So be it. His death will then be a burden on your soul, not on that of my man, may he rest with Ischyros.' In a way, Adelais was relieved. It took the matter out of her hands.

'Please, Pateras.' The soldier turned to d'Eivet. His skin had begun to shine like stale cheese; the fever was progressing fast and the man could feel it.

'What do you need?' D'Eivet still sounded unconvinced.

'I will wash the wound now with wine, and with vinegar if you have it. From an apothecary, white willow bark for the fever. Betony, or woundwort, to ease the pain. Wormwood. Best of all, vervain, which some call the herb of grace for it eased the wounds of Salazar in Alympos. It should have been blessed with the sign of the God before it was picked, and dried swiftly. They may also have a salve made with verdigris to pack the wound. If not, honey, and fresh cobwebs to seal it.'

The soldier looked at the priest with the big, pleading eyes of a wounded animal, and Malory d'Eivet turned to hail the boat's captain.

The next day there were times when Adelais and Humbert had enough privacy to talk. Adelais's treatment of the wounded soldier, who they learned was called Thierry, made the men suspicious. After all, a consecrated priest had called her a witch. Thierry lay on sacking just forward of the mast, lost in the depths of his fever. From time to time she mopped his face with a cloth dipped in the river, and trickled a honey-sweetened infusion of wormwood and white willow bark between his lips when he would take it. Adelais took care to make the sign of Ischyros and be seen to pray as she tended him, for the rest of the soldiers watched from further aft, glaring at her sullenly. They all understood wound fever, which could turn an apparently survivable cut into a mortal hurt. From first sweats to death could be less than a day, which was about as long as Thierry had survived, so far.

Even the boatmen avoided her now. In some stretches, a nervous boy would be sent to the bow to watch for the sandbanks that shifted with each year's floods, but few came willingly forward of the mast. When not working the boat, they also clustered towards the stern, near the priest, where they were roundly cursed by the helmsman for obstructing his view. Once Adelais saw a soldier talking to a river man on a bench near the stern, their heads low and close together. The soldier made a wrenching motion with his fist over his gut, and the river man looked swiftly up at her, his eyes wide. She stared back, and he looked away, hunching his shoulders.

'They think I could strike them down with a look.'

Humbert stirred beside her. 'Smile at them. The best way to counter the suspicion of witchcraft is to let them see your piety and innocence. Perhaps you are indeed a Blessèd One of Ischyros.'

It was hard to let him think that, whatever the consequences. 'I'm not a Blessèd One, messire. I shared my body with Arnaud, and it was...' She paused, trying to find a word that did not debase their love. 'Wonderful. So wonderful I would not even unburden it, though the priests would say it was a sin. It would be a lie to seek pardon for a something I do not regret.' But she wasn't going to let him know she did not believe in Ischyros.

'You think only chaste women find favour with the God? Good deeds are pleasing, whether by matron or maid, whether they are healing, or defending the faith against the infidel. And whether or not you are a Blessèd One, I suggest you act like one. For both our sakes. What you are doing for Thierry is an excellent start.'

'And it is hard for me to forgive those who slew Arnaud.'

'Remember the men who killed Arnaud also killed four of my brethren, but I hold them no ill will. They did their duty, no more.'

'Just one moon, I knew him. But...'

'But you still miss him.'

Yes, she missed him. She missed that sparkle in his eye, as if he was always on the edge of laughter. She missed the feeling of being whole, and complete, and content, when all the world shone like sunlight on frost. She even missed being called his 'little youngling', now that he couldn't call her anything. And even after her injury she missed his body; the broad shoulders poised above her, and, below that taut belly, his manhood straining for her...

An ache started within her, the wrong sort of ache, and she stood, turning to look at the view down the river. *Mustn't have those kind of thoughts. They hurt, in every sense of the word.*

'Yes, I miss him.'

She could stand easily, now. Walking pulled painfully at muscles within her, but there wasn't much need for walking in the boat, and the chain rubbed her ankle. Steps were a greater problem; the pain of lifting a leg and raising her weight on it meant that Humbert had to carry her in and out of the boat like a baby. But if she stayed still she was comfortable, and she knew her body was healing. She hadn't felt the need to open Elyse's phial, not even for a single drop. She could feel it against the inside of her thigh, a gentle contact only a little harder than the fabric, and it gave her confidence.

There had been another gift from Agnès. Sewn into the belt around Adelais's waist were five gold crowns. Enough, Agnès hoped, to bribe a guard, if not to release her then at least to make it a swift end and spare her the sin of self-murder.

Adelais steadied herself with one hand on the rope running from the stem-post to the top of the mast. The boat was sliding slowly through the water, just enough to make a light waterfall noise under the bow, but it moved swiftly against the land; islands near the shore trailed wakes as if they were vessels sailing upstream. It was a place and a scene that inspired reflection.

'Messire, how can a pious man like you serve the same God as the anakritim?'

Humbert also stood, planting his feet wide apart against the movement of the boat. He leaned his head close to hers to speak.

'We serve the same God, but not with the same faith. Salazar taught us to seek the God within us, whom the present age has named Ischyros. The disciples who came after, like Tanguy, were more militant, and those that followed Tanguy harsher still, each competing to show their rigour. In five generations a faith that was pure and sacred has been subverted in man's lust for power. Kings use the faith as an excuse for conquest. The episkopes decide what is heresy and the anakritim enforce that with torture. That would not have been Salazar's way, though I would be burned for saying so. The Guardians have tried to remain faithful to Salazar's ideal, and perhaps that was why the high priest abandoned us to King Aloys's greed.'

'Yet you still believe, and your brothers were willing to die to save a relic.'

'My brothers found a death that will be pleasing in the eyes of the God. They met their ends with joy, and they will have been welcomed across the bridge into the company of martyrs. I rejoice for them, that they found such honour.'

'And Arnaud?' Or the life that had quickened so briefly within her? 'He wanted to protect me, not find martyrdom.'

'Who can know the mind of the God? Perhaps He has a greater purpose for you than as an armourer's wife. In taking l'Armurier, He blessed the man and released you to His purpose.'

'If I believed that, I would curse Ischyros for taking him from me.'

Adelais expected Humbert to be angry, but he laughed, smiling at her with gentle eyes. 'And Ischyros would pardon your curse, the way a parent pardons an infant for its rage.'

The rope's coarse fibres scratched at her cheek, but she rested her head against it, listening. It was tight as a lute string and hummed in her ear as if singing to her. She'd found its tune changed with the strength of the wind and the movement of the boat in the water; now it was a gentle purr, as soothing as a sleeping cat.

'Why are you so happy, messire? You have lost the Hand, you have lost your brothers, even if they are now with Ischyros, yet all this voyage you have laughed and smiled as if Salazar himself awaited us both in Daija, not the anakritim.'

'Perhaps he does. The anakritim would be but the doorway to Ischyros, for I would cross the bridge with hope. And we did not lose the Hand. We delivered it safely to a good custodian, so perhaps my life's work is done. No, my joy is in the hope that *you* might be spared.'

'How so, messire?'

'I think my end is certain, for I led our party, and, as I have said, that does not concern me. But de Fontenay will intercede with the high priest. You are a curiosity, you see? When you lay wounded, Lady Agnès and I prayed to Salazar to spare you, and you lived. You are the living proof of the power of prayer, the woman who survived a crossbow bolt in the body. How can you say you are not a Blessèd One? You are no mere thief to be handed over to justice.'

'The anakritim will demand me. Demand us both.'

'And they may be given me, as a compromise. But the Angel of Death was always King Aloys's man, not the high priest's, and Daija is beyond the borders of Galmandie, in Yerísfaíra. That is the sacred domain of the high priest, where King Aloys's law holds no sway. You, I hope, will be allowed to live.'

'I am honoured that makes you so happy, messire.'

Humbert was silent. Adelais looked up at him, and was surprised to see him turn his face away awkwardly, even shyly.

'I never had a wife, nor a child, Adelais, but I would have been so proud to have had a daughter like you. You have been a blessing to me, these last days.'

Adelais put her hand on his where it rested on the rope, touched beyond measure by his words.

'And you have been a truer friend, Lord Brother, than any flesh and blood of mine.'

He put his other hand over hers, and they were quiet together, staring down the river, while Adelais wondered whether to tell him about the stone. Which was better, to let him keep his illusions or to tell him the unvarnished truth?

'Messire, I saw the Hand, in the stables after Arnaud was struck down.' She hadn't dared to admit that before. Now it came blurting out.

Humbert straightened, his jollity slipping away. 'How so?'

'The linen unrolled as Mathilde opened it. She meant no harm. I touched it. I wanted to bring it to Arnaud, to heal him, but it was too late.'

'Now I understand why you lived.' Humbert's face shone with the zeal of a true believer. 'You touched the Hand of Salazar.'

This explanation was going the wrong way. She only lived because he'd told her to pad her body like a man's, and she'd wrapped a sling and a stone around her waist. Luck. Plus a wise woman's skill.

'No, messire...'

But Humbert was not listening. 'You pulled a crossbow bolt from your own belly, and lived. Agnès said that you have no wound on your body. Is this so?'

Adelais nodded, reluctantly. 'But, messire...' She couldn't lie to Humbert any more.

'No cut?' The old knight's enthusiasm transformed his face.

'Only bruises. Messire, I must tell you...'

'You touched the Hand and were healed, of even so grievous a wound.'

'No, messire...' Adelais drew breath to explain but the rope by her ear changed its pitch, becoming angry as they rounded a bend in the river and met a stronger wind, and some instinct made her look over her shoulder.

Malory d'Eivet was stepping over the benches towards them. His face gave no sign that he had heard anything significant, only wonder that the soldier Thierry had pulled himself into a sitting position and was staring about, his eyes blinking but aware. He squinted into the sun, saw Adelais in the bow, and swallowed.

'Praise be to Ischyros!' Malory called. 'You have been saved by our prayers!'

Not prayer, Adelais thought, but wormwood, vervain, and verdigris. Perhaps Thierry knew that as well, for it was to Adelais that he turned.

'May I have a little water?'

It seemed that he was going to live.

Their passage was too swift. Cities that Adelais knew only as names, distant as Alympos, were already in their wake. Part of her dreaded their arrival at Daija; it was like waiting to be called to the eldest daughter for a beating, but so much worse. Mitera Chantalle had inflicted limited pain, a mere punishment. The anakritim would inflict unlimited pain, to break her. What if she was bound, and could not reach Elyse's bottle to save herself from talking? Should she take it anyway, before they had a chance to bind her?

Another part of her wanted it over.

Humbert was as calm as ever, perhaps even a little animated as they passed lands that he knew.

'Look, Adelais.' He waved his arm towards the right bank of the Naeva. It was always 'Adelais' now, never 'child' or 'girl'.

Adelais lifted her head. She'd been lying on her back, staring at the masthead moving against the sky, and dreaming up little, insulting speeches that she'd make to the anakritim with the bottle concealed in her palm. She'd go out with a last, defiant gesture if she could. She followed Humbert's pointing arm to the steep wooded hills that crowded towards the river beyond the floodplain to the west.

'That is Maycea. Beyond lies Arrenicia, my home. If Ischyros is merciful, I may one day ride its paths again.'

So he hadn't given up all hope of surviving whatever awaited them in Daija.

'This river marks the border of Galmandie. Over there is the land of Yerísfaíra.' Humbert pointed at the left bank. Beyond the plain, the land rose to more distant mountains that lay like clouds on the eastern horizon. 'Land that belongs to the high priest, not to King Aloys.'

'And does it stretch all the way to Daija?'

'And beyond.' He bent his head close to hers so that the nearby soldiers could not hear. 'Once we are landed on the left bank, we are beyond Aloys's law, and the high priest is reluctant to use torture in his domain.'

There were always people near them now, and had been ever since Thierry recovered. Once the soldiers and boatmen had lost their fear of her, they spread out to fill the available space. Even the skipper's son came to her, offering a running sore on his leg for her inspection. So far, Thierry's salve of vervain and verdigris seemed to be working equally well on the boy. That morning a boatman had pulled off his cap, bobbing his head in respect as he passed near her on some duty, and she'd looked up in time to see Malory d'Eivet glowering his resentment in the stern. She'd forced herself to make the sign of benediction at him. Her, an unbelieving novice, blessing a priest. She'd been rewarded by a flash of doubt. *Good.*

'The twin castles!' They'd entered a great, curving sweep of the river, and Humbert called her to see the landmarks as if they brought happy memories of his youth. 'Château Roquegris on the Yerísfaíra bank, Château Roquenoir on the Maycean bank. Roca Nera in old Occan.'

Ahead of them the Naeva divided around the base of a great rocky outcrop, crowned by a castle that rose as high above the river as the donjon of the Villebénie citadel. The lesser channel formed a natural moat between Château Roquenoir and a walled town to its west, while the main channel swung east at its base towards the far bank, a quarter league away. The side of Château Roquenoir facing them was not long, perhaps a single bowshot wide, but presented a cloud-scrapingly tall cliff that fell sheer to the water.

The boat began to edge towards it, out of the main stream in the middle of the river, pulled not only by the current but now by four oarsmen. Adelais looked over her shoulder towards the helmsman, not understanding the new direction, and found herself staring at Malory d'Eivet.

'Our journey is nearly over.' D'Eivet stood by the mast, gripping a rope for support while the wind whipped the skirts of his robe around his ankles. He'd spoken lightly, as if they were amiable travelling companions, but his eyes said 'here is where it begins'.

Humbert had also turned. 'We have yet some leagues to Daija. I know this place.' An edge of concern had crept into his voice.

'I had word from Pateras Ghislain at our last stop.' D'Eivet sounded almost apologetic. 'Daija is a little crowded, it seems. There is such an army of episkopes dancing attendance upon the high priest that there is no longer any spare room even for clerics. The anakritis-general has arranged alternative accommodation for you within the borders of Galmandie, where he will not offend the high priest's sensibilities about torture.' D'Eivet made a wry smile and gestured towards the towers slipping towards them, high on their cliff. He might even have regretted the end of their journey. 'Welcome to King Aloys's royal fortress of Roquenoir.'

Adelais turned her back on him, both to hide her fear and to see the castle that was to be their prison. Its dark, shadowed side faced them, dominating the river like a great armoured fist on the water, knuckled with squat towers. As they entered the secondary flow between the castle and the town, the southern aspect of the château opened up. Here the outcrop sloped to the water and the defenders could not rely on the cliff, so tiers of stone rose above her, walls within walls; a low perimeter enclosing a harbour, then the main bastion with five round towers. Higher still, if she craned her neck, more towers and the dome of a temple were outlined against the sky, so high she could not see the hand that would crown the dome.

But worst of all was the figure waiting for them on the jetty in his black-and-white anakritim robes. As they drew closer, Ghislain Barthram's unblinking eyes were locked on Adelais and his lips were pulled back into a thin line, like a snake's. As she watched, his tongue darted out to moisten them.

CHAPTER 12

12.1 MALORY

'Are you drunk?' Barthram frowned at Pateras Malory, pausing his benediction.

'Not so, Pateras.' Malory had staggered a little. After four days of swaying with the motion of the boat, his feet found the solidity of the land unsettling. 'The quayside seemed to move.'

Barthram sniffed and beckoned d'Eivet to walk with him, but Malory paused to watch Humbert Blanc lift the witch onto the quayside, where she seemed perfectly capable of standing unaided. The little harbour below Château Roquenoir was crowded; a constant stream of small craft plied between the castle and the town, trading vessels from further afield were unloading cargo, and a small, swift sailing boat was setting out with toll collectors to intercept passing craft. He was glad he had insisted that Blanc and the witch must be chained; it would be too easy to slip away. Now he had them, after so much difficulty, he didn't want to take his eyes off them.

'Come. The garrison will see to the prisoners.' Barthram gestured towards a group of soldiers tramping towards them, and led Malory up steps that climbed beneath an arrow-slitted tower to the castle's first gate.

'You have made no attempt to question them?'

'None.' Malory glanced around him inside the tower. The spaces between a fortress's first and second gates always made him nervous – the killing holes in the walls, and the funnels for burning oil above.

'Good. And you found nothing in their baggage?'

'No gold, save the de Molinot woman's jewels. It was... embarrassing. De Fontenay was most displeased.'

'He is a man of considerable influence. The high priest is taking a personal interest. He received a letter saying that the girl is no witch but is the walking proof of a miracle. He even hinted that she may be a Blessèd One.' Barthram's mouth tightened as if he had sucked a lemon.

'Things happened that I cannot explain, Pateras.' Malory looked up; they were passing through the third gate, inside another tower. More killing holes. Walking with the anakritis-general was bad enough, but Malory felt like a sinner on the bridge of judgement, waiting for the push.

'Such as?'

'She was hit in the belly with a crossbow bolt. I saw her go down. I saw the blood, and I saw her stand and rip it from her own body. Now, if the rumours are true, she shows no sign of a wound.'

More steps led through the first terrace, and up into a small garden where, finally, Malory could feel the sun again on his neck. They were now level with the curtain wall, and could see over it to the wide river and the green lands beyond.

'We will, of course, have her examined. You have her clothing?'

'With the cuts, and the crossbow bolt that made them.'

'This is powerful sorcery indeed.'

'Sorcery? Perhaps, Pateras. Or a miracle, as de Fontenay suggests.' Malory ignored Barthram's glare and kept speaking. 'She has power, and can use it for good. She healed a soldier of wound fever in the boat.' When she'd tended the man, bathing his wound, her face had softened and she'd been beautiful. She'd looked innocent, and he wished that she'd look at him like that instead of the tight-jawed grimace she usually gave him.

'More sorcery. And soon we shall prove it. You are too easily swayed. But let us sit awhile, here where we cannot be heard.'

Barthram led him to a seat against the north wall where someone, the castellan's lady perhaps, had cultivated a rose arbour that now held a cascade of blooms. A pitch-roofed well had been sunk in that corner of the garden, creating a secluded place, overlooked by no windows save those of the castle's temple, high on the rock's summit. A small almond tree shaded one corner. Malory was conscious of the honour of being invited to sit with the anakritis-general on the bench. Perhaps his work was not unregarded.

Ghislain Barthram closed his eyes, turning his face to the sun. 'The high priest himself wishes to meet her. He wants to see the evidence, and have her examined by his own physician.'

Malory breathed deeply, thinking through the implications.

'If the high priest concludes that there has been a miracle, will that not hinder us? Every episkopos in Daija and every priest in Galmandie will want to see her.'

'Then we must act swiftly, as soon as the high priest has gone.'

'He will come here?'

'He is in Daija, but a visit here was already planned; he plans to consecrate a fire temple in Arrenicia, and Roquenoir is on his route. It is tiresome, but unavoidable.'

Soldiers appeared on the far side of the garden, on the steps leading from the gates. In their midst came Humbert Blanc, carrying the witch in his arms. At the top step he helped her to stand on the grass and she squeezed his arm in thanks. Blanc leaned against the garden wall, recovering his breath. The day they'd captured him he had seemed a warrior. In the days since then his beard had thickened, growing almost white. Now, travel-stained, stripped of his armour, and clearly exhausted by the climb carrying the witch, he looked an old man.

Neither the guards nor the prisoners had seen Malory and Barthram, screened by the arbour and well. There was a moment before the guards jerked at the prisoners' chains, pulling them onwards, that was almost touching. The witch gripped Blanc's arm again, solicitously, and the look he gave her shone with affection, maybe even love. Blanc mouthed something at her that might have been 'courage, Adelais!', and they were pulled away. For the final flight of steps up to the highest level, by the temple, two soldiers made a chair of their arms to carry her.

'Do I see an old man's foolishness?' Barthram had watched the same interaction.

'They are fond of one another. I think the Guardian cares for her deeply, but there is nothing... inappropriate. He was of the Guardians' inner circle, and his vows will be sacrosanct.'

Barthram allowed himself a thin smile. 'A principled heretic?'

'Quite.' Malory watched the last of the escort climb the steps. 'The prison is up there?' Usually, the highest levels of a castle held its finest rooms, and the prisons would be in the cold depths.

'There is a tower up there where we can keep them safe and in isolation, with our own men. I want soldiers we can trust around them, not garrison guards, in case the high priest comes to any ill-advised conclusions. We will starve them to sap their strength, and wait for him to leave. Then we will need to act swiftly and rigorously.'

Malory winced. 'Rigorous' was the word Barthram used when relentless pressure would be applied, once it no longer mattered if the prisoner died. Malory wanted the witch to be punished, humiliated even, but he wanted her to be whole afterwards. Compliant. He'd indulged in this little dream of her kneeling before him, begging his forgiveness, with those blue eyes upturned and pleading. He'd embellished the dream with a strategic rip in her gown, exposing the rise and fall of her body...

Malory pushed the dream aside. 'But Pateras Ghislain, what if it is decided to send her elsewhere, to be examined in Daija, for example?'

'The high priest can wish all he likes. She is a prisoner of the king, in the king's castle, in Galmandie. We need to know what was taken from the temple, where it has been hidden, and who helped them. Once we have that, she can be killed attempting to escape, even if the high priest offers his protection. A fall from these cliffs would be so tragic.'

'But her body would bear the marks of torture.' Malory never thought he'd try and talk Ghislain Barthram out of harming her.

'Not necessarily.' Pateras Ghislain's tone was calculating; a touch of winter's ice among the roses. 'We have found, have we not, that fire is an excellent means of extracting the truth?'

'Indeed, Pateras, but the flesh will show the burns.'

'Not if the burns are inside the body.'

'Pateras?'

'All it takes is a hollow cow's horn, an iron rod, and a brazier to heat it. The hollowed horn is used to dilate one of the body's openings, and to hold it open while hot iron is inserted. There need be no outward signs. Sadly, the prisoner almost invariably dies.' Barthram paused and sighed. 'Eventually.'

Malory closed his eyes and swallowed. He didn't think he could do that. Especially not to her. It was, well, *sick*.

'The Third Great Council,' Malory found the courage to protest, 'ruled that no priest may shed blood.'

'No blood is shed. The wound is cauterised as it is made.'

'Nor order any man's death.'

'Yet we frequently condemn heretics knowing that the

secular powers will burn them. Pateras Malory, are you perhaps a little in love with this woman after your voyage?'

Malory shook his head, vehemently. 'She may not even know the answers we seek.'

'But the Guardian does.'

'He will die before he talks, I am sure. We have failed with others like him.'

'But Pateras Malory, I am learning from you.' The anakritis-general came as close to a smile as was possible, for him. 'Carel de la Tour would have died had we continued, but would probably have talked to save his son. A brilliant idea, if I may say so, although sadly flawed in its execution. No, I agree, Humbert Blanc will not talk, but I think he loves this woman. Will he stay silent if he has to watch such pain being inflicted on her? As you said about de la Tour's son, surely the mere threat will be sufficient?'

12.2 ADELAIS

By the sixth day at Roquenoir, Adelais was growing weaker, and the weaker she became, the more the fears crowded in on her. It was hard to sleep, now, but the cramps below her ribs were from hunger, not her wound. She was drinking water all the time to fill her belly, but that made it worse at night with the need to piss. The dark time before dawn was worst, when all her imaginings came crowding in and she'd clutch the little bottle through her gown. In those black hours she truly understood temptation; it would be so easy, so painless, just to fall asleep and drift away.

They brought her a little bread in the mornings, around the second office, and again before the Lighting of the Lamps; surprisingly good bread, fresh from the castle's ovens, and she'd fight the urge to wolf it down. The first day's rations were gone in three or four good mouthfuls, and left her craving more. Now she pinched a little of the soft centre at a time, pushing the flakes against the roof of her mouth with her tongue to savour them, and cradling the rest in her lap lest a crumb should fall. She'd nibble at the crust, crushing and sucking each morsel. Twice when Thierry was on guard, he'd managed to slip her a little of his own food – a scrap of cheese, and a chicken leg. She'd gnawed at that like a dog when the meat was finished, and when all taste was gone she scratched a shard of bone idly against the wall above her bed.

She did not consciously intend to draw runes, but they appeared within the pattern. *Thurs* was there, clearly.

Thurs, the rune of Thor. *Thurs* was the deepest rune carved into the *taufr* in her scrip. Elyse had cut it into the wax of the bottle hidden in her robe. Now she was scratching it on the wall. It was a strong rune, a rune of protection, but she could remember Yrsa's warning, hunched around a fireside in Vriesland. *Remember the nature of Thor and his wild, uncontrollable rages; do not unleash such strength lightly, for the damage that follows may not be mended.*

She was also leaving proof of her sorcery on the walls for all to read. Adelais was shocked that her thinking was so fuddled. She scratched at the rune until it had no more meaning than a child's scribblings with charcoal, and threw the bone from her window before she was tempted again.

She was privileged, Thierry said, to have a chamber in Brother Raymond's tower. She had a window as well, though it was barred with a thick mullion and there was no foothold on the other side, just a dizzying drop to the river. The window looked north, up the Naeva, and was set deep enough into the wall to have a little step up to a stone bench where she'd sit, watching the boats on the river, marking the passage of time by the bells of the castle's temple, and thinking. Thinking far too much. Summer heat was building towards a storm, day by day, making even this high-ceilinged room stifling, and her thoughts became like the inescapable cycle of a fever. *What will they do to me? Will I – can I – be strong?* That terrible unknown.

She used the step for exercise, when bread had given her brief energy, pushing against the pain because it was a good pain, a healing pain of muscle, not the ripping of damaged flesh. She set up a cycle, almost mindless. *Step up, rest, step down. Other leg. Repeat twenty times. Rest. Do it again.* She could climb stairs now, and each day the soldiers would unbolt the trapdoor to her chamber and allow her down the steep, wooden steps into the guardroom below for as long as it took to tend Thierry's wound.

The tower had just three rooms, each about four paces square, stacked one above another. The middle room, with access from an outside stair, was where all six soldiers now slept, pushed into that small space by the arrival of the high priest and his entourage. There were never less than three awake, day and night. They seemed to have lost much of their fear of her, though none but Thierry would risk giving her food, and thankfully none had tried to enter her room. Their leader, the sergeant, rarely spoke to her. She watched him carefully when she could, learning the unspoken language of his face and shoulders. When the moment came, he'd be the one they'd send to seize her, and she wanted to have those few precious seconds of warning.

One morning there had been an argument in the guard room below, Thierry protesting at the sergeant, pitching his voice too low for her to hear, and she'd thought they were coming for her. In her panic she broke the hard wax seal around Elyse's bottle, and loosened the little cork until it would come off with just a push of her thumb. She picked up the fragments of wax afterwards and pieced them together in the window, remaking the *thurs* rune.

Thurs er kvenna kvöl, ok kletta búi, ok vardhrúnar verr…

Thurs is the agony of women, the cliff-dweller, and husband of a giantess...

The poem didn't make sense. What was it that Yrsa had told her? The threads of fate, the *urlogthættir*, run through the runes; that which is past, that which is, and that which shall be. The *now* must be the cliff-dweller, for here she was, locked in her own eagle's nest. She'd never be a giantess, so was there agony to come?

You are just beginning, sweeting.

Another bolted trapdoor led down from the guardroom beneath to some kind of store where they'd thrown Humbert, and he was alive, for she heard his chants at the hours of prayer. It seemed unfair that the Guardian must sleep in a rock-cut cellar while she had been given a former Guardian's room above, with a window.

On the first day, when she was dressing Thierry's wound in the guardroom, she asked about Brother Raymond, who'd given his name to the tower and painted the walls of the upper room so delicately with birds and foliage. On its east wall was a large red lion, the lion salient of the Guardians, with both forepaws raised and clawed. This morning Thierry brought her an answer; Raymond, it seemed, had been an elderly brother, pensioned off by his order in the castle that Guardian money had built.

'What happened to him?' she asked, peering at Thierry's arm. She had packed the wound open to drain in the early days, but now allowed it to scab. They both knew he had no more need of her care, but she appreciated a moment of company, even the company of soldiers who had killed Arnaud.

'He died under questioning.' The voice of the sergeant made her look up, and she rose to her feet at the sight of two clerics silhouetted behind him. *Sætur Sif, was it to be now?* Elyse's bottle was still in its pocket, high under the skirts of her gown. She backed away as an ageing cleric entered the room, followed by Malory d'Eivet. The older man wore the flask badge of a healer on his chest. A scrawny youth with the first fluff of manhood on his face waited at the door, eyeing her as if she were some exotic animal never before seen in Galmandie. He carried her old herigaut and gambeson across his arms. Her bloodstained shirt and loin cloth lay on top, under a crossbow bolt.

'This is she?' The older cleric spoke with a heavy accent that Adelais couldn't place.

'That is the witch.' D'Eivet's loathing sounded a little forced. It might almost have been an act for the cleric's benefit.

The back of Adelais's thighs reached a table against the wall, where she could go no further. The guards had hung a cured ham above it, ready to slice, and even now the smell made her salivate.

'Sorceress, charlatan, or Blessèd One, we shall soon discover.' The speech was lilting, almost musical. It suggested a realm of sun and olives, somewhere eastwards towards Alympos.

Adelais looked around for a weapon, but there was only a water barrel and the guard's cask of wine. A line of cloaks hung from nails, but there was nothing she could use; no hanging swords, not even a knife for the ham. She began to gather the skirts of her kirtle up in one hand, lifting the hem, even though she knew she could not reach Elyse's bottle and drink before they intercepted her.

'I am Almundo Torrigiani,' the older cleric said. 'Physician to the high priest. I need to examine you.' Torrigiani was clean-shaven, a little stout, and old enough for the skin of his neck to be creased into lizard folds.

'Here? In front of the guards?'

The guards had stood out of respect but remained in the room. Thierry's wounded arm was bare to the shoulder, exposing the scab.

'The guards will wait outside. Young Florent de Chauliac

here is an apprentice surgeon, and should stay. Pateras Malory and I are clerics, so you have nothing to fear.'

'Really, *Pateras*?' Adelais was literally backed into a corner. 'I have nothing to fear from a priest whose profession is torture?'

Torrigiani made a slight nod of acquiescence and dismissed the room with a wave of his hand. 'Leave. All of you.' He stopped Thierry as he passed, turning his arm to the light with professional interest.

'That was deep. Sword thrust?'

'Yes, messire. It was like to kill me, but Mistress Adelais healed me of the wound fever.'

'And how did you do that, child?'

'Woundwort, white willow bark, and wormwood for the fever. I cleaned the wound with wine but kept it open to drain, using soft wax mixed with vervain and verdigris, then sealed with honey and cobwebs.'

'Excellent.' He tapped Thierry on the shoulder. 'You can go.' He looked at her with surprise and new respect, then glanced back over his shoulder.

'You too, Pateras Malory.'

'But—'

'Now, if you please.'

D'Eivet glared at her as he left, like a child robbed of his toy. Having him dismissed was such a wonderful, petty triumph, but one for which she would surely pay.

Torrigiani stared at her quietly, and she held his gaze, sensing that his examination had begun. Florent de Chauliac waited in the background.

'They are treating you well?'

'They are not beating me, but we have little food. I believe it is to make us weaker for the torture that must follow.'

'We? Torture?'

'My companion Humbert Blanc, formerly Lord Brother of the

Guardians, is in the cell below us. He has not seen daylight nor eaten a proper meal for six days.' This she knew. She'd have heard if they had brought him out. 'The anakritim and their torturers are waiting for the high priest to leave before they question us.' This also she knew, for the guards had talked, not knowing that the sound reached her through the boarded floors. She had nothing to lose by telling the physician, and perhaps something to gain.

Torrigiani drew the knife at his belt and she gasped, flinching away, but he merely reached past her shoulder to cut a thick slice off the ham.

'Bless you, messire.' Adelais looked at him in wonder as he put it into her hands. She was so light-headed she'd nearly added the name of a proscribed god. She had to swallow even before she tasted the ham; already her mouth was flooding with saliva.

'Sit. Eat.' He carved another hunk and lifted the trapdoor to the room below. 'Guardian! Top step.' He let the hatch drop, and bolted it again. 'These are the clothes you were wearing when you were hit?' He nodded at the pile in the young man's arms.

Adelais nodded, though her eyes were half-closed. She held the meat two-handed in front of her face, inhaling its aromas even as she chewed. From below came the low chant of a psalm of praise. Humbert, it seemed, had restrained himself long enough to give thanks before he ate.

'Then please strip and put them on.'

She stopped chewing, looking at them over the top of the ham.

'Come, child, we are physician and surgeon, not rapists. And we will turn our backs while you undress. It is either that or we call the soldiers to hold you.'

When they'd probably find the pocket with the bottle sewn into her gown, and perhaps even the gold in her belt. Adelais took another bite and turned her own back before she pulled off her gown.

The loin cloth and the shirt were stiff with dried blood, and patterned with stains that varied from thick crusts to watery marks the colour of a silted river. She began to push herself into a distant place; she was with Arnaud, face to face on a pillow, giggling with the delirium of new love.

'I am ready.' And eating, more thoughtfully now.

They turned to face her. 'You were wearing nothing else?'

Adelais gulped ham. Such a waste; it was still half chewed. 'Hose. It is not here.'

Torrigiani picked up the crossbow bolt and pushed it through the puncture in her herigaut. He reached inside, felt with his fingers, and worked it through the gambeson beneath until it met her shirt.

'I must lift the skirts of your herigaut.'

She did not protest. She was with Agnès, galloping over the fields near the Cheyne manor.

'It went through a gambeson.' That was a statement, not a question.

'He was only three paces from me.'

Torrigiani's finger, then the bolt, found the cut in her shirt, and probed through to the loin cloth.

And beyond. His fingertip touched her skin, just above her mound, exploring, not intruding.

'Come, de Chauliac, hold the material clear.'

The loin cloth was pushed downwards, though a finger still marked the spot where the crossbow bolt must have struck. De Chauliac held her clothing high, looking at her belly, blushing furiously. *By the gods, boy, if it is embarrassing for you, think what it is like for me.*

Torrigiani turned her a little towards the light of a window. She knew what they were seeing: a livid pattern of bruising, now fading to yellows, that blossomed madly above the darker gold of her bush. 'And when were you hit?'

'Fifteen days ago.'

'No bolt wound could have healed in that time.'

'Chain-mail inside the loin cloth?' Even the boy de Chauliac sounded as if he were clutching at straws.

'An armoured loin cloth?' Torrigiani let out a bark of a laugh. 'And inside a quilted gambeson? I think not. Besides, impossible for another reason; the rings would have been driven into the flesh. The clothes show a wound, and the blood from a wound, but the body shows signs only of a blow. No wound, no scab, no imprint.' He stepped back, still staring at her, and she made her eyes plead with him for it to end.

Torrigiani nodded at de Chauliac and the boy let her clothes drop. He even muttered thanks, his face burning, and turned his back again when she changed into her gown. That was kind, but a little ridiculous when he'd just been staring at her.

Torrigiani cut her another slice of ham and waved her to a stool. 'Come.' He drew a mug of the soldiers' wine and put it beside her. 'Why don't you tell us what happened?' He sat near her, his eyes locked on her face.

'The arrow threw me backwards.' She spoke around the meat in her mouth, like a tavern wench.

'You were seen to pull it from your body and throw it at the soldiers.'

'They had killed my man.' The wine was rough and strong, a tongue-loosening fire in her belly. 'I was angry.'

'So how do you account for the lack of a wound?'

Adelais stopped chewing. This time, she swallowed before she spoke.

'It was as if Salazar stretched out his hand, messire, like a rock against my body.'

Torrigiani's stare was kindly but penetrating. 'I do not think you believe that.'

She dropped her eyes, unable to meet his gaze. 'I do not know, messire. I fainted.' *Think, girl.* Fool that she was for accepting wine on an empty stomach. 'I believe Brother Humbert and Lady Agnès prayed to the Blessèd Salazar.'

Both Torrigiani and de Chauliac jumped as Humbert bellowed through the floorboards. 'But it took a greater power than prayer to work this miracle!'

Adelais flinched. Humbert must be delirious to come so close to revealing the truth, or the truth as he saw it.

Torrigiani stood. 'That is for the high priest to decide. He may wish to meet you himself.'

Adelais still had ham in her hands, and she pushed it into the sleeve of her chemise before the guards could return. 'How long will he stay in this place, messire?' *How long before the anakritim begin?*

'Two, three days. He has many matters pressing him.'

'You have been kind, messire. Will you intercede for us? I do not think we will be allowed to leave alive.'

Torrigiani paused with his hand on the door. 'As a physician, I can only present the facts as I see them for the episkopes to argue over.' He sighed, regretfully. 'The princes of the faith like their miracles safely in the holy texts, child, not in flesh and blood. It makes them uncomfortable. I cannot explain what I see. It is extraordinary, even miraculous. But it is also inconvenient. And an inconvenient miracle may be called sorcery.'

CHAPTER 13

13.1 ADELAIS

They waited two more days. Beyond Adelais's window, boats sailed slowly upstream, keeping inshore out of the current. In the room below, the guards played dice to pass the time, grew irritable in the heat, and quenched their thirst with water and with wine until the barrels had to be replenished. Even by her unshuttered window the air was oppressive, waiting for a storm to wash it clean.

She stank. She washed her body with a sponge and a bucket at night, and rinsed her chemise, but some rankness remained, and she'd had no fresh clothes since they left the hunting lodge. Adelais craved clean linen.

And food. Above all, food. She existed in a dream-like state where she stumbled even on the step to the window seat, too tired and too hot to exercise.

The waiting was like the coming storm; inevitable, long-expected, but she'd still jump at the first clap of thunder, when it came. The only preparation she could make was to move Elyse's bottle from her gown to inside the buttoned sleeve of her chemise. She practiced removing it; undoing a single button would let the phial fall into her palm, then a push of her thumb against the cork and it would all be over.

But not yet. The high priest was still in Roquenoir. She'd watch for the look in the sergeant's eye, and she'd know when to take it.

The bells for the noon office had not yet rung when they came. She knew the time of trial had arrived, even before the step on the stair. The noises below, the gathering of weapons, the low voices, all said *it is now*. She stepped up into the window, one last time, and toyed with her cuff. The river beneath her flowed like oil beneath a sultry sky, and orchards on the banks were spotted with the first ripening fruit. Should it be now, looking at beauty? It would be a good place and time.

But if she took her own life, Humbert would also die, horribly. No Blessèd One would commit self-murder. She'd damn him by her actions. And if this was fated to be her dying-day, then she would honour the gods by facing it with courage. Rather than unbutton her cuff, she tapped a rhythm on the stone of the window and, high on her cliff, began to mutter the song of the *thurs* rune. *Thurs*, the rune of Thor, the husband of Sif. The words hummed in her mouth, drum-like, and the call to the god was strong in her mind.

'*Thurs er kvenna kvöl, ok kletta búi...*'

Thurs is the agony of women, the cliff-dweller...

Come, defend your Sif.

She was filled with a mounting sense of dread, but the gods were silent. A boat rushed south, propelled out of her sight.

She turned as the trapdoor lifted. Thierry summoned her with a jerk of his head, and she stepped forwards to her fate, now moving her lips silently with the song, endlessly repeated.

Thurs er kvenna kvöl, ok kletta búi...

She was shocked at the sight of Humbert; he stumbled as he walked, hollow-cheeked, wincing at the light. She went ahead of him on the steps down from the guardroom to the courtyard, turning to face him for fear he might fall. Humbert gripped the rail, smiling his reassurance, but he was so weak he could scarcely stand; he swayed as all six soldiers formed a box around them for the short walk from their tower, past the temple, to another set of steps down to a garden. If this was how a grand commander looked, how must she appear? Could anyone believe them innocent, in this filthy, verminous state?

They were stopped by a temple guard at the top of the steps and told to wait for permission to approach. There had been roses in the garden below on the day they arrived, though now a pavilion had been erected, like the ones knights used at a tourney but striped in orange and white rather than the colours of heraldry. Its sides had been rolled up to allow a breeze; it seemed that even high priests suffered in this heat. Nearby the temple bell tolled for the noon office, yet the sun glared through a yellow haze and cast almost no shadow.

A queue of supplicants snaked back down the lower steps leading to the gates and the harbour, fanning themselves with their hats or their trailing sleeves as they waited. They inched slowly upwards to the pavilioned garden, to be met by ink-fingered clerics who sat under lesser canopies, scratching at scrolls and ledgers. Some in the queue were clerics themselves, others were sponsored into the sacred presence by diakones or episkopes, the nobles and princes of the faith, swirling scarlets and purples. The air was heavy and sultry enough to deaden sound. Adelais could no longer chant, even in her head, and she began to sway; boats on the river spun together with vestments, canvas and linen, pale brown sails and swirling colour.

Humbert caught her as she fell, not so much easing her to the ground as falling with her. He smelt, too, but she reached for his hand and they lay there together, tumbled over each other in strange, open intimacy. He turned his head on the gravel and smiled wanly at her.

'Courage, my lioness!'

Adelais curled her lip, pretending to snarl, and clawed one hand paw-like towards him. She began to speak, but turned her head away lest he be shamed by the tears that had sprung into his eyes.

Thierry brought them water mixed with wine that she sipped, then gulped, sucking courage from the mug. The soldiers pulled Humbert to his feet but let her lie there, even folding a cloak for her head; no one could see from the garden below. It was curious how their attitudes had changed; once she had been their enemy, the witch. Now, they were almost protective. They even offered to carry her down the steps when they were called.

They held her back, at the edge of the high priest's tent, while two temple guards pulled Humbert forwards and forced him to his knees in front of a dais. Swathes of scarlet silk had been hung over that corner of the pavilion, a canopy within a canopy, so that she had to peer into a darker space to see the supreme head of the faith of Ischyros, the inheritor of Salazar's vision.

Adelais saw gold before she saw the man, a jewelled chalice that caught the light when he raised it to his lips. It was large enough to hide his face, so at first she saw only a bald head with a badger-streak of darkness over the ears.

She'd expected a god-like figure with a white, flowing beard and a shining countenance, not this sick little man who blinked at the light and squirmed fretfully on his throne. As his chalice was refilled by a servant he seemed feverish; a pale, pasty face was disfigured by a rash that spread over both cheeks from the bridge of his nose, like the wings of a butterfly. Black eyebrows frowned into his drink.

Adelais should have listened as an episkopos raged his accusations against Humbert. What was being said would decide her life, and she could hear the words clearly enough. She might even be called upon to speak, but she was light-headed with hunger and it was hard to concentrate, even on the white-robed, fire-sashed man who sat in judgement.

Her gaze passed over the crowd of attendants around the throne, and one implacable face jolted her into wakefulness. Ghislain Barthram, Anakritis-General of Galmandie. The Angel of Death. To be sure, there were others. Many others. Soldiers ringing the tent. Servants. Priests. A purple-wrapped episkopos stood by the high priest's ear, whispering, his eyes on Humbert. A secretary, dressed in the scarlet robes of a diakonos, took notes; a man whose equals ran provinces of priests took the part of a scribe in the great man's presence. Almundo Torrigiani, the kindly physician, waited respectfully to one side with her old clothes in his arms. By him stood Malory d'Eivet, so obviously nervous amidst all this power that she might have laughed, but for Barthram's stare. She'd seen a snake like that, when she was a child. Men had trapped it in a pit, and thrown a mouse in after it, wagering how long the little beast would survive. The mouse went frantic, but couldn't climb out, and no matter what it did, the snake watched, slithering closer.

It took a long time.

In a strange way, the certainty that this was her dying-day became liberating. She could either squirm and squeal like the mouse, or go out in one great act of defiance. It didn't matter what she said, what she did, the end would be the same. Even the high priest himself could threaten her with nothing worse than that which was already promised in Ghislain Barthram's eyes. Adelais breathed deeply, squared her shoulders, and glared back at him while she sang her silent song, letting her lips frame the words. Let them think she was praying. *By the gods, if they knew...*

Thurs er kvenna kvöl...

The rune of Thor, the god of thunder. As if in response, a low rumble sounded, far away, like an empty barrel rolled over cobbles. The long-awaited storm was coming, but Adelais wondered if she'd live to feel rain on her face; the audience would be over soon. Already the high priest seemed bored. He began looking beyond Humbert at Adelais, and glancing sideways at the physician. The accusations of murder and desecration being hurled at Humbert were of less interest than a possible miracle. He began to lift his hand to wave Humbert away, but Humbert interrupted him.

'Wait, Your Holiness! For your soul's sake, wait!'

'For *my* soul's sake?' The high priest sounded affronted. His voice was reedy, the cry of an angry invalid, and he glared at Humbert with narrowed, intelligent eyes.

Humbert pointed at Barthram. 'When you dismiss me, that spawn of Kakos, your Angel of Death, will take my life as slowly and painfully as possible. I shall welcome the pain, for it will purge my sins and ease my passage over the bridge, but my death will be another burden on your soul, to add to all my brethren's deaths.'

'They were heretics.' The high priest spoke as if he was reminding a child of a lesson. He didn't take his eyes off Adelais. 'They denied Ischyros and spat on the holy texts.'

'That was what the torturers were told to discover. Think, Holiness, of all those brothers, your loyal servants, each held in isolation, each believing that this injustice was being inflicted only on him, or his commandery, and that the truth would be plain if only he was allowed to stand before you. And you abandoned them.'

'I set up a commission of inquiry under my chamberlain.' The high priest sounded tired, as if this was a matter that had been resolved long ago.

'You did. There were many who trusted your commission, and dared to recant those tortured confessions. They were burnt alive as relapsed heretics, sacrificed to King Aloys's greed.'

'Enough.' The high priest waved a hand in dismissal.

'Did you hear of Guerin's curse, Holiness? From within the fire the master called on you and the king to meet him soon on the bridge. Ischyros will send his Blessèd Ones to drag you to judgement. The pit of Kakos awaits you unless you make amends.'

The high priest flinched, and Adelais almost laughed with the knowledge that he was frightened. She gained a mad confidence.

Thurs er kvenna kvöl, ok kletta búi... She even stamped the rhythm into the turf.

Another drum roll of thunder, and the supreme ruler of the Ischyrian faith on Earth squirmed backwards in his chair, intimidated by the coincidence of a thunderstorm and a white-bearded old Guardian haranguing him like a reincarnation of Tanguy. In a flash of intuition, Adelais understood why; the high priest knew his own guilt, and the fate of the Guardians weighed heavily on his soul.

Humbert was relentless. 'Guerin and Cheyne endured their agony with such grace and courage that all men present knew them to be martyrs.'

'Take him away!'

Two temple guards seized Humbert by the arms and began to drag him backwards, but the episkopos whispered in the high priest's ear.

'Wait, Guardian.' The episkopos held up his hand to stop them. 'It is said that you desecrated the citadel's temple, and stole a golden idol. What became of that?'

A flash of irritation crossed Ghislain Barthram's face; Adelais guessed that he wanted to claim any treasure for the king, not see it taken by the high priest.

'I stole nothing, certainly no idol.'

More whispering. The high priest made brushing motions with his hand; he wanted to be done with this.

'What do you want, Guardian?' The episkopos assumed the bored air of one who is accustomed to haggling. 'Gold?'

'Never gold, Excellency. A knight whose heart is set on wealth will fear to die, for his wealth dies with him.' He'd used the same words to young Ordric Cheyne.

'Free passage out of Galmandie, then? What else do you want? Come, His Holiness has other matters to attend to.'

'Want, Excellency?' Humbert laughed. 'We all want something, don't we? King Aloys wants money. Othon de Remy wants power. Ghislain Barthram wants to be an episkopos. Me? I want peace. I should have died with my brothers on a bridge in Compeigne. Now I am done with it all, and I want to join my brethren in the blessed company of martyrs. I have no doubt that the anakritis-general is keen to grant me that wish.'

Humbert staggered as he spoke and dropped to one knee, apparently delirious with hunger. He twisted as he struggled to rise, caught Adelais's eye, and gave her a smile of such tenderness that her chant faded and her eyes filled.

'I tell you what I want, Excellency. I want freedom for this woman, though I fear that is as unlikely as Ghislain Barthram escaping the pit.'

The high priest made a small gesture of the hand that might have been irritation or boredom, and at a nod from the episkopos the soldiers dragged Humbert to the edge of the pavilion.

'The God forgive you, Guardian,' Barthram called after him, his tongue passing briefly over his lips. His narrowed eyes said '*but I will not*'.

The episkopos bent to the high priest's ear again.

'Ah yes, the woman,' the high priest leaned forwards, relaxing now Humbert had been pulled away, 'about whom such outlandish claims are made. Bring her to me, with the physician. And where's that young priest who saw it all?'

'Here, Your Holiness.' Malory almost fell over in his eagerness to present himself. 'Pateras Malory d'Eivet, Holiness. I saw the witch hit by a crossbow bolt at no more than three paces,' he gabbled, almost stuttering. 'She pulled the bolt from her own belly, I swear.'

The high priest stared at Adelais, frowning his curiosity, and she stared back, holding his gaze. An idea was forming; if he carried such a burden of guilt, perhaps he could be frightened into letting them go? And he'd flinched at thunder.

Thurs er kvenna kvöl, ok kletta búi, ok vardhrúnar verr... She began her chant again, silently. She even stilled her lips. Nothing must be heard or seen that would let them know she wasn't a Blessèd One.

'Her clothing shows the cuts and blood of the wound, Holiness.' The physician leaned forwards and touched her in the centre of her stomach, below her belt. 'About here. There is bruising, but no sign of the arrow penetrating.'

'And how do you explain that, Torrigiani?'

'I cannot, Holiness.'

Again, that stare. Again, she returned it, even tilting her head to one side like an unhooded hawk on the fist, watching, aloof. *Play the part, girl. Use the thunder. You have nothing to lose.*

'What are you staring at, woman?'

Wait for the rumble to pass. It was still building, rolling now like wagon wheels on stone. There was even the first flicker of lightning. *Even better.*

Mighty Thor, be with me. 'I think, *priest*, that before long it will be *you* who stands before Ischyros, justly accused by the soul of Guerin.' There were gasps around them, and flashes of purple as episkopes made the warding sign against Kakos.

Wait. After the flash would come the noise. Three... Four... Boom! And sweet Sif did he flinch. Was this how prophets worked? Sham mummers seizing their moment?

Or did she really have power, as Yrsa and Elyse had said?

'They are waiting for you, priest; the terrible shades of the Guardians, rank upon rank in their battle lines, all barring your way across the bridge. It will be soon, I think.'

There were cries of 'stop her!' from the attendant clerics, but the high priest had another question, mouthed with a face pulled tight by fear.

'Who are you? How is it that you live?'

'I am a messenger. One of the Blessèd.' Even she felt guilty at that sacrilege. *But by Thor, I will play to win.* A rush of cold wind sent the pavilion's skirts flapping. Raindrops began to fall on its roof, pebble-loud. The sound almost drowned Humbert's cry.

'And she touched the Hand of Salazar!'

'No!' Adelais rounded on him. Humbert was on his knees, but still swaying, and at the sight of her fury the look of holy joy on his face faded. He might be half mad with hunger, but he was putting Agnès in danger. 'Oh, you sweet fool!' Didn't he see? They had to fear *her*, and fear her so much they dare not risk keeping them imprisoned.

She looked at the faces around them. Who had heard? The nearest soldiers. Perhaps the episkopos, who frowned as if unsure. Torrigiani. Certainly Ghislain Barthram, the high priest, and Malory d'Eivet. Barthram and the high priest had leaned forward, eyes widening.

'So the old legends are true?' The high priest's face was now tight with pure avarice, as shiny and soulless as his golden goblet. Ghislain Barthram's blazed with a different kind of excitement, one that promised her agony beyond her worst imaginings until she earned her death with truth.

Fools, both of them. There was no wonder or joy at a miracle, only fear and greed. Now they'd unleash their minions on the de Fontenays, and Agnès's fate would be as sure as her own.

She'd have to distract them. Cover Humbert's mistake.

Fools.

There was a passage from the holy texts about fools and greed and death. What was it that Humbert had said?

'On the day his soul is demanded...' She couldn't remember.

Lightning. Close. Bright enough to make the canopy blaze white. Very soon.

Sterkur Thor, leidha tunguska mína. Guide my tongue.

'You fool!' She hurled the words at the high priest himself, hollowing her body to become divine fury personified. 'Your greed is pointless, for this very day your soul is demanded.' Maybe she hadn't got the words exactly right. 'And all the gold on Earth will not buy you passage over the bridge.'

The thunderclap split the sky, so loud that, all around her, men cringed, lifting their hands to their ears, but it seemed to shake the high priest clear of his throne, lifting and dropping him back on the cushions. Even Adelais flinched, but hardened her gaze, glaring into eyes that were now wide and bulging. *Play the part. Snarl. Let him fear the wrath of his god.* A mighty aftermath of sound reverberated through the heavens as if the château itself had begun falling onto the rocks at its base, and the high priest clutched at his chest, screwing the white robe like a napkin.

Adelais relented, straightening. The high priest seemed to be suffering some kind of fit, and she had a ridiculous urge to apologise because she'd only wanted him to let them go, not frighten him to death. But the high priest's eyes rolled upwards and he made a choking, rattling noise in the back of his throat like a drunkard who hawks phlegm to spit. The choke became a long sigh and he slid forwards off his throne to crumple in front of her at the edge of the dais.

There was an awful silence in which no one moved or spoke. As the last rumbling echoes of thunder faded towards the horizon, the crowds appeared to be released from some stupor, and divided. One group rushed inwards, clustering around the high priest's body and lifting him, bearing him away amidst cries of concern and shouted orders. The others backed away from her, making the warding sign, until she stood at the centre of a circle beneath the applause of the storm, pleading with their staring faces that she was sorry, she didn't mean to hurt him. Temple guards had drawn their swords and were pointing their shaking tips at her. And from the rim of this enclosure of chain-mail and scarlet, linen and steel, came the voice of one in the black and white of an anakritis. Even he hid behind the warding sign as he spoke.

'What have you done, witch?' Ghislain Barthram un-looped his rope belt, dragging it into his hands to bind her.

Still, the rune song flowed through her mind in an unstoppable, endlessly repeating chant.

Thurs er kvenna kvöl.

Thurs is the agony of women.

Adelais understood what was coming. Her death was now inevitable; it could be slow and excruciating, or swift and painless. She reached for the cuff of her chemise, knowing with absolute certainty that it had to be now.

13.2 MALORY

Malory d'Eivet had never realised that Pateras Ghislain was so courageous. He was a hard man, to be sure, and merciless when needed, but of all the assembled priests and soldiers, only Barthram dared approach the witch, pulling his rope belt from his waist as he went. She stood isolated on the edge of the chaos around the high priest, looking lost and frightened as if she hadn't really meant to do it. Her mouth was working, but her words could not be heard over the rain drumming on the canopy. Already the canvas was sagging into valleys between the poles, sending waterfalls gushing from its edges, and still the thunder rolled, as if Ischyros Himself was vexed at what He had just witnessed.

The witch saw Pateras Ghislain approaching. She shook her head, mouthing 'no, no', and began to fumble with the buttons on the cuff of her chemise, but Pateras Ghislain threw a loop of rope around her wrists and yanked it tight, binding her hands in the attitude of prayer. Her eyes were wide with fear; how could such innocence, such dawn-blue perfection, hide such vile guilt?

But Pateras Ghislain would not meet her eye. His courage

did not extend that far. A sorceress's curse, it was said, was made with the eyes and with the hand sign of Kakos.

'Sergeant, bind her eyes, before she strikes someone else dead.'

The sergeant hung back, looking around him for material.

'Quickly, man. Use your helmet liner. Reverse it.'

Oh, how she squirmed as it was pushed over her face, napeside forwards so it hung to her nose. The sergeant half strangled her tying the cords around her neck.

'Take them back, and guard them well. I will send for them very shortly.' Barthram was breathing heavily. So far, only he seemed capable of coherent speech. 'Then bring two benches to my chamber, and rope.'

'Benches, Pateras?' Like all of them, the sergeant was stunned into stupidity by what had happened, and the thunder made children of them all.

'Yes, fool. Benches, big enough that you could tie a man's length to one. Do you hear me?'

'Yes, Pateras.' Understanding dawned in the man's eyes.

'Come, Pateras Malory.'

Malory d'Eivet moved in a daze, content to be led through the temple guards still crowding the edge of the canopy, out onto saturated grass where water splashed over his sandals. Strange how some instincts are maintained even amidst chaos; the high priest had collapsed and might be dead, and yet in the absence of leadership, clerics still sought shelter from the storm, soldiers pulled cloaks over their armour against the wet, and all huddled, waiting for news. As they left, the murmurs of talk began, the buzz of a crowd who need to tell and retell the events they had all just witnessed.

'You heard?' Barthram beckoned Malory alongside him. '"She touched the Hand of Salazar." She had it. May still have it.'

'We searched their baggage...'

'Bones can be small and easily hidden; it would be insignificant without its provenance.'

'Perhaps the Guardian spoke figuratively?' But it rang true. How else could the girl still live?

Malory had to drop behind as groups of men ran past, servants and clerics, all rushing towards the chapel and the high priest's apartments, consternation stretching their faces.

Pateras Ghislain pushed open a door in the base of the castle's westernmost tower, and entered the room he had accepted for them both. Malory had not understood why so distinguished a man as the anakritis-general had chosen such mean accommodation, even at a time when the high priest's entourage had taken the best rooms. It was the circular base of the tower, with rough rock for its floor, and it was dark, lit only by three unshuttered arrow slits whose embrasures were cut into walls as thick as a man's height. It had the advantage of being cool even when the upper levels baked, though crossed by draughts at night despite the spare cloak that Malory had stuffed into the windward arrow slit. They had been given a table, which rocked on the uneven floor, two three-legged stools, and straw mattresses. But for the brazier against the nights' chills, it might have been a prison.

'We must act quickly before they are taken from us.' Pateras Ghislain sat at the table, where an assortment of tools lay scattered as he had left them. 'And I am not yet prepared.'

'Why would they be taken from us, Pateras?' Malory watched as Barthram gripped an old drinking horn between his knees and dropped the bit of an augur into its open end. The augur was a carpenter's tool, used for boring holes in wood by sawing a bowed string backwards and forwards to spin the cutting end.

'Even if the high priest lives, there will be a trial. Sorcery, of course. I can handle Roquenoir's chatelain, but the local seneschal has the king's authority. He will demand they be handed over.' The augur made a rasping, snoring noise as Barthram began sawing at the bow. Malory swallowed, guessing the drinking horn's intended use.

'How long do we have, Pateras?'

'Word will reach him tomorrow. We may have a day to uncover the truth ourselves. Then they will be taken from us, tortured, tried, and burnt. Our chance to recover the Hand will be gone.'

'How may I help?' Malory offered out of duty. He truly did not want to be part of this.

'Light the brazier.'

Malory found flint and steel, char and kindling. He was still stacking charcoal around the flame when there was a pounding at the door; not gentle deference, but fist-on-wood urgency.

'If you please, Pateres!'

Two of their own soldiers stood there, rain streaming down their faces. Two benches and a coil of rope lay on the ground behind them.

'Begging your pardon, Pateres, but the high priest is dead!' Fear tightened the man's voice.

Malory made the sign of the God. 'Ischyros accept him over the bridge. Come inside.' He was scared, too, but he knew how to maintain the appearance of authority.

'We met temple guards on the way.' The soldier was gabbling. He came into the room backwards, holding one end of the two stacked benches. 'They said His Holiness's body had been taken to the castle temple, where they are saying the Office of the Dead.'

'Put one of them over there.' Barthram pointed at an embrasure. 'Wedge it upright, on its end, so it can't fall over. Good.' While the men were arranging the bench, he sighted through the hole he had made in the horn and nodded his satisfaction.

'Give me your blade,' Pateras Ghislain said to one of the soldiers, pointing at the rondel dagger on the man's hip. The anakritis held the weapon upright and threaded the horn over its point. The horn rattled downwards, leaving a full handspan exposed when it finally jammed against the broadening, triangular shaft.

'Perfect. You may bring them both now.' Barthram's smile did not touch his eyes.

The two soldiers looked at each other. 'Forgive us, Pateres, but the witch might curse us.'

'She is blindfolded, and you will have two priests here to guard against any works of Kakos,' Malory assured them.

The soldier's look was eloquent. If she could kill a high priest, what use were a couple of anakritim?

Barthram grunted his irritation. 'Very well. Wait for Pateras Malory. He will cover her ravings with prayer. He will be with you directly, but go now.'

He waited until the door had shut behind them, and pointed the dagger at the upright bench wedged into the embrasure.

'When you return, Pateras Malory, I want the Guardian strapped tightly to that. It is important that he watches.'

'And the woman?'

'Is expendable. We must know for sure what this relic is, and where it is hidden. After that, she need only live long enough to confess her guilt in front of any episkopes we can find.' He picked up a file, rasped a rough edge off the tip of the horn, and blew away the dust.

'And to what do you want her to confess?'

'That the Guardians are in league with Kakos and plotted this blow at the heart of the faith.' Satisfied with the horn, Pateras Ghislain began to file down the sharp point of the dagger. Seeing Malory's look, he added, 'We don't want her struggles to kill her prematurely, do we?'

'And if there has been no such plot?'

Ghislain Barthram sighed, as a parent might with a dull boy.

'Pateras Malory, I have found that you need to learn the same lessons many times. As regards the relic, we seek the truth. As regards the Guardian plot, we merely seek evidence for something we already know to be the truth.' He tested the point with his thumb and plunged the blunted weapon into the brazier. 'Now bring them.'

Barthram picked up a set of bellows and nurtured the charcoal into greater heat.

Malory opened the door onto a world that seemed little lighter than the gloom inside the tower, though it was not yet even the time for the afternoon office. Malory tugged the hood of his habit further forwards; the rain was lifting but the clouds hung dark as old iron, grumbling, not yet spent.

The sudden flare of lightning was so bright that he lifted both arms to shield his eyes, and the thunderclap that came at the same instant made him crouch as if against some almighty blow. The very air around him seemed to swing a scorched fist into his chest, and he looked up, cringing, to see fragments of the temple roof spinning away as if struck by a mighty hammer. The golden Hand of Salazar that had crowned its dome arced away, trailing erratic spirals of smoke.

For several heartbeats the world held its breath, stunned into silence, but as Malory straightened, lowering his arms, the first cries of alarm carried to him along the terraces from the chapel. In the near darkness the wrecked temple roof flickered as if some vestige of lightning had been trapped within its timbers; flickered, became flame, and took hold.

13.3 ADELAIS

The soldiers pushed Adelais onto a stool by the table in Brother Raymond's tower, kicking her legs from under her to make her sit. At least, she thought it must be Brother Raymond's tower; the way back seemed to be the same as the way out, but inside the stinking helmet liner it was hard to be sure. It was foul with years of crusted sweat and tied close to her face, so she breathed through her mouth, tilting her head back in a vain effort to see beneath it.

There had been a lot of shouting and jostling, making her stumble, until hands seized her arms and almost dragged her along. In their roughness and the smell and the confusion she hadn't had time to think, but now, sitting at the table, she was hit by the full enormity of what she'd done.

She'd sung the rune song of the thunder god, but had she summoned the storm? Could she really do that? Or would the storm have happened anyway? At its heart she'd felt such a power within her that she might have cast thunderbolts with her hands or thrown men backwards with a look. The high priest had seen that power and he'd been so *fjakkinn* frightened that he'd collapsed. But now, bound, blindfolded, she felt weak and helpless in its aftermath, a child cowering while giants clashed above her.

And to the Ischyrians she was a heretic, a blasphemer, and a murderer.

Now they'd burn her.

Skit, skit, skit!

After she'd faced the anakritim.

Sætur Sif, help me.

There were shouts from the direction of the door. 'That's her, that's the witch!' It was slammed with an oath from the sergeant.

Adelais had heard Humbert pushed down into the store-room. His prayers rose through the floor, but she couldn't make out the words amidst the noise and confusion around her. She wondered why they hadn't returned her to the room above, with its wall paintings and Guardian lion. Perhaps they thought she might fall if her hands were still tied. And Barthram had said he'd send for them 'very shortly'.

There was no hope left. Adelais could feel the glass phial still jammed between her wrists, and pushed her arms under the table. It had to be now. She thought she'd managed to undo a button before the rope was pulled tight, but she wasn't sure. She began to move her wrists together, within their binding, slowly working the bottle forwards until its bottom was at the base of her palm. There she could fold her fingers over and touch it and knew that she could draw it out. It left a slight stickiness behind it; had it broken? Leaked? Would there still be enough to cheat the anakritim?

One of the soldiers was nearby, close enough, in that small space, for her to hear the creak of leather and sense his warmth.

'Thierry?'

'What?' The single word was gruff, angry, betrayed.

More pounding at the door, and a bellow from the sergeant to 'go shaft yourselves'.

'May I have some wine? I fear the pain that must come.'

He snorted, but she heard liquid splashing into the leather mug.

'In front of you.' His voice was in her ear. 'Get it down you before the others notice.'

Adelais reached her hands over the table, fumbled until they could grip the mug, and took one long swallow. The wine was coarse on her tongue but spread fiery warmth in her belly, and she moved the mug out of sight beneath the table, gripping it with her knees.

The phial came out easily into her palms and she held it there, her heart pounding. Her wrists and palms were slick with sweat, or was it potion? Self-murder. Would the gods forgive her? Would it be their will if she dropped the bottle and it shattered on the floor?

Adelais rolled it between her palms until it was upright, and the cork was by her thumb.

Pause. Think. Be sure.

More knocking, more voices, and the sounds of two men being admitted.

'The high priest is dead. Pateras Ghislain wants the prisoners. Now. But we're to wait for Pateras Malory.'

Adelais gasped. *The high priest is dead.* What unthinkable punishments would be inflicted on her?

It had to be now. She pushed off the cork with her thumb, found the mug with her knuckles, and poured, shaking out every last drop.

She let the bottle fall into the folds of her gown. It would drop and break if she stood, but then she wouldn't be standing up any more, would she?

Adelais lifted the mug onto the table, letting it rest in front of her, feeling tears well in her eyes as her resolve hardened. *Amma Yrsa, forgive me. Sætur Sif, accept me.* Two deep breaths. Three. *Now.*

Another thunderclap hit the room like the wrath of the gods, so loud that until a rumbling aftershock filled the sky, she thought that the building had collapsed.

The silence in the room lasted until a soldier muttered 'Salazar's wounds!' Cries of alarm came from outside, growing suddenly louder as one of the soldiers pulled open the door.

'Hit the chapel.' It sounded as if he'd stepped outside. 'There's priests and episkopes running everywhere!'

It was only thunder. I will do this. I will not endure the torture. Adelais reached for the mug, and seized empty space. Panicking, she moved her hands from side to side, feeling for it. *Gently, gently, mustn't tip it over.* Wider. Nothing.

And behind her, a soldier's voice. 'By Tanguy, I needed that.'

And another. 'Give it here, then.'

'No!' Adelais turned towards the voices.

The blow caught her by surprise, striking her on the ear and bending her sideways across the table.

'One more word out of you, witch, and I'll gag yer.'

Adelais began to weep, as profoundly as she had for Arnaud. She wept for the soldiers, who might now die, even though they'd killed her man. She wept in frustration at being thwarted, and she wept in fear for the pain she would have to endure.

The soldiers ignored her. Outside, the shouts resolved into a single word, screamed by a hundred overlapping voices. 'Fire!'

'You two.' The sergeant's voice. 'Go and see what's happening.'

What was it that Humbert had whispered? *Courage, lioness.* She pushed herself more upright on her stool and wiped her snivelling nose against her arm, smearing snot inside the leather mask. She would face this; she had no alternative. She would not give them the satisfaction of tears.

It seemed unnaturally quiet in the room. Adelais listened,

trying to separate the noises around her from the tumult outside. She thought she heard a muttered *'by Tanguy's bones'* and a thump as if a body had sat down heavily on the boards, but nothing else; no muttered conversation, no sounds of movement from leather harness or chain-mail. She angled her head, straining. There were muffled sounds of prayers from below.

And nearby, unmistakably, someone snored.

'Thierry? Sergeant?'

No reply.

Slowly, fearing another blow, she reached behind her head and tugged at the helmet liner's laces.

One soldier lay across the table, asleep. The sergeant was slumped against the door, drooling into his beard, and a third man was trying to lift himself onto his knees, steadying himself with one hand on the corner of the table. He lifted the other towards her in what could have been either a plea or a threat, and toppled sideways, slack-faced.

Adelais stood up, unsteadily, and the glass phial dropped to the floor. She frowned at it like a drunkard. She'd been about to take her own life. She hadn't thought she'd stand again. There was another soldier in the shadows, backing away from her, whimpering. He'd drawn his sword but held it limply at an angle, a barrier rather than a weapon.

'I'm not going to hurt you.' *Play the part. Take control. Don't let him run.* 'Open the trapdoor.' Adelais pointed at the hatch to Humbert's storeroom, surprised to find that she needed to do it with both hands. Of course. Still bound.

Unbelievably, he obeyed.

'Come out, Lord Brother.'

Humbert paused on the steps, staring around at the room in disbelief. 'How?' He made the sign of the God.

'Now you get in,' she ordered the soldier. 'Swiftly, if you want to live.'

The man scuttled to obey, and Adelais kicked the hatch

shut after him. She staggered a little as she slid the bolt home
with her foot; she still felt disoriented, as if awakening from a
fever and not sure what was dream or reality. The soldiers had
said something important. Must remember.

'D'Eivet is coming. Now.' Yet she stood in a daze, blinking
at the room. It all seemed so sharp, so clear, down to the single
ring of chain-mail that caught the light, winking silver, as a
soldier snored.

'You must move.' Humbert seized her by the arms and
shook her.

'I did not kill myself.' The reality was dawning on her. She
felt rooted to the spot, breathing air, dazed with wonder.

'Move! Now!' Humbert cut Adelais's bonds with a dagger,
pulled a sword belt from one of the unconscious soldiers, and
wrapped a cloak around himself. Adelais stood staring at her
hands, flexing her fingers as if they were the most wondrous
thing she'd ever seen. She was alive!

'Hitch up your gown.'

She frowned at Humbert, not understanding.

'You must have the appearance of a man again, Adelais.'

He strapped another sword belt around her hips and pulled
her gown up over it until the skirts fell only to her knees, like a
man's cote-hardie. Still she stared at him, even when he placed
the filthy helmet liner over her hair and draped another cloak
around her shoulders. It smelt of wet wool as he tugged the
hood forwards to hide her face.

'Keep the cloak wrapped around you. Ready?' There were
soldiers' rations of bread and cheese on the table and he grabbed
them, rolling them in his cloak before dragging the sergeant out
of the way and opening the door.

Her first, delirious thought was that the sky was beautiful,
and she was alive to see it, though weak with relief and hunger.
The horizon was clearing, and the sinking sun blushed the
undersides of the clouds, rose on steel. A breeze came from the

southwest, its after-rain freshness pushing at the stink of
burning wood, and she turned her nose into it. Towards the sun
the smoke of the town fogged the evening, pierced by the dome
of a temple. Boats were rushing from town to castle, presumably
bearing clerics for whom there had been no suitable lodgings
within the castle walls. She inhaled deeply. *Takk til gudhanna.*
Thanks be to the gods. *Takk til Thor. Sætur Sif, takk, takk, takk.*

'Come, Adelais.' Humbert tugged at her cloak, pulling her
towards the chaos around the temple. She followed in a daze,
dragged along rather than walking. Flames raged above the
skeleton of the temple roof, scattering smoke and burning fragments downwind, over the river.

'Take longer strides.' Urgency rushed Humbert's voice. 'Put
your shoulders back. Swagger a little.'

'Just like Villebénie all over again,' Adelais giggled. It was so
wonderfully glorious to be *alive.*

In front of them, a chain of soldiers and servants carried
buckets up the steps from the well in the garden, though such
was the heat that they could only throw their contents through
the temple door, lifting their arms to shield their faces as they
staggered away for more. There were more people than could
help, and too few buckets to go around; the press of onlookers
spread over the garden and down the steps to the harbour. And
breaking through them onto the less crowded terrace came
Malory d'Eivet. Two soldiers followed at his heels.

His eyes flew wide at the sight of Adelais and Humbert, and
he stopped, floundering in his shock.

'How?' D'Eivet stared at them, his jaw slack.

'Remember, priest.' Humbert sounded as if he was on the
verge of laughter. 'Remember the deeds of Salazar, who was
imprisoned by the Saradim. As *he* was led to freedom by a
Blessèd One while his guards slept, so am I.'

Did Humbert really believe that? He sounded so
convincing that d'Eivet hadn't yet raised the alarm, but there

were a hundred more soldiers within as many paces. If he pointed her out as the witch, she and Humbert would probably be torn apart by the crowd. Her euphoria drained away.

Blessèd One. She'd play the part, to the end. Adelais composed her face into an expression that she hoped radiated serene, calm superiority.

'Who are you, woman?' D'Eivet did not dare to meet Adelais's eye, and stared at her hand where it held her cloak closed. 'The high priest's body burns and none can reach him...'

Humbert answered for her.

'By Ischyros's grace, this is the vengeance of Grand Master Guerin. The high priest burns as so many martyred Guardians burned. Now stand aside or receive the retribution you deserve.'

D'Eivet did not move. Behind him, the two soldiers fingered their sword hilts, their eyes flicking everywhere in their fear. One, she saw, was Thierry.

Finally, d'Eivet found the courage to look her in the face. '*What* are you?'

He must not cry out. His eyes were full of fear, and beyond the fear there was something else; a need, perhaps a loss, and that look triggered words that flowed from her in an inspired delirium.

'I am one who would give you peace. Kneel, Malory d'Eivet.'

To her surprise, he did. Adelais put her hand on his head and bent down to whisper in his ear. The dizzy madness made her speech unthinking, as light and unstoppable as the sparks on the wind. A piece of burning timber crashed into the terrace beside them, scattering fragments. It lit an idea within her.

'I forgive you.' She didn't really mean that. The words were somehow detached from her feelings.

'I offer you the gift of unburdening. *Apó ti chári tou Ischyros, sas xefortónomai tis amartíes sas.* By the grace of Ischyros, I pardon you of your sins.' She picked up a piece of smouldering wood, ignoring its burn as she crumbled ash into her palm, and made the print of pardon on his forehead with her thumb. 'Ash from the sacred flame. *Zíste mia kalí zoí apó aftí ti stigmí. Sto ónomá Tou, amín.* Live a good life from this moment on. In His name, amen.' And by the rules of the Ischyrian faith, she was now damned for playing a part reserved for the priesthood.

Malory d'Eivet's face folded. He rocked back on his heels and began to cry in great, shaking sobs that could be heard above the crackling of the fire and the shouts of the water carriers. It seemed appropriate, now, for the two soldiers behind him to kneel as she passed, baring their heads. She paused in front of them and made the sign of their God. *Mind, soul, body. Play the part to the end.*

'Ischyros bless you, Thierry.'

They left them there, a trio of weeping men with their knees in the mud.

CHAPTER 14

14.1 ADELAIS

Adelais sat on a cloak on the hillside above a former Guardian preceptory, watching the road below. The sun was rising, setting light to mist in the valley so that it seemed she was sitting on an island floating in cloud. The road and the preceptory's cluster of buildings were indistinct, sometimes appearing, as if through fine muslin, sometimes vanishing. The outlines of trees formed along the road, became troops of soldiers in her mind, and faded. Behind her the preceptory's humble, thatched-dome temple sat benign and empty in the sunlight, the dawn office long since sung. Its stone walls were already warm.

In between glances at the road, she used a soldier's dagger to trim an ash staff that she'd cut from the woods; a lance-straight shaft thick enough to fight with, if necessary. Still green, of course, but long days on the road would dry it out. From time to time she paused to soothe her burnt hand in the dew, as she had trailed it in the water from the boat the evening before. It would pass.

She looked up again. Even on the higher, sunlit slopes she could see no one, not even brothers tending the vines. There had been a wolf earlier, staring at her from the far side of the valley, ghost-grey with a white bib. It could not have been the same wolf as the one outside the sisterhouse, surely? Yet she had stood, opening her arms wide, returning its stare. *I'm coming, Yrsa. I have many things to learn.* It had turned and trotted away to the north, turning once at the forest's edge to look back over its shoulder in a way that invited her to follow. She was learning to believe in such signs; like runes, they were glimpses of a greater mystery beyond. It was not always necessary to understand, only to be aware.

This was the first time she'd been outdoors and alone since she walked into Villebénie from the sisterhouse. The knowledge was liberating; she could make choices. She and Humbert were still too close to Roquenoir and must move on, but she could decide her own path. When Humbert returned, she'd tell him her decision.

The Roquenoir boatman had refused to take them beyond the mouth of a small tributary of the Naeva, even for one of Agnès's gold crowns, and even though a south wind filled his sail. It was too dark, he said. The waters were treacherous near the shore, where they'd have to sail to beat the current; even now, he'd have to wait for dawn to see his way back. *Gold's no use to my family at the bottom of the river.* He'd eyed them suspiciously but shared his skin of wine in exchange for some of their bread and cheese. She and Humbert had eaten gloriously, laughing around mouthfuls until the boatman clearly thought them mad. His eyes had widened at the portions they ate. Adelais only stopped when she felt ill.

Adelais had slept afterwards, lulled by the rocking of the boat, but had fevered dreams of the anakritis they'd seen staring down at them from the top of the westernmost tower of Roquenoir's castle. The black-and-white habit had broadened, as if Ghislain Barthram was spreading wings and about to take flight, but it was only to swing an arm backwards and throw something at them, long and thin like a stick or a dagger. It had bounced on the rocks below with a metallic ring before it dropped at the water's edge.

Humbert had been unconcerned to be left so close to Roquenoir. 'Can you walk two leagues?' he'd asked her, and the bread and cheese and rough wine had said yes. She'd had to lean on him after one, and he'd carried her in stages for much of the last, faltering half-league into the hills. By then they were both staggering under the bright light of the barley moon, hanging in a newly washed sky. 'There's a small preceptory,' he'd said. 'They know me there. Not far now.' The brothers had welcomed them with food, and more wine, and fresh straw to soften her nightmares of pursuit. Before King Aloys's persecution these men had been simple lay brothers, working the land to support the Guardian knights. Now they were pardoned, accepted into another order, and worked the same land to support the king. Their greatest suffering had been to see a proud order brought low, but they remembered their old allegiances and could be trusted.

There was movement on the road below Adelais, growing stronger, fading, solidifying again. She stood, and began to back towards the temple, nestled into the hillside above her. One man among the trees, or many?

One. Humbert, carrying a sack or a roll of cloth across his shoulder that for a moment reminded her, impossibly, of another roll of linen. She watched him climb the hill to her, and realised that the spry, vigorous knight who'd led Agnès de Molinot's group out from the Villebénie house with a resounding 'Forward, in the name of Ischyros!' was now a gaunt old man, leaning into the hill and climbing slowly. Only the sword at his hip marked him as a man-at-arms.

But the smile was the same. It creased his face into fanned lines behind shining eyes, and folded his untrimmed beard into grey-white bristles around his mouth.

'See what the brothers have found you, Adelais!' He laid

clothing across her cloak to save it from the dew, like an indulgent father spreading gifts for his daughter. 'There is a herigaut, and hose, loin cloth, and linen shirt. A cap to cover your hair...'

'Let us sit, Brother.' She omitted 'Lord' deliberately. A simple 'Brother' was more intimate, more like family.

In response, he searched her face as he lowered himself stiffly to the ground. He sighed as if he expected bad news.

'They will come after us, Brother.'

'But they will not find us, Adelais. Ischyros would not let you lead me out of the prison, only for us to be retaken.' He spoke like her counsellor, not her leader. So much had changed since the miracle of her wound.

'Perhaps we must give Ischyros a little help.' She toyed with the hem of the cloak, seeking kindly words. 'They will look for us both together, a man and a woman.'

'So we will be an old man and his son. It would be an easy and welcome deception for me.'

'You are more valuable to them than me. You can tell them about the Hand. I think you should ride west, through Maycea, and seek sanctuary among your friends in Arrenicia.'

Humbert chuckled. 'I have no horse. Nor do these poor brothers have one to give me.'

Adelais took off her belt and used the dagger to prise two more crowns from its lining.

'It will not buy a destrier, but it is enough for a sound horse, one that will put some leagues behind you.'

'But you?'

'I have two more. They may buy me passage in a boat, or food on the road north if I must walk.'

'Or another horse! We can ride together.'

'I could not ride, Brother. I am not yet healed.' This she knew instinctively. She could walk, though the journey from the river had been punishing. She'd rest every league until she was stronger. She could even lengthen her stride to look like a man, but she could not yet endure a saddle and the movement of a horse. It would pull her apart. Besides, her path lay to the north, his to the west.

Humbert frowned at the coins in his palm. He let his hand lie open, not yet accepting them.

'I once offered you silver for your journey, Adelais. Now you give me gold for mine.'

'Don't thank me. Thank Lady Agnès. For the gold and for the potion that saved us.'

Humbert made a little wry laugh. 'She is a remarkable woman.'

'And, like you, a true friend whose company I crave. I think Château Fontenay must lie on the way to Vriesland. I will go north that way.'

'You are determined?'

She took his hand in hers and closed his fingers around the gold. 'We must part, and you must find powerful friends. Swiftly. And I must find other friends, in a land where I can walk openly as a yellow-haired woman.' Adelais was sure of one thing, after the past days; it was time to fulfil the destiny of the *taufr*. There was a power within her that Yrsa could help her understand. The barley moon was still full, the days were long, and with luck she might reach Vriesland before winter set in. Perhaps Agnès or Elyse would help her on her way.

Humbert sighed. 'I would protest, but I think you are protected by a greater power than any I could offer. Sometimes I wonder if you are truly a Blessèd One.'

Adelais snorted. 'I am too flawed for that.' *And much too heathen.* 'You think too highly of me, Brother.' She dropped her eyes, embarrassed to admit her crime. 'Yesterday I tried to commit self-murder with the medicine.'

'And Ischyros saved you from that sin.'

'But not from others.' Why was this farewell turning into a confession? And a confession she must frame in the words an

Ischyrian would use. 'I gave pardon to Pateras Malory, as if I were a priest. That's heresy, isn't it? I even said I forgave him, though I didn't mean it.'

Humbert squeezed her hand. 'Well, I did ask you to behave like a Blessèd One. Now Malory d'Eivet believes himself unburdened and may be a better man for it.'

They were silent together, staring down into thinning mist, both of them prolonging the moment of parting.

'Where do you suppose it is, Brother? The Hand?'

'We cannot tell.' Humbert said it in a way that also meant *we cannot be forced to say*. 'De Fontenay will have it safe, beyond the king's reach, and the anakritim do not have enough evidence to move against so great a lord. A more pious age may come when it can be shown with reverence and without greed, but I do not believe that will happen in my time.'

'A lot of lives have been lost for a few bones.'

'That saved your life.'

She looked at him. His eyes were full of a gentle, loving faith, and she knew she could not rob him of that. She'd let him keep his illusion.

'Perhaps one day you will see it again, Adelais. You have proved a worthy protector.'

'Even though I am a woman, and not a virgin?' She smiled at him, teasing.

'Even so. But do not seek it, if you reach Lady Agnès. Let Ischyros reveal Himself to you in a time of His own choosing.'

They were quiet again, close enough on the single cloak for their arms to touch.

'I will miss you, Brother.' She nudged him with her shoulder.

'And I you, Adelais.'

'I will change in the temple.' She jumped to her feet before her resolve weakened.

. . .

When she emerged he was waiting outside the door, holding out a soldier's cloak.

'I cut off the king's badge. The nights will be cold.'

Adelais embraced him long and fiercely, and stood back, blinking away tears. She turned away, not trusting herself to speak, and walked down the hill, keeping her eyes resolutely on the path ahead.

'Shoulders back, Perrin Wilg! Swagger a little.' The humour did not cover the emotion in his voice.

Adelais lifted one arm above her shoulder in farewell, and swung her hips like a harlot.

His laughter seemed to clear the mist before her.

A LETTER FROM G.N. GUDGION

Thank you so much for reading *Hammer of Fate*.

After my previous novel *Draca* was published, my agent (Ian Drury at Sheil Land Associates) encouraged me to write a book with a female protagonist. I was researching fourteenth century Europe at the time, an age when the only empowered women were either royal or religious, and the character of Adelais leapt into my mind as if she'd always been there, waiting for me to let her out; a rebellious, independent-minded woman in a world of mail-clad, sometimes-chivalric knights. The magic came shortly afterwards; I gave her rune lore in the way that I might give another hero a shining sword, and the alignment of character and capability took hold.

I think before long I fell a little in love with her, in a Humbert-ish sort of way; she seemed so determined that I should tell her story. Perhaps we told it together. *Are* telling, for her adventures continue in *Runes of War* and *Blood of Wolves*, and I am excited to show you how a weaver's daughter could become the woman who shapes the fate of nations.

I hope you stay with us on that journey. If you want to hear about future releases, please sign up with Bookouture at the following link. Your email address will never be shared and you can unsubscribe at any time.

www.bookouture.com/gn-gudgion

If you liked *Hammer of Fate*, could you do me a huge

favour? I welcome feedback, and reviews really help new readers discover the books. Reviews don't have to be long; a few words and a star rating on the website of your retailer is all it takes. Thank you.

I have another invitation. Would you like to know the story behind the story? Snippets of history that inspired scenes in the book? More about my writing process? You'll find some free short stories to download and a growing collection of short, Adelais-related articles on my web site:

https://geoffreygudgion.com

There's also a 'contact me' page, so if you'd like me to talk to your book club, or have comments/questions you'd like to make directly, I'd love to hear from you.

Happy reading!

 facebook.com/geoffrey.gudgion.author

twitter.com/GeoffreyGudgion

instagram.com/GeoffreyGudgion

ACKNOWLEDGEMENTS

My first thanks go to my wife and family for their understanding when I stepped off the corporate ladder and away from a safe, predictable income in order to release time to write. Without that support Adelais would never have been born.

More recently, two people above all have encouraged me to keep going with *Hammer of Fate* and its sequels *Runes of Battle* and *Blood of Wolves*: my son James, and my agent Ian Drury at Sheil Land Associates. They are Adelais's godfathers. James even helped me name her, sitting around a table with his lovely wife Faith in their home in Sydney, Australia. James became so absorbed in an early chapter that he missed two stops on the train, and has been demanding more ever since.

Ian guided my writing towards the fantasy genre and has been an enthusiastic supporter and mentor. He always believed that Adelais would live in print and, most importantly, he introduced her to Jack Renninson at Bookouture. Jack's editorial input has been intense and insightful; he has invested a huge amount of thought and effort to take a book that I thought was ready and turn it into the story you have in your hands. He has also co-ordinated the outstandingly professional team at Bookouture/Second Sky; Alex Holmes, Mandy Kullar, Natalie Edwards, and Lizzie Brien for editorial, Angela Snowden for forensically detailed copy editing, Faith Marsland for proof-reading, Melanie Price and Ciara Rosney for marketing, and powerhouse Noelle Holten for publicity. Huge thanks also to

Lance Buckley for the wonderful cover design. Together this team has ensured that Adelais sets out into the world well dressed and prepared.

Several other friends read earlier versions and commented along the way, including Gill Thomas, David Rolfe, Marcus and Susie Bicknell, and Vee Walker.

While building Adelais's world I read many sources about medieval life and beliefs, in particular:

- Malcolm Barber and Keith Bate, *The Templars* (Manchester University Press, 2002). Their transcripts of the trials of the Knights Templar gave me ideas and contemporary rhetoric for the persecution of the Guardians.
- Geoffroi de Charny, *The Book of Chivalry*, mid-fourteenth century, translated by Elspeth Kennedy (University of Pennsylvania Press, 1996). Before de Charny died a hero's death as the French standard-bearer at the battle of Poitiers in 1356, he wrote *The Book of Chivalry* as a guide for young knights. It is a wonderful insight into the mindset of a pious, medieval warrior and it helped me to form the character of Humbert Blanc.
- Toni Mount, *Medieval Medicine* (Amberley Publishing, 2016). So useful for concocting effective cures.
- *Whispers of Yggdrasil*, a blog by Arith Härger. There is a wealth of published material on runes and *seidhr*, the practice of sorcery in pre-Christian Nordic cultures. Among the frequently contradictory sources, I have found Arith to be a rich and credible mine of information at both the academic and esoteric levels. A novelist weaves facts into imaginary worlds, and while

acknowledging Arith's considerable input, I make no claim that he endorses the warp and weft of my story. https://arithharger.wordpress.com

- Wikipedia for the public domain, Icelandic versions of rune poems and their translations.

Printed in Great Britain
by Amazon